the MAGE'S MASTER

FINLEY FENN

The Mage's Master

info@finleyfenn.com

Cover design by Sylvia at The Book Brander
Proofreading by Emmy from @brabedrebelt

Sign up at www.finleyfenn.com for bonus stories and epilogues, delicious artwork, complete content guidance, news about upcoming books, and more!

ALSO BY FINLEY FENN

THE MAGES

The Mage's Maid

The Mage's Match

The Mage's Master

The Mage's Groom (Bonus Story)

ORC SWORN

The Lady and the Orc

The Heiress and the Orc

The Librarian and the Orc

The Duchess and the Orc

The Midwife and the Orc

The Maid and the Orcs

The Governess and the Orc

The Beauty and the Orcs

The Widow and the Orcs

The Artist and the Orc

Offered by the Orc

Tryggred by the Orc

Yuled by the Orcs

Tales of Orc Sworn

ORC FORGED

The Sins of the Orc

The Fall of the Orc

PROLOGUE

Like every day that week, Fasta spent the morning holding back tears, and pretending everything was fine.

"I'll need those labourers you mentioned," she told her client, a grey-haired man whose name had utterly vanished into the fog swarming her brain. "And the exact coordinates of where you'd like the cottage moved."

The man nodded, speaking something Fasta didn't hear, and once he was gone, she spread her hands against the cottage's cool stone wall, and breathed. Felt her magic search and settle, feeding back a steady stream of images and information. This wall needed to be braced, the roof had to come off, she really should investigate that corner...

It should have been a fascinating, gratifying project. Fasta had recently finished her studies at Vakra's prestigious Earth-Magic Academy, and despite the deep disapproval of her father—the wealthy, powerful Earl of Dalreagh—she was finally starting a real career in magic, doing the work she loved best. Period restoration and reconstruction, mostly, like fixing up this beautiful old stone cottage, and moving it off this muddy flood plain, so it could be properly used again.

But instead of enjoying the job, or revelling in the fact that she'd finally bested her father on this, Fasta was thinking only of Elgin. Elgin, with his dark hair and lean body and beautiful eyes, his clever hands that so easily shaped earth and stone. Hands that had also run so eagerly over Fasta's skin, exploring and caressing, sparking pleasure unlike anything she'd ever felt in her life.

But last weekend, Elgin had been busy. Again. With work, with friends, with a variety of crucial commitments he couldn't possibly escape. Finding only enough time for a brief visit, hurling Fasta full of that swarming pleasure, and leaving again, amidst empty apologies and practiced cool smiles.

So finally, after two whole years of believing they'd truly been friends, *partners*, Fasta had gathered her courage, and ended it. And even Elgin's protests had felt careless, half-hearted, enough to reveal the rest of the miserable truth. He hadn't cared. He wouldn't miss her. He probably had someone else lined up, or several someones. It was for the best. It was *fine*.

Fasta pressed her hands harder against the cottage wall, and squeezed her eyes shut. It had to be fine. She just had to keep going, pretend and nod and smile, until it was fine.

"Lady Fasta Valgeirr?" came a deep voice beside her, and Fasta flinched, and whirled around. Toward—someone new. A big blond-haired guy around her age, wearing shabby, ill-fitting clothes, and assessing her with deep grey eyes.

"I'm Henrik Hallen," he said, holding out a large, work-roughened hand. "Schmidt sent me. Said you needed help moving this cottage?"

Right. A labourer, come to help. Fasta shook herself a little, and belatedly clasped the guy's outstretched hand. His big fingers gripping hers felt strong and capable, and the taste of magic beneath his skin was undeniable, simmering bright and heated and powerful.

"Um, yes, thank you," Fasta replied, drawing her hand away,

as a strange warmth prickled in her cheeks. This Henrik was unquestionably good-looking, with his strong stubbled jaw and broad shoulders and tousled golden curls, but he also looked a bit wolfish, what with the dark shadows under his eyes, the hollows in his cheeks, and the way his ill-fitting clothes hung loosely off his large frame.

"Well, should we get at it, then?" Henrik asked, as he turned and thrust his big hands to the cottage wall, fingers spreading wide. And again, Fasta could taste his magic, flaring hot and succulent in the air around them, as his blond head tilted, his hand sliding up the wall, and down again.

"Although, d'you think this will hold once it's lifted?" he asked, with a glance toward Fasta. "Or the roof? And that corner"—he nodded toward it—"is a bit shite, yeah?"

Fasta twitched, and forced her scrambling thoughts to follow the question. "Yes, I was planning to remove the roof first," she replied, settling her hand to the wall beside his, fighting to ignore the taste of his lingering magic on the stone. "And no, that wall certainly isn't going to hold, but"—she fumbled in her pocket for the paper she'd stashed there—"I've run a few calculations, and as long as we brace it like this, it should suffice to get the cottage moved, at least."

She snapped the paper open, frowning down at her neat diagram, and Henrik stepped closer, and peered at it over her shoulder. "Oh," he said, with distinct surprise in his voice. "Yeah, that could work. Good thinking."

When Fasta looked up, he was glancing between her and the paper, and his big hand carefully came to grasp the paper's other corner, tilting it up to the sunlight. "How'd you figure it, though?" he asked, carefully. "What's this?"

He jabbed at Fasta's quickly scrawled equations, all down the side of the sheet, and she briefly explained, her face still strangely hot, how one could calculate the rigidities of each wall, along with the shear force likely to occur when they were lifted, minus the stabilizing force of the roof. While this

Henrik's blond eyebrows rose higher and higher, and once she'd finished her little speech, she could see him swallow, his throat bobbing above the neck of his shabby tunic.

"Well, aren't you useful," he said, with a furtive, appreciative look at Fasta's eyes. "Did you work it out about that wonky corner, too?"

Fasta shook her head, and lurched over toward the corner. "It's been bothering me," she told him, "but I can't determine why. The stones are fine, the mortar is still intact, and it feels solid, right?"

Henrik had followed her to the corner, kneeling and thrusting both hands against it, while that taste of his magic again filtered through the air. "Yeah, not quite," he replied. "This stone's gonna crumble, the second you move it."

Fasta blinked, and then knelt down to join him, spreading her hands close beside his. And with his magic now lingering on one of the wall's largest stones, suddenly she could feel the cracks, almost imperceptible, but most certainly there. "Right, then," she heard herself say. "Very good, Mr. Hallen."

It sounded like something one would say to a student, or a child, and Fasta's face heated again—but Henrik didn't seem to take offense. Instead, he glanced at the plain all around them, and then strode a short distance away, and waved his hand toward his feet. And as the taste of his magic flashed through the air, beneath him the ground cracked and rumbled, turning up mud and earth, and then—

A stone. A large new stone, spinning easily in midair. And with another wave of Henrik's hand, its rough edges sheared off without a sound, leaving it the exact shape and size of the cottage's cracked stone.

"That should work, yeah?" he asked, but Fasta's voice had entirely failed her, and she jerked a shaky nod. Watching as Henrik strode back to the cottage, pulled out the broken stone with a single glance of his eyes, and slid the new one back in, where it fit perfectly.

"Oh," Fasta said, numbly, earning a brief, amused glance from Henrik's grey eyes. And then he spread his hands against the wall, and—Fasta gasped—the roof carefully lifted off the cottage in one perfect piece, hovering in midair before dropping to rest gently on the ground beside her.

"D'you want to do your bracing next, then?" he asked, his eyes still amused and twinkling on hers. "And then we'll move the cottage?"

Fasta fought to find her breath, her focus. "Um, well," she began, "before we can move it, we'll need at least a few more labourers, and a cart. Schmidt said he was managing that?"

But Henrik's mouth quirked into a wry smile, and he shook his head. "Nah, no need," he replied. "We can handle it. That is"—he winked at her—"if you don't mind taking a few orders from a commoner, Lady Valgeirr?"

What? It was an audacious thing to say, from this equally audacious earth-mage—but Fasta only nodded, and stammered an incoherent reply. Earning a swift, stunning grin from Henrik in return, and another sly wink.

"Good girl," he said, husky. "Now c'mere, and do what I tell you."

And as ridiculous as it was, Fasta obeyed. Following Henrik's orders one by one, pouring her magic into the stone alongside his, lifting and shoving and heaving. Pushing herself and her magic harder than she'd done in months, or maybe years.

But when they finally finished, late in the afternoon, the cottage was nestled beautifully into its new home, perfectly intact, without a single stone out of place. And both Fasta and Mr. Henrik Hallen were covered in sweat and mud, breathing hard, their clothes filthy and soaked—but Henrik was broadly grinning at Fasta, and she couldn't stop herself from grinning back.

"Look at you, Lady Valgeirr," he said to her, his voice warm, as his big hand gripped brief and approving at her shoulder.

"Never woulda thought such a pretty, proper noble like you would be willing to work so hard, or get herself so dirty."

Fasta made a face, but Henrik only laughed, his hand firing more of his bright, warm magic into her shoulder. Feeling like relief, like peace, like *home*, and Fasta inhaled, deep, her body leaning just slightly into his touch.

"Never woulda thought you'd be so willing to follow orders, either," he murmured. "You like being told what to do, Lady Valgeirr?"

Oh, *gods*. The gasp escaped from Fasta's mouth before she could stop it, the heat pooling hard in her groin—and before her, Henrik's grin slowly faded, slipping into something just as hot and hungry as she felt. And that big hand gently slid down her shoulder, still spread wide and strong and almost *familiar*, and Fasta swallowed, leaned a little closer—

But then Henrik stumbled backwards, jolting and abrupt, almost like he'd been shoved. And his hand clapped to his mouth, rubbing hard against it, as his big bony shoulders rose, and fell.

"*Shit*," he breathed, his voice hoarse, "I mean, sorry, I didn't mean that, I should—"

He broke off, his shoulders still heaving, and his eyes squeezed shut, as if something hurt. "Look, I—I'm actually on the hunt for work, Lady Valgeirr," he said. "My ma's been ill, and my brother and sisters gotta eat. I don't suppose—I mean, I don't want to ask, but"—his eyes opened, fixed on hers, with unmistakable misery in them—"if you—if you liked my work today, is there any chance you might be willing to recommend me, going forward? Or keep an eye out for me?"

Oh. Something plunged deep in Fasta's belly, and she blinked, fought to reorient her scrambling thoughts. Henrik was looking for *work*. She was someone with education, someone with influence and access, who could find him work. And that was all.

But that was still—*something*, better than nothing at all, and

Fasta looked at Henrik's rangy form, his hollowed cheeks, the shame in his eyes. And he *was* brilliant, more brilliant than perhaps any earth-mage mason Fasta had yet met, whether within the Academy, or without. And his magic tasted like *that*, he'd made her smile more than she had in weeks, and—her shoulders sagged—she hadn't thought about Elgin or her father in *hours*. And that alone had been a true gift, a glorious, ridiculous relief.

"Well, your work today has indeed been exemplary, Mr. Hallen," she said thickly. "In fact, now that you mention it, I actually do have another similar job lined up for tomorrow. And then another next week, if you might happen to be free?"

It was as if her own relief was reflected in Henrik's blinking grey eyes—and the smile that slowly spread across his face was so grateful, so stunning, Fasta could barely breathe.

"You mean it?" he asked, his voice choked. "Really, Lady Valgeirr? You really want to keep working with *me*?"

Fasta couldn't help smiling back, her eyes oddly wet again, and she snapped up a loose rock from the earth beneath her feet, and gripped it tight. Everything would be fine. It had to be fine.

"Yes, of course," she replied. "I think we make a good team, don't you?"

Henrik was still smiling at her, perhaps a little regretful now, but his answering nod was earnest, almost fervent.

"Yeah," he said. "We do."

1

Fasta stalked up the corridor to Henrik's bedroom, her teeth gritted, her papers clutched tight in her trembling hand.

It was fine. Everything was fine.

"Henrik?" she called, as she rapped firmly on his closed bedroom door. "Do you have a moment?"

She could hear the murmured voices inside, the shift and shuffle of movement. Of Henrik getting out of bed, maybe, and Fasta clamped her papers tighter, raised her chin, and silently counted to ten. She needed to talk to him. It didn't matter if it was almost midnight. It was *fine*.

She twitched at the sound of his door latches spinning and clicking—they were his own brilliant metalwork, of course—and then the door finally drew open. Revealing the blond, bulky, familiar form of Henrik Hallen behind it.

Fasta's breath hitched, because even now, the sight of Henrik still caught her speechless. With his tousled golden curls, his stubbled square jaw, and his big, broad, powerful body, now dressed haphazardly in trousers and a loose tunic. He'd probably doubled his weight since they'd first met five years before, and it made him look every bit the huge, powerful earth-mage he was, impossibly strong and skilled, still maybe the most brilliant earth-wielder Fasta had ever met in her life.

But now—Fasta's eyes flicked over his shoulder, toward that glimpse of his bedroom behind him—Henrik wasn't alone. And there, in his bed, was another woman. *Ilsa.* A lovely, dark-haired water-mage, and, if the gossip was to be believed, a very eager, enthusiastic bedmate, too.

"What is it, Fass?" Henrik asked, his voice still low and husky from—from doing *that*. With *Ilsa.* "Anything wrong?"

Fasta drew herself taller, and shoved down the twisting bitterness in her gut. "I just wanted to talk over tomorrow's job with you," she replied, as smoothly as she could. "I've done some new calculations, and I wanted to review them together."

Henrik blinked at her, and shot a brief, betraying glance over his shoulder. To where Ilsa was looking downright poisonous, glaring back and forth between them, and Henrik exhaled, and rubbed a hand at his mouth. "You need it right now?" he asked Fasta, under his breath. "It can't wait until morning?"

A wild, sudden fury flared through Fasta's chest, and for an instant, there was the almost overpowering urge to shout in Henrik's face. To tell him yes, she needed him now, because he was *her* partner. *Her* protege. *Her* best friend. And if it wasn't for her, Henrik wouldn't even be here, living and working at Vakra's highly prestigious Coven Manor. He wouldn't be sharing his bed with girls like Ilsa. He would probably still be doing heavy labour back east, hauling bricks and *starving*.

But gods, the way Henrik was looking at her. His grey eyes glittering, his jaw flexing in his cheek, his big hand running through his tousled curls. He looked—frustrated. Annoyed. *Disappointed.* As if Fasta had spoken all her horrible, selfish thoughts aloud, and betrayed all the sheer desperate jealousy reeking behind them.

Fasta's stomach plummeted, and she jerked a step backwards, shaking her head. "Actually, never mind," she said, too quickly. "I—it's fine. You're busy. I'll see you in the morning, Harry."

She winced as the *Harry* escaped her mouth, because even that was probably more jealous desperation, wasn't it? Giving her colleague—some might say her *employee*—a personal pet name, as if trying to make him hers, when it was so painfully obvious that he wasn't. When he'd made it so damned clear that he would rather have Ilsa, or any of the dozen other women he'd bedded this past year. Women whose magic would always linger for days on his big beautiful body, clashing painfully with his own.

But Fasta wasn't supposed to care, because Henrik wasn't hers. And maybe he never would be.

She didn't wait for his reply, and instead spun around, and rushed for her own room down the corridor. Even as she could hear Henrik's heavy sigh behind her, could almost feel his frustration in the air.

"Fass, wait," called his voice, but it was frustrated too, and Fasta shook her head, and walked faster. It was fine. *Fine.*

She opened her own bedroom door with an angry swipe of her hand, and then glared at the door, slammed it shut. Because it was lined with Henrik's latches too, just like her bed was Henrik's steel, her flickering lamps were Henrik's iron, and her floor was made of Henrik's perfect, paper-thin stone tiles. Henrik was everywhere, in her brain, in her work, all over her damned bedroom.

But in all their five years of working together, studying together, travelling together, spending almost every damned day together—it had never gone beyond friendly. Respectful. Professional. And even if Henrik looked at Fasta the way he did, or teased her, made sly comments about Lady Valgeirr taking orders from a commoner—he'd also made his wishes very clear. He didn't want more than that, with her. He never had.

And just like with Elgin, years ago, Fasta finally had to face it. Let go. Move on. It was fine. It had to be fine.

"Fass?" came a low voice from beyond the closed door, along with a firm rap. "It's me."

Henrik. Fasta's legs suddenly wavered beneath her, and she sank heavily down onto her bed, clasping her hands tight. "Come in."

There was an instant's stillness, and then the sight of the door's latches spinning and whirring, opening beneath Henrik's magic from the other side. Of course he still knew all the combinations, because curse her, Fasta hadn't changed them. Because maybe she'd wanted him knowing them, wanted him coming in whenever he pleased.

Fasta gripped her clammy hands tighter as the door swung open, and Henrik eased inside. He still looked dishevelled, his tunic hanging baggy and crooked, his curls askew. "Hey," he said, his eyes shifting on hers in the lamplight. "You still good to go over the job?"

Right. The job. Fasta jerked her head toward the papers she'd thrown onto her desk, and Henrik strode over to pick them up, sifting through them one by one. "Looks good, Fass," he finally said, once he set them down again. "As always."

He twitched her his warm, crooked smile, though it was fainter than usual, his eyes searching hers. "Was there anything else?" he asked, after an instant's silence. "You good?"

That wild, bitter rebellion surged again through Fasta's chest, and she pursed her lips, shook her head. "Perfectly fine," she replied, a little too sharp. "You can go back to Ilsa now."

Henrik's eyes briefly closed, and Fasta didn't miss his hard swallow, spasming in his throat. "No, I can't," he said thinly, "'cause I sent her away. Told her my boss needed me for *work*."

There was a faint stress on that word *work*, and Fasta couldn't stop her brief, baleful glare toward him. "I'm not your boss, Harry," she snapped back. "I don't pay your salary. I'm your colleague. Your *friend*."

Henrik sighed, but he didn't deny it. Didn't say any of the things he'd told Fasta a dozen times before. *You're the rich titled heiress with the fancy education, I'm the poor commoner who's worked every day of his life. There's no chance in hell I'd still be working here, in this place, without you.*

But he might as well have said it anyway, because Fasta's thoughts were already swarming with all the things she'd done for Henrik, all the money she'd surreptitiously spent. Leveraging every possible connection to keep him on, to get him all the proper certifications, to drag him along with her wherever she went. Including here, to Coven Manor, the most prestigious magical research and training facility in all of Vakra. Its placements were nearly impossible to obtain, and its forty-odd live-in mages—across all five disciplines of earth, air, fire, water, and healing—were said to be among the most gifted and accomplished in the world.

Fasta shook her head, and shoved it all away. No. Henrik deserved to be here. He was quite possibly the most skilled earth-mage in the entire country. And he wasn't her employee, he shouldn't be, and…

And gods, she couldn't stand him looking at her like that. Still with too much awareness in his eyes, and something not unlike disappointment.

"Look, please, just—forget it," Fasta told him, with a resigned wave of her hand. "And go back to bed. I'm sorry I interrupted you. It won't happen again."

Henrik was silent in reply, and Fasta stared morosely down at her knees, waited for him to leave. But he didn't move, his gaze almost strong enough to be a touch, and Fasta twitched at the warm, delicious taste of his magic, furling out between them. Tightening that pesky loose bolt in her bed frame, and then sealing it off, too.

Fasta murmured a reluctant thanks—even now, her metal-working was no match for Henrik's—and again waited for him to leave. But instead, he began prowling around the room, trailing his hands against the wall, smoothing out an imperceptible ridge in the plaster, shifting something in the beam behind.

"Look, Fass," he finally said, his voice rough. "I don't know why you even care about Ilsa. Didn't you just go off alone with Johan Falk after supper?"

Fasta's head snapped up—Henrik had known about that? But yes, damn it, his eyes on hers were too knowing, his blond brows raised. Challenging her, commanding her, *judging* her. As if again, he could see straight through all her petty jealousy, down to the shameful truth beneath.

And also—he was accusing her, right? Accusing her of interrupting him and Ilsa on *purpose*?

Fasta's face flooded with painful heat, and she took a deep breath. "But, well, it wasn't—anything, with Johan, earlier," she stammered. "It really wasn't. It was just—"

She winced, shaking her head, as something flashed across Henrik's eyes—and in one swift step, he lurched to stand before her, his warm callused hand gripping her chin, tilting it up with firm, steady fingers. His touch so easy, so familiar, the way it so often was, as the command again flared in his eyes.

"Tell me the truth, Fass," he ordered. "You brought Johan here. I can smell his magic all over this room. Can still smell him on *you*."

Fasta winced again, and her face burned even hotter. "Look, it wasn't serious," she said, speaking far too quickly, and why was she telling Henrik this, why did he care, either? "He didn't even stay long. It wasn't"—she took a breath—"a *success*, between us, if you must know."

She didn't miss the distinct relief flashing across Henrik's eyes, and he dropped his hand from her chin, dragged it through his messy curls. "You all right, though?" he asked, a little stilted. "Johan didn't hurt you, or upset you, did he? That's not why you came to me, just now?"

Fasta swallowed hard, and she briefly considered lying,

telling Henrik that yes, she'd had a horrible time with Johan, and she'd only come to him afterwards for comfort and protection—because of course he would give it, with all his usual stubborn thoroughness. Gods, he'd probably go track down Johan at once, and crush him into dust before Johan even saw it coming.

"No," Fasta replied, through her clenched teeth. "It was fine. He was fine. It just—didn't feel right. I didn't like the smell of his magic, and I don't think he liked mine, either. I'll try again with someone else."

But damn it, maybe that was yet more petty vindictiveness on her part, and she could see Henrik bristling, his shoulders hunching. His big body turning, as if he was about to leave— but then he stopped again, looking back toward her, his jaw spasming in his cheek.

"Why now, though?" he asked, clipped. "Why Johan, or someone else? You've never been into—flings, before. As long as I've known you."

Fasta stared at Henrik for an instant too long, and then barked a strange, bitter laugh. "I suppose not," she said. "I've always been—preoccupied, these past five years. With... *work.*"

Henrik betrayed a faint but visceral flinch—because yes, of course, Fasta meant she'd been preoccupied with *him.* With his brilliant magic, his impossible skill, his bulky body, his stunning grin, even his cool, careless commands. And how the hell was she ever supposed to have a real relationship with someone else, when she was working with Henrik every damned day? When no one else would ever measure up?

But as she blinked at Henrik's face, her bitter rebellion suddenly faded, sinking into misery and regret. Into... guilt. Gods, she was a mess over this. And yes, she was petty and vindictive, and hopelessly jealous, because she'd watched Ilsa flirt with Henrik all through supper, and she'd known exactly where it had been heading. And in her frustration, her ever-deepening loneliness, she'd turned her attention to Johan, who had previously made his interest toward her very clear.

And maybe—maybe she'd even wanted Henrik to notice. Maybe she'd wanted to see if he would care. But of course he'd gone off with Ilsa anyway, because he saw Fasta as his boss. His friend. Nothing more.

And Fasta finally needed to accept it. Move on. It would be fine. *Fine.*

"Look, Harry, I'm sorry," she said now, squaring her shoulders, dropping her gaze to her knees. "If you really want the truth, I suppose I have been feeling a bit—lonely, lately. It's been a long time since I've had any kind of—well. And I just—I miss it, that's all. I want to be touched again. I want to be— *wanted.*"

It was indeed all truth, bare and shameful, and Fasta's face was burning again, her eyes risking a glance up at Henrik's unreadable face. "And it's clear that I need to find a—a better outlet," she added thickly. "Something... appropriate. Away from... from *work.*"

Henrik's big body twitched, because yes, she'd just come out and said it, hadn't she? She needed to find something apart from him. Someone who wasn't him.

But Henrik didn't look... surprised by that. Did he? No. If anything, he looked... uneasy. Unsettled. His hand again running through his hair, his breaths heavy and harsh.

"But—you've always seemed happy, Fass," he finally said, into the taut silence. "I never thought you..."

He didn't finish, and another bitter laugh escaped Fasta's mouth. "What, you never thought I'd want to be intimate with anyone?" she demanded, too sharp. "Or maybe, like so many other people here, you think I'm a frigid arrogant ice queen, who no one could possibly want to go to bed with?"

It was indeed something Fasta had heard whispered more than once, and Henrik grimaced, shook his head. "'Course I don't think that," he replied, hoarse. "Nobody could. You're just—really smart. Sure of yourself. And good at keeping your thoughts to yourself, too."

It sounded like another accusation, and Henrik grimaced again, and took a step backwards. "Look, any of them would jump into bed with you in a second, Fass," he added. "Gods, if nothing else, you look like—"

His big hand waved up and down Fasta's seated form, and she darted an uncertain glance downwards, toward her simple, unstylish tunic and trousers, and her soft body beneath it. Far softer than it should have been, because she'd been eating to keep up with Henrik these past few years, and he'd always liked that, *wanted* that, but...

Fasta shook her head, and shot Henrik a hard, accusing look. "You don't need to lie to me, Harry," she snapped, before she could bite it back. "I mean, *you* still won't go to bed with me, will you?"

Henrik stilled, his eyes snapped wide and hunted on Fasta's face, and too late, she heard what she'd just said. How she'd finally just hurled this all out into the open between them, and now it just kept hanging there, like a living thing. Like a beast that Henrik now had to face down and conquer, and he looked like he felt it too, his hands clutching to fists, his jaw clenched tight.

"Look, it's not that I don't *want* to go to bed with you, Fasta," he said finally, stiffly. "It's that I *can't*. Because whatever you want to call it, you're still in charge of this. Of *me*. You're Lady Valgeirr, and I'm here at your whim, to help you. To serve you. And I *need* this job."

Fasta winced, even as something leapt, sharp and strange in her belly. Henrik really meant that? He... he *wanted* to go to bed with her? Or he would, if things were different?

And maybe he saw the look in her eyes, because he sighed, and shook his head. "You don't understand what it's like," he continued. "I mean, look at your father, your education, your coin, that massive inheritance still coming to you someday. You have all the freedom and opportunities you could ever want. Any work you do is a *choice* for you. But for me"—he took a shaky breath—"this job is *everything*. It's the only thing keeping my entire family fed, and educated, and *alive*. And I can't put them at risk like that."

Fasta nodded, as her heartbeat kicked in her chest, and yet more miserable guilt coiled in her gut. Because yes, after so many years, she knew all the details of Henrik's family situation back east—his continually ill mother, and his four younger siblings, three of them triplets, who all needed food, shelter, schooling. Not to mention the fact that Henrik's brother Andreas was now attending the vaunted Earth-Magic Academy itself, because Andreas really was that good, just like Henrik. And wait, had Fasta ever asked who was paying Andreas' tuition at the Academy? Henrik couldn't be paying it all himself... could he?

"Do you need money, Harry?" Fasta asked, too sharply. "For Andreas, maybe? You know I would be happy to—"

But Henrik cut her off with a snort, and waved the offer away. "Fuck, no," he replied, impatient now. "You've already done enough. More than enough. I'll sort it out, yeah?"

Fasta blinked—what did he mean, he would sort it out? Did he mean he *did* need money, then? And she knew that look in his eyes, that flat forbidding stubbornness, and...

But then Henrik squeezed his eyes shut, and rubbed his hands at his face. "And look, Fass, I *like* this job," he added, faster. "I like working with you. We know each other, we understand each other, our magic is good together. *We're* good together, yeah? And I don't want to take it further, and risk losing it altogether. Don't want to risk losing *you*."

Fasta's thoughts kicked and swirled, and she tilted her head, studied Henrik's familiar face. "But why," she began, "why do you think... *furthering our relationship* would risk anything? Why couldn't it be... good, between us? Or even better?"

Henrik laughed, sudden and harsh—but then it faded just

as swiftly, his mouth grim. "Because there's no future in it, Fasta," he said curtly. "It would only go one way. And it's not a way that benefits me. Ever."

What? Fasta blinked at him, the hurt and confusion flaring together, and Henrik exhaled, frowned at the floor. "Look, let's be honest here," he added, quieter. "We both know rich heiresses like you don't settle down with your employees. It would only last until you got sick of me, and found some rich lord to marry. Or maybe"—he took a ragged breath—"until I get too comfortable, and take it somewhere I shouldn't. And then I'm alone, without you, without a job, with my family still needing me. I'm *fucked*, Fass."

Fasta desperately wanted to argue that, all of it, but her scattering brain was somehow caught on just one part of it. *Until I get too comfortable, and take it somewhere I shouldn't.*

"What... what do you mean?" she croaked, through her convulsing throat. "What would you do that you shouldn't?"

There was a breath of choked silence, and then another harsh laugh from Henrik, a wild, reckless hunger flaring in his eyes. "Really?" he asked, his voice low and strange. "You have to ask?"

Oh. Heat flared up Fasta's spine, sudden and sharp, because yes, oh gods, she did know that look in Henrik's eyes, that tone in his voice. And her swirling thoughts suddenly flipped backwards, to a day on a job several weeks before, when she'd argued one of his orders. And Henrik had looked at her just like that, and flipped his heavy steel shovel in his fingers.

I oughta give you a paddling for that, Lady Valgeirr, he'd drawled at her. *I oughta bend you over my knee, and teach you who's boss around here.*

Afterwards he'd of course laughed it off, played as though it was just a joke, like he always did. But he wasn't laughing now, and Fasta couldn't stop staring at him, as her heart thudded in her chest, and her thoughts frantically hurled the pieces together. Henrik didn't truly *want* such things with her. He hadn't *meant* all those jokes and comments. He couldn't. Could he?

But he was intently looking away now, his jaw tight, his hands in fists. "I can't risk it," he said, quiet, toward the floor. "Please, Fass, *please* don't push me on this."

His voice was rough, his mouth twisting, his unhappiness far too clear in the air around them. And gods, suddenly Fasta just felt cold, and alone, and miserable. Henrik had truly thought all this about her, all this time? He thought she would use him like that, and then dump him, either for some rich lord, or over a few commands in bed? That she would cut him off, forever, and let his family be *impoverished,* when she *knew* how much they mattered to him?

But the look in Henrik's eyes said that he did believe all that, and more, and Fasta squeezed her eyes shut, counted to ten. She'd finally pushed for Henrik's truth on this, and he'd given it. And clearly it was only her own privilege that had kept her from seeing this before now, because Henrik truly did have everything to lose, if it went wrong. He would lose everything, and Fasta would only lose him.

But suddenly that *did* feel like everything, and Fasta had to count to ten again before opening her eyes, blinking at the floor. It was fine. It had to be fine.

"Thank you for telling me, Harry," she said, wooden. "I understand, of course, and I'll do my utmost to respect your wishes."

There was only more silence from Henrik, and Fasta blinked again, took a hard, bracing breath. "Um, so are you still planning to work tomorrow?" she asked, her voice wavering. "I'll be starting soon after sunrise, but don't feel obligated to join me, you'll likely be tired."

The words were met with yet more silence, and now with the sound of Henrik's shifting feet. And Fasta desperately wanted to look up at him, to search his face, but found that she couldn't move, couldn't breathe. Could only sit here on the bed, blink at his perfect tiled floor, wait for him to leave.

"Look at me, Fass," came Henrik's voice, but she didn't look up—and in a breath, he was there. *Here.* Standing close before her, his big callused hand warm on her face, tilting her chin up, making her look at him.

"Look at me," he said again, quieter. And Fasta was looking, her heartbeat skipping, but Henrik wasn't talking. Just looking back toward her, with his ruffled curls and strong jaw and shifting, too-dark eyes.

"Look, if you want," he breathed. "If we're still doing this, when the girls are done, and on their own—then, we can try it."

When the girls are done. Henrik's little sisters Hilda and Elsie and Chloe were ten now, Fasta knew—she'd sent them all gifts on their birthday—so Henrik meant another six years, at minimum? Probably eight? Or ten?

Fasta should have shoved away—should have said, *Thanks, Harry, but no thanks, you just told me you don't trust me, and I just told you, I'm so sick to death of being alone...*

But instead, she just kept looking. Looking up at how Henrik's throat bobbed, his breath hitching, as a faint pink stain crept up his cheeks.

And when his hand moved again, pulling her up and close, Fasta had no thought of resisting. No thought of anything but Henrik Hallen drawing her against him, his hand spreading wide and possessive on her face as he leaned down, took a shuddery breath, and—*kissed* her.

It exploded through Fasta all at once, the taste the smell the bright sheer magic of him, and her mouth groaned against his, her hands gripping at his tunic. Drawing him closer, harder, and like in everything else, he just *knew*, was just *there*, tilting her head and sliding his tongue deep. Sliding his big strong arms around her, too, folding her into the safe broad heat of his chest, and also—Fasta groaned again—pressing her against that shocking bulging hardness in his trousers. Saying he did want her, proving he wanted her, and fuck, nothing had ever felt so good in her entire *life*—

Until suddenly it was snatched away, those hands pushing instead of pulling—and when Fasta's eyes blinked open again, Henrik was halfway across the room, breathing heavy, rubbing his hand against his mouth. Almost like that first day they'd met, like he was—appalled, somehow, and Fasta still couldn't speak, could still feel the ghost of his breath on her lips.

"*Damn* it," he whispered, and Fasta flinched, her body suddenly shivery and cold. Because it was Henrik—*again*—saying he regretted that. He shouldn't have done that. And his big body was already confirming it, sidling toward the door, his eyes distant and strained.

"Uh. So yeah, I'll probably be a bit late tomorrow," he said, his voice hoarse. "Sorry. You don't have to wait for me, I'll be along."

Fasta nodded, because she couldn't trust herself to speak, and Henrik jerked a nod, too. "Sorry," he said again. "I really am. Can we just—pretend this all never happened tomorrow? Please?"

Fasta didn't reply, but the look in her eyes must have been enough, because Henrik nodded, and twitched her a wan little smile. And then he slipped out the door, shutting it quietly behind him, even as the too-strong taste of him kept sparking, all over Fasta's skin.

2

Fasta slept horribly that night, with visions and smells of Henrik swirling in her head, her room, her bed.

It was bad enough that he'd kissed her, but making it even worse was the fact that he'd also prowled around the room like that, touching her walls and her bed. Ensuring that Fasta's every breath filled her with Henrik's eyes, Henrik's hands, Henrik's magic.

She was already far too sensitive to his magic, having worked with it every day for the past half decade, but now it was like it was swallowing her, consuming her whole in its too-powerful wake. Even the judicious use of Fasta's current favourite bedfellow—a long, polished stone cylinder that she could barely get her fingers around—only briefly helped, and filled her head with desperate, unwelcome memories of that hard, thrilling bulge in Henrik's trousers.

But Henrik had told her his wishes, more clearly than he ever had in all their five years together. He didn't trust her. He couldn't risk it. He would lose everything. And that kiss—that glorious, impossible kiss—was all she was getting from him, probably forever.

Finally Fasta gave up on sleep, and dragged herself out of

bed, and through her usual morning routine. First making her bed, then brushing and braiding her long blonde hair, pulling on the clothes she'd selected the night before. And then she sat with her legs crossed in the middle of her room, and felt the earth, the stone, the push and pull of magic in the air around her. She was still in control. It was fine. It had to be fine.

When she went to leave, there was another unwilling vision of Henrik, thanks to all those latches lining the door—all of them now freshly polished and gleaming. And when had Henrik even *done* that, and Fasta gritted her teeth, snapped the latches open with a flick of her hand, and stepped out into the dim, quiet corridor.

Her mood finally lifted a little as she walked out of Coven Manor's front gate, away from the lingering taste of Henrik, and into the early morning sun. Their project this week was excavating and restoring the exterior of an old ruined chapel, and so far it had been an intriguing, rewarding job. Enough that along with Fasta's usual daily diagrams and calculations, she'd also begun a detailed paper documenting the process, and a series of addenda to her own comprehensive notes on ancient construction methods.

Also, restoring old buildings was just plain fun. And once Fasta had arrived on-site, reviewed her previous night's notes, finished sifting the earth for artifacts, and properly set to work, she finally forgot Henrik entirely in the ebb and flow of it, the studying-drawing-calculating, alternated with the actual laying on of hands, pulling up the magic. Watching as the chapel's walls rose and straightened, a long-lost secret brought back to life again.

When Henrik finally showed up, it was mid-morning, and Fasta had finished with three of the chapel's granite exterior walls, and was currently chewing on the end of her pencil, considering the fourth. And being distracted enough, thankfully, that she twitched a smile toward Henrik, and waved him closer.

"So I know where this last wall was," she said, without preamble, "but it's disintegrated, and I can't get a grasp on it. Can you feel enough to isolate what's left?"

Henrik's shoulders relaxed a little—had they been tense?—and he gave a hesitant smile back, a careful clap to Fasta's shoulder as he passed by. Swirling her full of his bright, succulent magic, but she clenched her teeth, and dragged her thoughts away. She was respecting his wishes, and pretending last night had never happened. It was fine.

"Yeah, I can feel it," Henrik said now, kneeling beside her, spreading both hands against the earth. "Though it's different from the other walls—cheap limestone, which is why it's disintegrated. Must have been knocked down at some point, and rebuilt. Wouldn't you rather just start over with granite, to match the rest?"

Fasta would, of course, and after a few more minutes of discussion and review, they were standing shoulder to shoulder, carefully rebuilding the wall together with the stones the quarry had sent. Sometimes speaking, sometimes communicating only through touches and glances, and sometimes through the earth and stone itself.

"This is a bit off, right?" Henrik asked, touching a twinge of his magic into the corner he was working on, showing Fasta what he meant. "That's not our fault, is it?"

Fasta was already walking around to the other side of the wall, trailing her fingers along it. "Definitely not our fault," she said, and in reply a head-sized peephole swirled open in the wall between them, showing her Henrik's wry smiling face on the other side.

"Show-off," she murmured, though she was smiling too, and running an appreciative finger along the intricate bevelled edge of the peephole. "This looks like it was originally crooked by a few degrees, to line up with this door frame."

"Shoddy," Henrik said, with a grave shake of his head, but

the entire wall moved accordingly, jumping over a hands-breadth. "Better?"

Fasta touched it again, nodded her agreement toward him. "Perfect. As always, Harry."

Henrik shot her another grin through the peephole, and then it swirled shut, as though it had never been there. Matching the texture of the surrounding rock beautifully, with just a splash of extra colour, and Fasta pressed her hand against it, and breathed. It would be fine. It *had* to be fine.

By noon Fasta's stomach was growling, and as usual Henrik brought out his lunch, which as usual, was far too much for one person. But it was familiar, it was fine, and Fasta managed to keep talking about work as they ate, to keep her thoughts away from heated kisses and big hands and bulging trousers in the dark.

"You're gonna finish that, right?" Henrik pointedly asked, once Fasta had started fiddling with her bread, rather than eating it. "We both know you didn't eat breakfast, so keep at it, buttercup."

Fasta bit into the bread again, her face warming, and she meekly accepted the hunk of cheese Henrik handed over, too. Food was something else Henrik had casually given her orders about for years, because while Fasta still cared—sometimes—about fitting into her old dresses, or Society's standards, or her father's expectations, Henrik had always scoffed at all of it. And it had become a surprising relief to have him deal with it, rather than Fasta having to face off against the mess it still sometimes made in her head.

"Stop worrying about it, Fass," Henrik said gruffly, his eyes glinting with too much awareness on her face. "You need to eat, to keep your strength up. And you look great."

His eyes had briefly, surreptitiously dropped to Fasta's full breasts beneath her work tunic, and for an instant, she froze in place, her thoughts again flailing toward the night before. His hands spreading against her, his tongue hot in her mouth, *it's not that I don't want to go to bed with you...*

But—no. No. They were pretending it had never happened. So Fasta belatedly ducked her head, and ate the rest of her lunch as quickly as she could. It was fine. *Fine.*

She kept repeating that as they set to work again, first finishing that last wall, and moving to the roof. Until finally, late in the afternoon, she and Henrik both stepped back, and gazed up at their lovely little chapel. Which looked just as though it had been standing there whole and untouched, for thousands upon thousands of years.

"Thanks, Harry," Fasta said, once they'd had a short, satisfying debrief with their suitably impressed commissioner, and set out together back toward Coven Manor. "I'm really pleased with how that one turned out."

Henrik flashed her a tolerant smile, and nudged her shoulder with his as they walked. "Yeah, me too," he replied. "Thanks, Fass."

His voice hitched a little, as if hinting at some deeper meaning—but when Fasta shot him a look, he was looking straight ahead, his jaw set. And surely she was imagining things, and she needed to get over this, and move on.

"Well, now that this job is complete, we'll need to choose the next one," she told him, keeping her gaze on the road. "Have you looked at any of the new proposals Kjaran's received?"

Ms. Ellin Kjaran was the interim Director of Earth-Magic at Coven Manor, which meant that she was technically Fasta and Henrik's supervisor. She'd been brought on to replace their previous director, who had made an untimely exit the year before, in a mess that had involved several of Fasta and Henrik's friends—but while their friends had moved on quite spectacularly, Fasta and Henrik had been left behind with the ongoing scourge of Kjaran, who was a vapid Council appointment, and very near to useless.

"Nah, you know I'm not gonna subject myself to Kjaran if I can help it," Henrik said now, with a shrug. "You pick. Some kind of new build might be fun, we've been doing a lot of repairs and reconstructions lately."

Fasta nodded, and suggested a few possibilities she'd seen come through. Which, thankfully, led to more talking about work, and no more memories of last night. They were pretending it had never happened. It was *fine*.

When they arrived back at Coven Manor, it was supper-time, and their fellow mages were milling about, making their way to and from the dining hall. As usual, Henrik greeted many of the people they passed—mostly other women—and Fasta raised her chin, ignored them all, and fought to shove down that bitter, familiar surge of jealousy. Henrik was her colleague, and nothing more. That was all.

Neither of them spoke as they stepped into the baths together, the way they always did after a day's work. Of course they'd never fully bathed together, but they always used the room's washbasins and plentiful clean towels, and left their work clothes for the laundry. And though Fasta didn't look at Henrik as she peeled off her baggy tunic and trousers, she could almost feel the prickle of his eyes, lingering on her much finer, much closer-fitting regular clothes beneath.

"Hey," Henrik said, once she'd finished. "Fass. C'mere."

Fasta blinked, and then immediately obeyed, as though compelled. Holding herself perfectly still as Henrik's big hand reached up, and gently wiped his damp rag beneath her chin.

"Missed a bit," he said, with a twitch of a crooked smile, and Fasta felt her face heat as he kept doing it, maybe more than was necessary? But then he tossed the rag away, over with the rest of the laundry, and waved her toward the door.

They went to supper in the large, wood-panelled dining hall together, like they always did, and perhaps for the first time, Fasta wondered if this was something their other colleagues regularly did, too. Travelling to work together, eating together, washing up together, eating together again? Certainly some of the others would do so, wouldn't they?

But as Fasta headed for their usual table, a little apart from Coven Manor's other forty-odd mages, she wasn't quite sure—and even more so when Henrik came over with their plates. He knew what Fasta liked, and didn't like, and he always brought way too much, which again, at his prompting, Fasta usually ate anyway.

"What does *he* want?" Henrik said suddenly, halfway through a continued discussion of their last new build—and Fasta blinked over her shoulder toward the sight of none other than Johan Falk. The same tall, dark-haired fire-mage she'd taken to her bedroom last night. And he was currently stalking straight toward their table, with two of his fire-mage colleagues at his back, and something not quite pleasant on his handsome face.

"Hey, Fasta," Johan said, with a brief, meaningful glance down toward her, and then a harder one toward Henrik. "Hallen."

Henrik didn't stop eating, though his eyes had gone forbidding, his big shoulders squaring. "Falk. You need something?"

Johan curled his lip, and crossed his arms over his chest. "Yeah," he said. "I want you to give me my money back."

His money? Henrik briefly stilled, his jaw flexing in his cheek. "And why would I have your money?"

"Because you were in my room last night," Johan replied coldly. "While I was down in the common-room. Your magic's signature was on the door, and where I keep my pay. And now the last two weeks' worth is missing!"

Two weeks' pay wasn't an insubstantial amount, especially for a high-performing mage of Johan's calibre, and Fasta shot a worried look at Henrik. Who was now warily eyeing Johan, and shaking his head. "Look, it wasn't me, Falk," he said, his voice flat. "I've never been in your room in my life. I barely know where it is."

"Oh really?" Johan asked, clipped. "Then explain how the hell *your* signature got inside it last night, precisely when that much coin went missing!"

Fasta's shoulders stiffened, because Johan was hinting—as many of their fellow mages often did—that Henrik was poor. That Henrik hadn't come from the same kind of background that most of them had. And that if anyone would need to steal money, it would be him.

"Yeah, well, maybe you were drunk, and imagining shit," Henrik shot back. "I wasn't in your room, Falk."

His voice had deepened, carrying through the dining hall, and already multiple sets of eyes were glancing toward them. Until Runar Alariaq, a few tables over, stood to his feet, and sauntered over to join them.

"Trouble, boys?" he asked, and in reply all three fire-mages—and even Henrik—twitched away a little. Runar was something of an outsider here too, with his mysterious back-ground and his decidedly post-mortem areas of study. But he was also a brilliant healer, and—most pertinent, for the moment—he had an unnerving ability to detect small changes in a person's body that could indicate they were lying.

"Falk is accusing me of breaking into his room and stealing his coin," Henrik finally replied, his voice hard. "And I *didn't*."

Runar's dark eyes narrowed on Henrik, and then he gave a dismissive shrug. "Yeah, he's telling the truth," he told Johan. "Or at least, he thinks he is."

"Well, his signature was in my room!" Johan replied, louder. "I *felt* it. I went upstairs for a bit with Fasta"—he shot a sidelong glance toward her—"and when I stopped in, everything was fine. Went back downstairs for another drink, came back up around midnight, and there it was. *Him!*"

"Hmmm," Runar said thoughtfully, eyeing Johan with dispassionate dark eyes. "How fascinating. He's telling the truth too, folks."

He's telling the truth. Throughout all this, the panic had been simmering low in Fasta's stomach, but now it lurched higher, louder, screeching in her ears. If Johan really *was* telling the truth, that meant trouble. It maybe meant—*disaster*. Because Johan's uncle was a wealthy, titled, influential landholder, just like Fasta's father. And as much as Fasta hated to admit it, that meant Johan's truth, Johan's testimony, would be worth far more than Henrik's.

And a credible accusation like this could cost Henrik *everything*. Not only his job, but his earth-magic accreditations, and his entire career. Maybe even his freedom. It could take him away from here, from Fasta, *forever*.

And even after last night, after that kiss, Henrik didn't *trust* her—suddenly the thought of losing him, forever, felt overpowering enough to choke on. No. *No.* Fasta needed to fix this. She needed to do something. Say something. Henrik was *hers*.

And—wait. *Midnight*, Johan had said. And that was around when Henrik had been with Fasta, right? When they'd had that fight—that kiss—in her bedroom?

Fasta didn't miss that sudden warning flare in Henrik's eyes on hers, that brief shake of his head. Not wanting her to mention it, maybe not wanting to publicly admit to last night. *Can't we just pretend this all never happened...*

But—no. Fasta needed Henrik. He was her partner. Her protege. Her best friend. *Hers.*

"No, Johan," Fasta said, her chin raised, her voice cold and firm. "Henrik couldn't have been in your room last night. Because he was with *me*."

3

Fasta's words echoed through the suddenly quiet dining hall, as multiple heads snapped toward her.

He was with me.

It had come out sounding possessive, maybe even smug, and Fasta could feel Henrik's stillness across the table, the sharpness in his eyes. But she kept her own gaze coldly on Johan, who blinked back toward her, with something almost like hurt twisting on his mouth.

"Hallen was with *you*," he repeated, hollow, his dark eyes piercing on hers. "You were with *me* last night, Fasta."

Fasta's face heated, but she nodded, kept her chin lifted. "Yes, for a short while," she replied. "But immediately after that, Henrik came to my room instead. And I can assure you, there was no taste of *your* room, or your possessions, anywhere on his person whatsoever!"

It was again making a very public implication, or maybe even an announcement. Because for Fasta to be that certain, it meant Henrik's visit to her room wouldn't have just been a respectable collegial visit. It would have been... intimate. Touching. *Kissing.*

No one else spoke, though Fasta could still feel Henrik's

eyes burning into her, just as sharp as Johan's. But she held her eyes to Johan's face, and even gave him a cold little smile.

"If you don't believe me," she said, "you're welcome to come back upstairs and check for yourself. You'll easily feel Henrik's signature all over my room. Now, tell me"—she raised her brows toward him—"can you prove the same with yours?"

Johan's eyes narrowed, suggesting—as Fasta's distant thoughts had been rapidly calculating—that no, he couldn't prove any such thing. Because if Henrik's signature was still traceable in his room, he would have started with that point, and probably would have gone and reported it to the directors, besides.

"It was only trace amounts of his magic," Johan replied, his voice hard. "But it was definitely Hallen's, and definitely *there*. Where it sure as *hell* wasn't supposed to be."

Fasta's simmering anger flared higher, and she frowned up at him, pushed her plate away. "I told you, Johan," she said, "he was with me, and I can prove it."

She shot a sidelong glance toward Runar, who was still standing there listening—and thank the gods, he gave a slow, thoughtful nod. "She's telling the truth too, Falk," he said toward Johan, with a shrug. "Sorry."

Johan glared between them, as the distinct smell of smoke filtered through the air—but then he spun on his heel and stalked away, his friends trailing close behind him.

Fasta let out a slow, heavy breath, and finally risked a glance across the table at Henrik. But he was staring down at his half-empty plate, his jaw tight, his cheeks stained splotchy and red. Looking almost—angry. Disapproving. As if Fasta had betrayed him somehow, by defending him, and *saving* him. Helping him avoid charges of theft, and maybe even a Coven inquiry, or a horrifying public *trial*.

But Henrik still wasn't looking at her, wasn't even pretending to thank her. And when Fasta darted a sideways glance toward Runar, who was still standing there beside them, his expression clearly said what he thought, too.

"Look, Harry, I've got to go work on that paper," Fasta said now, her voice stiff. "I'll see you in the morning?"

Henrik glanced up, his eyes dark and narrow, and then frowned back down at his plate again. "Right," he said, hoarse. "See you then."

That was that, then, and Fasta stood, and strode out. Suddenly feeling irrationally and thoroughly furious, so much so that she didn't even notice Runar had followed until he was walking in step beside her.

"I covered for you back there, Fasta," he said, quiet, "but I can't do it again. My job is already on the line enough around here."

Fasta grimaced, because yes, Runar had gone above and beyond for her, and for Henrik, too. "I know," she replied, with a sigh, and a sideways glance at his handsome brown face. "Thanks. I really do appreciate it."

Runar shrugged, and turned with her to climb the stairs. "It's not you who should be thanking me," he said flatly. "You really need to make sure Hallen wasn't stealing."

Fasta shot Runar another look, sharper this time. "Henrik wasn't stealing," she replied, with a firm shake of her head. "He wouldn't. He told you so, and you yourself said it was true."

"Yeah, but Falk was telling the truth too," Runar countered. "And Hallen sure as hell wasn't with you that entire time, because we all saw him going off with Ilsa. And, let's be honest"—he flashed Fasta a cool smile—"you leave the common-room last night with Falk—which had Hallen in a towering temper, by the way—and a few short hours later, money is missing from Falk's room? It's suspicious, don't you think?"

Fasta's panic lurched again, swirling with the anger, and she jerked another hard shake of her head. "Henrik wouldn't steal," she insisted. "Never. He won't even take my money on a *loan*. Even when it's something important to him."

Her thoughts reluctantly flicked back to the night before, to when she'd offered to help Henrik. To that familiar stubborn look in his eyes as he'd said, *Fuck, no. You've already done enough. I'll sort it out...*

"Yes, but that's you," Runar said. "And you're not exactly impartial where Hallen is concerned."

They'd reached the open door of Fasta's second-floor workroom, perhaps her favourite place in all of Coven Manor, and she let out a slow breath at the familiar sight of its oversized desk, its wall of bookshelves, its neat piles of paper, its organized rows of stone and textile and wood.

"I'm not that partial," she replied, as she lit one lamp, and then the other, filling the room with a cozy flickering glow. "I'm well acquainted with Henrik's flaws. Stealing just isn't one of them."

Runar had followed her inside, half-shutting the door behind him, and he leaned against Fasta's desk, studying her. "You *are* partial," he said. "If you weren't, you'd be acting like everyone else in here, and actually *enjoying* your life. Rather than burying yourself in work and pining after Hallen, while he fucks around with almost every girl here except you."

"*You* fuck around too," Fasta snapped at him, but then closed her eyes, rubbed at her temples. "And look, I—I'm really trying, all right?"

She could feel Runar still watching her, his lean body shifting on her desk. "Are you?" he asked. "Then why'd you turn down Falk last night? He's a decent enough guy, considering. He'd be good to you. Would probably be faithful, honest, all of that."

Fasta made a face at the floor, shook her head. "I *know*, which is partly why I did it," she said testily. "But I didn't like the taste of his magic."

Runar shook his head, and huffed a low, knowing chuckle.

"And let me guess. The only person here whose magic you like is Hallen's?"

Fasta glared across the desk at him—why was he even still here?—and crossed her arms over her chest. "Of course not," she replied flatly. "Plenty of people are fine. *Yours* is fine."

There was an instant's silence, and when Fasta glanced up, her cheeks felt unusually hot. While Runar's head tilted, his eyes flicking briefly down Fasta's front, and up again.

"Is it, now?" he asked, his voice light, and Fasta swallowed at the sight of him coming around the desk, and then—her entire body twitched—he brushed a light, careful finger up against her cheek.

"Still?" he asked, soft, and Fasta swallowed again, looked at his long-lashed dark eyes—and then made herself give a slow, shaky nod.

Saying... *yes.*

And gods, this was definitely a bad, bad plan—but then again, maybe it wasn't. Because Henrik had made himself very clear last night, hadn't he? And then again today, too, between pretending nothing had happened, and then that mess with Johan. He wasn't hers, he didn't want to be hers, and she needed to remember that...

And Runar was here. He was a friend. He was handsome, and kind, and clever. And by all accounts he was a good—if prolific—lover, to boot. And besides, Henrik had just bedded Ilsa last night, hadn't he?

"You'd actually—want to?" Fasta asked, breathless, as Runar leaned closer, his mouth not quite touching her cheek. "You're sure?"

"If you are," he whispered back, and there was the touch of warm lips, soft against her cheekbone. "Nothing serious, though, you understand? Just between friends?"

Fasta jerked a shaky nod, because yes, that made sense. And maybe that was what she needed in all this, something without ties and commitments, without the pressure of seeing each other every damned day…

But then Runar pulled back, his eyes shifting on Fasta's face. "And not an ongoing thing, either," he murmured, "and no telling Thora. All right?"

Thora was the quiet, blonde-haired mage Runar worked with most, and someone Fasta considered a friend—and she yanked back too, and frowned at Runar's face. "Thora wouldn't like it?" she demanded. "Why not? You two aren't—?"

She didn't finish, because Runar pulled her close again, and pressed a soft, open-mouthed kiss to her jaw. "No," he said smoothly. "I just prefer keeping work and my personal life separate."

That was fair, and clearly something Fasta needed to embrace, too. And when Runar kissed her cheek again, she let her eyes flutter closed, let her body sink into the feel of this, the taste of it.

And it was… pleasant. Pleasant to feel Runar's warm, clever mouth on hers, and he did taste good, smell good. Much better than Johan, and perhaps much more practiced, too, with slim hands that knew very well what they were doing, and a mouth that seemed to fit so easily against hers…

But then, without warning, flaring in Fasta's thoughts, there was Henrik. Visions and memories of Henrik, of how it had felt with Henrik, of what Henrik's mouth had done instead. Of how it had felt more—*real*, somehow, more primal, with none of this cool self-awareness. And even the memory of Henrik's big hands touching her was making Fasta gasp into Runar's mouth, her body pressing up hard against him—

"*Fasta?!*" demanded a deep, familiar voice from the doorway. "What the *hell?*"

And even before Fasta yanked backwards, the horrified certainty shot through her body, slammed her like a boulder to the chest.

It was Henrik. And he'd seen *everything.*

4

Henrik advanced into the room, his hands in fists, his grey eyes bright and blazing with rage.

"You conniving *bastard*," he breathed toward Runar. "You make Fasta doubt me—let her think I'm a petty *thief*—and then you follow her up here, and make your move? Are you fucking *kidding* me?"

He looked damned near ready to punch Runar in the mouth, oh gods. And after a panicked glance at Runar's face, Fasta darted in between them, and clutched her clammy hands at Henrik's huge, twitching arms.

"Runar didn't plan anything," she said firmly, holding Henrik's flashing eyes. "I started it, Harry."

Henrik blinked at her, and then shook his head back and forth, like he couldn't quite follow. "*You* started it," he repeated. "With him? You actually want *him*?"

He shot a sharp glare toward Runar, and Fasta could feel Runar stiffening. Reading, surely, into that disbelief in Henrik's voice, and Fasta tightened her grip on Henrik's arms, and glowered at his face. "Yes, with *him*," she snapped back. "He's handsome, and kind, and very smart. And also, Harry, he could be an *ogre*, and you would have no right to an opinion, because this has *nothing* to do with you!"

Henrik blinked at her again, and his mouth dropped open, his eyes wide and incredulous. "Nothing to do with me?" he demanded. "We had an *agreement*, Fasta!"

A what? Something in Fasta's jaw was twitching, and she spun around, away from him, toward where Runar was watching all this with dispassionate eyes. "Forgive me, Runar," she said tightly, "but can you excuse us for a few minutes? Perhaps we can continue this later?"

"Oh no you won't," Henrik growled from behind them, prompting Fasta to shoot another furious glare over her shoulder—but Runar gave Henrik a chilly smile, his eyes flicking from him to Fasta and back again.

"Of course, beautiful," Runar said lightly, and then—to Fasta's jolting astonishment—he learned forward, and pressed a soft, lingering kiss to her mouth. "Come to my room anytime."

Henrik cursed under his breath, but Fasta ignored it, and held her eyes to Runar's. "Thank you," she said. "And thank you, again, for what you did tonight to help Henrik avoid theft charges, and a Coven inquiry, and possibly a public criminal *trial!*"

Henrik had finally gone silent, and Runar gave Fasta another cool smile. "Anytime," he replied, and then he strode out, shutting the door a little too hard behind him.

Fasta watched him go, and then slowly, stiffly turned herself around. To where Henrik was still watching her, his face flushed, his eyes glittering and hard.

"What the *hell*, Fasta," he snapped. "You're really with him now? And you're going to his *room* later? What if—what if you get *pregnant*?"

The fury lurched higher in Fasta's gut, and she met his glare with one of her own. "I've been on a pregnancy prevention spell for *years*," she shot back. "Not that it's any of your business, Harry, because we work together, and that's *all*. A fact which you made very, *very* clear last night, when you told me you'd consider a physical relationship with me in ten years, and then asked me to forget you'd said it at all!"

Henrik rapidly shook his head, like he was trying to knock something out of it. "Look, I didn't mean that," he said, with a grimace. "Didn't want you to forget *that*."

"Oh, really?" Fasta replied, putting her hands to her hips. "Then what *did* you want me to forget, Harry? The part where you said work was too important to risk? Or the part where you said you didn't *trust* me, and that I might leave your family *impoverished*?"

Henrik groaned aloud, rubbing at his eyes, but he didn't reply. And Fasta was finally following the full extent of this now, all of it, and she lurched closer toward him, and glared up into his familiar, handsome face. "Or," she continued, "the part where you apparently expect me to be alone and miserable for ten years while I wait around for you. While *you* get to keep running off with whoever the hell you want!"

Her voice rose sharply at that, making something catch and flicker in Henrik's eyes, and Fasta realized, distantly, that she couldn't remember ever yelling at him before. That she'd always kept it all buried deep inside, kept it calm and professional, just the way he wanted—but right now the jolting fury was far too powerful to ignore.

"Look, I didn't mean it like *that*," Henrik said, his eyes plaintive, almost pained. "I meant for it to be a—a good thing. A promise. Not a message that you should start fucking the first random arsehole who offers!"

"Yes, well, it wasn't a good thing for me!" Fasta shot back, her voice wavering, high-pitched. "It was you showing me exactly what I'm missing out on, and then telling me that maybe—if I keep you gainfully employed for the next ten years—I'll finally get to experience the rest of it!"

Henrik flinched, his shoulders hunching up tight. "It had

nothing to do with you keeping me employed," he said, through gritted teeth. "I swear to you. And you have to see"—he drew in a shaky breath—"this is exactly why it would be such a bad plan. It's all mixed up and mashed together, and if you're the only thing keeping my family out of the poorhouse, then I absolutely should *not* be fucking you!"

He was right, of course he was, and Fasta nodded, blinking away the irrational wetness suddenly lurking behind her eyes. "You're right," she replied. "You're absolutely right, Harry, and I agree with you. For my own sake, as well as yours, because I'd probably never know for certain whether you truly wanted it, or if you were just doing it to keep your job. So it's entirely logical for me to move on! And entirely *illogical* for you to be angry about it!"

There was no way Henrik could argue that, and thankfully, he didn't try. But his big chest was heaving, his eyes strangely glinting, and his swallow convulsed hard in his throat. "So you're telling me," he said, low, "if I don't fuck you, you'll go fuck someone else. Probably Runar. Probably tonight."

Fasta's chest was heaving too, and she took a breath, held his glittering eyes. "Yes, Harry," she replied, "I am saying that. And I'm sorry if it bothers you, but I've barely been touched in five whole *years*! And now that you've made your intentions very clear to me, why the hell should I keep waiting?"

Henrik didn't reply, didn't move, but his eyes on her were still so distant, so strange. With something in them Fasta had never seen before, in all the years she'd known him. And oh, she could scent his magic, too, swirling up taut and peculiar and powerful between them.

"And if I did it," he breathed, his voice almost a growl, "you wouldn't go to Runar? Or anybody else?"

The room suddenly seemed very small, the walls very close, and Fasta was oddly aware of the closed door, of that too-strong scent of Henrik's magic in the air. Tasting almost of rage, or maybe even desperation, his hands in fists, his eyes flashing in the flickering light.

"No," Fasta replied, her voice cool, distant. "Not if you did it."

The fury lurched again through the air, tight and hard and barely contained—and with it, suddenly, was the feel of Henrik's hands, gripping tight to her shoulders...

"Fine," he breathed, hot, furious, desperate. "Have it your way, you spoiled-rotten little brat. *Again.*"

And then he yanked Fasta close, and crushed his lips to hers.

5

Henrik Hallen was kissing her.

It was unexpectedly rough, hard, his mouth hot and demanding on hers, but Fasta instantly opened to it. Clinging back to him just as hard, just as hungry, even as his appalling words raged and echoed through her chest.

Have it your way, you spoiled-rotten little brat. Again.

She should have been offended. Should have shoved him away, and demanded explanations and apologies. But somehow it felt shockingly close to all those comments, all those commands, *I should bend you over my knee, show you who's boss*—and Fasta gasped at the bite of Henrik's teeth on her lip, and yanked him closer. Wrapping one arm tight around his broad hard back, sinking the other hand up into his tousled silken curls.

Henrik growled into her mouth, and his big hands on her shoulders shoved her backwards, toward her desk. Until she was pinned up deliciously tight against it, with nowhere else to go—except closer into Henrik, pushing back against him. But he was so damned big, so strong, and he was everywhere, in her mouth and all up against her, trapping her, his fingers gripping so hard she felt like she was about to crack—

A sharp bite of her teeth to Henrik's lip wrenched him backwards a little, his grey eyes stormy and incredulous on hers—but now he was here again, all his angry powerful bulk pressing down against her, and there was nowhere to go except backwards. Until Fasta was lying on her back on the desk, crushed between Henrik and the hard wood, with his mouth ravaging hers, his hands both clutched to her shoulders.

But there were still no thoughts of resisting, not even a glimmer. Only the heady furious craving for more, needing more, Henrik was so angry, Fasta was so angry, his raging magic leaking all over her and into her. And the only thing left was to bite and push and cling at him, to take more and more of this, whatever it was, whatever he would give her, *please.*

"You still want it," Henrik breathed, suddenly, his mouth yanking off just long enough to spit the words—and Fasta frantically nodded, even as Henrik's lips caught hers again, his teeth sinking down hard enough that she tasted blood. "Fine," he gasped, almost spat, into her mouth, and then—Fasta couldn't help a strangled cry—he bodily lifted her, turning her with his big strong hands, until she was facedown on the desk, her cheek her breasts her hips pressed painfully into the hard wood.

"Still?" his hoarse voice demanded, and Fasta was already nodding again, silently pleading, needing this so much she couldn't think, or breathe, or speak.

"*Fine,*" Henrik spat again, while the fury dragged against hunger, against heat, against a surging flying craving—and then his hand snapped to her trousers. Wrenching them down with a fluid jerk, and then yanking her long tunic up—and suddenly Fasta felt cool air, all up and down the skin of her back. Because she was bare to the room. To... to *Henrik.* Her friend. Her colleague. Her employee...

And oh, gods, Henrik was looking. She could feel him looking. And while part of her wanted to crouch and cower in shame, the other part risked a desperate glance back over her shoulder. To where yes, Henrik was looking down at her, his breath heaving, his face a furious shade of red.

And now he'd caught her looking, as yet more fury flashed across his eyes—and with a purposeful yank of his hand, one of Fasta's trouser legs pulled entirely off, as his booted foot kicked her legs apart. Exposing her even more, every secret place spread wide open to him, this couldn't be Henrik doing this, it *couldn't*—

But it was, and the craving was everywhere, all-encompassing, swallowing Fasta alive. And she was still looking at him, and he was looking at her, his eyes angry, blazing, stunning.

"Still," he hissed, even as he shoved her legs a little wider, as his eyes dropped, lingered. As the air felt even cooler, because she was soaking wet, her body waiting, pleading, begging—

"Tell me, Fasta," he growled. "The truth."

"Yes," she gasped back. "Yes. *Please*, Harry."

There was something wrong, suddenly, flashing in his eyes—but then he yanked down his own waistband, maybe just far enough. And gods, Fasta wanted to see him, needed to see what he *looked* like—but she couldn't, because his other hand was pinning her to the desk again, and because—he was already there. Already thick, and hard, and hot, and *there*.

And then—pressure. So much pressure, bearing down, breaching her. Making her cry out with it, scrabbling against the desk, but Henrik kept holding her, kept taking her. Pushing in, spreading her open, splitting her apart, so much, too much, pleasure and pain and Henrik actually doing this, holy mother of *fuck*—

"You like that?" his voice demanded from above her. "You want this?"

Gods, yes, and Fasta frantically nodded again, even as he pushed in deeper, harder. As her body fought, resisted, broke— and then Henrik was *there*, punching all the way inside, his hips pressed hard to her arse, his full bollocks grinding below.

"*Fuck*," he breathed—and oh gods, oh hell—he was fucking

her. Driving in and out of her, hard and fast and merciless, Henrik, Harry, her best friend, her colleague, her own brilliant earth-mage, everywhere, inside her, he had to be as big around as her *arm* and she had never been so open, so stretched and exposed, in so much perfect pain from so much heady glorious impossible craving pleasure.

Her body was fighting to keep up with him, to meet the wild pounding pace of his driving hips, but the desk was hard and forbidding and his hands had almost lifted her lower half off of it, holding her hips up while he slammed inside again and again. So there was no doing, only surrendering, only sinking into the feel of this, the truth of this, Henrik doing this, fucking her, finally making her *his*—

And with one final, gouging slam inside, he cried out, his body inside her swelling even fuller—and then he was pulsing out, hard and deep, with his hips pressed tight and close. Filling her with him, with his own hot surging ecstasy, and Fasta's groans were almost as loud as his, because there was nothing like this, no pleasure like this, nothing better than this in the entire damned *universe*—

She'd already felt impossibly full, stretched and raw and open, but now she could feel that wetness leaking out, squeezing itself around Henrik's hot, rapidly deflating invasion. And in a sudden, sharp movement, that heat jerked away altogether, leaving only cool air and emptiness behind, and—oh. The impossible, mind-bending feel of Henrik's thick seed, oozing out slow between her legs.

There was an instant's hurtling stillness, filled only with their heaving gasping breaths—and then more movement. Henrik moving, backwards from her, away. Leaving her cold, untouched, exposed, her head pounding, her face still pressed into the desk's hard wood.

It took Fasta too much effort to push herself up—her hands were jittering, her arms oddly unreliable—and already her body was aching, especially down between her legs. Where that wetness was still dripping out, and was Henrik still *watching*—

Fasta's feet felt just as unsteady as her hands, especially since one leg was still caught in its trousers, but she managed to turn around, gripping behind her at the desk for balance. And yes, Henrik was still there, but—oh. He was somehow already fully dressed, with his trousers tied up again, his body stiff, and his face redder than Fasta had ever seen it.

But he was still here, his eyes flicking up and down her shaky body, which—to Fasta's distant gratefulness—was still somewhat covered by the generous length of her wrinkled white tunic. But the wetness creeping down her leg was too present, too visible, now holding Henrik's arrested, wide-eyed gaze like it was something obscene.

"Um," Fasta said, her voice hoarse. "Harry. Do you have a rag?"

Henrik's whole body twitched, and he fumbled at his trouser pocket. Yanking out a rag, and thrusting it toward her, though his hand was visibly shaking now, perhaps just as badly as hers.

"Thanks," Fasta croaked, as she fought the sudden, bizarre urge to turn away, to hide. And instead, she just made herself wipe up the worst of it—gods, there was so *much*—under the too-heavy scrutiny of Henrik's dazed, strange eyes.

When she finished the rag was sopping, and—she blinked down toward it—tinged with dark streaks of red. Not unexpected, she supposed, considering the fact that it had been years since she'd done that—but before she could ball the rag up, hide it away, somehow Henrik was there, *here*, and plucking it out of her hand, and looking.

She still couldn't read him, couldn't follow that expression on his face, but something lurched in his magic, tasting harsh, and wrong. And when Fasta put her shaky hand to his arm, she was sure of it, because what had been the anger was now something else, something like regret, or like... grief. But then he yanked his arm away from her, sharp and frantic, almost like he'd been stung.

"I... hurt you," he whispered, looking down at that rag, and then up to her eyes. "I—*hurt* you, Fasta."

Fasta blinked, and then shook her head, so hard the room seemed to spin. "No," she said. "I'm *fine*, Harry."

"Don't lie to me!" he growled, so loud and unexpected that Fasta flinched, reeled back against the desk. And too late Henrik was there, steadying her, but his hand had gripped to her shoulder, to the same place he'd grabbed her before. Where it was now decidedly sore, enough to wring a sharp, unwilling gasp of pain from Fasta's mouth.

And gods curse her, because Henrik immediately released her, so abrupt that she stumbled, and had to cling at the desk to stay upright. To which Henrik betrayed a visible flinch, even as he kept staring at her like that, with that godsforsaken agony in his eyes, and that awful taste curdling in his magic.

"I'm fine," Fasta said again, but Henrik's head was shaking, back and forth. Saying no, no, and no again, and he backed up, away from her, with that red-streaked rag still in his hand.

"You're not fine," he said, his voice thick. "Tell me the truth, Fasta, *please*."

Fasta's head was shaking too, she wasn't going to tell him, she *wasn't*—but an odd noise scraped from Henrik's mouth, and he crumpled the rag in his fist. "Stop lying for me, Fasta," he rasped. "Stop covering for me. I'm not your servant, or your responsibility, or your *pet*. I don't need your pity, or your fucking *protection*!"

What? Fasta blinked at him, at his miserable eyes, at how he was now backed flat up against the door, fumbling for the latch. Trying to leave, *no*, and that sharp spike of fear was enough to wrench her upright again, to yank the trousers back up and tie them tight around her waist.

"Stop this, Harry," she told him, her voice surprisingly

calm. "I'm fine. I wanted that. I *enjoyed* that. You're over-reacting."

"I said, stop *lying* to me!" Henrik bellowed back, his eyes blazing. "Stop protecting me, stop condescending to me. Stop always acting like you control fucking *everything*, because you *don't!*"

The words hurt, but more than that was the tone of them, the look on his face. Saying that this—this wasn't only about what they'd just done. And did he truly think Fasta was condescending to him? Trying to *control* him?

Have it your way, you spoiled-rotten little brat. Again.

"Fine," Fasta said now, raising her hands in what she hoped was a gesture of conciliation. "Fine, Harry. I'm sorry. Whatever it is, I'm sorry."

But that only seemed to make Henrik shrink inward, his big body gone strangely small. "Don't apologize to me," he breathed. "Oh gods, Fasta, don't apologize, oh *gods*—"

And then he turned, and grabbed for the latch, as the spike of panic in Fasta's gut rose to a towering scream. "Harry," she gasped, as she lurched closer, gripped for his arm. "Don't go. We can work this out, *please*—"

But he shook his head, shook her off, and the bitter, broken taste of his magic was almost sickening in the air. And without another word, he stepped out the door, and swept it shut behind him.

6

Fasta spent another sleepless, miserable night. Not even bothering to go to bed this time, but just sitting there, alone in her workroom, staring at her desk.

She'd botched this. Badly.

It had only been a suspicion at first, dark and bitter in her gut. But the more she considered it, weighed Henrik's words against his actions, the more certain it became.

Have it your way, you spoiled-rotten little brat. Again.

And curse her, maybe Fasta *had* been a brat to Henrik about this. She had all the money in their relationship, all the power, all the control. And even if Henrik technically wasn't her employee, he still only had this position at Coven Manor because Fasta had demanded it. Because she had liberally thrown around her father's wealth and title and influence. And if she were to leave here, for whatever reason, Henrik would ultimately be expected—or forced—to leave, too. And while he could surely find other employment elsewhere, without the prestige of Coven Manor attached, it would likely involve far more tedious heavy labour, at a fraction of his current income. And they both knew it.

So Henrik *did* need Fasta. He needed this job, for his

family's livelihood, for his siblings' future success. He was obligated, cornered, trapped. And Fasta had ignored all that, and demanded more from him, when he hadn't wanted to give it. She'd made her displeasure known to him. She'd gone off with Runar, just like she had with Johan, because she'd wanted Henrik to know. She'd wanted him to respond. She'd maybe even wanted him to lose his temper, and do exactly what he'd done. Even if he'd clearly been furious, and desperate, and miserable.

And no, Henrik certainly hadn't been faultless either, but gods, what else had Fasta expected? Even that first kiss, that offer he'd made of trying it in ten years, had probably just been about keeping his job, because what else could he conceivably have told her? *No, I don't want you? Once my sisters are through school, I'm finished with you? I'd really rather have someone like Ilsa, and not a spoiled-rotten brat like you?*

Fasta groaned aloud, and rubbed at her aching eyes. Because maybe—maybe now she'd ruined this for good. Ruined five good years of friendship, of understanding, of easy camaraderie between them. Because she'd been jealous of Henrik and his other women. Because she'd used her position and her influence to try to get him to herself.

She'd seen the pattern far too often in her old life, where there had been an epidemic of older, wealthy men pursuing young naive women, who on the whole had held very little choice but to comply. Fasta had always found it highly enraging, and deeply immoral, and now here she was, doing the exact same thing to Henrik.

Fuck.

By dawn she was on her feet again, walking doggedly out Coven Manor's front gate, and toward the nearest town, a mid-sized hamlet called Skent. It was only an hour's walk away, a walk Fasta was well accustomed to, and she ignored the morning bustle of horses and vendors and children as she strode through the dusty streets.

Her goal was the town's main bank, one that had access to both her and her father's accounts in the capital, and a brief meeting with a courteous clerk had things arranged in very short order. And then—Fasta initially walked past, but then relented—she stopped by the office of her usual healer, and paid double to be seen on such short notice. And then stood naked and red-faced while the healer fussed over her, and asked who'd dared to be so rough with her, and whether she didn't want to arrange a meeting with the constable.

Fasta vehemently rebuffed all his questions, and she left feeling admittedly better, the ache between her legs entirely vanished, and her thoughts far clearer than they'd been yet today. She would offer to make amends. And she would accept whatever path Henrik decided to take from here.

Of course, that meant having yet another unpleasant conversation, but Fasta was determined to get it over with, and when she arrived back at Coven Manor, she followed the faint trace of Henrik's magic toward the dining hall. But upon stepping inside, she was confronted with the sight of Henrik on his feet, his eyes furious, his hands in fists. And he was facing off against—Johan?

Fasta hesitated for an instant, as more memories from the night before barged through her thoughts. *Stop covering for me. I'm not your servant, or your responsibility, or your pet. I don't need your pity, or your fucking protection.*

But the entire scene was surrounded by curious onlookers, and Henrik looked cornered, raging, ready to snap. And with one wrong flare of magic, one flying piece of metal, he could so easily kill Johan where he stood—and that would be the end of everything. Of Henrik's job, his family's security, his *life*.

No. *No.* Henrik might hate Fasta for this, but she needed to try. Needed to be the spoiled-rotten brat, again.

So she squared her shoulders, and elbowed her way through the gathering crowd of onlookers. Until she could shove herself in between Henrik and Johan, facing off against

Henrik's furious, tensed-tight form. "What's this about?" she asked, too sharp. "Is there some kind of problem?"

And thank the gods, Henrik didn't snap back, or move her away. Instead, his stiff shoulders slightly sagged, his eyes sharp and searching on hers.

"Falk is saying I was in his room again," he replied, his voice hollow. "Stealing."

Gods damn it. Fasta choked back her curse, and spun to face Johan, holding herself as straight and tall as she could. "When?" she demanded. "Last night?"

"Yes," Johan replied, his eyes narrow and glittering. "And don't try and play that he was with you this time, Fasta, because we all saw him getting drunk down in the common-room last night!"

They had? Fasta's thoughts skittered and spun, but she dragged in a deep breath, and rapidly counted to ten. "And do you actually have any proof this time?"

"No," Johan spat back. "But I brought Konsta in"—he gestured at one of his fire-mage friends behind him—"and he tasted it too. But only for a few minutes, because Hallen was obviously hiding himself, again. And instead of coin, he helped himself to every valuable piece of stone and metal in my room!"

What? Fasta shot a sharp look at Henrik over her shoulder, but he was slowly shaking his head, his jaw jumping in his cheek. Because no, of course he hadn't done any such thing, he *wouldn't*—but Fasta could almost taste his hurt, and his simmering shame. His miserable awareness that every person in this room believed him to be a stupid, petty thief, and there was nothing—*nothing*—he could do about it.

It flared Fasta's own fury even higher, and she spun to glare back at Johan again. "Have you informed the directors yet?" she demanded. "Or conducted a search for the missing items?"

"Not yet," Johan replied flatly, "because I know exactly where to look, and Hallen's refusing to let me into his room!"

Fasta had to take another breath before turning back to face Henrik, who was now nearly spitting with fury. And no wonder, because for any earth-mage—and especially a builder of Henrik's calibre—a room wasn't just a room. It was a sanctuary, a solace, even a work of art. And letting it be invaded, searched, would feel like a sacrilege. An attack.

"No," Henrik hissed, his voice deep and vicious. "This prick is *not* stepping foot inside *my* room!"

But curse it, even more curious people were filtering over to watch the hubbub. Including Runar, now with his blonde colleague Thora in tow, and behind them—Fasta bit back a groan—was the smug, portly form of Kal Merton, the only other earth-mage currently working at Coven Manor. And Merton was a slimy pompous toad, who had previously been caught red-handed in some *highly* illegal activities, and who had gotten off scot-free thanks to atrocious amounts of his wealthy father's money.

"This *priiiick* is *naw* steppin' foot inside *mah* room," Kal repeated, in a high-pitched, sing-song voice, mimicking Henrik's accent with awful, spiteful accuracy. "Gods, Hallen, you sound like a mewling *peasant*. If you're really telling the truth about being innocent, what are you so scared of? That they'll see your wanking rags?"

Almost all the onlookers laughed, except Runar and Thora, while Henrik's magic tilted and flared in the air, shuddering with that humiliated, desperate rage. Strong enough that Fasta's own heartbeat kicked and surged with sheer rising panic, because *fuck,* this was bad. This was going to destroy Henrik's job, his family, his entire *life*, and Fasta had to fix this, had to make it *fine*—

"Hey," said a soft voice, close beside Fasta, and when she twitched to look, it was Thora. Runar's blonde, pale colleague. And she was placing a careful, surreptitious hand against Fasta's arm, her blue eyes gone glazed and distant, because— oh. She was casting. Using her strange, deeply impressive magical skill of delving into the future, to project where this whole mess might lead next.

"It's all right," Thora said, her eyes blinking, her voice soft. "Let them search."

Let them search. That was all the confirmation Fasta needed, in this moment, and she spun back to face Henrik. Who was now staring at her with raw, incredulous disbelief in his eyes, because maybe he'd heard what Thora had said, he knew what Fasta was about to do...

"No, Fasta," he hissed at her, through his teeth. "You don't get to decide this."

But yes, Fasta was a selfish spoiled brat after all. Because even if Henrik hated her for this, she still couldn't stand for this to take him away from her. She couldn't. He was *hers*.

"Actually, yes, I do," she told him, with as much haughty coldness as she could muster. "Now take us to your room, Henrik. And that's an order."

7

There was no way Fasta and Henrik were coming back from this.

Henrik hadn't argued Fasta's order, her very public proclamation that yes, she was in charge, and yes, Henrik was as good as her employee. But she could again almost feel his hurt, his betrayal, his bitter fury. And he hadn't once looked at her as he'd led them up to his room, his big shoulders hunched, his hands in fists.

"Gods, Hallen, your room is a *dump*," Merton announced, once Henrik had snapped open his latches and stalked inside, with the rest of them following behind. Not only Fasta and Johan, but also Konsta and Merton, who Johan had insisted accompany them as so-called impartial observers.

"Then don't fucking look at it," Henrik snarled back, as the fury in his magic flared hotter, shot through with frustration and shame. "Or better yet, *leave*."

But of course Merton wouldn't leave—he was enjoying himself far too much—and Fasta followed his contemptuous eyes across Henrik's room. Like her own, it was beautifully outfitted and furnished, full of Henrik's own stonework and metalwork—the tiled wall and floors, the iron bed, the delicately wrought lamps. But yes, at first glance, the room was indeed also a mess. There were stacks of wire crates lining the walls, bursting with rocks and ore and tiles and books, and every available surface was covered with yet more rocks, everything from gravel to polished gems to massive rough-cut boulders.

But the reason for that, of course, was because in all Henrik's years at Coven Manor, he had never been given a proper workroom to study and practice in. There had always been some excuse, someone else who needed the space more urgently, and was just another way that Coven Manor had not-so-subtly pegged Henrik as a second-class citizen. As Fasta's *employee*. And of course Henrik had always refused Fasta's offers to share her own workroom, because that would make it even more obvious, wouldn't it?

Fasta's own anger lurched higher, and she whirled around to glare at Merton, her chin up, her jaw set. "Henrik is one of the most highly skilled earth-mages in this entire *country*, Merton," she told him, in frigid tones. "And most certainly the best one presently here at Coven Manor. I wonder why that could be? Perhaps due in part to the fact that he chooses to work and study in his spare time, rather than relying on his father's *money* to compensate for his failings?"

Merton glared back at her, muttering something unintelligible under his breath, but Fasta ignored him, and turned her attention to Johan and Konsta. "*You* were the ones who wanted to do this," she said sharply. "Can you at least proceed in a timely manner, and get this farce over with?"

Thus commenced a deeply unpleasant morning of searching, mostly led by Merton, whose goal was clearly not only to tear Henrik's room to pieces, but also to provoke him as much as possible. Making snide comments about how filthy the place was, and how there was no way Henrik had actually *read* all these books, and how someone had to keep an eye on Henrik, to make sure he wasn't surreptitiously moving around his contraband with magic while they weren't looking.

"All right, so maybe it's not in here," Merton finally admitted, with palpable misgiving, once they'd searched through every drawer, under every tile, and even—with Fasta's reluctant help—into the walls themselves. "But Hallen could also have stashed the loot elsewhere. He could easily hide a hoard behind any wall in this manor."

Merton shot Henrik a look of deep dislike as he spoke, but to Henrik's credit, he didn't acknowledge it, or respond. Instead he just kept standing and glaring in silence, with his arms crossed tight over his chest.

"You're grasping, Merton," Fasta cut in, her voice cold. "You've taken this entire room apart, and as expected, there's nothing here. Johan, if you really must pursue this matter further, you should go make your reports to the appropriate authorities, and stop wasting our time!"

Johan clearly wasn't convinced, but even he was looking at Merton with obvious distaste by this point, and after a few muttered words to Konsta, the two of them finally left, with Merton trailing along behind. Not even giving the slightest apology for the mess they'd made of Henrik's room, let alone offering to help clean it up.

Fasta glared after them, her heart still skipping in her chest, her hands in clammy fists at her sides. How *dare* they. How dare they treat Henrik like this. He was brilliant, he was hardworking, he was *hers*—

But—no. No. Because gods curse her, she hadn't been much better than Merton or Johan in this, had she? She'd treated Henrik like a pet, like an employee, like a *servant*. And she'd just done it again, publicly, before all those watching witnesses. Called him to heel. Made him obey.

Suddenly Fasta couldn't bear to look at Henrik, to see the judgement or the disappointment in his eyes. And instead, she spun away from him, and shoved her hands against the nearest wall. Feeling the broken tiles, the crumbling plaster, the sinking miserable guilt. The regret.

"Look, I'm sorry, Harry," she said toward the wall, her voice cracking. "For this, and for—for yesterday, too."

There was an instant's strange stillness behind her, but Fasta didn't look, couldn't turn her head. "I was—inappropriate, last night," she went on. "I shouldn't have pressured you. I shouldn't have taken advantage of my position, and treated you like—like a servant. A *pet*. And"—there was no air, why was there no air—"I want to make it up to you. To do better by you. So—"

There was more silence, still so strange and stilted, and when Fasta risked a glance over her shoulder, Henrik was staring at her, eyes unreadable. But he didn't speak, so Fasta dragged in more breath, forced out the rest.

"So I've set aside a sum under your name, at the bank in Skent," her hollow voice said. "It should be enough for you to take your time and find other profitable work, and ensure your family is well taken care of in the bargain. If I can help in any way, please let me know, I'll of course give you an excellent reference. Anything you need."

But Henrik still didn't reply, so Fasta turned away, back to the wall. Gripping her hands against it, feeling the strength of it beneath the broken plaster. "Thank you for being such a—an exemplary colleague, these past five years," she whispered, her voice wavering. "I've truly loved being your—your—"

But gods, she couldn't even say it, she was about to break down sobbing—and too late, she wrenched away from the wall, toward the door. She'd said it, she'd done it. Henrik wasn't hers, he wasn't, it was done.

Until—a hand. Henrik's hand, warm and strong and familiar, curling around Fasta's wrist. Holding her here. And now gently drawing her back toward him, turning her to face him, his shadowed eyes searching hers.

"Look, you know I'm not taking your coin, Fass," he said, his voice strained, thin. "But—is this what you really want? For me to *leave*?"

Fasta hesitated, swallowed, because maybe her honest answer would be more condescending, somehow—but now Henrik was guiding her backwards, toward the broken wall. Until her back was pressed flat against the dusty plaster, with both Henrik's hands settling to the wall on either side of her head. Feeling it, needing it, because it was always easier like that, maybe for both of them.

"Tell me, Fass," Henrik said, lower. "The truth."

That cursed wetness prickled stronger behind Fasta's eyes, and she held her gaze safely over Henrik's shoulder, on the wall behind him. "Of course I don't want you to leave," she managed. "But I botched this, Harry. I have to—make amends. Have to respect your wishes, and stop—condescending to you. Trying to control you. Being a—a rich spoiled brat."

It came out bitter, and a little broken, and Henrik groaned aloud, and brought his hand to Fasta's face—but then he snatched it away again, too quickly, and shoved it back to the wall. Remembering, maybe, what had happened last time he'd touched her.

"You didn't fuck up, Fasta," he replied, quiet. "You didn't do anything. I'm the one who fucked up. I'm the one who—lost my temper with you. And *hurt* you."

Fasta had already opened her mouth to deny it, but then her eyes caught on his, and she choked back the words. Because maybe that was more lying to him, more protecting him, and if she was being honest, he *had* hurt her. With the aches and bruises, yes, but more than that, with the way he'd been afterwards. The way he'd left.

"Yes, but I pressured you into it," she told him instead, raising her chin. "You asked me not to push you, but I did anyway. I took advantage of my authority over you."

Henrik huffed a heavy sigh, his hand briefly covering his

mouth. "No," he said. "I took advantage of *you*, Fasta. I wanted you. I've wanted you for—*forever*."

What? No. Fasta stared at him, as something surged and screeched through her skull. *I wanted you. I've wanted you for—forever.*

"And you not seeing anybody all these years," Henrik added, "keeping all your attention for me—well, that suited me just fine. More than fine. Even though I had no right."

Oh. Fasta's thoughts were still wildly blaring, but she swallowed, shook her head. "But you—you never actually asked for any of that, or pushed it with me," she countered. "I was the one who pushed *you*. And I had no right, either, because yes, fine, maybe you *are* essentially my employee—and you made your wishes toward me very clear!"

Henrik's mouth twisted, and he huffed a low scoff. "Look, my wishes can go to hell," he said, impatient, "because yeah, maybe that's what I told you I wanted—but what I actually wanted *was* for you to wait around for me! You were right, me expecting that from you—and then losing my shit over it like I did yesterday—is fucked up, and way out of line. Especially with everything else you already do for me!"

Fasta couldn't find a reply to that, and Henrik took a deep breath, his chest expanding. "*I'm* fucked up," he added, stiffly now. "What I did to you yesterday was unforgivable. The worst thing"—he hesitated, his throat convulsing—"I've ever done to somebody I care about in my life. You should get me fired. You should report me. You shouldn't be defending me and putting up with all this bullshit today and trying to give me coin and *apologizing* to me!"

His voice rose at the end, his eyes blazing bright and furious on hers, and damn it, and they were back to this again. To the quietly creeping despair, now lurking low but unmistakable in their mingled magic, choking the air between them.

"I—I didn't know," Fasta finally said into it, against it, her eyes dropping down to his chest. "That it bothered you so much. Me defending you, protecting you. Being... in charge. In control."

Henrik's chest heaved, straining a little at the leather laces of the tunic covering it, and Fasta shoved back the inexplicable urge to reach for those laces, to loosen them. "It shouldn't bother me," Henrik replied, his voice rough. "You've been so good to me. I owe you more than I'll ever be able to pay back."

And maybe that was something, right there, and Fasta's eyes darted back up, searching his. "But it's not fair, is it?" she said. "You're just as good as I am at this job. Better, even. Me being in charge is just—family. Money. The opportunities I've had. It's entirely arbitrary."

Henrik didn't reply, but there was something in his eyes, something... resigned. Because yes, of course he already knew all that, and maybe he'd learned to live with it—but he'd clearly still found it chafing, lacking, wanting.

But he still wasn't speaking, so Fasta kept following it, feeling her way. "So maybe—how things stood between us," she said slowly, "before yesterday, with me waiting for you—made it better for you. More—fair. Gave you some power back."

Henrik's eyes shifted, changed, and Fasta knew she had it now. And yes, of course, it was so damned obvious, why hadn't she seen it before?

"And then," she continued, careful, "me seeing other people—threatening to see other people—took that away from you."

Henrik still didn't reply, but he didn't have to, and Fasta grimaced down at those too-tight laces again. "That makes so much sense," she whispered. "I'm sorry, Harry."

But Henrik was shaking his head now, swift and furious. "*Don't*," he hissed. "Don't apologize to me, Fasta. I fucked up, I hurt you. You're not responsible for setting me off, making me treat you like that. That was all me, I guarantee you."

There was an unmistakable flare of misery in the air, in his voice, and his eyes were pained, his mouth tight. "And like I said before, that's another reason why this"—he waved between them—"is such a bad idea, right? Why it's the *worst* fucking idea. The last thing I should ever, *ever* do."

Fasta blinked uncertainly toward him, and Henrik shook his head again, and choked a harsh, bitter laugh. "You have this ridiculous idea of me as someone—*safe*," he said. "Someone reliable, and trustworthy. Someone who'll always treat you like you deserve. Right?"

Fasta nodded, because yes, she did feel that way—but Henrik laughed again. "Well, you're wrong," he continued, harder. "You think you know what I really want in bed? You *don't*. You can't *imagine* the shit that goes through my head about you, Fasta. The things I think about you. The things I'd be tempted to *do* to you."

Fasta's body quivered to a stark, sudden stillness, her eyes trapped on his. "Like—like what?" she stammered, because were there really *more* things? Even beyond rough handling over a desk, beyond all those sly comments and commands? *I oughta give you a paddling for that. I oughta bend you over my knee, and teach you who's boss. Do you like taking orders from a commoner, Lady Valgeirr?*

Henrik hesitated, maybe regretting that he'd admitted that. But Fasta needed to know now, so desperate that she *did* hook her finger through that leather lace at his throat, and pulled him closer. "What things do you want to do to me, Harry?" she whispered. "Things like what we did yesterday?"

Henrik grimaced, his eyes briefly closing, his chest heaving against her finger. "Not just like that," he replied, flat. "Way worse than that. Shit you'd only ever do at certain kinds of places. Not *here*, and especially not with the perfect brilliant generous girl you owe your entire damned *life* to."

The air in the room had stretched thin, and Fasta searched for thoughts, for breath. "Like what?" she said again, her voice sounding oddly composed, even as her finger pulled harder at his tunic. "What places do you go to, Harry?"

She hadn't even known he sought out encounters like that, or that he ever even *would*, when he already had so little difficulty finding regular bedmates here at Coven Manor—but his face was flushing red now, his throat spasming. "Secret places," he replied, hoarse. "With people who are actually into all that. And you can set up rules, and play those kinds of games with them. Have your way with them. Have them listen to you, obey you, serve you."

Oh *gods*, and even as Fasta's stomach churned, something else tightened, hard and low in her belly. Because yes, it made so much sense now, all of it, and she fought down the sudden urge to laugh, or maybe sob.

"Well," she began, cleared her throat. "I suppose you wanting that—from me—does have a certain logic, doesn't it? That if I'm the one in control the rest of the time, that it would be—*appealing*—to you, if our roles were reversed?"

Her finger was still hooked on Henrik's tunic, her eyes searching his, and he blinked at her once, twice. And then he shook his head, like he was trying to escape his own thoughts, and he grasped Fasta's hand, guided it away, back toward the wall behind her.

"You're still doing it, Fasta," he said, his voice hard again. "You're still covering for me. Did you not *hear* what I just said to you? That I want to play games where I order you around, and do whatever the hell I want with you? Even worse than I did last night? When I shoved you onto a desk and forced myself on you until you *bled*?"

Fasta dragged in a slow breath, let it out. "But I *wanted* that last night, Harry," she insisted, the truth of it ringing through her voice. "And no matter what, you're still—*you*. I *know* you. I *trust* you."

"No," Henrik shot back, and his hand clutched to her chin, giving it a firm little shake. "You don't know me, and you shouldn't trust me! Do you really want to know the shit I think about doing to you, Fasta? Is that what it's gonna take for you?"

Fasta should have said no, should have finally backed down, let this go, like she'd originally meant to do—but Henrik's hand was still on her chin, tasting so strong of his magic, swirling up too-powerful memories of the night before. And before she'd even caught it, Fasta's head fervently nodded against his fingers, saying—yes. *Yes.*

Henrik's grip on her chin tightened, his eyes briefly closing in something almost like pain. "Fine," he hissed. "*Fine.* I think about fucking you until you scream. About making you gag on me, about spraying off all over your face. I think about pinning you down with rocks and shackling you spread-eagled to a wall and spanking you, until you're covered with my handprints. I think about making you suck me while I work, slamming myself up your tight little arse and making you like it. I think about stretching you out so much you'll never feel anyone else inside you *again.* I *dream* about"—that hand on her chin slightly shook—"making perfect, proper Lady Fasta Valgeirr kneel and grovel for me, begging for my spunk. Begging to be knocked up by a poor fat *commoner.*"

The words came out fast, rushed, jumbled, *wrong*—but as he spoke them, it was like each one leapt fully to life in Fasta's thoughts. Like she could envision them, could see Henrik doing them. And would he actually do them, did he do them with the women in those secret places, threaten to *knock them up*, was that a *game*—

There was something almost like a smile on Henrik's mouth now, grim and cold, and he released Fasta's chin, his hand dropping to his side. "And I would do all that," he said, his voice lower, like a threat. "If you let me. I would ruin *everything* with that shit, Fasta. You can't *trust* me."

The words hung in the air between them, potent and powerful and perhaps—perhaps actually *true*, and Fasta couldn't seem to come to terms with them, with Henrik saying them. Her Henrik, her Harry, her best friend. Her protege. Her... *employee*. Wanting that? Thinking that? Maybe even... *doing* all that?

But then again, the signs had all been there for years, hadn't they? All those teasing comments about punishing, about paddling, about high and mighty Lady Valgeirr? All those little orders, so casually given throughout their workdays, that he fully expected her to follow? And then, of course, last night, when he'd shoved her over that desk, and had his way with her?

Henrik was waiting, watching her, still with that strange grimness in his eyes, tinged with something like triumph. Like he'd thoroughly made his point, and maybe he had. But Fasta couldn't stop looking at him, at his mouth his shoulders his hands, at those smile lines all around his grey eyes. Because Henrik did smile, he grinned at her all the time, he teased her and brought her lunch every day and made beautifully bevelled peep-holes, just because he knew she'd like them.

"But," she said, and even that one word made something change, flickering in those eyes. "I still just—*like* you, Harry."

His eyes shifted again, and Fasta pulled in more breath, more courage. "And I know you don't believe me, but I—I liked it yesterday, too. I liked how strong you were, how confident and commanding you were. I've always liked that about you. And getting to finally experience you like that"—she exhaled in a shuddery huff—"it was so *good*, Harry."

Something sparked and charged in the air, hot and close between them, and Fasta raised her hand, dared a brief, furtive touch of her fingers to Henrik's chest through his tunic. "So maybe," she added, quieter, toward her hand, "maybe I would like the rest of it, too. If we tried. Especially if it really was"—her eyes fluttered—"just a game."

That heat between them flared higher, and Fasta let her hand go flatter against Henrik's chest, fingers spreading wide. Feeling the rise and fall of his breath, the too-rapid thud of his heartbeat. And she hadn't even gotten to touch him yesterday, or see him, and what would he look like under all these clothes, what would he *feel* like, did he really want to *knock her up*—

"No," Henrik growled, so sudden that Fasta flinched. "*No*, Fasta. This is still you covering for me, still making excuses for me. I am fucked up, what I did to you was fucked up, there's no way I'm letting you martyr yourself for my twisted power-trip *bullshit*. I will scar you for *life*, and ruin *everything!*"

Fasta opened her mouth to protest, but Henrik shook his head and staggered backwards, away from her, out of her reach. "Please, just go," he said, with a wave toward the door. "Please, Fasta. We're done with this conversation. Forever."

Fasta's stomach plummeted, and she stared at Henrik, caught in that look on his face, that bitter command in his voice. He really was ordering her to go? Now? Forever?

"But—what now, Harry?" she asked, pleaded. "What do you want to do?"

Henrik closed his eyes, his hands clenched tight at his sides. "I want you to move on, and start seeing other people, like you wanted," he gritted out. "I want to forget any of this ever happened. And if we can't forget it, then maybe I *should* leave."

"*No*," Fasta breathed, as a sudden, horrified fear spiked through her chest. "Wait, I mean"—she had to force herself to stop, close her eyes—"whatever you want, Harry. Of course."

The laugh that barked from Henrik's mouth was cold, mocking, entirely unfamiliar. "Oh, of *course*," he repeated, and the tone was unfamiliar, too. "Because you would *never* lie to me, would you, Fasta?"

And there were no words left, no thoughts, nothing but that look on his face, that miserable jolting pain. So Fasta turned, and covered her eyes, and fled.

8

Fasta should have spent the afternoon writing up her paper on their finished job, and reviewing proposals for the next one. But after an hour spent pacing alone in her room, trapped with her miserable thoughts, she packed her overnight bag, and set out due south. For her cottage. *Their* cottage.

It was almost three hours' walk from Coven Manor, tucked away by a stream in a hidden, fully forested little valley. And when Fasta had first stumbled upon the spot several years before, she'd immediately fallen in love with it, with its hills all around, the rich deposits of earth beneath.

"You need to see this place I found," she'd told Henrik, and on their next day off, she'd taken him there, and they'd explored it together. And as always, Henrik had soon pointed out the best place for a house, well out of the stream's flooding range, on an almost-level sheet of bedrock.

"I think I can level this," he'd said, walking around and kicking at the earth covering it. "It would work, Fass."

Fasta hadn't even had to say what she'd wanted it to work for, and together they'd begun mapping out plans. Taking far more care and time with it than was truly needed, but the unspoken agreement between them had been to create something more than just work, or just a building. Something that was entirely theirs.

So Fasta had arranged the paperwork, and despite Henrik's protests, she'd bought the land—plus acreage all around—from its distant titled landholder, and put it in both their names. And then they'd begun the still-endless debates over materials, over window placement, over weather and earthquake resistance, over flow and feel and all the tiny meaningless things that most non-mage builders never even noticed.

The cottage still wasn't done—Fasta had a feeling that it would never be done. But it was weathertight, and cozy, and *wonderful*, and her favourite place in the world.

Really? Henrik had asked when Fasta had told him that, after a long day's hot work clearing space for a garden. *You grew up in a mansion, Fasta.*

Fasta had shrugged and waved said mansion away, because yes, she'd grown up there, and it was supposedly home—but it had always been her father's house, not hers. Which meant that despite her repeated pleas, she'd never been permitted to touch it, let alone restore it or change it or do something as banal as plant a garden. Because if she was truly pursuing *that magic foolishness*, as her father called it, she was going to do it properly, with architecture and mathematics and the best engineers on the continent.

But here, Fasta could do whatever she wanted, however she wanted. And Henrik had always firmly supported that, and helped her in it, though he would still sometimes uneasily ask whether Fasta wouldn't prefer it to be bigger, or better situated, with more expensive finishes, because what if her father, or her family, ever came to visit?

And curse her, Fasta was thinking about Henrik again—she'd been thinking about Henrik for a good half-hour—and she let out a long, relieved breath when she finally caught sight of the cottage's gabled roof, barely visible through the cover of leafy greenery. She was home.

She jogged down the hidden stone stairs they'd built into the steep hillside, and followed the familiar grassy path through the tall oaks and pines. Drinking in the beloved sights of the cottage's arched entryway, its sheltered little porch, its mismatched but perfectly plotted stone walls. Its encircling clearing, complete with a sheltered working area, a fire pit, an outhouse, and—of course—the garden, with green shoots just beginning to poke up through the soil.

The heavy oak front door was locked from the inside, with a complicated set of Henrik's best steel latches, but Fasta put her hand to the solid wood, drew up the magic. And after a few seconds of clicking and sliding, the door swung open, and she stepped inside.

Their main great room was just as lovely as always, with the rows of long slitted windows letting in dappled bars of sunlight onto the pale, brilliantly polished floor. The floor was a single unbroken slab of stone, which they'd found after weeks of digging and searching, and which had taken another week of intermittent heavy labour to bring back. A task that Henrik had tackled with good grace, despite the fact that it had been brutally exhausting, and he'd often had to get in a full night's sleep outdoors somewhere, with the slab parked nearby, before moving again.

Fasta smiled to herself at the memory—how he would just find the softest place, and collapse—and how she would then walk around him, put up some makeshift walls and tarps, stuff her rolled-up coat under his head. And then, sometimes, she would just sit there and watch his barrel chest rising and fall-ing, his golden curls splayed in a sweaty mess over his forehead.

But it had never, ever gone beyond that. Even in all those years travelling together, constantly moving from one job site to the next, they'd never so much as shared a tent, let alone a bedroom. And Fasta had seen Henrik with his shirt off a handful of times, but nothing more, and even that had always been by accident, and swiftly followed by awkward mumbled apologies.

So—Fasta walked across the great room, sank down on one of their temporary stools—how was it possible that Henrik could have wanted her? *Forever*, he'd said? How could he truly think all those shocking things he'd said? Wanting to bind her and punish her, wanting to make her beg, stretch her out so she could never feel anyone else again, fill her with his *child*—

The visions rose again behind Fasta's eyes, so close and vivid and tantalizing. And the longer she lingered on them, the more the shock of them faded, edging away in favour of something like hunger. Like... *longing*.

Her hand trailed down to her groin, her thoughts now lingering on those impossible minutes in her workroom, when Henrik *had* done some of those things. Manhandled her, pounded into her, made her scream. And gods, even the memory of it was so good, impossibly good, and it only took a few sharp strokes over her trousers until she was trembling and gasping, almost bent double with the pleasure of it.

But once it dissipated, she was alone again, gazing around at the room she and Henrik had made. And Henrik's other words suddenly jostled up again, far too loud and bitter and cold.

I want you to move on, and start seeing other people. I want to forget any of this ever happened. Maybe I should leave. You spoiled-rotten little brat.

Fasta's throat tightened, and abruptly she stood and went for the cozy side room, the one she'd claimed for her own. Henrik had a room too, on the opposite side, and their unspoken agreement was that while everything else in the cottage was up for debate, these were their own private spaces, to be set up however they pleased.

And Fasta's room—she stepped inside, took a long,

cleansing breath—was all bookshelves and woven rugs and polished warm wood. With a carefully sculpted brass bed against one wall, facing the wall opposite, which was made up of an intricate, half-finished mosaic of tiny stone tiles. It was Fasta's own statement to herself that mathematics could be beautiful, if you did it properly, and since she'd planned and sourced and cut it all herself, there were no traces of Henrik anywhere in it.

But Henrik would come in and look at it sometimes, maybe trace a finger along the patterns. And gods, Fasta lived for that look on his face, that hint of unmistakable awe in his eyes. *You're brilliant, Fass*, he'd said once, with that look, and a strange huskiness in his voice, and Fasta had never forgotten that, maybe never would—

She stumbled toward the wall, and with fumbling fingers grasped the next tile, held it up. Needed to take it one piece at a time, one minute. She could do that, she could learn to accept this, to control this, it would be *fine*. Right?

The rest of the afternoon plodded by, creeping into evening, and then into night. And once Fasta had lit the stone fireplace in the great room, the cottage felt warm and cozy, a refuge from the outside world.

But it was also quiet. Empty. And though Fasta had stayed here alone multiple times before, it had always been with the knowledge that Henrik was either visiting his family, or working. And that he would meet her there once he was done, and she would hear the latches click, see his big body filling the doorway.

But there was no sign of Henrik now, and why would there be? He'd told Fasta what he wanted, and she'd promised to respect that, and accept it. He only wanted to be her colleague. Her... *employee*. And maybe even their friendship was lost to this now, destroyed beneath all those horrible new truths.

You spoiled-rotten little brat. You would never lie to me, would you?

Sleep didn't come easy that evening, and after another fitful night, Fasta again woke at dawn. Her usual morning meditation went just as badly, with no composure to be found, and by the end of it she realized she was just straining to hear movements, jumping at every sound.

Because—curse her—she still *wanted* Henrik to come. She wanted to see him so desperately it hurt. And gods, why couldn't she accept this? She was supposed to be forgetting it forever, and she'd come here to escape him, to forget. Not to wonder where the hell Henrik was, or what he was doing. Or whether maybe he'd taken Ilsa to bed again, or even worse, whether he'd gone out to one of those secret establishments he'd mentioned, to do everything he wanted with someone else...

Fasta wiped at her wet eyes, and stalked outside again. They'd been talking about building a cookstove for ages now, and that was something, anything, to take her mind off this mess.

So she set herself up outside at their sheltered worktable, with a sheet of plans, and a pile of pre-formed cast-iron plates. And finally, thank the gods, this was difficult enough, consuming enough, that by midday, Fasta had finally, thankfully, stopped thinking about Henrik at all.

At least, until she felt an odd prickle on her neck. And when she snapped her head up, there he was, standing awkwardly at the edge of the clearing, and looking at her.

Henrik had come.

9

For an instant, Henrik didn't speak, and Fasta's hungry eyes roved over his form, drinking him in. He looked red-faced and ruffled, like he'd come in a hurry, and he was only carrying his small pack, and none of the heavy building supplies he usually brought on his trips here.

But he was here. He'd followed her, after all. And though the relief almost staggered Fasta on her feet, she couldn't seem to speak, or even smile. Could only drop her eyes, grip her pencil tighter, make herself keep working.

"Hey, Fass," Henrik said, and Fasta was keenly aware of him coming closer, peering over her shoulder at the paper. "This the stove? Looks great."

Fasta tried for a smile—at least, forced her mouth into the proper shape—and frowned back down at her work. She'd been attempting to re-form heavy plates of cast iron to match the plans, and while she'd been somewhat successful, one of them had gotten badly warped, and it was taking far too much of her limited energy to fix it.

But now Henrik's big hand reached over, spreading flat against it—and with that single touch, he finished what she'd spent half the morning trying to do. And it was Fasta's cue to smile, or thank him, or call him a cocky show-off, but at the moment she couldn't muster any of it at all.

"Hey," Henrik said, his voice lower. "Fass. You all right?"

Fasta's fingers twitched on the iron plate, and she took a shaky breath, dropped her hands. "Fine," she replied, turning toward the cottage. "Could you bring those in, please?"

Henrik murmured his assent, but Fasta didn't look to see how he managed bringing the plates in—whether carrying them, or levitating them. Because if she was going to forget this, control this, she needed to learn to stop looking, stop wanting, stop drinking up the closeness of Henrik's body, his concentration, his skill. Right?

Henrik shut the cottage door behind them, clicking all the latches into place, and Fasta could hear the thunk of the iron, stacking on the floor. "Hey, Fass," he said again, and Fasta's steps hesitated, from where she'd already been halfway to her room. And she should have kept going, locked herself away—but it was too late, because Henrik stepped in front of her, blocking her, making her finally look at him.

And he looked—tired. Worn. Not at all his usual easygoing self, but then again, Henrik hadn't been much of his usual self lately, had he? And maybe Fasta now had to find a way to accept that, too. Like how she needed to accept moving on, seeing other people, trying to forget any of this had ever happened...

"You're not fine," Henrik said now, his hand circling gentle—very gentle—around her wrist. "You're lying to me again."

Lying to me again. And why did he keep harping on that, why couldn't he leave Fasta in peace with her lies? Why didn't he see that telling the truth would only make everything worse?

So Fasta just stood there, blinking down at his chest.

Trying, and failing, to hide the sniff that came from her nose, the single streak of wetness that escaped from her eye. Gods, it was pathetic, she'd never been such a mess in her entire *life*, what the hell was wrong with her...

"I'm trying," she said, her voice hitching, "to move on. To forget. To see you as just—my employee. Like you *wanted*, Harry,"

There was something dangerous lurking in her throat, threatening to escape, but when she jerked toward her room again, Henrik's hand tightened, holding her in place. And when she glanced up through wet eyelashes, he was blinking down toward her, and it was like her own misery was reflected there, glimmering too strong in his grey eyes.

"I'm sorry," he said, maybe for the first time in all this, and in a sudden, jerky movement he pulled her close. And Fasta should have resisted, but his arms were so strong and his body so warm, his chest so safe that she could bury her face in it, press her ear against the rapid *thud-thump* of his heartbeat.

"I'm so sorry," he whispered again, as one hand spread against her back, the other stroking at the nape of her neck. "For everything."

Fasta didn't speak, couldn't, but just breathed in his voice, his smell, his strength. Feeling her own hands still hovering in the air behind him, like they didn't know what to do, and finally she let them settle, tentative, against his broad back.

"I've been such a complete bastard to you lately," he said, his voice hoarse against her neck. "You don't deserve it. You shouldn't have to put up with it. I should just leave you the hell alone."

But his arms around her tightened, maybe betraying his words—and maybe he'd realized that, because he abruptly released her, and stepped away. Not quite meeting her eyes, but his chest was heaving, his hands balled up, his weight shifting on his feet.

"Is there anything I can do to try and make it up to you," he said, quiet. "As a—friend."

A friend. Fasta's heart skipped, her eyes searching his face, because that was still better than an employee, right? That was still—something?

But it still didn't settle the misery lurking in her throat, and she pulled in a breath, let it out. "Well," she began, as steady as she could manage, "if you really do still want to be friends, maybe you could start by telling me the truth."

Henrik's feet were still shifting, his eyes flicking up to hers. "About what?"

About what. As if he were an innocent virtuous *schoolboy*, and the anger jolted up fast and irrational in Fasta's thoughts. "About all of that!" she exploded at him, before she could choke it back. "About everything you've been hiding from me, all this time! That you resent me being in charge of you, being given more opportunities than you. That you think all those things about me. Even that you patronize secret—*sex dens*, or whatever the hell they are! When did you even have time to *do* that?!"

Henrik's shoulders heaved, his eyes briefly closing, and he jerked toward their small dining table, which was off to the side of the room, under its own greenery-filled window. The table was a perfect square, cut perfectly by Henrik from yet another solid slab of stone, and he yanked over one of their makeshift wooden stools, and sank his big body down onto it.

"I go late at nights," he said, toward the table. "If I can't sleep. And I don't do it that often, either. Just once in a while. If things get to be too much, and I need to settle myself down again."

He didn't elaborate, didn't say what might be too much, and after an instant's silence Fasta went to sit opposite him, gripping her hands to the table's cool stone. Thinking, now, of those mornings when Henrik would show up looking exhausted, with bags under his eyes, and a grim satisfaction on his mouth.

"Then why did you keep it all such a secret?" she demanded, toward the metal tray of random rocks and earth they always kept on the table. "Especially when you keep accusing *me* of lying to *you*? Was it because"—she took a shaky breath—"you really have seen me as just your boss, all this time? Or as a *spoiled-rotten brat* who might retaliate against you? Or fire you?"

It came out sounding bitter, or even hurt, and Henrik grimaced, and shook his head. "Gods, no, Fass," he replied, with a sigh. "We *are* friends. Best friends. And I never once thought you'd fire me over something like that. I just..."

He grimaced again, and then reached for the tray, snapped a handful of stones into his palm with the barest flick of his fingers. "It's just—all the worst things about me," he continued, quieter. "All the things I didn't want you to know. I suppose I liked you seeing me as someone decent. Trustworthy. *Safe*."

He huffed a dark, sad little laugh, his eyes fixed on his hand, on the streams of fine-grained sand now trailing through his fingers. Not even trying to show off, because it was just that easy for him, always.

"Did you get a healer to check you over for any infections, at least?" Fasta finally asked, into the silence. "After you went to those—*dens*?"

Henrik brushed the sand off his fingers, frowned down at the tray. "Sometimes," he replied. "It's expensive, and I don't always have the coin, and"—he stopped and glanced up at Fasta, his face flushing red. "Shit. I haven't lately. I'm sorry, Fasta. *Fuck*."

Fasta couldn't seem to meet his eyes, and jerked a shrug. "It's fine," she said, and at Henrik's responding telltale twitch, she winced, and shook her head. "And I'm honestly not lying, that's what the healer told me."

Henrik twitched again, his body leaning closer across the table. "Wait. You went to a *healer*? Because of me? *When*?!"

Fasta swallowed, rubbed her hand against the table's smooth edge. "Yesterday morning."

There was an instant's silence, in which all the rocks and sand on the tray snapped together into a small boulder, and hurled itself onto the floor, where it smashed into a thousand tiny pieces. "Fuck," Henrik growled, as the pieces crunched back together, soared upwards into the air, and then smashed again. "Fucking *hell*, Fasta. I'm so fucking sorry. Again."

Fasta desperately wanted to lie to him, to pretend everything was fine, but she choked back the urge. While Henrik sighed again, and with a wave of his hand, the broken stone on the floor filtered back together, soared back up to land in a neat pile on the tray.

"Listen, Fass," he said, quieter. "Maybe—maybe you *should* fire me, after all. Maybe that would be—better for you. Safer."

What? Fasta's head snapped up, her eyes narrowing on his face. "Is that what you want?" she demanded. "To *leave* me?"

Henrik let out a heavy breath, and ran both hands down his face. "Look, I don't *want* to leave you," he replied. "I just think maybe it would be for the best. I hurt you. I *forced* myself on you, Fasta."

Not this again, and Fasta groaned, and snatched for a handful of sand from the tray. "You did not," she shot back. "You did exactly what I wanted you to do. Exactly what I *told* you I wanted, because you kept asking, multiple times, demanding I tell you the truth!"

Henrik blinked across the table at her, like he'd forgotten that part, and Fasta rolled her eyes, clutched the sand tight in her fist. "And I *am* telling you the truth, Harry. I keep telling you the truth, and you refuse to believe me!"

Henrik opened his mouth, maybe to deny that, but Fasta shot him a quelling look, dropped her newly made rock on the table. "Because," she continued, "like everybody else, you really *do* think I'm a cold sex-hating ice queen, or maybe at best, a clueless innocent virgin! And don't try and deny it!"

Henrik didn't, but his eyes were still uneasy, maybe forbidding, and Fasta frowned across the table at him. "When in truth," she snapped, "I've just been too wrapped up with *you* all this time to get serious about someone else. And unlike you, I'm just bad at sleeping around! So instead, I've been stuck alone all this time, and craving it so much that I've started building an entire *army* of stone phalluses to keep myself busy with!"

Henrik blinked, and too late Fasta clamped her mouth shut—had she really, really just said that?! But if she wasn't mistaken, Henrik's mouth quirked, his eyes suddenly almost amused.

"You've built an army of stone phalluses," he repeated, deadpan, and Fasta felt her face flush hot—but she lifted her chin, made her eyes meet his.

"A small one," she said thinly. "It's really quite easy, for an earth-mage."

The amusement was still there, quivering on Henrik's mouth, but so was the disbelief, flaring in his eyes. "It is?" he asked. "What, you mean you *make* them?"

It took all Fasta's composure to hold her head up, her eyes steady. "Yes," she managed. "I do."

"Really," Henrik replied, in a cool, challenging tone that clearly suggested he didn't believe a word of it. "How?"

The low, lurking anger surged up, so swift Fasta felt dizzy with it, and after another dark look across the table toward Henrik, she snatched up the rock she'd just made, along with another handful of sand. And after a few sharp swipes, a strategic twist of her fingers, the rock was already looking decidedly phallus-like, complete with a softly bulging head.

"There," she said, tossing it across the table toward Henrik, who easily caught it. "It needs polishing, but you get the idea."

He did, if the slow stroke of his hand down the length of it was any indication—and now his eyes on Fasta were sharp, searching, maybe even incredulous. "And you have *more* of these?" he asked, his voice strange as he glanced down again, watched his fingers trace the smooth bulging head of it. "How many?"

Fasta's eyes seemed fixed on his hand too, her body clenching up tight and hungry, and she attempted a shrug. "I don't know," she replied, a little unsteady. "I haven't counted. More than any decent person should, I'm sure."

The amusement flicked across Henrik's eyes again, but with it was still the suspicion, the too-obvious disbelief. "Do you have any here?" he asked, his voice cool again, like he truly thought she was still lying. And Fasta's anger surged again, enough that she didn't care what he knew anymore, and she shoved to her feet, and strode toward her room.

It took an instant for Henrik to follow, but he did, leaning his big body against the doorway. While Fasta yanked open the drawer of her desk, and rummaged inside until she found a feathered stone writing quill, and threw it across the room toward him.

He caught that easily too, turning it over in his fingers before giving her a searching, bemused look. "This is a *quill*, Fasta," he said, still with that tone in his voice, and Fasta rolled her eyes, stalked over, and yanked off the sharpened writing tip. Revealing another blunted, polished end beneath, not unlike the fingers that were now turning it over between them.

"Use your imagination, Harry," Fasta snapped. "You don't think I'd just leave them lying around here in the open, do you? When *you* can sniff out rock formations from a hundred fathoms away?"

Henrik blinked, still turning the quill over in his fingers, like he still didn't believe it. So next Fasta yanked out what appeared to be a polished round paperweight, and with a few practiced strokes, she gave it its true shape—long and slim, but with an embarrassingly large head.

Despite the heat in her cheeks, she tossed that over too, and without waiting to see Henrik's reaction, she lurched for her little dressing table, which held a small collection of glass bottles. Mostly filled with various tinctures and oils, but one bottle—Henrik's hands were probably full, but Fasta threw it toward him anyway—was all one piece, with a gently tapered base. And unless you looked closely, you wouldn't realize that there was no stopper, and the tinted liquid inside had no way to get out.

"This is *fake*?" Henrik's voice asked, high-pitched, and when Fasta glanced over, he was tilting the bottle side to side, watching the liquid slosh around uselessly inside. "What's in it?"

"Water," Fasta replied thinly, "with a bit of cinnamon for colour."

Henrik looked almost impressed, still tipping it back and forth, and before Fasta lost the nerve, she went for the most revealing, most humiliating one of all. Her lovely brass bedposts, one of which—she could feel Henrik staring again— she'd built to twist off at the top. And now, in her hand was a good eight inches of silken polished brass, carved into a series of large decorative beads. Growing progressively larger as they went, with the bottom one too thick for Fasta to even get her fingers around.

Henrik followed her across the room, and dropped the rest of her collection on the bed. And without asking, he plucked the bedpost from her hand, tracing his finger down the row of smooth bulging spheres. Until he was encircling the bottom one with his fingers, which didn't quite meet on the other side, either.

"You—*use* this," he said blankly. "For... *fun*."

Fasta pulled in a bracing breath, made herself meet his disbelieving eyes. "Yes," she replied. "I mean, not all the time, that one's a bit much for every day, but—yes."

Henrik stared down at it again, at where his fingers still

couldn't quite reach around the bottom. "All of it?" he asked, his voice thin. "All the way?"

Fasta's face heated even more, and she attempted a shrug. "A few times," she managed, "but usually not, it's pretty intense."

Henrik swallowed, blinking down toward it, and then his eyes darted upward, narrowing on the other three posts of Fasta's bed. "Do *all* of them come off?" he demanded, sounding almost personally affronted, and Fasta shook her head, tried for a half-smile.

"No," she replied, "just that one. Not like I can use more than one at a time anyway."

She couldn't follow the look Henrik gave her, or the strange little flicker in his magic. "You can't?" he murmured, with a brief, telling glance down toward her arse, and Fasta couldn't quite breathe, had to grip at her shortened bedpost for balance.

"Well," she said, and her face had to be bright red now, because the heat felt furious, licking all over her skin. "I mean, not with that one, but"—she gave a vague wave at the assortment on the bed—"something smaller, yes, sometimes."

Henrik stared at the pile on the bed again, and something jumped in his jaw, his throat. "You couldn't just"—he began, swallowed again—"use your hand, like everybody else?"

Fasta couldn't tell if the question was accusing, or maybe just still that same disbelief, but she was deep in this now, so she might as well just keep digging. "I do," she said. "But it's just—better with something else. Feels more... real."

Henrik's chest rose and fell, his cheeks perhaps just as flushed as hers, and he swallowed again. "How often?" he asked. "Would you use one of these?"

Fasta swallowed too, and couldn't quite keep her eyes on his face. "Every day, usually," she said. "Sometimes more."

That strangeness flared through Henrik's magic again, pulsing almost like a heartbeat, and when Fasta met his eyes, it seemed to pull tighter, closer. While her thoughts suddenly swarmed with the vision of him in her workroom, striding toward her, shoving her down over the desk—

"You're lying," Henrik said, breathless, his eyes dazed, remote, desperate. "You *have* to be lying."

Fasta should have snapped back at him, but the anger felt blunted, somehow, smothered by the rising curling heat. And instead, she drew herself to her full height, and met his stunned staring eyes.

"I'm not lying," she said. "And I can prove it."

10

She could prove it.

Those shocking words had barely escaped Fasta's mouth before she regretted them. Gods, what was she thinking? After she'd promised Henrik she was moving on, keeping it professional, just like he wanted...

But beside her, Henrik's big body had gone very still, and his only movement was his eyes. Darting between Fasta, and the collection on the bed, and the brass bedpost, still clenched in his hand.

He—hadn't argued. Hadn't said no. And perhaps he wasn't about to, either, because his gaze flitted down to the front of Fasta's loose tunic, to where—she let out a slow, shaky breath—her nipples were easily visible, jutting against the thin fabric toward him.

"You can prove it," he repeated finally, his voice hoarse. "Really."

And despite the breathlessness in those words, they were without question a challenge—the kind of challenge they would often use on each other in the field, throwing up walls and digging out boulders. And Henrik couldn't possibly mean it, or could he—

"Really," Fasta repeated, confirmed, just as breathless. "If you really don't believe me."

The disbelief flared again through Henrik's eyes, as more of that taut close strangeness lurched in his magic. "I really don't," he said, low. "So prove it, then."

Prove it. He really meant it, oh gods—and that meant Fasta was doing it. Because there was no thought of refusing, not with her heart hammering like this, her whole body clenching at that disbelieving, downright hungry look in Henrik's grey eyes.

"Fine," she replied, her mouth suddenly bone-dry, but she still couldn't seem to move, to begin. How did one begin with such things, how did one go about pleasuring oneself while one's colleague watched, she couldn't even *think*—

"And it doesn't count, if you keep your clothes on," came Henrik's voice, taunting again, and it was enough to raise Fasta's eyes, her chin. Enough to make her reach for the hem of her tunic, and swiftly pull it up, up, and off, over her head.

She hadn't been wearing anything beneath it, meaning that her heavy breasts were now hanging bare and exposed, the pink nipples puckered and hard. And Henrik was looking, his eyes glittering, and Fasta was suddenly, distantly grateful for the half-closed shutter over the window, at least partially hiding her in its shadows.

Henrik kept staring, still not speaking, and whether that was good or bad, Fasta couldn't tell—until her own eyes darted, belatedly, down to his trousers. Which were looking very full in front, the hard line of him easily visible. As if—he liked this. He wanted this.

It was enough to relax Fasta's shoulders a little, and she kicked off her short leather boots, and then the socks beneath. And then it was just the trousers left, with Henrik still staring, watching, *waiting*.

And this was the part of her Henrik had already touched, already seen, already *fucked*, gods damn it—so why were her hands shaking? But they were, and it took too much effort to untie the trousers' waist, and then the string of the underpants beneath. But finally all of it was sagging over her hips, and Fasta took a fortifying breath, pushed the fabric down, and kicked it all away.

She couldn't remember the last time she'd been naked with someone else—years ago, that was certain—and her body had most certainly filled out since then, almost entirely thanks to Henrik's ongoing prompting on the subject. Her hips and breasts fuller, her arms and legs smoother and softer, and she fought the strange, faltering urge to cover herself, to hide. To apologize, perhaps, to say, *I used to control every bite I ate...*

But the way Henrik was looking at her wasn't critical, or judgemental. Instead, it was almost the way he looked at ancient stonework, or at a masonry job he was particularly proud of. Except now it was *her*, and his appreciative eyes openly lingered on her breasts, her hips, the patch of brown hair at her groin.

"Take your hair down," he murmured, soft enough that Fasta almost couldn't hear it—but her still-trembly fingers immediately went to her braid, and unravelled it. Working up and up, until she could shake her hair out, now tumbling in thick blonde waves over her shoulders.

Henrik's hand rose to rub his mouth, his eyes now locked onto her hair, and it occurred to Fasta that she almost never took it out around him, or anyone else. She'd never been good at styling it in the first place, and it tangled so easily that it almost wasn't worth it—but maybe it was, if Henrik would keep staring at her like this, with those dazed, hungry grey eyes.

"Turn around," he whispered, with a purposeful motion from his hand—and after an instant's hesitation, Fasta obeyed. Feeling Henrik's eyes on her bare back, her arse, and how much of this had he seen last time, what had she looked like, as he'd bent her over the desk—

When she turned back to face him, the taste in the air was

even stronger, tighter, and Henrik's hand briefly, casually adjusted himself in his trousers. The sight of it firing a surge of heat all through Fasta's body, and perhaps something almost like bravery. She could do this. She would.

So she walked closer toward him, her bare feet silent on the stone floor, while Henrik's dazed eyes followed her slightly jiggling breasts toward him. "Where?" she asked, putting a single, daring finger under his stubbled chin, tilting his head up. "On the bed?"

Henrik's throat convulsed, his skin feeling hot under her finger, but he jerked a curt nod. So Fasta lowered herself onto the bed, as gracefully as she could, curling her legs beneath her as she reached and slid the little pile of implements toward her.

"Which one?" she asked, her voice husky, as she let her fingers trail suggestively over them. While Henrik watched, his throat spasming again, his hand clenching around the largest bulb of the brass one, still gripped tight in his fingers.

"All of them," he murmured, and Fasta closed her eyes, let out a heavy breath. *All of them*, he couldn't possibly mean that, want to see that—could he? But he wasn't taking it back, was just still standing there, watching, waiting. And at this angle, the bulge in his trousers looked enormous, so thick, and so *close*—

And it seemed easier to look there, than at his eyes. Easier to reach for one of her implements—the quill, first, perhaps— and spin its familiar weight in her fingers.

There was no sound from Henrik, no movement, and Fasta spun the quill again, building her resolve around this. She didn't want to perform for him—did she? No, not with him so caught on the lying, on proving it. Better to just do what she would truly do, if she were alone, and craving it. And perhaps if she had set herself a challenge, to not allow herself to finish, maybe, until she'd gone through all of them.

Fasta had always done better with strategies and plans, and with that decided, she relaxed a little more, her eyes fluttering closed. While her fingers began tracing the smooth stone of the quill, the silken soft feather at the end.

The feather was long, rather more than necessary, but that had been intentional, because—Fasta's breath shuddered as she brushed it against her neck—it felt good. Teasing. Unpredictable. And she stroked it lightly down her neck, her shoulder, feeling her skin quiver, the gooseflesh trailing behind.

Next she teased it against her breasts, lightly at first, but then harder, swirling around her nipples. Watching it through half-lidded eyes, brown feather brushing against pink skin, against nipples that were now so hard they ached. Jutting out hungry and peaked as the feather twined further down, to her belly, her hips, her thighs.

She was still sitting, rather demurely at that—but she wouldn't be doing so if Henrik wasn't here, would she? So she took another fortifying breath, and made herself slowly rise up, to her knees. So she could part her legs enough to trace the feather up the insides of her thighs, and then to let it linger and twirl up even higher, harder, closer.

This was where—she swallowed, risked a glance up at Henrik—she was already tiring of the feather, wanting more, and at the moment Henrik's eyes were steady, intent. Maybe wanting more, too. So she slowly turned the quill over, and brought its rounded end up between her legs.

She just slid it back and forth at first, feeling its cool hardness rub against her, coating itself in her wetness. While the feather juddered forward, almost close enough to touch Henrik's muscled thighs. And that was a sight, so Fasta let her eyes linger there, and then glanced further up, to that beautiful, still-bulging hardness behind Henrik's trousers.

And it was with her eyes still there, still caught, that she slowly, carefully, slid the quill up inside. Hearing herself gasp with it, and Henrik gasped too, maybe because she wasn't slowing, wasn't stopping. Not until the still-cool stone had sunk in all the way, entirely concealed, but for the long feather, now brushing down against her bed.

Gods, it felt good, all slim smooth hardness, and Fasta revelled in it for a breath, clenched her body tight around it. Making the feather move, angling itself up toward Henrik, and at his choked hiss, a distant, hungry part of her did it again, and again. While her hands slid up to stroke and tease at her heavy breasts, bringing more gasps to her mouth, and maybe putting on a show, after all.

She wasn't supposed to be doing that, but her hungry body was already pushing the quill back out again, almost all the way, until it dangled between her thighs. And then, with just a twinge of magic, a glance at Henrik's eyes, the quill sank itself back up inside, smooth and deep and powerful.

Henrik hissed again, perhaps not quite realizing the usefulness of earth-magic with such an endeavour, and Fasta shot him another brief glance, and kept going. Touching and stroking her breasts—Henrik liked her breasts, right?—while the quill sank in and out. Hovering in midair between her thighs for just an instant each time before driving back up again.

She was already close, so damned close, and with a grimace, she let the quill drop back to the bed. There were still three more to use before she could finish this, and she'd barely made it through one. And even the sight of Henrik's slightly twitching trousers was almost enough to set her off alone...

So she pulled up the next smallest implement—the slim stone, with the bulbous head—and this time, she brought it up first to her mouth. Truly showing off now, because the wetness between her legs was already almost dripping, but Henrik betrayed a low, hitching groan as she sucked the stone head between her lips—so she did it again, deeper this time, and again. And then she pulled it out enough that she could kiss it, could run her tongue all over it, before it slammed back inside on its own.

Henrik groaned again, the sound firing straight to Fasta's groin, and with a shuddery flick of her hand the stone dropped downwards. Turning itself, angling itself upwards, and then—Fasta gasped aloud—nudging its rounded head up between her parted legs. And she had to spread her thighs further, had to use her hands to help, and let out a sharp cry as it breached her, and sank deep inside.

Fuck, that felt good, and Fasta made the near-fatal mistake of glancing up again, meeting Henrik's eyes. Which were looking stunned, now, greedy and glazed, his lashes fluttering as Fasta slid the stone all the way out, still with no hands, and slammed it back up inside.

She did it again, and again, harder each time, until the taste of Henrik's magic in the air felt thick and powerful and impossibly intense. And she was so close now, her body sparking, shuddering, craving it, enough that she had to drop the stone to the bed, gripping her hands to her thighs as she pulled in deep, dragging breaths.

That was two down, two to go, and another look up at Henrik's eyes showed him glancing sideways, toward where the glass bottle was still lying on the bed. It looked inert, harmless, deceptively innocent, but Fasta knew better—so after another gasping breath, she lowered herself down onto her back on the bed, and spread her knees wide.

Henrik twitched, maybe shuddered, and he even stepped sideways, giving himself a better view. Flooding Fasta with more flares of heat, and she had to make herself breathe, and hold her legs open. He'd seen it before, he'd been inside it before, he wanted this, there was nothing to hide...

So she shifted on the bed, got comfortable, as the glass bottle floated through the air, and came down to nudge up between her legs. Easily, at first, thanks to the tapered tip, but soon slower, harder, tighter. Until it had stopped entirely, jammed halfway up inside her, stretching searing friction all the way around.

Fasta had to reposition herself again, force herself to relax, to use her fingers to open herself more. And then she took a deep breath, and tried again. And gods, why the hell had she shown Henrik this one, when it wasn't easy on the best of days, let alone with him standing there like that, watching—

But then the hard glass finally sank a little further inside, making Fasta's body arch up, cry out, and she kept pushing, until her body could almost—almost—close around it, concealing it from Henrik's eyes. And suddenly she wanted to do that, desperately needed to show him that, so she used her fingers again, pulled herself wider, while the glass kept driving up inside.

When she finally managed it she was shaking all over, her feet and fingers gone tingly and almost numb, her breath coming in sharp shuddery gasps. While Henrik maybe wasn't breathing at all, his eyes just held between her legs, staring with something like disbelief, or maybe even wonder.

So Fasta pushed the glass out, slow, using her body rather than magic, while Henrik's lips parted, letting out a low moan. Almost like *he* was the one fucking her, and maybe he really *had* felt a little like that, but instead of the cool smoothness he'd been hot, quivering, *alive*.

Suddenly Fasta was done with the glass, and she shoved it away from her, down to the foot of the bed. And then her breath caught again, because—her body clenched, its wetness audible now—Henrik was still holding the length of brass in his hand, his fingers curled around its bulging circular base.

But Fasta needed it, craved it, so urgent that she had to bite her lip to keep from begging. And fuck, she wasn't supposed to be putting on a show, but her fingers slipped down to her thighs, spreading them wider. And then spreading her slick, swollen folds wider too, opening herself up, silently pleading with Henrik with her eyes. Saying, *please, I'm ready, look at me, give it to me.*

The brass bedpost slightly trembled in Henrik's hands, and

for a short hanging instant, Fasta thought he would refuse. But then the tautness in his magic wrenched even tighter, impossibly strong, where was the *air*—and the post lifted from Henrik's hands, and floated slowly down between her legs.

Fasta gasped aloud, but maybe he was just handing it over, maybe she would have to take things from here—and then, oh *hell*, the cool smooth metal brushed lightly up against her swollen aching wetness. Making her cry out, and then again, oh *fuck*, because there was already pressure behind it, pushing it slowly inside.

Fasta's breath was heaving again, and maybe so was Henrik's, but he wasn't even lifting a hand, not a single finger. Just doing this with his eyes, his thoughts. And fuck, that was hot, quite possibly the hottest thing anyone had ever, *ever* done—

That was, until the hard, rounded end did a little corkscrew spin against her. Shocking enough that Fasta gasped out a curse, which made Henrik huff a strangled laugh—and then he did it again, more purposeful this time. Not just driving the hard brass inside, or spinning it inside, but making it circle out, around. Pulling her further open, spreading her wider apart. And as Fasta felt the first, smallest bulb sink inside—oh *fuck*— her thoughts flashed backwards to Henrik's room, to all those shocking things he'd said. *I think about stretching you out. I think about fucking you until you scream.*

And maybe that was exactly what he was doing, in this moment—and curse her, but Fasta's trembling fingers fluttered back down there, *helping* him. Pulling herself wider apart for him, until she could feel that second bulb easing inside.

Something almost like approval flickered across Henrik's eyes, so Fasta raised her knees more, spread them even further apart. While the hard brass kept circling, now corkscrewing further inside, up to the third rounded bulb, oh gods.

This was where Fasta often, usually, stopped, because this was already almost as tight, as full, as the glass had been—but she only sucked back more breaths, pulled herself wider. Breathed through the stinging heat, the tension, the impossibly circling hardness pushing stronger, deeper, oh—

"Fuck," she gasped again, her eyes fluttering, fighting to focus on Henrik's flushed face. "Oh fuck, Harry, oh *gods*—"

Henrik huffed another low, strangled laugh, firing even more blood to Fasta's stretched-out quivering body, as she felt that fourth hard bulb finally sink inside. Circling again, moving again, he was going to drill it all the way inside her, holy mother of *fuck*—

"Still good?" he breathed, even the sound of his voice shooting more heat to Fasta's groin, and she desperately nodded, and pulled her knees up higher, further apart. Spreading her legs as far as they could possibly go, showing Henrik absolutely *everything*—but all that mattered now was how this felt, how her entire body was on fire, and screaming for more.

The stone's circling felt harder now, more painful, with a constant raging pressure behind it. Trying to get all the way in, while Fasta begged and pleaded for it, and one of Henrik's hands spasmed against his own groin. And then his other hand—oh gods, oh *hell*—came down to settle between Fasta's legs, she could feel him touching that last bulb, giving one last firm decisive push—

And with a cry from Fasta's mouth, it was in, all the way, her body stretched and invaded and impossibly full, while Henrik's big, work-roughened hand cupped her swollen wetness, and held it there. Henrik's *hand*, between her *legs*, and Fasta was writhing on the bed, gasping, shouting. Because there were no thoughts, no hesitations, nothing but Henrik's fingers, Henrik's pressure, Henrik filling her up so full she couldn't even breathe—

Henrik's other hand was moving now, over his trousers, and Fasta desperately wanted to see more of him, all of him—but he only gave a choked chuckle, an insolent little pat between her legs. "You haven't even come yet," he breathed, "have you?"

And his voice, his eyes, blazing on her like that, challenging her. Making her rise to it, to him, oh gods almighty—and Fasta's body finally choked, screaming, shuddering its release. Pleasure that throbbed and swung and exploded, blocking out everything else, the room, the light, the *world*.

"Oh," she gasped, "oh, Harry. *Fuck*."

Henrik stiffened all over, his eyes rolling back, his hand gripping at the front of his trousers—and then he was gasping too, his body bent, his eyes closed tight, as a pool of wetness spread slowly across the front of his trousers.

Oh. Fasta was still trembling, her eyes fixed on the sight, her own hunger teetering itself up again—but damn, she was exhausted, and increasingly tender, too. And with a hiss, she pulled out the hard brass, and kicked it down to the end of the bed.

"Fuck," she said again, pressing her palms almost painfully to her eyes. "*Gods*, Harry."

Henrik barked a laugh, and when Fasta looked up his eyes were still dazed, and maybe disbelieving, too. "What the *hell*, Fass," he croaked—and then he swayed a little on his feet. Enough that he had to put a hand to the bed for balance, so close...

And maybe it was wildly inappropriate, but Fasta clutched for him, and dragged him down toward the bed beside her. Because he couldn't leave, she couldn't stand for him to leave, not after that. Not like last time.

Henrik didn't even try to resist, and he sank his big body heavily onto the bed beside her. Even tucking his bulky arm under her head, and Fasta let out a long, shaky breath at the glorious smell of him, the feel of his warm strength all up against her. He was still fully clothed, of course, but that wetness at the front of his trousers didn't lie, couldn't.

"You still good?" he asked now, hoarse. "Was that... too much?"

Fasta shook her head against him, too relaxed and contented to care if her face was burrowing into the heady scent of his neck. "No," she murmured. "That was *amazing*, Harry."

Henrik let out another hoarse chuckle, his other hand tracing down a lock of her still-loose hair. "So you really do like it," he said, low. "Sorry, Fass, but you were right. I never would've thought. You've done a damn good job of hiding it, all this time."

Fasta probably should have been offended, and managed to at least lift her head, and attempt a glare toward him. "It's not like you tried very hard to find out."

Henrik's brow furrowed, his gaze dropping to his fingers stroking against her hair. "No," he said, with a heavy sigh. "Safer not to."

Safer. Fasta grimaced, and opened her mouth to counter that—but then Henrik shook his head, his eyes flickering to something beyond her. "Still, though," he added, louder, more casual, while his fingers gently pulled out a knot in Fasta's hair. "It would take a mind even filthier than mine to suspect that prim and proper Lady Valgeirr, lone heiress to the Earl of Dalreagh, would have a secret dildo obsession."

Fasta's head tilted into Henrik's touch, her mouth twitching into an unwilling smile. "It's not a *dildo* obsession," she countered. "A dick obsession, maybe, if you must."

"Sure it is," Henrik replied, voice dry. "Didn't see much dick involved just now, buttercup."

A surge of heat shot down Fasta's back, and she felt her smile go wider, warmer. "There could have been, if you'd wanted," she said, soft. "Would have made it even better."

Henrik's jaw flexed, his eyes briefly closing—and then he abruptly sat up, and turned away. About to leave, after that, and curse her, but Fasta grabbed his arm, held him there. "Harry," she said, breathless, toward his broad back. "You *did* want that. Didn't you?"

Henrik didn't turn around, but his shoulders rose and fell. "I did," he replied. "I just—I need some time to think about it."

Fasta nodded, and swallowed hard, let go of his arm. And then watched as he stood up, ran a hand through his rumpled curls, and strode toward the door. Walking a little awkwardly, perhaps due to that mess in the front of his trousers.

"We should go back soon," he said, stiffly, once he'd put his hand to the door. "Kjaran wants us on a new job tomorrow."

Fasta barely heard it, but nodded again, watched him step outside, and shut the door behind him. And then she dropped herself back onto the bed, dragged in a deep, shuddering breath, and rubbed both hands hard against her face.

He needed some time to think about it.

And that... meant something. Something important. Right? Because if Henrik was thinking about this—rather than just saying no—then this was still an option. Still a possibility. Still... *there.*

And suddenly, swarming in Fasta's gut, there was determination, and certainty, and—hope. Maybe she could still make this happen. Maybe she could still have Henrik, after all, as more than a friend, more than an employee. Maybe she could prove to him that she could be everything he wanted. Even if that meant obeying, being punished, stretched out, serving and begging a commoner...

Yes. Yes. Whatever it took, Fasta was going to make this work. She was going to make Henrik Hallen *hers.*

11

When Henrik emerged from his room some time later, he was freshly washed and dressed, his eyes carefully fixed on the wall behind Fasta's head.

Fasta was fully dressed too, waiting in the kitchen with her pack in her hand, and an easy smile fixed to her face. Just as she usually would have been, because she was proving this to him. And as part of that, she was going to show him how they could still be friends and colleagues, despite what they'd just done.

She was going to make Henrik *hers*.

"There you are, Harry," she said lightly. "Good to go?"

Henrik rubbed his mouth, his eyes darting uneasily toward hers, and away again. "Yeah. Just give me a minute to do the circuit."

Fasta nodded back, and then watched, with something tilting in her chest, as Henrik did what he did every time they locked up the place. Walking around it, tracing his hand along every wall, lingering on the latches and seams, setting his own subtle wards. Making sure their house was guarded, protected, safe.

He ushered Fasta out the door ahead of him before he did

the latches, while Fasta put her hand beside his, feeling the new combinations. Committing them to memory, like she always did, because it was always different, every time.

It was proof that Henrik loved this place, just as much as she did, and Fasta added that thought to the rest as she followed his silent form across the clearing. Did he think, maybe, that by doing this with her, he could risk losing the cottage, too? Along with his job, his family's stability, his siblings' futures? Because he clearly still didn't trust her, right?

Fasta swallowed, and picked up her pace until she was beside him, matching his strides. She needed to prove this to him. To be a friend, a colleague, and maybe then...

"Are you hungry?" she asked, as cheerfully as she could. "You haven't eaten a thing since you showed up here, right?"

It had been the right question, because Henrik was almost always hungry, and he shot a telling, baleful frown down at his pack. To which Fasta chuckled, fished in her own pack for some dried meat, and tossed it over toward him.

"You're a genius, Fass," Henrik said, with genuine-sounding appreciation, as he took an eager bite. "Thanks."

Fasta smiled and waved it away, though her gaze again dropped to Henrik's slack-looking pack, bouncing against his hip as he walked. It was odd that he hadn't brought any food, as if he hadn't meant to be gone long at all—but then again, he'd also mentioned a new job, hadn't he? Something Kjaran wanted done?

"So what's the new job tomorrow, then?" Fasta asked. "I hope it's something important, for Kjaran to throw it on us at the last minute like this?"

She didn't try to hide the edge of genuine exasperation on her voice, because this wasn't the first time Kjaran had inserted herself into their usual bidding process. Typically, potential clients would submit proposals, and Fasta and Henrik would choose what projects to take on, based on factors like costs, distance, time to complete, and how the project fit into Fasta's ongoing research. It also went without saying that they only chose the most interesting and difficult projects, and anything that could be done without earth-magic was an immediate hard no, on all counts. A fact which Kjaran had, to date, seemed repeatedly unable to grasp.

"Sounds like it's another one of Kjaran's bullshit political things," Henrik said flatly, around a bite of his meat. "Some new noble just took over the lands at Hartmoor, and apparently wants a bunch of period reconstructions, and new builds to match."

Fasta sighed, and gave Henrik a sympathetic bump with her elbow—the period reconstruction point wasn't so bad, but nobles were almost always unpleasant to work for, with absurdly high expectations and corresponding stingy payments. "Did you get a sense of how long the project will take?" she asked. "Or what the payment looks like?"

"Three months," Henrik replied, even flatter. "At least. And payment to be determined, upon completion."

Upon completion. Which meant—Fasta's steps faltered, halfway up the hill they'd been climbing—that neither of them would be paid for months. Their wages at Coven Manor had always been based on commission, a system that had previously worked just fine—but again, that had been because they'd chosen the jobs, and Fasta had always made sure there was steady money coming in. Not for her own sake—she had plenty of savings, and spent very little of it—but, of course, for Henrik.

Henrik hesitated too, glancing briefly back toward her, and there was something wrong in his eyes, something tired, stubborn, resigned. Something that looked... familiar, and Fasta's memories flicked backwards, to that night in her room, before Henrik had kissed her. When she'd asked if he'd needed help, and he'd looked at her just like this, and said, *You've already done enough. I'll sort it out...*

Fasta lurched forward to catch up with him again, gripping

at his arm. "What bills do you have due?" she demanded. "You already paid for the girls' schooling for the next term, right? But what about Andreas?"

Henrik's mouth spasmed, but he didn't reply, and Fasta searched his face, that deepening tired tension in his eyes. Suggesting that yes, there was something more to this. Something else he wasn't telling her, something that had to do with his brother. And maybe she shouldn't be pushing it, but suddenly she couldn't bear not to. They were still friends, right?

"What's going on, Harry?" she asked. "Please, tell me. I told you my horrible embarrassing secret, didn't I?"

She attempted a wry smile, but Henrik's face flushed, his hand rubbing at his mouth. And after another instant's awkward stillness, Fasta reached for her waterskin, and passed it toward him. Watching in silence as he took a long drink, his throat bobbing as he swallowed.

"Got a letter from Andreas last week," Henrik finally said, handing back the waterskin. "His tuition's almost due for his next term at the Academy, and between us, I thought we had it covered. He's had a few good scholarships, and some loans, and that rich titled patron—Cutler—who's been supporting him, too. But..."

Fasta waited, searching Henrik's hard profile, and he closed his eyes, let out a breath. "But it turns out Cutler wasn't some *benevolent supporter of underprivileged magical youth*, like Andreas told me," he continued bitterly. "The guy was making Andreas *work* for that coin. And not with earth-magic, either."

Oh. Fasta winced, her stomach churning, because along with being an extremely gifted young earth-mage, Andreas was also excessively handsome—but unlike Henrik, he was meek and soft-spoken and compliant. An easy, appealing target for a noble with plenty of money and no scruples.

"And you know Andreas, it sounds like he's just smiled and put up with it, all this time," Henrik added, even harder. "Until apparently this prick took it too far, even for him. And when Andreas finally said no, the bastard cut off all the coin, and called in everything Andreas owed. And now my brilliant little brother is gonna be kicked out of school, when he's only got two years left. Unless he can magically come up with all that coin, and it's due in a fucking *fortnight!*"

Gods damn it. Fasta winced again, and shook her head, searched for some kind of answer. "And Andreas can't seek out an extension with the Academy?" she tentatively asked. "Or does he have any other savings? Access to loans? Or anyone else who could help him?"

"No, he doesn't," Henrik shot back, as frustration flared in his voice, his eyes. "We don't have rich family members and massive bank accounts and favours and connections hiding round every corner. It's a miracle that he's even gotten this far, but after all this, he's probably fucked for good. And that was *before* this whole damned mess with Johan!"

With Johan? Fasta blinked, and clutched again at Henrik's arm. "What, you mean Johan's theft accusations toward you?" she asked. "But what does that have to do with anything?"

Henrik's arm flexed beneath her grip, and around them the loose rocks on the ground had started to skitter, rolling and bouncing against their feet. "Because it gives me a *motive,* Fasta," he replied, his voice hard. "Because if anyone finds out I'm desperate for coin for my brother, I'm *done* for. And I'm starting to think somebody here *does* know about it, because rich people always know all the other rich people, and that damned manor is *swarming* with the bastards!"

Fasta fought to follow this, to not to take it personally, and she snapped one of the bouncing stones up into her hand, squeezed it tight. "You mean—you think someone is framing you? Trying to get rid of you?"

There was an instant's silence, another shudder of the earth around them. "Yeah, I do," Henrik snapped back. "And it's working, because after you left yesterday, Kjaran called me in.

And she told me if there's one more incident, with *any* proof whatsoever, I'll be out on my arse for good!"

"You'll *what*?" Fasta demanded, the sudden fury too sharp in her voice. "What the hell, Harry! She honestly *said* that?"

"Yep," Henrik replied flatly. "Even after I told her I had an alibi, and Johan already searched my room, and found nothing. But she still said Coven Manor's had too much bad publicity lately, and they can't risk any more."

Gods *damn* it. "I'll go back and sort it out," Fasta said, with as much certainty as she could muster. "They can't threaten to fire you based on Johan's unsubstantiated claims. That's ridiculous."

Henrik didn't look even slightly convinced, and huffed a low, bitter laugh. "You think? Especially when word gets out that my brother's gone and crossed one of *theirs*, and I'm on the hunt for coin to get him out of it?"

Right. Fasta groaned, and hurled the rock she'd been holding toward the earth. Because Henrik was brilliant, and Andreas was brilliant, and neither of them should have to wheedle and hustle for education or a job, let alone tolerating this kind of absolute rubbish.

"Well, do you have any idea who could be behind Johan's accusations, then?" Fasta's thin voice asked. "Anyone who could have somehow left your signature in his room?"

Henrik sighed, and jerked a shrug. "Anybody could have, if they'd just dragged something I've touched around with them," he replied. "The trick would be hiding their own signature, and there are spells to do that, aren't there? Or, if they're already one of Johan's friends, and in and out of his room anyway, they wouldn't even need to bother."

It was true, damn it, and Fasta was already running a mental list of Johan's friends, of people who could have had access to his room. Johan didn't seem to sleep around much, which was one of the reasons Fasta had considered him as a romantic possibility in the first place—but it meant that the suspects were mostly his male fire-mage friends, none of which, admittedly, held Henrik in high regard.

"We should make a list of possibilities," Fasta said, squaring her shoulders. "Cross-reference it with who has connections—"

But Henrik cut her off with a loud groan, a dismissive wave of his hand. "All the paperwork in the world isn't going to help, Fasta," he snapped. "Whoever it is, if they want to get rid of me, they will. They're already halfway there, remember? One more incident, and I'm out!"

Fasta pinched her nose, pulled in a breath. "Right," she said. "Fine. So let's go back, spend as much time as possible out on the new job, and focus on getting Andreas' tuition sorted. Maybe once that's finalized, whoever's doing this will at least lose that as your motive. Maybe they'll even decide to leave the entire thing alone."

"But I can't get Andreas sorted," Henrik replied, voice tight. "Remember? I have no money. Andreas has no money. Nobody has any money, Fasta, and there's no way in *hell* I can get it in time!"

That was it, damn it, and Fasta pulled herself straighter, met Henrik's desperate eyes. She was going to prove this. She was going to fix this, and make Henrik hers.

"You can," she said. "If you'll let me help you."

12

Henrik's reaction to Fasta's offer of help was predictable. So predictable, in fact, that she pulled up a nearby boulder, sat down, and waited in silence while he sputtered, and protested, and spectacularly smashed a flurry of rocks against a nearby cliff.

"Very impressive," Fasta said, as she waved the dust and debris out of her face. "Are you done?"

Henrik glowered down at her, his hands in fists. "No," he snapped. "I'm not. Because I'm *not* taking your coin, Fasta, and that's all there is to it. You are not floating in and rescuing me, *again!*"

Fasta took a slow breath, considering him, while her hand pulled up some earth, ran it between her fingers. "Then I'll give the money directly to Andreas," she replied, voice cool. "And tell him it's from you."

Henrik stared at her, his mouth falling open, his face flushed a deep red. "*No*," he growled. "*No*, Fasta. I'll *quit* before you do that. I will fucking walk away from this forever, I swear to you."

There was a strange, distant detachment in Fasta's thoughts, smothering the fear lurching up below. "Would you?"

she asked, somehow managing to keep the hurt out of her voice. "You would quit your job and leave me forever, just for helping your brother? Helping him escape from this swine who's been taking advantage of him, so he can finish his education? And helping to keep *your* name clear of whoever's trying to frame you?"

Henrik glowered toward the trees, his arms crossed over his chest. "Yeah," he said. "I would, Fasta. I keep telling you, I'm not your responsibility, or your charity case, or your *pet*. You don't get to walk all over me, waving your money in front of my face!"

Of course, *that* was what Fasta was doing, and the hurt sharpened, sank in a little deeper. "Fine," she countered, though her voice wavered. "Then please tell me, Harry, how I can help you. I know you're very busy having your pride offended right now, but perhaps you could take a moment to consider that I am apparently very close to losing your very singular professional skills, and am more than willing to pay whatever it costs to keep them!"

Henrik shot her a baleful look, his arms still folded tight over his tunic. "Don't try that bullshit on me, Fasta," he snapped. "You've already done way more for me than you should, and gods only know what you've done that you haven't even told me about. I am *not* taking even more of your coin for this!"

"So that's it, then?" Fasta demanded, jumping to her feet, pacing back toward him. "You're going to just—give up? You're going to tell Andreas you can't help him, and he needs to drop out of school, and forget about a career in earth-magic, forever? And you're going to just roll over and wait until you get *fired*?"

Henrik's hands twitched, his eyebrows furrowing. "I didn't say that."

"You didn't?" Fasta asked, voice cold. "Then what *did* you say, Harry? Please, tell me how I am misunderstanding you! Do you have *any* plans to address this *whatsoever*?!"

Henrik didn't reply, but his eyes were mutinous, his crossed arms flexing against his chest. And Fasta couldn't stop staring at him, her heartbeat pounding erratically, because he didn't see where this was going? He would truly *leave* her, already, when he was supposed to be hers, she was supposed to be fixing this, controlling this...

"Why can't I loan Andreas the money?" she said, a little desperate. "Not as a gift. An investment."

Henrik yanked a hand through his hair, jerked a shake of his head. "You have no way of knowing if he can ever pay it back," he replied thinly. "What if he can't finish school for whatever reason, or if this mess with this bastard keeps coming back to haunt him? And also, he's already carrying way too much debt over this, and I don't want to make him beholden to you for what could be *decades*, or the rest of his *life*."

Fine, fine, and Fasta pulled in a breath, tried again. "Well, then why can't I loan the money to *you*, then. Since you keep saying you're beholden to me already. And if Andreas can't pay it back, *you* could, with extra jobs on the side. With work that needs doing."

"Look, even if I could sort out extra work, when the hell am I going to do it?" Henrik shot back. "While I'm sleeping? It's not like magic is just unlimited, Fasta, especially mine, with the kind of work we do!"

He had a point, of course, and he kept glowering at her, shaking his head. "Besides," he continued, "even if I did take extra work, it's still not going to bring in enough coin. I can barely cover the rest of my family's expenses right now as it is, and the amount that's due"—he sighed, and another rock hurled itself against a nearby tree—"it's more than I make in a year. It's just not possible."

Not possible. But there was a nagging, twitching thought, circling in Fasta's head, and the longer she looked at Henrik's slumped shoulders, his distant angry eyes, the stronger it became. Quashing the many, many obvious objections under the sheer brutal perfection of it.

She could fix this. She could fix all of it, and get exactly what she wanted.

"Then what if," Fasta began, slow, careful. "I paid you to be—intimate with me."

Henrik's eyes blinked, once—and then, oh gods, he laughed. Loudly, nervously, his eyes darting to Fasta's, and away again.

"That's a joke," he said, and the smile on his mouth didn't reach his eyes, not even close. "Right?"

But Fasta wasn't joking, and Henrik's smile faded as he took in the truth of it, his big body coiled and tense. "Wait," he hissed, low. "You actually mean that. You actually want to pay me? To fuck you? *Especially* after these past few days?"

Fasta's distant detachment was filtering back again, enough that she could turn around, and finally start walking again, on the familiar rocky path back toward Coven Manor. "Yes," she told him, over her shoulder, "I do. You need money, Harry, and you don't want charity. Well, as it happens, I have money, and you have something I want, very much."

Henrik had to jog to catch up to her, but Fasta didn't look at him, and kept walking. "And I'm not being charitable," she said coldly. "I'm being horribly and immensely selfish, and just as awful as that bastard who's been taking advantage of Andreas. And, I'm being overly profligate with my father's excessive and unearned wealth. I want you, Harry. And I'm tired of waiting."

A glance at Henrik's face found him looking pale, his throat swallowing, and his steps beside her were jerky, off-kilter. "And you actually expect me to go along with something like that?" he demanded, his voice strained, incredulous. "To—to sell myself to you? To be your—your personal *harlot*?!"

Fasta swallowed too, but kept her head high, looked straight ahead. "I'm not expecting you to do anything," she replied, clipped. "I'm offering. You've repeatedly expressed reservations about combining personal and professional with me, haven't you? Well, this would keep it all thoroughly professional. I pay you for your services, you can take the job or leave it as you see fit, at any point. And"—she frowned, felt her brow furrowing—"I wouldn't threaten you, or expect repayment, or punish you in any way, if you chose to leave. I'm willing to promise that, in writing."

Henrik didn't reply, his steps still uneven beside her, and Fasta took a breath, kept going. "You've also expressed discontentment with my authority and power over you," she added, "and I believe this proposal could address that as well. As the provider of said services, you would have the ultimate control over whether to continue providing them, or not."

Her heart was hammering now, at bizarre odds with the cool certainty in her voice, because yes, this truly was the perfect solution, wasn't it? It helped Andreas, it might help the theft accusations, it would create clear plans and boundaries and reassurances. It would give Henrik the power back. And Henrik wanted that power, right? Henrik wanted...

Fasta's heart skipped a beat, and she dragged in more breath, more courage. "And as part of the agreement," she added, "I would wish you to—exert that control over me, in intimate interactions. With the types of—um, *games*—that you've previously mentioned."

Henrik's breath caught, and suddenly Fasta could taste that familiar tension in his magic, bubbling hard and hot. "You want to pay me," came his voice, flat and disbelieving. "To play games with you in bed."

Even the words bloomed sudden craving through Fasta's groin, and she nodded, kept walking, staring straight ahead, fighting to ignore the rising flush in her cheeks. "If I'm paying," she managed, "I should get to decide what kind of treatment I receive. And what I want"—she sucked back another breath—"is for you to treat me just like you treat the women at those secret establishments you visit. For you to set up rules, and be my—my *lord*."

That word rang through the air, deep and powerful, and

Henrik's hand grasped for her arm, pulled her to a stop. "Fuck *off*, Fasta," he breathed. "This is ridiculous. There's no *way* you would actually *want* that."

"Isn't there?" Fasta replied, whirling around to face him. "Just the same way I couldn't want sex, either? The way I couldn't *possibly* enjoy using stone phalluses in bed? Or the same way"—she dragged in more breath—"that I've already been willingly deferring to you for *years*? About work, about food, even about not *touching* anyone else?"

Henrik stared at her in silence, as mingled disbelief and anger flared through his eyes, and Fasta leaned forward, raised her brows. "Ever since our first day together," she said. "You've *wanted* me obeying you, and I've done a *spectacular* job of it. For *years*. So try me on this one, Harry. I *dare* you."

The anger flashed higher in Henrik's eyes, and it distantly occurred to Fasta that maybe challenging him was the wrong angle, the wrong approach. So she pulled down another breath, stepped closer, made herself say the rest of it.

"I loved it, Harry," she said, her voice cracking. "When you took me the way you did, on my desk. You were so big, so powerful, so *everywhere*. It was—*incredible*. Better than anything—or anyone—else."

Henrik's eyes shifted, stuttered, and his magic flickered, too—so Fasta took another breath, another step closer. "And then just today," she added, quieter. "What we just did in my bedroom. It was so damned *good*, Harry. I will never, *ever* forget it."

Something hitched again in Henrik's magic, swooping lower, and Fasta dragged in another breath. "And you were right, I do control a lot of things," she went on. "And whether you believe it or not, maybe"—she searched for words, for truth—"maybe I don't actually *want* that all the time. It felt so good to give it up for a while. It was such a *relief*. It felt like serving you, and pleasing you, like—like a good little servant, was the only thing left in the *world*."

Henrik still didn't speak, but that taste in his magic kept quivering, deepening. Enough to make Fasta lick her lips, and Henrik's eyes were watching, lingering...

"It would work for both of us," she said, soft. "You get what you need, I get what I need—and we can still be friends and colleagues, too. We both win."

Henrik's eyes were unreadable, now, but he still wasn't speaking, and maybe he wasn't going to. *I need some time to think*, he'd told her earlier, and she still wanted to respect that, she was so close...

So she swallowed, and lifted her chin. "There's no obligation whatsoever," she told him. "You're in charge, so you decide. And if you decide to pursue it, you know where to find me."

And with that, she spun around and away from him, and strode off alone through the trees.

13

Fasta had no idea what she was doing.

The certainty of that kept growing as she walked through the forest, straining to listen in the silence. There was no noise behind her, no feeling of movement, which meant that Henrik was still back there, alone in the trees. Doing what? Thinking? Raging? Still deciding to walk away from her, forever?

More than once, Fasta almost turned around and went back, perhaps to beg him to forget everything she'd just offered. To say, *I don't want you obligated to me, I don't want to be that wealthy person taking advantage, I want you to want me for me, not for my money.*

But every time her steps slowed, she just made herself keep walking, her heart pounding too loud in her chest. Because Henrik hadn't refused, had he? He was thinking about it. And the thought of that, the distant hanging possibility of it—of Henrik wielding that kind of power over her—it was so powerful, so intoxicating, that Fasta couldn't bear the thought of taking it back.

And Henrik needed the money, didn't he? And he'd chafed at her control over him, and wanted the power back? It was still a neat, tidy solution, an excellent plan—and most crucial of all, it would finally get Fasta exactly what she'd wanted, all this time. She would get to feel Henrik's hands on her again. She would feel him inside her again. She would finally make him *hers.*

But something about it still twisted low in her gut, no matter how she fought to shove it away. And it was a long, lonely walk back to Coven Manor, wondering where Henrik was, what he was thinking, what he had decided...

By the time Fasta finally arrived at Coven Manor, she was in a truly foul temper, and she strode straight for Kjaran's office, her mouth set, her chin lifted. No matter what, she was at least going to handle this.

"I hear you've threatened to fire Henrik," she snapped, once she was seated on the other side of Kjaran's desk. "For no cause, other than him being the innocent victim of *demonstrably* false accusations!"

Kjaran stared at Fasta across the desk, her mouth pursed, and Fasta stared straight back. Kjaran was the daughter of some minor noble with connections in the Coven, and though she looked the part of a Director of Earth-Magic, with her businesslike attire and gem-heavy jewelry, her actual magical skills were sorely lacking. A failing that Fasta might have forgiven, if Kjaran had ever recognized that it rendered her utterly unqualified for her current position.

"I understand your concerns, of course," Kjaran said now, her voice crisp. "But let me be clear. Having an accused thief on staff is a liability to our entire facility, and particularly to our esteemed Earth-Magic department. I cannot be seen to allow this to stand."

"Then have you begun a proper investigation?" Fasta shot back. "Surely, if you're so concerned about having thieves on staff, you'll do your utmost to determine the real culprit at once?"

Kjaran looked at Fasta, eyes unblinking. "I am afraid," she

replied, "that calling a public investigation will only draw further attention to this deeply unfortunate matter."

Fasta's patience was wearing thinner with every breath, and she leaned forward in her chair, pressed her feet against the bracing stone tile of the floor. "Please, Ms. Kjaran," she said. "Henrik is this facility's best earth-mage. He has been an exemplary employee for years, and his work brings this department regular accolades and funding. He is *innocent*. He has an *alibi*. There was *nothing* found in his room when it was searched. *Please*, order an investigation."

Kjaran only kept gazing back across the desk, and Fasta's stomach plummeted, the furious comprehension sinking through her thoughts. Kjaran didn't care. She would willingly destroy Henrik's career, his entire *life*, if it kept people from questioning *her*.

"I am deeply disappointed in you, Ms. Kjaran," Fasta hissed, as she swept to her feet. "Such a response reeks of cowardice, and complete and utter ineptitude. You may rest assured, I will be reporting as much to my father."

Kjaran knew very well who Fasta's father was, and how much money he gave to the Coven each year, and finally that seemed to crack her composure, her mouth betraying a slight spasm. "Perhaps you are not aware," she said, "that Mr. Johan Falk has also promised the same attention to this matter from his uncle."

Gods damn it. Johan's uncle wasn't nearly as well-off as Fasta's father, but he was rather higher-ranking, and had been a full member of the Coven's ruling Council for years, if not decades. And how was Fasta supposed to counter that, she needed to fix this...

"Then I will inform you," she said thinly, "that if Henrik is fired, I will be entirely unable to continue taking on projects of our current calibre and quantity, including the one you have apparently committed to, without consulting me. You may expect to reduce my commission income—and therefore this department's expense budget—by a good two-thirds, or more. And of course, I will readily share the true reasons for these developments with my *many* influential contacts!"

That seemed to dig the matter further, and Kjaran frowned down at her desk. "I remain unable to call for an investigation at this time," she said, her voice clipped. "However, I will not prevent you from conducting your own investigations, as long as they are not openly apparent. If you are able to discover the true perpetrator, then of course I would be happy to proclaim Mr. Hallen's innocence."

Of course she would. And as much as Fasta currently loathed Kjaran, she had to admit that it was a well-played answer. Now Kjaran could openly say, to anyone who asked, that she was supporting Fasta, while putting all the work on Fasta as well, and relieving herself of the entire enraging mess.

"Very well," Fasta said flatly, because at this point, she just needed to get out of this damned room before she crushed something. "I will expect your assistance in my investigations, as required. I also expect to be included in any and all meetings between you and Henrik, going forward."

With that, she leapt to her feet, and stalked for the door—when behind her, Kjaran loudly cleared her throat. "I truly wish I could do more to help you," came her voice. "But if I were you, I would ensure that Mr. Hallen does not wander about alone, especially at nights. And that he does not have access to resources or hiding places that may be suspect. Or be seen as in need of funds."

Fasta whirled around, her eyes narrowing—Kjaran couldn't know about Andreas, could she? "In that case," she snapped, "you should be willing to offer Henrik an appropriate advance for this months-long project you've thrown onto us, with no warning whatsoever!"

Kjaran's mouth opened and closed, and distinct exasperation flared across her eyes. "I will have you know," she replied, "that particular request came from the Coven's Council itself.

Perhaps you would like to go inform them that you refuse to take the job? Especially when your primary colleague has been credibly accused of theft, and the victim's uncle sits on said Council?"

Gods curse her, curse them all, and with effort Fasta held herself still, and glared down her nose at Kjaran's infuriating face. "I require a month's advance for Henrik," she gritted out. "And you *will* arrange it. *Today*."

Kjaran finally nodded, and Fasta spun on her heel and stalked out. Not sure if she was angrier at Kjaran, or Johan, or this entire appalling situation, *damn* it.

She was still furious when she got to her bedroom, so much that it wasn't until she'd undone the latches that she tasted it. There was someone inside. *Henrik.*

Fasta's heart skipped, and her fingers trembled on the last latch—but then the door swung open, hard enough to bang against the wall behind it. And there, indeed, was Henrik. Standing there inside her room, looking huge, and powerful, and just as furious as she felt.

"Get in here," he breathed, and Fasta obeyed, her steps swift and lurching. While the door slammed shut without Henrik even touching it, his magic swirling tense and crackling in the air. Flaring a long, rippling shudder up Fasta's back, the heat pooling hard and sudden between her legs, because this already felt familiar, the magic, the tautness, that telltale look in his eyes.

"If you really want to hire me to do this with you," Henrik hissed, "you need to prove to me you want it. You need to get naked, and get on your knees, and make me fucking *believe* it."

Oh hell, he wanted her to prove it again, and Fasta's frantic thoughts were floundering in the vision of that, her breaths coming short and shallow. "Um," she gasped. "Right now?"

"Yes, *now!*" Henrik growled at her, eyes blazing, his hands clutched to fists. "You told me to come to you, well, here I am. What, is all this some kind of *joke* to you?"

Fasta's heart skipped a beat, her eyes trapped in the anger in his voice, his magic, his eyes. *Is this all some kind of joke*, as if she'd been taunting him, or taking advantage. As if she'd been mocking him, trying to control him, showing herself a spoiled-rotten little brat.

Fasta gulped and shook her head, and then tossed aside her pack, and fumbled for her braid, raking out her hair. "It's not a joke," she breathed. "I still want it, Harry."

Henrik's eyes kept burning on hers, like he didn't at all believe it, and what had he just said? *Get naked, get on your knees, prove it*—and yes, yes, Fasta could do that. She would do that. This was her chance. She would make him *hers*.

So she shook out her hair, even as she shucked her trousers, and yanked off her tunic, throwing it to the side. Now standing there entirely bared in front of him, her chest heaving, her nipples peaked and aching.

"Please, Harry," she gasped, as she held her eyes to his, and stepped closer. "Please. I want you. So much."

Henrik's eyes didn't change, and Fasta risked a tentative touch of her hands to his tunic, feeling the hard muscle of his chest, the rapid beat of his heart. "I've wanted you for so long," she breathed. "Can't tell you how many times I've pleasured myself to thoughts of you. Thinking about your orders. Pretending those stones of mine were *you*."

Henrik just kept watching, his body stiff, forbidding, and Fasta slid her hands downwards, toward the softer expanse of his belly. "But I kept it hidden from you," she said, "because I knew you didn't want it, and I needed to keep being near you, keep working with you. Because you're the best, Harry, abso-lutely brilliant, and some days I just want to stare at you, want to touch you, just want to *worship* you."

The words sounded shocking to Fasta's ears, choked and appallingly true, but Henrik still seemed entirely unmoved, even when her hands slid down further, against the hollows of his hips. "You could be my lord, Harry," she breathed. "I would pay alms to earn your attention, your favour. I would beg for your guidance, your direction, your"—she took a breath, risked sliding a hand toward his groin—"your discipline."

And oh, he was hard, and huge, his thick cock twitching against Fasta's fingers, and she felt the heat dip and surge, rising to her cheeks, pooling heavier between her legs. "I would serve you," she whispered, as her fingers circled closer, tighter around him. "I would give you my body, my adoration, my loyalty. My obedience."

Her hand trembled as she risked an experimental stroke upwards, and if she wasn't mistaken, something swerved in the magic, in Henrik's eyes. And as she kept touching him, driving up her own hunger, his lips parted, his mouth letting out a hard huff of breath.

"Your obedience," he murmured, "so far, is shit. Told you to get on your knees."

Oh, *gods*, had he actually just *said* that, and Fasta immediately dropped to her knees on the hard floor. Keeping her hand on that thickness in his trousers, keeping her eyes fastened to his shadowy beautiful face.

"Forgive me," she breathed. "Please, my lord, I beg of you."

Henrik's breath huffed out harsh and ragged, his cock flaring up against Fasta's fingers, she couldn't bite back her own low, shuddering groan. Because yes, he liked this, yes, she was proving this—so she kept looking up at him, bringing her other hand to stroke up against the hard bulk of his thigh.

"Please, my lord," she said again, earning another shudder from that thick cock in return. "Teach me what you need. Show me how to please you and honour you. Make me your favourite servant."

Henrik's breath sounded more like a groan this time, his cock swelling out strong against her fingers. And in return Fasta stroked firmer against it, brought up her other hand, tentative, to cup against the heavy bollocks underneath.

"I want you to have your way with me," she whispered, as

she felt his magic pulling up tighter, breathlessly close. "I want you to show me who's in charge, who's in control, who's really the boss between us. I want to serve you. Want to obey you. *Please*, my lord."

Henrik growled low in his throat, something snapping harsh and powerful in the magic—and then his hand swept down, and nudged hers away. And with a quick fumble of his own fingers, there was—

His cock. Right there, *here*, in front of Fasta's face. And there was only an instant to register the deep ruddiness of it, the thick veined heat of it—before it slid itself between her parted lips, and shoved deep into her throat.

Oh gods, oh fuck, and Fasta groaned around him, around the impossible girth of him, invading her mouth. Tasting of musk and seed, leaking against the back of her throat, even as it swelled a little fuller against her tongue, her stretched-apart lips.

"Look at me," Henrik's voice whispered, ordered, and when Fasta raised her eyes he was watching her, his face flushed, his eyes glittering. "You always look at me, when my dick's in your mouth."

Oh, *fuck*, and Fasta groaned again, tried to nod. As much as she could, with her mouth full of his cock, and he gave a smile that wasn't a smile at all. "Good," he breathed. "Now suck on it."

The world juddered, tilted, but Fasta managed to stay upright, to draw in air—and then she sucked, as hard as she possibly could. Making Henrik's eyes flutter, his breath hitching, his big hand skittering against her hair.

That meant he liked it, so Fasta did it harder, deeper. Sinking all the way to the base of him, driving him deep against her throat, and breathing in the heady sight and feel and smell of that coarse brown hair at his groin. She was sucking Henrik's cock, her face was in Henrik's groin, she could stay like this all day, all night, please—

But Henrik's hand on her hair tightened, holding her there, and then he pulled backwards, sliding his thick, glistening length back out between her lips. Not all the way, but enough, before sinking back inside. Making them both groan this time, while Fasta fought to suck him deeper, her hands now fluttering around to grasp at his still-clothed arse, and pull him closer.

"Good girl," he rasped, tangling his hand deeper into her hair, grinding himself harder into her throat. "You like that?"

Fasta nodded around him, groaned again—and again he slid out, slower this time. "Good," he breathed, and he kept pulling back, holding Fasta's head still, until his slick cock bobbed fully free of her mouth. "Now beg me to do it harder."

Fasta's whole body shuddered, the wetness already dripping between her legs, and she had to lick her lips, try to catch her breath. Her jaw was already sore, her lips stretched and tender, but she held her eyes on Henrik's, strained against his hold just enough to slide her tongue against the silken blunt tip of him.

"Please, my lord," she whispered, and when he slightly released his hand's pressure, she brazenly kissed him, lingered her tongue against his smooth leaking slit. "Please, do it harder. Make me suck you. Use my throat until I *choke* on you."

That drew another groan from Henrik, a jolt as his other hand came to tangle with the first into her hair—and then, oh hell, he was doing it. Holding Fasta's head still while his cock sank in and out, dragging thick and tight against her stretched-out lips, feeling even bigger, harder than before.

Oh, it was good, even if Fasta could hardly breathe, could hardly keep the suction on him, and the saliva was leaking from her mouth, making loud slurping noises that should have been appalling. But it only seemed to make Henrik groan louder, his hands tightening in her hair, his eyes fluttering closed, his head tilting back—

And then, oh gods, he was pumping out, filling Fasta's

mouth with his tangy thick bitterness. Tasting so strong it was almost enough to make her gag, and her eyes watered as she struggled to swallow, to make her throat work. While Henrik just kept bearing down, pulsing into her throat, filling her so full that she couldn't keep it in, couldn't keep it from spilling out, and dribbling down her chin.

When he finally eased backwards, she was still fighting to swallow it all, to lick off the mess on her lips. And damn Henrik, but he even gripped his hand to her chin, and tilted her head up. Watching with dazed, dispassionate eyes as she finally got it all down, and wiped at her still-swollen mouth.

"Now clean me up," he whispered, hoarse. "And finish yourself off."

Fasta had to close her eyes, find the air, and when she looked up again, Henrik was holding—a bottle. Another one of her glass bottles with no stopper, this one slimmer than the one back at the cottage, with its trapped liquid tinted yellow rather than red.

Fasta couldn't seem to speak, just blinking at it—of course Henrik had found it now, how many others had he found along with it—and when he shoved it toward her again, she finally took it. Curving her shaky fingers around it, slipping it down between her spread legs.

And as it began sinking itself up inside, now with only Fasta's magic guiding it, she leaned forward and breathed in the smell of Henrik again, his cock now soft and slack against those dark curls, but still undeniably wet, with lingering strings of white. And he'd wanted her to clean him up, so Fasta drew him into her mouth again, licked and suckled at him, while that hard rounded glass pressed up inside, further and further, suck him deeper, harder, lick him clean, oh, *oh*—

The pleasure flared up without warning, consuming her, swallowing her in wave after wave. So strong she had to cling to Henrik's hips to stay upright, to keep his slightly-twitching soft cock in her mouth. Fuck, it was good, he was good, *gods*, yes.

She stayed there for far too long, basking in the truth of it, the relief. And even as the reality of it all slowly filtered back again—she was naked, impaled on a bottle, sucking desperately on Henrik's flaccid cock—the entire world around her was suddenly warm, glowing, impossibly content. And whirling even brighter at the feel of his hands stroking her hair, soft and approving, sinking her ever deeper into his touch, his peace.

Finally Henrik gently guided her away, and then tied up his trousers with shaky, fumbling fingers. And wait, that meant Fasta still hadn't seen him naked, and also—she looked up, held his dazed eyes—she'd done it. Proven it. Hadn't she?

Maybe Henrik had followed the question, because his arms crossed over his bulky chest, and something like awareness, or even distance, flickered across his eyes. As if he was judging her, weighing her, deciding...

"Fine," he said, hard, decisive, *wonderful*. "Fine. I'll do it."

14

He would do it. Henrik Hallen would finally be hers.

The delighted relief surged through Fasta in a rush, and she couldn't help a swift grin up at his face. "You will?" she gasped. "Truly, Harry?"

There was an instant's stillness, and then Henrik's throat convulsed, and he nodded. "But with conditions," he said, as he groped for Fasta's nearby pack, fished out her waterskin, and thrust it toward her. "You feel good enough to go through them now? Or we can wait until..."

His voice trailed off, his eyes flicking down toward Fasta's still-kneeling, still-naked body—but she rapidly nodded, and took a long, fortifying drink from the waterskin. "I'm fine," she said, and at Henrik's brief grimace, she smiled at him again, took another drink. "Really, Harry, I am. What are your conditions?"

Henrik took a deep breath, and ran both hands through his hair. "Well, first off," he began, "like you said, I can quit, with no consequences, whenever I want. And second, for payment"—he took another deep breath—"I want double what we made last year, and I want it up front. Non-refundable, no matter what happens."

Oh. That was a hell of a lot of money, but then again, that was the entire point, wasn't it? So Fasta jerked a nod, and kept her eyes easy and calm on his face.

"Fine," she said, as steadily as she could. "Anything else?"

Henrik grimaced, his eyes briefly closing. "Yeah," he said. "You need to know where this is gonna go, if you really want me to play these kinds of games with you. Because if you give me my head in this, it's not gonna be a few friendly orders and a little swat on the arse now and then. You get that?"

Fasta nodded again, perhaps too quickly, because Henrik's eyes narrowed on hers. "I mean it, Fasta," he said, lower, dangerous. "If you let me, I will *use* you. I will boss you around. I will fuck you every way I can. I will make you kneel and crawl and beg for me in the dirt, and push limits you never knew you had. I will teach you some fucking *lessons*, Lady Valgeirr. And you will learn, and *obey* me."

Gods. Fasta's breath shuddered out harsh, and she nodded again—but now Henrik's hand caught on her chin, gripping a little too tight. "It won't be sweet," he hissed. "It might not even be *safe*. And afterwards, you will *never* see me the same again. So are you sure"—his eyes fixed on hers, boring into hers— "are you *sure* you want all that. You *agree* to all that."

Fasta rapidly, fervently nodded, as a thrill of heat raced up her spine. "Yes, Harry," she said, her voice still markedly calm. "I understand, and I agree. Shall I draw up the paperwork?"

"No," Henrik replied, dropping his hand from her face. "No. No paperwork. That's your way, not mine, and if we're doing this, it's gonna be my way."

Oh. Another flare of warmth shot up Fasta's back, but she nodded again, and Henrik frowned away from her, toward the opposite wall. "But I still want rules," he added. "Rules I need you to keep, while we're doing this."

Fasta blinked, but made herself nod again. "What kind of rules?"

Henrik's eyes darted back toward her, toward where she

was still kneeling on the floor at his feet, with no clothes on. But something whispered at her not to get up, not yet—and he glanced away again, rubbed a hand at his eyes. "We keep it separate," he said. "Separate from work, and from being friends."

Fasta nodded again, twisted her fingers in her lap. "How so?"

Henrik sighed, his mouth twisting. "Like—this is just an agreement," he replied flatly. "It's a contract, a business deal, and that's *all*. It's not a relationship. We're not together, beyond work. I'm not your boyfriend, or your responsibility, or your *pet*. None of it."

That again. Fasta fought down her wince, the odd clenching in her gut, and fought to keep her gaze steady on Henrik's face. But he was still looking away from her, his jaw tight and set. "So we don't spread it around," he added. "We only do it when we're alone—either here, or at the cottage. We don't talk about work in the bedroom, and vice versa. And I'm *not* gonna cuddle and coddle you like I'm your boyfriend."

Oh. Fasta could handle that, of course she could—right? But when she nodded again, Henrik still wasn't even looking at her, instead just glowering toward the wall. "And you don't call me Harry while we're doing this," he said. "You don't use your magic in this unless I tell you to. You don't touch me or undress me unless I tell you to. And you don't get yourself off unless I tell you to. You don't even *touch* these without me."

He waved toward the glass bottle, which had rolled away a little on the floor. And Fasta nodded again, easier this time, as more of that heat flickered low in her belly. Because it meant he was going to use them, he was going to touch her with them...

"And most of all, you have to be honest with me," he continued, harder now. "Always. Both in the bedroom, and out of it. If I ask you to tell me something, you tell me. You don't hedge, don't talk around it, don't try to protect me. If you're really giving me control, you're gonna start telling me the *truth*."

Fasta nodded again, but Henrik's hand gripped back at her chin, making her meet his eyes. "And you *especially* tell me the truth when we're doing this," he said. "If something actually hurts, or scares you—or even if you decide you want to stop—you're gonna tell me, every time. You're gonna say, *No. Stop.* And then I stop. Because I can't read your mind, and these kinds of games can get dangerous—and I know when I'm lost in it, I *will* keep pushing it, pushing *you.* But I sure as hell don't want to actually hurt you, or scar you forever with my shit. You understand?"

His voice had gone deep and demanding, his eyes intently searching hers, and Fasta nodded. "Yes, my lord," she whispered. "I understand. I'll tell you the truth."

Henrik's eyes flickered, but he nodded, too. "Good," he replied, curt. "Now, tell me what you *didn't* like about what we did, just now."

What you didn't like. Fasta blinked at him, and opened her mouth to tell him there was nothing, it had been perfect, wonderful—but then she snapped her mouth shut again. Because Henrik was testing her, of course he was. He wanted to see if she could obey. If she could really keep her word on this.

So Fasta drew down a shaky breath, and held Henrik's glittering eyes. "Well," she began, "your taste is very—strong. And when you say we're not together, and no one will know"—she took another breath—"do you mean... would you still... keep seeing other people?"

Gods curse her, it was too much truth, bitter and thin in her voice. Because surely he hadn't meant that, surely he wouldn't...

But something dark and grim flared across Henrik's eyes, almost like satisfaction. "Yeah, I do mean that," he replied. "You said I'd have the power in this. And this is completely professional. So that means you have no say over my personal life. *None.*"

Oh. The shock and the jealousy flashed through Fasta's

kneeling body, sharp and astonishingly painful, and she had to squeeze her eyes shut, look away. Take deep breaths, count to ten, it would be fine, it had to be fine. Because if Henrik was touching her, bound to her, he would still be *hers*, right? And she could handle him having the occasional fling... couldn't she?

"Is that a problem?" Henrik asked, his voice cool. "Do you want to call it off?"

Fasta grimaced, and blinked up at his familiar face, his mouth, his glinting grey eyes. While desperately fighting down the vision of him looking like this at someone else, doing this with someone else, maybe with more women at his *establishments*, or with Ilsa, oh gods...

Fasta swallowed hard, counted to ten again. "Um," she said, "no. As long as you—get regularly checked, I—I'll deal with it."

Something shifted in Henrik's eyes, and his hand briefly brushed against her hair. "Good girl," he said, his voice oddly gruff. "You can get dressed now."

Fasta ducked her head and nodded, and then groped for her clothes, and shoved to her feet. Feeling Henrik's eyes on her as she began dressing, and gods, it still was so surreal, so strange. To know that he'd just been in her mouth, he'd just sprayed off down her throat, and made her lick him clean. It was hard to even think about, hard to look at him, to see how much this had changed...

And maybe Henrik felt the same, still standing there so stiff and silent—and Fasta's thoughts flitted back to what he'd just said, before all that. How he wanted to keep this separate from their work, and their friendship. Suggesting, maybe, that he did still want to be colleagues, and friends.

And yes, yes, Fasta needed to cling to that, because that was something those other women didn't have, right? That was another way Henrik was still hers. *Hers*. And she would show him, he would see...

So once she'd finished dressing, Fasta finally made herself

look at him, at his watching unreadable eyes. "Um, have you eaten?" she asked, in what she hoped was her usual, normal voice. "Because gods damn it, Harry, I'm starving."

Henrik's eyes blinked, changed, and the stillness stretched out wide—but then he nodded and looked away, too quickly. "Right. Yeah. Want to try for a late supper?"

"Hell, yes," Fasta replied, with emphasis, as she reached around him, and yanked the door open. "I thought you'd never ask. I can never sweet-talk the cooks into feeding me after hours without you."

Henrik huffed a laugh as he stepped out the door, and then waved Fasta through it before shutting it and fastening the latches, all without touching it. "Yeah, because you terrify them, Fass," he said, as they headed down the stairs together toward the dining hall. "All that looking down your perfect nose at them, lording your title and your coin over them, using all your long complicated words."

Fasta winced, and despite Henrik's teasing elbow in her side, she could only manage a halfhearted smile toward him. "I might have thrown all that at Kjaran earlier, too," she said. "When I first got back here. Used my father, and her budget, and everything else I could possibly think of."

"I figured," Henrik said dryly, but a sideways glance at him showed his eyes weren't angry, just resigned. "What'd she say?"

"She was useless, as usual," Fasta replied, with a frown. "She refused to order a proper investigation, because Johan's gone and involved his uncle, and she doesn't want this to reflect negatively on her. I did get you a month's advance on your pay, but she otherwise said we'll need to look into it on our own, and I need to do a better job of babysitting you. Oh, and apparently"—she shot Henrik an irritated look—"that new job? It was actually a request straight from the *Council*."

"Great," Henrik said, with a roll of his eyes, but again there was no anger, just the light, thrilling touch of his hand to her back as he swung open the dining hall door. "Go sit, I'll get supper."

It was their usual routine, their usual way, and despite her lingering annoyance at Kjaran, Fasta felt herself relaxing as she went to their usual spot in the now-empty room. And then she watched with reluctant appreciation as Henrik sauntered over to interrupt the cooks' washing-up, made some cheerful jokes and small talk, and soon walked away with two overflowing plates of food.

"You are *incorrigible*," Fasta said, as Henrik plopped one of the plates in front of her, and sat down across the table. "This is enough food for a *party*, Harry. What the hell did you say to them?"

"Hey, you were the one who said you were starving," Henrik replied, with satisfaction. "I'm just being considerate. Don't I even get a thank you?"

Fasta shot him a mock glare—there was no way she was thanking him for being a manipulative flirt—and he flashed back a broad, teasing grin. "You like it," he said. "And you know what? You're gonna eat all of that. Or else."

Or else. The room caught, tilting slightly around them, but when Fasta blinked across the table, Henrik was all innocence, spearing some green beans onto his fork. While Fasta was still twitching, still fighting to breathe, to come back from that. To escape the visions of herself kneeling on the floor, with his cock in her mouth.

"Thought you wanted to keep it separate," she managed, breathless, giving him a light kick under the table. "Didn't you?"

Henrik glanced up, and the look in his eyes was warm, wicked, triumphant. Even as his foot kicked her back under the table, and stayed there.

"No idea what you're on about, Fass," he said lightly. "Now are you eating, or what?"

And with a low, hopeful thrill in her chest, Fasta nodded, and obeyed.

<h1 style="text-align:center">15</h1>

enrik slept in Fasta's bed that night.

It was the first time they'd ever done such a thing, in all the years they'd known each other. But after they'd finished eating, and Henrik's eyes had lingered on Fasta's empty plate, she'd dredged up the nerve, or maybe the foolishness.

"Look, Harry," she'd said, keeping her eyes carefully on the table. "Thinking about how Kjaran said you shouldn't be alone at night—I was wondering if maybe you should—stay with me. For a while."

The last words had come out in a rush, fast enough that she'd thought maybe Henrik hadn't heard—but then his eyes had lifted to meet hers, and he'd sighed. "Yeah," he'd replied. "Maybe."

He'd then followed her up to her room, and Fasta watched as he clicked the latches into place on her door, neither of them saying aloud what they were both thinking. That this was as much to keep Henrik trapped inside than anything, a way for Fasta to be able to say to a truth-seer, *No, we locked the door, I was with him the entire time, all night long.*

But Henrik still didn't seem angry or impatient, the way

Fasta had expected him to be. Just quieter than usual, maybe, and when she asked what he wanted to wear to bed, he just shrugged, and waved down at the clothes he was wearing.

Fasta hated wearing day clothes to bed, and had already had her silk sleeping shift in hand, eyeing the adjoining water closet—but Henrik dropped himself down onto her suddenly small-looking bed, and made an all-too-clear gesture with his hand. *Put it on*, it said. *Right here.*

So Fasta changed as quickly as she could, her cheeks burning, while Henrik stayed there and watched. But he didn't speak, didn't hint at anything close to what they'd done before. Keeping it separate again, maybe, but it didn't quite feel separate as Fasta padded over to the bed, now dressed only in her thin sleeping shift, and looked down at Henrik's eyes.

He shifted over, lying down and making room, so Fasta sank down too, taking care to leave a respectable distance between them. But then came the glorious, impossible feeling of Henrik's arm, settling heavy over her waist, and pulling her body close.

They slept like that, with Fasta's back curled against Henrik's broad chest, with him snoring softly into her hair. And it was so strange, so stilted and precious, somehow, that Fasta almost didn't want to sleep, just wanted to lie there and revel in it, the close warm wonderful safety of it. Of being in bed with Henrik Hallen, the one person—Fasta's breath shuddered in the dark—who was everything, who'd always *been* everything, since that first day he'd walked onto her job site.

Morning came slow and quiet, and far too late. Fasta was typically an early riser, but she'd slept terribly the last few days, and sleeping in Henrik's arms somehow seemed far easier, far more relaxing, than sleeping alone ever did. And when she finally yawned and squinted at the morning sunlight, Henrik was already awake, his hair loose and tousled on the pillow, his eyes lazy and content on hers.

"Finally awake?" he asked, husky. "Thought you were always up at the crack of dawn."

Fasta made a face at him, but she couldn't help a warm smile, too, especially when he gave her arse a light little slap in return. And then he left his hand there, his fingers spreading wider, and Fasta's breath caught, her heart beating faster in her chest.

"You like it in the mornings?" he murmured, and it took Fasta an instant too long to realize what he meant. But he meant this, them, *now*, and the heat thrilled her all over, surging from her head to her feet.

"Maybe," she whispered, her eyes trapped on his. "You?"

Henrik's mouth quirked up, and his hand on her arse spread a little wider. "Wouldn't say no," he replied. "But fair warning, you'll be on top. I'm a lazy arse in bed in the mornings."

Henrik had always hated mornings, in all the years they'd worked together, and Fasta couldn't help a choked laugh, a roll of her eyes. "You don't say. I'm *shocked*, Harry."

And damn it, she wasn't supposed to be calling him *Harry* in this, but he didn't seem to notice, and only shot her a snide little smirk. And then he raised his eyebrows at her, like he was waiting to see what she would do next, and Fasta gave a pointed glance downwards, toward where his still-clothed body was well hidden under her blanket.

"Thought I wasn't supposed to touch the clothes," she said. "Or are mornings exempt?"

Henrik seemed to consider that, his forehead furrowing, and finally he shrugged, gave an imperious wave toward the blanket. "Somewhat exempt," he replied. "Enough to get the job done, at least."

The heat swirled again, pounding louder with every thud of Fasta's heartbeat, and she carefully slid her hand toward him under the blanket. And there—her eyes closed, her breath exhaling sharp—there he was, so thick and hard below the coarse fabric of his trousers. Wanting this, actually wanting her, and she still couldn't believe it, couldn't quite breathe.

But Henrik's eyes on hers were still warm, easy, and she drew in a shuddery breath, and yanked the blanket downwards. Revealing his trousers beneath, with a highly prominent bulge, and Fasta's too-eager fingers fumbled for the drawstring, yanking apart the knot. And then—she dragged in more air, more courage—she slipped her hand inside, and drew him out, into the dappled morning light.

Gods, he was gorgeous, and Fasta's whole awareness drew in, close and hot and breathless. Just looking at this, experiencing this, the incongruous impossible sight of Henrik Hallen, sprawled casually in her bed, with his trousers pulled down, and his hard cock jutting out, thick and flushed and veined all over. Waiting for Fasta to touch it, to actually take it *inside* her, and she couldn't seem to stop staring, couldn't make her brain work again.

"Having second thoughts?" Henrik's low voice asked, making Fasta's eyes dart up. To where he was watching her, his eyes distant and careful. As if he was—worried. As if he thought, maybe, that she didn't want to do this.

Fasta managed a shaky laugh, a wave of her unsteady hand. "No," she breathed. "Gods, no. Just—looking. Wishing I could see the rest of you."

She shot a brief, hopeful glance at his tunic, and if she wasn't mistaken, Henrik's cheeks flushed rather pink—but he didn't make any move to take the tunic off, or push down his trousers any further. "Too bad," he replied. "This is all you're getting, buttercup."

The heat surged even sharper, especially when Henrik's hand reached over, tugged a little at Fasta's shift. "You, though," he added, soft, "never fuck me with your clothes on."

Damn. Fasta had to fight for composure, take a long breath, because it was one of those power things again, a way for Henrik to be in charge, even as he lounged here and made her do all the work. And it was almost shocking how arousing it was, how desperately she wanted this, needed this.

She'd already pulled herself up to sitting, enough to yank the shift off over her head. Leaving her kneeling fully naked beside him, while he openly looked his fill, his eyes lingering, flicking up and down. And then he shifted and stretched on the bed, sprawling his muscled arms up behind his head, like he really was just going to lie back and watch the show. And even as Fasta rolled her eyes at him, she was almost trembling, her heart pounding so loud she was sure he could hear it.

"C'mon, then," he said, with a nod, his voice gentler than she'd expected. "Wanna see you take it."

It was enough to make Fasta nod too, and she lurched her body over him, one leg straddling either side of his hips. Fully exposing herself to him, oh gods, and what if he didn't like what he saw—but she squeezed her eyes shut again, and hauled in more air. He'd already seen it all, in far more vivid detail than this. He liked her looking like this. She could do this. She wanted this. She was making him *hers*.

So she opened her eyes again, made herself look at his shifting eyes as her hand slipped down between them. Finding his hot swollen hardness, tightening her fingers around it, lifting it up. And then—she gasped, bit her lip—she settled it just there, between her spread legs.

It shuddered against her at the touch, strong, and somehow that was enough to flash the certainty, the focus, back to Fasta's thoughts. Henrik wanted this, too. Henrik had done this to her before, over that desk. And now he wanted to see her take him, and she was damn well going to show him, and please him, and obey.

So she kept her eyes on his as she lowered herself against him, nudging that hard blunt head against her slippery wetness. And oh, there was a lot of him, so much of him, and she sucked in a breath, willed herself to relax, to sink a little further.

"Good girl," Henrik's voice rumbled, and the sound of it made Fasta's whole body clench up, hard. Enough to push him all the way out again, and he chuckled, gave a little roll upwards of his hips.

"C'mon, buttercup," he whispered. "Seen you take way more than this. Just yesterday."

Gods curse him, but Fasta pulled in a breath, and silently counted to ten. And then she pushed back down against him, feeling the pressure building and building. She could do this, she just had to breathe, relax, spread herself wider, arch herself backwards, how was there so fucking *much*—

But then the pressure shuddered, broke—and with a single shocking, burning thrust, he was suddenly *there*, plunged all the way up inside, hot and hard, skin to skin. And Fasta cried out, shivering all over, while Henrik flashed an approving grin toward her, and gave a smooth painful *glorious* circle of his hips.

"Fucking *right*," he breathed, even as Fasta cried out again, damn near shouted with it. Because it felt impossible, overwhelming, everywhere, everything, there were no thoughts, no nothing, but this—

"Tell me," he whispered now, circling his hips up again, deep, raw, powerful. "How's it feel."

Gods damn him, he was expecting her to talk in this, to make coherent sentences, but Fasta could only keep gasping, choking on her breath. While her shaking, prickling hands scrabbled to his still-covered chest, sought to brace herself against the warm solid strength of it.

"Tell me," Henrik said again, his eyes intent, compelling, on hers. "C'mon, Fass. Truth."

Truth. Fasta gulped for breath, fought to think, to find words. But there was still nothing, except the power of this, the fullness of it, the taut swollen everywhere invasion. Her Harry was inside her, fucking her, looking at her, *hers*, and this was everything, *everything*—

"Say it," he ordered, with another purposeful, almost-painful circle of his hips. "What's in your head right now."

Fasta shuddered all over, her body clamping even tighter on him, making him swell even fuller inside her, fuck, *fuck*. "Everything," she gasped, finally, because that was a word, that was truth. "*Everything*, Harry."

It came out choked, pleading, and Fasta was shocked, or maybe not, to feel a streak of wetness, slipping down her cheek. "Everything, Harry," she gasped again. "I'm sorry, I just—"

She couldn't finish, couldn't breathe, just shook her head, bit her lip. While Henrik's still-clothed chest heaved under her hands, his eyes gone still, arrested, strange.

"Aw, it's all good," he murmured, and his hand came up, curled familiar and safe around the back of her neck. "It's so good, Fass. You're such a good girl, aren't you?"

And then he pulled, pulled her all the way down over him, and his mouth found hers, his lips and tongue warm, alive. While Fasta clung to him, frantic, kissing him back, needing his tongue invading her just like his cock was invading her, needed him here, now, all of him, *please*—

It was all this now, all the shocking sweeping sensation of him, the tension the fullness the pressure rising, swinging up wild and uncontrollable. And Fasta could only kiss him, clutch at him, silently beg for more of him, while the whole world pulled in tighter, tighter, hot and close and—

And it collapsed, reverberated, so powerful that she bit down, hard, against Henrik's lips, even as her body wrenched itself against him, flaring out its furious blazing pleasure all around him. Making him arch up even tighter, fuller, deeper, his mouth under hers groaning aloud—and oh, fuck, he was right there with her, emptying himself out up inside her, his big hand clamping tight on her neck, his shuddering cock commanding her, controlling her, consuming her.

But then it was over, the invading fullness between Fasta's legs shrinking, becoming something normal, bearable again.

And her mouth still against Henrik's seemed to find air again, heaving in shaky breaths, while her body went limp and sated and boneless all over. *Fuck.*

Henrik's chest rose and fell under her, his breaths harsh against her lips, but there was something strange, something new, hitching in his magic—and when Fasta pulled back to look at him, his eyes were strange, too. Distant, even, as if he couldn't quite bear to look at her.

Fasta's stomach plummeted, as sudden awareness flashed through her thoughts. Because maybe—maybe—she'd already botched this. Maybe she'd already broken those rules Henrik had set out. Because that—that had been her and Harry, just now. Not a business deal, not professional, and not a lord and his servant, not in the least.

She groped a shaky hand for the frame of her bed, just needing to feel the brass, the earth—but then she blinked, and stilled, because the bedpost wasn't there. Instead, all four brass bedposts were now pointed in toward them, bending the entire bed's frame, curving in at them as if they'd been a magnet, or a sun.

"Um," she said, and she pulled up a little more, feeling Henrik's still-soft body shift inside her. "Was that you? Or me?"

Henrik's glance toward the bed frame was perfunctory, entirely unsurprised, and Fasta realized that unlike her, he must have felt it as it had happened. "Not sure," he replied, reaching overhead to grip at it, and Fasta felt the mattress under them straighten again, returning to its proper flat state. "Both of us, probably."

Fasta bit her lip and looked at him, at that still-distant unease in his eyes—and then her gaze caught on where there was a distinct new cut on his lip, surely from where she'd *bitten* him. And—she frowned downwards—she'd somehow managed to tear his tunic, too, at the neck. And when had she done that, had he noticed that, but his angling eyes said that yes, surely, he had.

"Well," Fasta said, and tried for a smile. "Sorry. It's, uh, been a while."

Henrik's eyes shifted, betraying something else Fasta couldn't quite read. "Don't apologize," he said, his voice gruff. "Occupational hazard."

He half-smiled, like that was supposed to be a joke, but Fasta could only stare back down at him, as a sudden tightness clamped against her chest. Because Henrik was referring to the fact that he was being *paid*. That this was his job now. That him making her want that, and feel that, just now, had been *work*.

His eyes betrayed it too, and he cleared his throat, and took a breath. "But next time, you'll remember about not calling me Harry, yeah?" he asked, a little too steady. "And you know"—he took another breath—"I think it might be better if I sleep on the floor from now on, too."

Oh. *Oh*. Fasta flinched, and her body suddenly shoved up, off, away from him, all on its own. Leaving her empty again, but for Henrik's now-dripping wetness, slipping down her thigh. Feeling like hers, but it wasn't, he wasn't, this was just a job for him, with rules, rules he didn't want her to break...

Gods, this was messing Fasta up, swirling up a rampant rioting mess in her head. And where only minutes ago she'd felt drunk on that heady wrung-out contentment, now there was only distance, and loneliness, and something too much like shame.

"Right," she finally said, staggering on her too-shaky legs. "We should probably get ready, we have that new job today, right?"

She didn't wait for Henrik to answer, didn't even meet his eyes, and she swiped for her wardrobe, for her clothes. Clutching them to her chest as she dodged into the water closet, and slammed the door behind her.

16

When Fasta stepped back into her room again, she was tall and composed, her hair braided back, her eyes swollen but dry. She could still make this work. She was fine. This would be fine.

Henrik was waiting for her, sitting fully clothed on her bed, which—Fasta's eyes flicked across it—looked mostly as it originally had, but still with posts that curved slightly inward at the corners. Like he'd fixed it, but not quite all the way, and she couldn't find the space to think about that right now, couldn't bear it.

"You all right?" Henrik asked her, a little gruff, as he rose to his feet, and briefly touched a hand to her arm. "Can I... do anything? Get you anything?"

Fasta waved it away as casually as she could, and waited while Henrik washed up and dressed in the water closet, changing into a set of fresh clothes he'd apparently had in his pack. And then she silently accompanied him down to the dining hall, where they ate in silence too, while this thing, this weight, hung heavier and heavier between them. So much that Fasta was deeply relieved when they finished, and she could finally stop feeling Henrik's eyes, Henrik's body, across the table.

"Listen, Fass," Henrik said, once they were walking on the road toward Hartmoor, and the noble's estate. "About that payment, I..."

His voice trailed off, and Fasta pulled in a lungful of air. "Right," she replied. "Once we're done today, we can stop into the bank at Skent, and I'll make the transfer. You could send it off to Andreas from there, too."

There was silence from Henrik beside her, and when she glanced over, he was frowning straight ahead, and twitching a curt nod. Not saying anything else, not even a thank-you, and Fasta surreptitiously snapped up a rock into her hand, clenched it tight. She would be fine. This had to be fine.

"So who is this client again?" she asked Henrik. "You said he'd just taken over the place?"

Henrik's shoulder shrugged, sharp and jerky. "The Earl of Valkin, apparently," he said. "Whoever that is."

Fasta usually knew which nobles belonged to which titles— that was her father's regular circle, after all, and the world she'd grown up in—but she vaguely remembered hearing that the Earl of Valkin had died a few years back, and that the title and lands had been contested. If she ever discussed such matters with her father, she would probably have found out who'd finally gained it, but her brief visits to her father's estate were already tedious enough, without adding in painful parlour gossip about which far-off persons were squabbling over whose houses.

"I suppose we'll find out," Fasta said glumly, and Henrik shrugged again. Letting the silence spiral out again between them, and it was so stupid, because they'd always talked as they travelled, even if it was just empty comments, or teasing, or pointless debates over what kinds of stone and ore deposits were buried nearby.

But finally, after what felt like an interminable journey, they reached the edge of the estate's grounds, and announced themselves at the gatehouse. Which seemed permanently and expensively staffed, with a proctor who was clearly expecting them, and immediately took off to find "his lordship".

"Great," Henrik muttered, as they watched the proctor's livery-clad form jogging up the long, curving drive, and disappearing behind the sheltering trees. "Any noble who makes his underlings call him *his lordship* is gonna be a real treat."

Fasta elbowed Henrik in the side, while trying to clobber down the memory of herself calling Henrik *my lord*, just the night before. While she'd been on her knees, and he'd slammed his cock into her mouth, made her clean him up, afterwards...

She cleared her throat, attempted a glance past Henrik toward the closest outbuilding, which felt like a carriage house—but instead, her eyes caught on Henrik again. Or rather, on his lip, which was still red from where she'd bitten it. And when she glanced up at his eyes, he was watching her. Looking at her looking at him, and he took a breath, opened his mouth—

"Well, if it isn't the great Lady Fasta Valgeirr!" came a voice. A familiar voice, one that set something skittering in Fasta's chest—and when she whirled around to look, she found herself staring at a handsome, astonishingly familiar face.

"Elgin?" she asked blankly, even as her traitorous eyes darted down his slim, muscular form, and back up to his laughing dark eyes. "What are *you* doing here?"

Elgin flashed her a grin, just as swift and stunning as it had always been, and then swept into an elaborate bow, along with a graceful flourish of the silken riding cape he was wearing. "The Earl of Valkin, Lord Norberg, at your service," he replied. "My lady."

Fasta blinked at him—Elgin Bryant might be Lord Norberg, but he was *not* the Earl of Valkin—was he? But he flashed her another knowing grin as he stood tall again, tossing the riding cape over his shoulder. "It sounds ludicrous, I know," he said. "Eight months in, and I'm still not used to it."

Fasta kept staring at him, still not following, and Elgin tilted his head, as unmistakable awareness flicked across his eyes. "Your father didn't tell you, did he?" he said slowly. "Gods, Fasta, you must have been losing your mind over this demanding entitled maniac who wanted you to come in and restore his entire estate."

It felt like icy water had dumped over Fasta's head, but finally the comprehension was sinking in, twisting low in her gut. Her ex was now the Earl of Valkin. He now owned this entire estate. And he now wanted her to restore all of it, in a project that would take *months*?

But Kjaran had said there was no getting out of the job, and Fasta's relationship with Elgin had decisively ended five years ago. So she took a deep breath, squared her shoulders, and shot an assessing glance over Elgin's shoulder at the estate's manicured grounds and gardens. The house itself wasn't even visible yet, but she could feel it there, situated large and heavy at the end of the curving drive, beyond that patch of trees. She could also feel an excessive number of outbuildings—sheds, stables, that carriage house, a kennel. Enough to make this one of the larger estates she'd seen, rivalling even her father's.

"How did *you* end up with this place?" she asked Elgin, as steadily as she could. "I don't even remember you being related to that earl."

"Distantly," Elgin replied, which was fair, because all that crowd was interrelated somehow, if you went back far enough. "And the stingy bastard left no legitimate heirs, and no instructions, and after an excessively tedious barrage of negotiations, here I am. Coming to terms with the fact that my gigantic new estate"—he gestured irritably behind his head—"is a complete and utter *dump*."

Despite herself, Fasta twitched a wry half-smile, and

glanced over the estate again. "It can't be that bad, can it? The grounds look great."

"Yes, that's because our old Earl was all about the look," Elgin replied, "while he let the buildings he didn't use run to rack and ruin. And he plastered over the interiors of the buildings he *did* use, meaning there's now rot and damp behind everything. Some of it might be salvageable, but most of it needs to be redone from the bottom up. So please, Fasta"—he gave her that grin again, broad and wheedling—"please, rescue me, and do it properly, for the love of the gods. Otherwise I'll end up trapped here forever, raging at shoddy workmanship into my dotage."

Fasta couldn't help a laugh this time, because Elgin had always been excessively particular, and she could easily picture him waving a cane and shouting at his crumbling walls. "Well, we'll see what we can do," she said, with a sideways glance at Henrik—and then her brain caught, suddenly, on the fact that Elgin hadn't once spoken to Henrik in all this, or acknowledged his existence. And the look on Henrik's face said he hadn't missed that, and he wasn't happy about it, either.

"Oh, Elgin, this is Henrik Hallen," Fasta said, with a brief, apologetic touch to Henrik's elbow. "My partner. And Harry, this is Elgin Bryant, who I used to know as Lord Norberg, but apparently"—she smiled toward his dancing dark eyes—"is now also the Earl of Valkin. We used to, um, study earth-magic together at the Academy."

"Though Fasta was always way out of my league," Elgin said, reaching out a hand toward Henrik, and giving Fasta a too-obvious wink. "So you're her partner? With work, I presume? Unless I'm missing something here?"

His voice stayed light, teasing, but Fasta could see the sudden tension in Henrik's bulky forearm, the muscles straining as his big hand briefly gripped Elgin's. "Yeah, we work together," he replied. "For five years now."

Elgin tilted his head at Henrik, seeming to consider that.

"You know, I think I've actually heard of you," he said, with a sudden smile. "Earth-mage too, right? You do Fasta's heavy lifting?"

Henrik's shoulders went stiffer—he'd always hated being likened to a common labourer, for good reason—and Fasta cleared her throat, and again touched Henrik's elbow. "Actually, Henrik specializes in resource identification, extraction, and refinement," she told Elgin. "And sedimentary and metamorphic rock transitions. He's also extremely gifted with period and artisanal masonry and earthwork."

Elgin's eyebrows snapped up, but he kept the smile on his face. "Impressive," he said. "Where did you study, then?"

Fasta bit back her wince, while beside her Henrik went even stiffer, his mouth thin. "I'm self-taught," he said, voice curt. "Through actual experience."

Elgin blinked, maybe reading that for the insult it was, and Fasta stepped slightly between them, and drew herself to her full height. "Henrik has all his certifications," she said firmly, "and he earned some of the highest marks ever on the Academy's masonry exams. Afterwards, the supervisor couldn't even tell what work was his, and what was original."

She shot Henrik a quick smile, because that week they'd spent in the capital, while Henrik had consistently dumbfounded all the so-called masonry experts at the Earth Academy, was still one of her favourite memories. They'd spent the week exploring the city together, sharing meals and playing around with earth-magic, and one very memorable evening had involved Henrik getting very drunk, and telling Fasta that no one had a right to be as rich and smart as she was, while also having a face and a body like that.

"Nice," Elgin said now, smiling again, like he meant it. "Well, there's plenty of old masonry here, and half of it's gone to shit. Come on, let me take you around, show you the damage."

They spent the rest of the day touring the place, going from building to building, laughing at Elgin's amusing, self-deprecating commentary. Or rather, Fasta laughed, while Henrik was all business, only speaking when necessary, and focusing all his attention on the admittedly dilapidated state of the estate's masonry. Which, as Elgin had said, encompassed everything from the storage sheds to the beautiful old manor house.

"I do love the house," Elgin said, trailing a reverent hand along the wall as he led them up its grand central staircase. "If you ignore the mess, it's beautiful underneath, right?"

It was, with its tiled floors and matching sandstone walls, and intricate stonework and carvings in every room. The original building team had clearly been artisans, as well as earth-mages, but the neglect was clear here in the house too, with copious amounts of damp and broken mortar, and crumbling, haphazard repairs. Fasta could even feel that the entire house was slightly tilted, sagging toward the northeast corner, and she knew Henrik felt it too, judging by the way he kept frowning toward that side.

"You're aware you have foundation issues, right?" he said abruptly to Elgin. "That corner should've been dealt with years ago."

Elgin stiffened on the staircase, and aimed a cool smile over his shoulder. "Yes, I'm well aware," he said lightly. "And as I keep telling you, the place is a mess, and here I am, getting it dealt with now. Unless you don't think you can fix it?"

There was an unmistakable challenge in his voice, which only served to make Henrik's mouth go tighter, and Fasta put a quick hand to his arm. "I'm sure we can fix it," she said firmly. "Though it would be good to go down and take a look at the foundation, right, Harry?"

Henrik nodded, and they followed Elgin back downstairs, through the kitchen full of young, well-dressed servants, and then further down into the basement. It was large and open, and studded throughout with multiple hefty slabs of stone, mostly marble and granite. Some of them were rough and untouched, fresh-cut from the earth, while others were smoothed and finished, carved into detailed shapes and sculptures.

"This is your work, right, Elgin?" Fasta asked, and then immediately wished she hadn't, from the way Henrik's eyes darted up, and narrowed on hers. He'd been frowning down at one of the sculptures, a carved set of geometric shapes that seemed to be floating on top of one another. And while it wasn't Fasta's own preference—too stark and angular, typical of Elgin's work—it was very well done, and an undeniable showcase of the sculptor's impressive earth-magic skills.

"Yes, this is all mine," Elgin replied. "I still keep up with my sculpting, when I can. Sell a few pieces here and there, too."

There was a trace of pride in his voice, and Fasta couldn't begrudge it, because she knew how vehemently Elgin's family had disapproved of his magical studies. His parents had made her own father look almost supportive, and it was one of the reasons she and Elgin had first become friends, and then lovers, back at the Academy.

But then it had ended with all those weeks of sobbing, with Elgin only occasionally there in Fasta's bed, and almost always gone off elsewhere. And now that Fasta was faced with him like this, all these years later, she found herself feeling almost fondly tolerant toward him, while also being utterly certain that their breakup had been for the best.

However—she briefly met Elgin's eyes over his sculpture—it had occurred to her, more than once today, that Elgin might have had regrets, after all. Because the way his dark eyes lingered on her wasn't unappreciative, or uninterested, and Fasta almost wished she'd worn her baggy work tunic, rather than her more finely spun, close-fitting day clothes.

Henrik had noticed too, Fasta was certain, and he scowled as he prowled around the basement's corner in question, running his hands along the walls, and biting out questions that Elgin couldn't answer. Things like when was this part of the manor built, had any of it been replaced, had the mortar ever been redone, had the house ever been struck or attacked.

Elgin's replies were steady and cool, even as Henrik became more curt, more distant. Not even bothering to hide his contempt at the fact that despite being an accomplished earth-mage, Elgin clearly knew little to nothing about his grand mansion, and hadn't given nearly enough attention to admittedly significant structural problems.

"So are you living here alone, then?" Fasta asked Elgin, too loudly, once Henrik had finally finished his interrogation, and they'd climbed back out into the afternoon sun. "With just your staff? Is there anyone else we'll be reporting to?"

"Nope, just me," Elgin replied. "Though I've been told I need to start hunting for a good woman to manage things, keep the old place in line. Don't suppose you know anyone who'd be interested?"

He winked at Fasta as he spoke, making his point rather too obvious. And though she kept her face carefully blank, beside her Henrik was viciously glowering, the angry dislike billowing off him in plumes.

"No," Henrik snapped at Elgin, "we don't. And we have an appointment we need to get to before sundown."

It was unquestionably rude, and Elgin clearly didn't approve, his eyes narrow and glinting on Henrik's face. Prompting Fasta to jump in with future plans, and thank-yous, and promises to return and start properly working in the morning.

Henrik listened to it all in stony silence, his arms crossed forbiddingly over his chest. And when Fasta finally turned to leave, Henrik didn't spare a single glance at Elgin, just spun on his heel, and strode out the gate.

"What the hell," Henrik demanded, once they were well out of earshot, "was that all about?"

Fasta shot him a disbelieving look, and picked up her pace. "What, the job?" she asked. "Or you being openly rude to the influential client we have to deal with for the next three months?"

A growl hissed from Henrik's throat, and his hand caught Fasta's arm, drew her to a stop. "Don't," he said, a low warning in his voice. "We agreed to this, Fasta. You don't lie to me anymore. You don't try to protect me, you don't dance around the truth with me. You know *exactly* what I mean."

That tone in his voice set Fasta's eyes fluttering, but she pursed her lips, pulled herself straighter. "Fine," she said. "Yes, Elgin is a flirt. And yes, he was dismissive and rude to you at first, and that isn't appropriate—but that's just what these rich nobles are like. You *know* that, Harry."

But Henrik's expression didn't change, and his hand caught Fasta's chin, and tilted it up toward him. "No," he snapped. "You look me in the eyes, Fasta, and tell me the *truth.*"

Fasta blinked up at him, her shoulders heaving, her breaths coming fast and shallow. She had told him the truth. Hadn't she?

"Um," she said, and then swallowed, her throat convulsing against his fingers. "We were—together. Years ago."

Henrik's hand jerked away, as something like triumph, or maybe contempt, flared in his eyes. "Yeah, there it is," he said, on a heavy exhale. "For how long?"

Fasta held his eyes, and drew in a ragged breath. "Two years."

Henrik stared at her for another empty, hanging instant, perhaps waiting for some kind of explanation, or even an apology. But Fasta couldn't seem to find one, and finally Henrik shook his head, and spun away from her. Heading down the road, as if he was *leaving* her, and he couldn't, he was *hers*—

Fasta twitched and jogged to catch up, gasping at his too-tense shoulder. "Look, it was *years* ago, Harry," she said. "Before I even *met* you. It means nothing to me now, and there's no reason you should even care!"

"No reason, is there?" Henrik snapped back, keeping his

eyes straight ahead on the road. "Five years we've worked together, Fasta, and you've never *once* mentioned this guy to me. And how long were you gonna keep pretending? *Lying* to me?"

Fasta grimaced and shook her head—she hadn't been lying, had she?—while Henrik huffed a low laugh, rubbed his hand at his mouth. "I'm gonna be doing the 'heavy lifting' at this arsehole's house for *months*," he added, harder. "While he insults and ignores me, fucks you with his eyes, reminds you about the good old days, and all but asks you to be his *wife*! And you were just gonna keep lying to me, all that time? After that promise you made me yesterday?"

Fasta grimaced again, and fought for an answer, for truth. "Look, I didn't think it mattered!" she countered. "It's not like you've told me every detail about your past lovers, have you? Or like you've been celibate all this time? Or like you're even willing to be *faithful* to me?"

Henrik blinked at her for an instant, and then barked another brittle, humourless laugh. "We're still *friends*, Fasta," he said. "If I'd ever been with anyone for two whole years, I sure as hell would have told you about her by now. And I *definitely* wouldn't have marched you up to her door, and then pretended to you like there'd been *nothing* between us!"

Fasta shook her head, shoved down the irrational surge of jealousy at even the thought of it. "Well, with everything going on right now," she shot back, "I just wanted to keep the peace, keep our heads down, and focus on the job! Because Elgin is our employer now, so we need to nod and smile, and do whatever he wants!"

"Yeah, and you don't think he *knows* that?" Henrik retorted. "You didn't hear the part where he said he specifically wanted you for this? And you don't remember how you told me, just last night, how Kjaran said this job came straight from the *Council*?"

Right. Fasta had forgotten that point, and Henrik scoffed,

not at all a laugh this time. "He ignored our process, and went straight to the Council," he snapped, "and probably *paid*, so he could get you there, alone, on his estate, for three whole months, whether you wanted it or not. And what he does *not* want out of the deal is *me*, and if you didn't notice, he made that very fucking clear!"

His deep voice rumbled through the air around them, and without thinking, Fasta grabbed for his arm, yanked him toward her. "Stop this, Harry," she said, darting a furtive glance around them, to where a cart was coming up the road. "Look, can we just—"

She tugged him off toward the nearby trees, into the thick cover of the neighbouring forest. If they were really getting into this right now, she would rather not do it in front of spectators, or where Elgin might hear about it. And also, it was just easier to think in the forest, even if she stumbled over roots as she walked, even if they'd be too late for that damned transfer at the bank.

"You're overreacting, Harry," Fasta continued, whirling around to face him again, once they were deep in the trees. "Yes, it's unfortunate that Elgin used his money and his influence to get his way, but"—she pulled in air, met Henrik's eyes—"we all do that. I do that. I'm doing it right now, with you!"

Henrik's eyes shifted, narrowed, and he opened his mouth—but Fasta wasn't done, and she spread her hand flat to his chest. "And look, I *am* good at the kind of work he wants done," she said. "And he probably thought I wouldn't accept the proposal if he submitted it the usual way, because of our history. So he went around the rules. Which is unfair, Harry, I know, but it's not worth caring about!"

Henrik barked another one of those laughs, and shook his head. "And why isn't it?" he demanded. "Is it just my opinion that doesn't matter, because I'm just here to do your *heavy lifting*? It doesn't matter if I don't want to do this job, because you're still the one who's *really* in charge of me?"

Fasta winced, shook her head, but Henrik came a step closer. "I don't want to do this job, Fasta," he said, deeper. "I don't trust this guy. I don't want to work for him for the next three months. And I want us to walk away from this. *Today*."

What? Fasta blinked at him, her mouth opening and closing. "Walk away?" she repeated blankly. "You mean, you want to back out from the job entirely? *Now*?"

"*Yes*, I want to back out from the job!" Henrik growled, and Fasta could feel his magic unspooling around her, close and tight and reckless. "What don't you understand about this? I don't like it, I don't feel good about it, what else do you need to hear? I thought we were supposed to be partners!"

"We *are* partners!" Fasta snapped back, and it felt like his anger was seeping into her, curdling deep and bitter inside. "That doesn't mean you have the right to refuse jobs and risk your entire *career* just because you're *jealous*!"

The words swung through the air, and she could almost feel them hitting Henrik, striking him straight where it hurt most. In his pride, his relentless work, his hard-earned accolades and accomplishments. And striking at that new agreement between them, too. The one where she'd promised she would give him control back...

"Good enough," he said, his voice wooden, his eyes glinting too bright on hers. "Have it your way, then, Fasta. *Again*."

And without another word, he spun around, and strode away through the trees.

17

Damn it. *Damn* it.

Fasta stared at Henrik for too long, his broad back growing smaller and smaller—and then she rushed after him, tripping over roots and twigs, until she could grasp at his stiff shoulder.

"Harry," she said, breathless. "Don't be like this. That's not what I meant, you know it isn't—"

"Oh, really?" Henrik asked, incredulous, as he whirled around to face her. "What am I supposed to know? How you're lying to me again? You don't care about my opinion? And"—his mouth twisted—"you really think I'm just *jealous* of this guy? *This guy*, with his snide attitude and his crumbling tilting house? And how he's clearly absolute *shit* at earth-magic, if he could really stand to live for even a single damned *day* in that deathtrap?"

He wasn't wrong, and gods, this was a mess, and why were they even fighting? And Henrik was hers, *hers*, and how could she fix this, what would sway him, please—

She flew at him without thinking, tackling him backwards, and she could feel his sudden confusion, could taste it in the skin of his neck. But she was kissing at him, desperately touching at him, because he was hers, and *this* was what they'd agreed to, hands and bodies and mouths, hungry lips against slick skin.

Henrik's body against hers shuddered, once—but then he was in it with her, his big hands gripping against her back, his mouth crushing hungry and furious against hers. As a low growl rumbled from his throat, vibrating through his chest, and damn, that was good, and they both tumbled down to the damp cold ground, twisting and tangling together.

"I only meant you're jealous," Fasta gasped into his mouth, her breath heaving, "because I fucked him."

Gods, why had she said that, and another deep growl reverberated through Henrik's chest. But something shifted again in his magic, and his strong hands settled her flat to the earth beneath him, his bulky body close over her.

"How much," he breathed, his eyes so strong, so intent. "Did you fuck him."

Fasta groaned into his mouth, pulled him down harder. "Don't know," she gasped, into the demanding heat of his still-kissing lips. "Dozens of times. Hundreds."

Henrik growled again, and his hands swiped for Fasta's wrists, and pinned them powerfully against the ground over her head. And then—her whole body froze—something else curved over her wrists, too. Something cold and hard and smooth. *Stone.*

Fasta's eyes snapped upwards to look, and found—*cuffs.* Big, bulky stone cuffs, curving out of the earth, pinning each wrist firmly in place.

Henrik was looking too, his breaths heaving, his eyes blazing on hers. "Good?" he gasped. "More?"

Fasta frantically nodded, and with another low groan, Henrik grabbed for her trousers, and yanked them all the way downwards. Exposing her swollen, quivering groin to the cool air, oh gods—but he still kept going, pulling off her boots, tugging the trousers over her feet. Baring her entire lower body for him, and then—she moaned—more stone rose from the earth, pulling her legs wide apart, trapping her bare ankles in place.

"Now tell me the truth, my spoiled little brat," Henrik breathed, as he shifted himself up over her again, hands flat to the earth on either side of her head. "You really *liked* that smug skinny bastard? You liked him touching you? Fucking you?"

Fasta couldn't quite hide her flinch—of course he would go right there, damn him—and she bit her lip, strained against the stone constricting her wrists and ankles. What could she say to him, maybe just *forget him, forget that, it's you*—

But Henrik shook his head, looking disdainful, insolent. "The truth, Fasta," he ordered, hovering so close over her, as the ankle cuffs drew her legs even wider, flooding her bare body with even more cool air. "Tell me."

Fasta kept straining upwards, her hips bucking, trying, failing, to reach him. "It was—" she began, and then she stopped at the look on Henrik's face, the warning in his eyes. *It was awful*, she'd been about to say, *it was nothing*—but no, no, that wasn't true, and her thoughts swarmed with memories of Elgin's lithe, smooth body, moving hungry and fluid against hers...

She shook the visions away, but Henrik saw too much, knew too much. And his big hand slid toward her, curved against her cheek—and then drew back, and gave her a light, gentle slap.

Fasta jolted all over, gaped up at Henrik's face. He'd never once done something like that before, and fuck, it should not have felt so good, thrilling through her chest, her groin. Making her arch harder up against him, and his eyes flashed as his hand drew back and landed again, just a little harder this time.

"Tell me," he growled, his voice at utter odds with the way his warm callused hand was now stroking her cheek, perhaps rubbing the redness away. And then that hand slid down her front, all the way, until it curved between her spread legs, his thick fingers gently nudging against her slick opened heat. "*Now*, buttercup."

Fasta arched and gasped again, and somehow her head was shaking, saying—*no*. No, she couldn't tell him that, what if he—what if he *left*—

And then his hand drew back, and landed in another firm little slap, straight between her spread legs. While Fasta flailed and cried out, her opened body trembling and convulsing, maybe needing more—and oh, he drew his hand back, and did it again. And again, and again, until Fasta was fully shouting and writhing with it, and Henrik's eyes were blazing on her face, his pupils blown wide.

"Look what's become of you," he breathed. "High and mighty Lady Valgeirr, turned into such a greedy, shameless little brat. Defying her lord, because she's enjoying her punishment too damned much."

He accompanied it with another slap between her legs, his hardest one yet, and Fasta could hear the wetness, could feel her desperate body clinging back to his lingering hand. Betraying her with shocking brazenness, and Henrik huffed an insolent little laugh as he shook his head.

"Naw, that's all you're getting, buttercup," he drawled, and his hand drew away, his body shifting over her. "We're gonna try this another way."

Another way? Fasta gasped for air, nodding, needing whatever he would do next—and then, oh hell, something new touched her. Something *there*, prodding straight against the inflamed convulsing wetness between her spread legs. His—his bare *cock*.

"You like that, Lady Valgeirr?" he asked, his eyes slightly fluttering, and she could feel his blunt silken head fluttering too, nudging him closer against her. "You like that even more than being slapped, don't you?"

Fasta nodded again, and fought to shove herself

downwards, to take him deeper—but the stone cuffs still held her in place, and Henrik laughed as he watched, the sound cool, contemptuous. "Yeah, you do, Lady Valgeirr," he drawled. "You want my fat commoner dick fucking you, don't you? You want me pouring you full of my filthy commoner spunk."

Oh, fuck, and Fasta's body was writhing and shouting on its own now, needing all of that, yes, *please*—

But Henrik shook his head, and just held himself there over her, with his thick blunt crown just nudged slightly inside her. "You keep trying, you greedy little brat," he purred. "But you're not getting it until you tell me the truth."

The truth. Fasta's shouting whirling thoughts couldn't even follow anymore—what had he wanted again? But that was a warning glitter in his eyes, and oh, hell, he drew slightly back from her, taking it away from her, *no.*

"Time's running out, buttercup," he hissed. "The longer you take, the less of it you're getting. Now answer my fucking question."

His question. His question, what had he wanted, what was Fasta supposed to say? She was supposed to protect him, to make him hers—but that awareness kept flitting away, lost beneath the strength of him, the power of him, that brief tantalizing nudge between her legs...

"You liked him?" Henrik supplied, clipped. "You liked having that smug little lord fuck you?"

Damn it. Damn it, there was no lying to Henrik, not like this, not with her thoughts screaming, her every nerve frantic and aflame. And his brutal powerful body taunting her, so close and yet so far away...

"Yes," Fasta finally gasped, squeezing her eyes shut. "Yes, I liked him. I wanted him. It was—good, between us. But—"

She forced her eyes open, forced herself to see that shadow across Henrik's eyes, that sudden bitterness on his mouth. To find more truth, even when he looked like that, and facing it felt almost like panic.

"But—now I want you," she choked, holding his eyes. "I want you, Harry. You're gorgeous, you're brilliant, you're better than any other earth-mage I know. I want you so much"—she pulled in air—"I'm *paying* you to be with me. So please, please, just *do* it!"

Henrik's eyes changed again, going somewhere Fasta couldn't follow, but then, finally, finally—he bore down. Pushing that huge solid bulk against her slick spasming heat, and Fasta fought to breathe, to relax, to open. And then she almost screamed aloud at the thrilling feel of her resistance breaking, of Henrik finally driving deep and full and burning inside.

"Fuck," she moaned, her still-clothed chest heaving up against him. "Fuck, Harry. *Gods.*"

A strangled noise escaped from Henrik's mouth, again something Fasta couldn't quite catch—but then he dragged himself out, and sank back in. Shocking, soaring, everything, and she cried out again, pulled helplessly at her wrists.

"Oh, *Harry*," she groaned again, and Henrik's hooded eyes snapped to hers, held with glimmering intensity. Maybe still wanting to hear her truth, and why was it so difficult, why couldn't she just say it?

"So good," she choked out, her breath gasping with every driving strike of his hips, of that too-strong cock inside. "So good, Harry. So much better than it *ever* was with him. I swear to you."

Henrik's eyes flashed, his body held up taut and thrilling over hers on those muscled forearms, and Fasta turned her face to one of those arms, breathed in the scent of it, the nearness of it. Wishing she could touch it, and she could say that, too. She should.

"I wish I could touch you right now," she gulped at him. "Wish I could kiss you, taste you, *worship* you, Harry."

The feeling was impossible, the thinking impossible, everything scattering away, but for the firing consuming drive of that cock, so deep, so powerful. "Please, Harry," she rasped, and it felt like her whole body was begging, arching, on fire. "Please, fuck me, make me yours, *please*—"

Her voice lurched, choked, lost in the sudden thundering relief. In the pure, streaming ecstasy charging through her, lighting her up, writhing her body against the earth, and against Henrik's shuddering, invading strength. Needing him with her, needing him to give her this, now—

But suddenly—he was *gone*. That hot stretching fullness was gone, away, because Henrik had—pulled out. Pulled backwards, up to his knees, as his hand roughly moved downwards, stroking up, once—

And then he was pulsing out, spurts of slippery white spraying onto the earth beside them. Some of it catching on Fasta's tunic, stringing her to the wet tip of him, while he groaned and shuddered above her, his chest heaving with his breaths.

Oh. Fasta couldn't think, couldn't follow. Could only stare, blink at him, try to force away the sudden breathless tightness in her lungs. What—what was he doing? Why had he done that? He was supposed to be hers, *hers*...

But his eyes were squeezed shut, his breaths still heaving, and with a shaky jerk of his hand, he yanked up his trousers. Leaving her lying there untouched, but for the stone cuffs still circling her wrists and ankles—but then those fell away, too, crumbling apart into the earth.

It meant—they were done. Henrik was done. Right?

Something plummeted in Fasta's chest, and after a long, silent minute of blinking at him, she took a deep breath, and made herself sit up. The forest spun around her at first, her body suddenly achy and strained, and she blinked down at the sight of her wrists, which had somehow gotten rubbed red and raw. Her ankles looked the same, and they'd begun throbbing, too—though she hadn't felt it at the time, hadn't even noticed.

And surely Henrik hadn't noticed either, because he was

now kneeling beside her, shaking his head, rubbing both hands at his eyes. Still not looking at her, or speaking to her, and Fasta's hand snaked out, brushed brief against his shoulder.

"What—what is it, Harry?" she asked, her voice small. "Did I—did I do something wrong?"

Henrik twitched at the touch, his eyes snapping to her face—and again, Fasta couldn't read that look, that twist on his mouth. "No, love, you were perfect," he said, hoarse, as he fished sideways in his pack for his waterskin, and thrust it toward her. "I just—need a minute, all right? You just—get dressed, yeah?"

He even briefly patted her cheek, and then lurched up to his feet, and staggered a few steps away. His back toward her, his shoulders still rising and falling, and Fasta had never seen him like this before, had she? But then again, he'd never called her *love* before either, and it shivered in her chest, brief and hopeful and desperate. Whatever this was, she could handle it. Right?

So she drank deeply from the waterskin, and then gingerly reached for her boots and trousers, and pulled them back on. Her trousers had gotten streaked all over with grass and mud, and her once-grey silk tunic looked even worse, especially with—Fasta wiped uselessly at it—those telltale streaks of white where Henrik had spattered it. But it was fine, it had to be fine. She was an earth-mage, she got dirty all the time, people would just think it was mortar, right?

She stood carefully to her feet, holding herself tall, taking a long, fortifying breath. And then she turned to where Henrik was still facing away from her, still not looking at her. "Should we keep moving, then?" she made herself say, her voice scratchy, thin. "Perhaps we can still make the bank in time?"

Henrik's shoulders rose and fell again, and when he turned around, his face was carefully blank. Even as his eyes flicked down her body, lingered on the mess of her clothes. She'd pulled down the sleeves of her tunic, at least, covering her wrists, and thankfully he hadn't noticed that, though his throat visibly spasmed, his hand again rubbing at his eyes.

"You can't go to the bank like that," he said, and then he grimaced, and fixed his gaze somewhere beyond her shoulder. "Sorry about the clothes. Do you—feel all right? Does anything hurt?"

Fasta waved it away, too quickly, and Henrik nodded and turned away again, his shoulders hunched. And it still felt so wrong, somehow, so awkward and stilted and miserable, and Fasta grasped for his hand, pulled him back toward her.

"You're still angry," she said, her voice cracking. "Aren't you?"

Henrik sighed, still not looking at her. "Not at you."

Not at you. Fasta tilted her head, considering that. "But you—the way you were with that, just now, it felt like—"

Henrik's eyes finally met hers, brief, and darted away again. "You said," he began, "you wanted me to play games with you. That's what you hired me to do, what we both agreed to. And that's *all*. Right?"

Oh. Fasta couldn't seem to find a response to that, especially with the visions flaring behind her eyes, the counter-arguments bubbling up. *You finished inside me this morning, you held me and touched me in bed last night, were those just games to you, too?*

But maybe Henrik had followed that, his eyes settling brief on hers again, his mouth gone tight and grim. "Look, we shouldn't have done it like that, this morning," he said, his voice hard. "With the cuddling, the bed, any of it. And you still shouldn't be calling me Harry in it, either, and"—he took a breath—"I *really* shouldn't have brought that arsehole ex of yours into this just now. It's not my place to care, because I'm not your boyfriend, I'm your *employee*. And we're supposed to be keeping it separate. Right?"

Right. The misery wrenched deeper into Fasta's chest, and

she made herself nod, though she couldn't meet his eyes. And then she spun around, and began walking away, back toward the road. She was supposed to fix this, but she couldn't even think, what the hell was she supposed to say, what was she supposed to do now?

She could feel Henrik jogging to catch up, falling into step beside her, but he didn't speak, either. Not even once they'd reached the road again, and she was earning strange looks from every single person who passed them by.

"Will you come and speak to Kjaran with me tonight?" she made herself say, finally, into the too-oppressive silence. "And see if there's any way we can possibly turn down the job?"

Henrik's steps faltered beside her, and it was an instant before he caught up again, his strides matching hers. "I thought," he said, voice stiff, "you didn't want to get out of the job."

Fasta shrugged, a movement which pulled the sleeve of her tunic painfully against her raw wrist, and she bit back a wince. "No, you were right," she said, toward the dirt road at her feet. "We're the best reconstruction team in the country, we're in high demand, and we have an established process—and Elgin is cheating on our process. And also"—she angled a sideways glance at Henrik's hard profile—"we're partners. And you don't feel good about the job, or Elgin's motives. So yes, we should try harder to extract ourselves from it."

There was silence from Henrik, just the sound of his footsteps, his slow exhale. "I—thank you," he said finally. "You really wouldn't mind?"

Fasta shrugged again, couldn't quite hide her wince this time. "No," she said, and she meant it—but Henrik abruptly pulled her to a stop beside him, and caught her face in his hand. Making her look at him, making sure she was telling the truth—and Fasta couldn't deny the thrill of heat that licked up her back, quivering her in his grip.

"No," she said, holding his eyes. "I don't mind. I'd much rather work a job you're happy with."

His breath came out slow, quiet, and his fingers almost felt gentle for an instant before they pulled back, away. And she could almost taste his relief as he kept walking, could almost sob at the feel of his hand again, this time brushing brief and warm against her back.

But he didn't speak, not until they'd reached the road forking off toward Skent, and Fasta nudged him toward it. Making him flinch, and then he frowned at her, his forehead creased. "Really?" he asked, with a jerky wave toward her messy state. "You still want to go to the bank like this?"

But Fasta squared her shoulders, and frowned straight back. "I don't care how I look," she replied. "And Andreas needs the money soon, doesn't he? And you've already started the"— she swallowed—"the *work*, right?"

Henrik's frown deepened, but he didn't argue, and accompanied Fasta through the town's streets toward the bank. It was approaching sundown, when most folks finished their work days, so there were plenty of people around, and plenty of them angled Fasta curious or disapproving looks, which she pointedly ignored.

The bank appeared to be closed when they arrived, but Fasta rapped loudly on the door, which was opened by a flustered-looking clerk. And upon hearing Fasta's name, the clerk instantly ushered her and Henrik inside, and things were arranged in short order. Including the payment of Henrik's sum, as well as a significant transfer to Andreas' account, halfway across the country. And if the clerk gave Fasta a few strange looks—perhaps wondering why she was throwing around this kind of money, when she usually dealt in far smaller amounts—he didn't comment.

"We're all set," the clerk finally said, with a reassuring smile. "Mr. Andreas Hallen will have his sum within the week."

Henrik twitched a nod, and then followed Fasta back out to

the road. And though neither of them immediately spoke, Fasta was far too aware of Henrik's eyes glancing toward her, the audible swallow in his throat.

"Thanks," he said finally, low. "This... really means a lot to me."

But when Fasta glanced sideways toward him, his eyes were straight ahead, his mouth tight, his shoulders hunched. And he'd looked so much like that today, tense and on edge and miserable, and Fasta bumped his arm with hers, let it stay there.

"It's my pleasure, Harry," she said, and she meant it. "Truly."

But if she thought that would help, it didn't, and he shook his head, bit his lip. "You're gonna regret it," he said, his voice so thin, so hoarse, that Fasta's hand twitched, and then went to his. Snaking around his warm callused fingers, squeezing tight.

"I won't regret it," she said into the darkness, taking courage from those strong fingers, clenching back on hers as they walked. "I don't think you understand, Harry, how much I—"

His hand flexed tight on hers, maybe telling her to stop, and when she glanced toward him again, his eyes were pained, glittering in the dark.

"Don't," he said, almost breathless. "Please."

So Fasta tried to nod, ignore it, keep walking, shove down that low lurking misery. It would be fine. It would. He would see.

18

It was past dark when they reached Coven Manor again, and Fasta wasted no time in heading for Kjaran's office, with Henrik in tow.

But when they arrived—Fasta pulled up short at the sight—there were two other people there, too. The tall, heavy-browed Argusson, the Director of Fire-Magic, and Mr. Luda, a quick little grey-haired man who was in charge of healing.

"Lady Fasta Valgeirr," Kjaran said, waving her inside, toward the chairs opposite her desk. "And Mr. Hallen. How precipitous. Please be seated."

This didn't bode well, and Fasta warily sat, ignoring the looks toward her mud-streaked ensemble. "What is this about?" she asked, while Henrik lowered his big body into the chair beside her. "Have we missed something?"

"We've had another theft," Kjaran replied, her voice flat. "In the storage room this time. A number of valuable metals and gems have been stolen, from a variety of owners."

Why anyone would keep valuables in a minimally guarded storage room had always been a mystery to Fasta, and she gave Kjaran her blandest look. "How unfortunate," she said. "Can the stolen items be traced?"

"We've been attempting it," cut in Argusson, frowning down his long nose toward them. "Without success. Yet."

Fasta kept her expression distant, and glanced back toward Kjaran's face. "I wish you the best of luck, then," she said. "Now, is that all? Kjaran, there is another matter we'd like to discuss."

Kjaran now bore a distinctly unpleasant frown, and Argusson loudly cleared his throat. "Mr. Hallen's name has been linked to the theft," he said flatly. "By multiple victims."

Henrik twitched beside Fasta, but she kept her back straight, her eyes steady. "And with what justification?" she asked. "Henrik has an excellent alibi, as he has been directly in my presence for the past thirty hours straight!"

The three directors exchanged glances, and Luda cleared his throat. "We're not certain of the exact time of the theft," he said. "It could have been any time within the past few days."

Gods curse it, curse them all, and Fasta gazed coldly at each of them, one by one. "Do you have proof?"

Each of them dropped their eyes, except Argusson. "The theft very specifically targeted items that only an earth-mage would be aware of," he replied. "There are only three earth-mages on site presently, and the logs indicate that no others have been admitted as guests in over two weeks."

Damn it. Those three earth-mages were Merton, Henrik, and Fasta herself, and she couldn't fight down the surge of sudden twitching fury. "If that's the case," she snapped, "then I presume Merton and I are under suspicion as well?"

The look in the directors' eyes said it all—of course their only suspect was Henrik, because Johan and his uncle had made it so. "How equitable of you," Fasta said, as coldly as she could. "Then please do inform us if you encounter any actual evidence. Now if you'd make some time for us in the morning, Kjaran, we have another matter to discuss with you."

Fasta had already stood to leave, with Henrik rising abruptly beside her, when Argusson stepped forward. "I'm afraid," he cut in, "that the Coven Manor Board has gone forward, and put Mr. Hallen on probation."

What? The fury jolted higher under Fasta's skin, her teeth clamping tight together. "Probation?" she repeated. "What kind of probation?"

"Effective now, Mr. Hallen is suspended from all new projects, and will be prohibited from earning any income through his work here," Kjaran supplied. "However, since he has already been contracted for this extensive project for the Earl of Valkin, we are willing to make a concession for him to continue until the work is complete. If his innocence is somehow proven before then, we will discuss appropriate backpay."

At this rate Fasta was going to crush something, and she choked down the shouting careening rage. "And if neither of us want to continue on the current job?" she demanded. "What then?"

"Then Mr. Hallen can pack his bags," said Argusson flatly, "and find work elsewhere. And you can hire short-term support to help you complete the project alone."

Fasta had to close her eyes, count to ten. Fight to think, to work through this, what would happen if Henrik actually *left*, what would she do, how could she possibly, *possibly* fix this—

"No," said Henrik beside her, his voice deep and sure of itself. "If you want to get rid of me, you can step up, and fire me properly. I'm not about to crawl away quietly and make this extra convenient for you."

He glared at Kjaran with clear contempt in his eyes, and in return Kjaran shifted in her chair, her hunted gaze briefly darting toward Fasta's face. No doubt remembering Fasta's own pointed threats from yesterday—alerting her father, drastically reducing the earth-magic department's income, and publicly tarnishing Coven Manor's reputation. And it was gratifying, if unnerving, to realize that those threats were probably the only reason they hadn't already gone and fired Henrik outright.

"So?" Henrik demanded toward them. "Am I fired, or not?"

The directors exchanged nervous glances, and finally Kjaran squared her shoulders, and met Henrik's eyes. "Not yet," she replied coldly. "But you *will* complete the job for the Earl of Valkin, who is very eager to have his renovations completed in a timely manner."

Right. Of course that was part of it, too. Elgin had clearly applied excessive pressure about the job, just like Henrik had said. And for all the directors knew, Henrik had been part of what Elgin had wanted, and they couldn't risk angering such an influential noble by firing Henrik before the job was done.

And clearly Henrik had followed all that, too, and he didn't hide his snort as he shoved to his feet, and strode for the door. Nobody made to stop him, and after another instant's glowering, Fasta leapt up too, and rushed to catch up with Henrik in the corridor.

"Harry," she said, breathless, while he kept walking, going for the staircase. "Are you sure about staying? I thought you didn't *want* to keep doing that job for Elgin."

"Yeah, well, now I don't have much of a choice, do I?" Henrik flatly replied. "You think I'm just going to let them decide I'm a petty thief, and force me out, and leave you alone with that shifty arsehole and his dangerous disaster of a house for three gods-damned months?"

Fasta's own anger was still bubbling close too, and she shook her head, took the stairs after him two at a time. "Elgin's not *dangerous*, Harry," she said, once they'd reached the next corridor. "But also, I wouldn't keep doing the job without you!"

"Oh yeah?" Henrik shot back, his big body whirling around to face her. "Then tell me, Fasta, what *will* you do, once they sack me? What happens when Kjaran calls you in there, and tells you that you have to keep at it, keep trotting off to Lord Earth-Mage's house every day, or else *you're* out next?"

Fasta faltered mid-step, as her thoughts dipped and spun. What *would* she do, if Henrik really was fired, permanently?

How far would she be willing to take her displeasure? Would she walk away from quite possibly the most prestigious, most enviable earth-magic position in the country? *Could* she?

Fasta couldn't seem to speak, and Henrik gazed back at her, his eyes glittering—when suddenly there was the sound of a door opening, right behind them. Making Fasta leap halfway across the corridor, and when she whirled around, she found— Runar. Standing in the doorway of his workroom, with his white work smock on, his arms crossed over his chest.

"As enlightening as this is," he drawled, "could you please do it elsewhere? Some of us are actually trying to—"

But then he wrinkled his nose, frowning down at Fasta. "What are you *wearing*? And also, were you recently *incarcerated*?"

He waved irritably at Fasta's wrists, and then stepped closer toward her, frowning down at her tunic. And particularly at where—she moved her hands to cover it, but it was too late— those dried splatters of white were still all too visible against the wrinkled grey silk.

"Ah," Runar said, looking partly amused, and partly nauseated. "Right. In here, then. Both of you. *Now*."

He jerked his head toward the door, and after a glance at Henrik's forbidding eyes, Fasta obeyed. Brushing her fingers against his arm as she went, making sure he was coming, too.

"Put your hands on the table," Runar told her, once he'd shut the door behind them. His workroom was clean and white and sterile-looking, and Fasta had been in it enough to know that the steel slab worktable was where Runar often conducted autopsies, and worse. But it was thankfully empty at the moment, and Fasta distractedly put her hands onto it, while Runar stepped closer, and began rolling up her tunic's long sleeves.

"What the hell," Henrik spluttered, "are you *doing*, Runar?"

Runar rolled his eyes, and pointedly nodded toward Fasta's raw, reddened skin. "Healing her, you great imbecile," he snapped, as he hovered his hand over her wrists. "You don't need to shear someone's skin off to have your way with them. For future reference."

There was an instant's stilted, pained silence, in which Fasta's cheeks flushed hot, her hands skittering on the table. While Henrik lurched closer, staring down at Fasta's wrists—and then his face rapidly paled, his eyes widening.

"Gods *damn* it," he breathed, and the glance he shot at Fasta's face was chagrined, or maybe even appalled. "Why—why didn't you tell me? Or loosen them? Or take them off?"

Fasta swallowed and shrugged, dropped her eyes from his face. "I didn't realize," she said, and that was mostly true, wasn't it? "Too distracted, I suppose."

She attempted a wan, conciliatory smile toward him, but he was still blinking down at her wrists. At where Runar's hands were hovering over the raw skin, which was slowly lightening, knitting itself back together. Until the redness had entirely faded, leaving only smooth, clear skin behind.

"Thank you," she said to Runar, but he only stepped back and looked her up and down again, his foot tapping irritably on the floor. And then he huffed an exasperated sigh, and knelt down, and did the same to her ankles.

"Anything else?" he asked, once he'd stood again. "Any other tenderness, or pain?"

He angled a meaningful glance down toward Fasta's groin, and she flushed again, shook her head. "No," she said, too quickly. "It's fine."

Runar pursed his lips, like he didn't at all believe her, and his eyes flicked back to Henrik. "Well, you need to take it easy on her for a few days," he said flatly. "Vaginal tearing and scarring is not fun, for either her, or you. Your dick is not a battering ram. Work her up to it, for fuck's sakes."

Fasta's cheeks flooded with more mortified heat, and her furtive sideways glance at Henrik found him looking just as unsettled as she felt. "Right," he said, his hand running over his pale face. "Yeah. I will. Although"—his throat convulsed—"you're sure it was from me? And not—"

And not someone else, he meant, maybe, or something else, one of those jars in Fasta's room? But Runar rolled his eyes, gave a dismissive flourish of his brown hand. "I'm a healer," he snapped. "I have eyes. Also, you two have been circling each other like vultures for months. *Years*, probably."

Fasta wanted to protest that—on Henrik's behalf, at least—but Runar was already striding away, toward the washbasin in the corner of the room. "Not to mention that little scene the other day in Fasta's workroom," he added, over his shoulder. "Which, by the way, Fasta, could have ended with you actually *enjoying* yourself in bed. Without any ensuing injuries, or unjustified verbal aggression in the corridor."

His voice had gone icy at the last, his eyes narrowing unpleasantly on Henrik before he started scrubbing at his hands. Clearly announcing that they were done here, so Fasta mumbled one more thank you, and turned and left, with Henrik close behind her.

They didn't talk the rest of the way to Fasta's room, didn't look at each other. Even when Fasta's door opened on its own accord for her, the latches clicking apart all at once, and she should have looked at Henrik, smiled, acknowledged him, something—she couldn't seem to. Could only go for the wardrobe, pull on the sleeping shift, and crawl, quiet, into bed.

Henrik had just stood there, silent and unmoving in the middle of the room, and a low, gnawing part of Fasta half-expected him to just leave—but then, he lurched a step closer, and another. Until his hand found Fasta in the dark, settling heavy and familiar on her shoulder.

"You still—want me?" he asked, quiet. "To stay?"

Yes, of course she did, and Fasta swallowed back that still-lurking lump in her throat, and reached for that hand. Pulled it down toward her, until he was down there too, lying fully clothed on the blanket, close against her back. Not on the floor, like he'd said, but here, cuddling in bed, his arm curling careful over her waist.

"I'm sorry," he finally said, his voice rough. "So sorry, Fass. I should've caught that, back in the woods. You know I never, *ever* want to hurt you."

It felt like the words pressed something, broke something, and Fasta couldn't help a shuddery sniff, a streak of wetness from her eye to the bed. "It's fine," she managed. "Really."

Henrik's arm pulled her closer, his breath coming out in something that might have been a groan. "Stop lying to me," he said, and he sounded tired, resigned. "It's not fine."

He was right, and Fasta still couldn't even explain why. It should have been fine. She'd asked for all this, agreed to all this. She was making it work. Right?

"I don't know how to do this," Henrik said, his voice hitching into something desperate, or even pleading. "I'm already fucking it up, and it's barely been a *day*."

Fasta's breath caught, another streak of wetness escaping her eye, and she could hear Henrik swallow, could feel the warmth of his face, maybe his lips, against her shoulder. "You—you're like a goddess," he whispered. "Beautiful and generous and so, so good to me. Doing everything you can to help me, in all this bull-shit. And here I am, *defiling* you. Taking your coin to drag you down into the mud and filth with me, and—and *hurting* you."

Fasta's breath would only come in gulps, and she tried to shake her head. "But I—I wanted it," she choked out. "Today, I mean, in the woods. I wanted you."

There was an instant's silence, maybe a shake of his head against hers. But now Fasta was finally letting herself think about it, about what they'd done there in the trees, and every-thing Henrik had said. *You like that, Lady Valgeirr? You want my fat commoner dick fucking you?*

It was enough to catch her breath, and fire heat deep to her groin, and she fought the urge to turn around, to beg him to do it again. "I wanted it, Harry," she said, her voice steady. "I wanted you taunting me like that. Punishing me. Using me. Making me obey you. Fucking me with your fat perfect cock."

It should have felt humiliating, maybe, but Henrik's breath caught too, and then exhaled shaky and slow. "Yeah," he said, quiet. "Damn good, wasn't it?"

Fasta fervently nodded, and gathered her courage. "The only thing that could have made it better," she began, "is just—if it could have been more—*us*, after. You and me."

Henrik was silent behind her, even his breath, and she made herself speak into it, against it. "I don't mean—all the time," she added, her voice cracking. "I know we agreed to keep it separate. But maybe just—sometimes? Like how it was this morning?"

She was thinking of how she'd taken him on the bed, of the warmth of his eyes and his voice as he'd praised and comforted her. And how it had felt when he'd released his pleasure deep inside her, making himself hers...

There was a harsh sound from Henrik behind her, maybe a laugh, or a groan. "Look, I want to make sure you feel good after, and your head's settled, all of that," he replied. "But I'm still not your boyfriend, yeah? And it's shit like this morning that makes me fuck it up. Makes me think I have any right to care who you fucked years ago, or who flirts with you too much. Or what jobs you want to work on, or even"—he cleared his throat, huffed a heavy sigh—"what you decide to do with your life, once I'm out of your way for good."

Oh. Fasta didn't know what to say to that, and she felt his chest expand, and then hollow. "It has to be separate," he whispered. "I'm sorry, Fass, but it *has* to be. I mean that. Otherwise we'll have to call it off, because I just—I can't. And that means"—she felt his weight shift, and suddenly his warmth was gone, away, *no*—"if you really still want this, we're not cuddling all night. We're not doing it like we did this morning.

You're paying me to fuck you, and be rough about it. And that's *all*."

He was standing beside the bed now, his form a looming shadow in the darkness. And the hurt felt almost real, like a powerful moving thing in Fasta's gut, and she squeezed her eyes shut. Just trying to keep her breath steady, keep it from betraying her, keep from breaking out into full-on sobs.

"Is there something else," he said above her, his voice hoarse. "Anything else I can do, to make it better for you. More—worth your coin."

Fasta fought back her grimace, and took a lurching breath. Yes, she was paying, and he was offering, and what could help fix this, please...

"Well," she began, "then could it be you—afterwards? Not while we're in it, but once it's done? As friends? I missed you so much today, Harry, we didn't talk, or laugh, or do any magic, or even eat a decent meal together. It was just you—walking away, not talking, turning your back. Like you didn't even *like* me anymore."

There was another shuddering breath above her, and then the feel of his hand again, resting heavy against her shoulder. "'Course I still like you, Fass," he whispered. "Always. Couldn't stop if I tried."

The tension in Fasta's gut slightly loosened, her body sagging into the bed, and Henrik's hand gently squeezed her shoulder. "I'll do better," he said, and it sounded like he meant it, his voice low and fervent. "You'll see."

Fasta twitched a nod, and he exhaled above her, hard enough that it rustled her hair. "And look," he said, "Fass. I *need* you to tell me if anything hurts. I know you want to be in it, and so do I, but I can't stand to actually hurt you. You need to *say*, and I'll stop whatever I'm doing, in a heartbeat. *Please*."

Fasta's body relaxed a little more, and she nodded again. "I know," she said. "I—I should have told you. I really didn't feel it at the time. I was just so distracted with the rest of it. With how damned good it was."

The truth of it quivered through her voice, and above her Henrik huffed a low laugh, curling warm into her skin. "Yeah, me too," he said, soft. "Well, then it's on me to do it better next time. Go over your sleeves, maybe. Use some kind of padding."

Next time. Fasta's mouth betrayed an unwilling gasp, and she attempted to cover it with a laugh of her own. "Good idea," she said, as lightly as she could. "Keep Runar from raging at you, and calling you an imbecile."

Henrik actually laughed again, the sound warm, thrilling. "That smug little bastard," he murmured. "He's just jealous. As he should be."

As he should be. Fasta blinked, and then twisted and pulled up a little, searching for Henrik's eyes in the dark. "You don't care?" she asked. "That he knows?"

There wasn't enough light to see his face, but she caught his shrug, and the tinge of dismissiveness curling through the magic between them. "Nah," he said finally. "Not if you don't."

Oh. It leapt in Fasta's chest, because it meant—Henrik was still breaking his rules, too. He still wanted this, wanted her. She could still do this. It would be fine…

And with that deeply reassuring thought, Fasta curled up against her pillow, and slipped slow into sleep.

19

Fasta slept late again the next morning, jolting awake only at the sound of the water closet door clicking shut. It was Henrik, getting up, and her bleary eyes blinked down toward the floor, to where there was the distinct trace of his magic, as well as the rumpled old blanket she'd had stashed in her wardrobe.

It meant Henrik had slept there—he could happily sleep on anything, especially if it was stone—and Fasta curled back into her own blanket, into the warm, reassuring certainty of it. Even if he hadn't slept in her bed, he'd still stayed. He was still here.

"Getting up, Fass?" came Henrik's voice, some time later, and Fasta blinked awake again to find him standing over her, looking amused. "Really, I thought you were the early one?"

Fasta made a face at him, but accordingly dragged herself out of bed, and off to the water closet. Giving Henrik a longing, lingering look on the way by, her thoughts swarming with unwilling visions of what they'd done the morning before—but he kept his eyes carefully neutral as she walked past, his mouth twitching into a vague, distant smile.

Fasta fought down the bubbling disappointment enough to

smile back when she emerged again, her face freshly scrubbed, her hair neatly braided. And if Henrik watched as she got dressed, first into her regular clothes and then into her baggier work clothes on top, he didn't let on.

"Wouldn't mind getting some clean clothes myself," he said, once she was ready. "My room next?"

His voice was light, the question seemingly innocuous, but the fact that he was asking—that he'd waited—meant something. That he didn't want to risk going alone, not now, not even when his room was only halfway down the corridor.

Fasta had almost forgotten about that disastrous meeting the night before with Kjaran, and Henrik's probation, and she frowned at even the thought of it. "Yes, of course," she said. "I assume you fixed it up, after Johan's search?"

Henrik jerked a tight nod, and followed Fasta out into the corridor, locking her door's latches behind her. And once they reached his own door, he unlocked yet another set of latches, and ushered Fasta inside with a thrilling little touch to her back.

His room still smelled slightly of dust inside, but beyond that, it looked almost precisely as it had before Johan's search. The books looked neater, perhaps, and some of the rocks had moved their positions, but the floors and walls appeared entirely untouched, as though no one else had ever been inside it at all.

It was just so typical, and Fasta fondly smiled as she reached and touched the nearest wall, feeling Henrik's signature all over it. He'd fixed it perfectly, seamlessly, even mimicking the slight variations in the plaster's original texture, something no one but an earth-mage would ever notice.

"This plaster work is excellent," she said, over her shoulder, but Henrik had his back to her, pulling on a clean tunic so quickly she only caught a flash of pale skin. "It must have taken you ages."

"Nah, wasn't too bad," Henrik replied, stilted, as he headed toward the water closet, clean trousers in hand. "Remembered exactly what it looked like before, so that helped."

Fasta bit back her grimace, and purposely turned her attention to something else, something safer. His haphazard rows of rocks, maybe, so she drifted around looking at them, trying to guess at Henrik's purpose with each one. All together, they did look rather a mess, with no unifying theme—but upon closer inspection, there was always some kind of loose order, with similar sources and types together, similar levels of refinement and roughness.

He kept similar kinds of projects together, too, and Fasta hesitated over his desk, which was scattered with a variety of delicate-looking metal and wire. She knew he only dabbled in finer work now and then, but the results were still brilliant, and she traced her fingers over an intricate silver chain that tasted of him all over.

"You like that?" Henrik asked, from behind her shoulder, and Fasta startled, then shot him a swift smile.

"It's lovely," she said. "I didn't realize you were still doing this kind of metalworking."

Henrik shrugged, but reached around her and picked up the chain. "Not much, it's too tedious," he replied. "And expensive. This should be gold, with a flashy cut jewel here"—he showed her where he'd made a clasp—"but no way in hell is that happening, right? Unless I want to risk even more hassle from our stingy overlords?"

He was referring to the Coven's extremely strict rules about earth-mages and precious gems and metals—even a single sale of valuables from a registered earth-mage required an arduous permitting process, and a conviction for unsanctioned mining was enough to land the offender in a labour camp. It was yet another way that Fasta's class had kept people like Henrik under their thumbs, making sure that even if he knew exactly where a brilliant gem deposit was hidden, he would never be allowed to touch it.

"Who cares about flashy jewels," Fasta said, her voice sharp. "You have plenty of other lovely stones here. Why not use one of those instead?"

She nodded at a nearby shelf, which boasted an impressive collection of shaped and polished stones of varying colours and sizes. None of them particularly valuable, of course, but they all showed off Henrik's incredible skill, each one beautiful in its own way.

"Yeah?" Henrik asked, his eyes flicking to Fasta's, and away again. "Pick one you like, then."

Really? The warmth licked up Fasta's spine, and she lurched closer to the shelf, first looking, and then touching. Picking up one stone, and then another, feeling the silken rounded softness of them, the calming quiet weight, the twinges of Henrik's magic lingering on each one.

"What's this one?" she asked, holding out a deep grey teardrop-shaped stone, streaked with flares of white. "Basalt?"

Henrik flashed her a tolerant smile, and shook his head. "Phyllite," he replied. "This is basalt."

He nudged at another similar-looking stone on the shelf, and Fasta smiled at him, warmer than she meant. "Right," she said. "How about the phyllite, then?"

The teardrop-shaped stone immediately rose from her fingers, hovering briefly in midair before dropping into Henrik's outstretched hand. And with a few twists, a delicious lilt of his magic in the air, the stone was attached to the silver chain, hanging elegantly like it had always belonged there.

Fasta couldn't stop smiling at him, shaking her head, and in return, Henrik beckoned her closer, almost near enough to touch. And then he lifted the chain over her head with both hands, and settled it against her skin.

It was heavy, warm with his touch and his magic, and the stone rested just between the upper swells of her breasts. Feeling solid, powerful, and quietly intimate, and Fasta blinked down at the sight of it, her fingers touching almost reverently at the silky grey stone.

"You could keep it," Henrik said, gruff. "If you wanted."

If she wanted. Fasta glanced up, sharp, to where Henrik was looking at the pendant too, his eyes and body gone wary and still. Like maybe he expected her to refuse, because it wasn't all gold and jewelled, wasn't at all the kind of piece a wealthy heiress would wear.

Something wrenched in Fasta's belly, in her throat—and before she'd even caught it, she hurled herself toward him. Circling her arms tight around his waist, burying her face deep into the heady scent of his broad chest.

"Of course I want it," she whispered, into his tunic. "Thank you."

Henrik's body briefly stiffened against hers, but then he relaxed again, his arms circling around her back. While his head rested warm against her hair, his breath exhaling heavy and slow.

It was probably inappropriate, probably not keeping it separate enough, but Fasta didn't make any move to pull away, and neither did he. Not until there was the sound of loud voices passing by in the corridor, and finally Henrik stepped back, his eyes careful on the door.

"Should get to breakfast," he said, and Fasta nodded, and followed him out. Still feeling the weight of that pendant, moving slightly as she walked, whispering of Henrik's magic, and maybe something like triumph. He'd given it to her. He'd made it for her. He wanted her to wear it.

It made it easy to smile at him when he brought over their overfilled plates, and then she asked where he'd come across a particularly rare rock he'd had in his room. Earning a warm grin in return as he replied, and soon they were caught in their usual easy discussion about rocks and deposits and extractions.

But as they spoke, Fasta couldn't quite ignore the looks they were getting, especially as more and more people filtered into the room. Looks that were uneasy, even angry, accompanied by whispers and elbows into friends' sides. No one had made any effort to come over, at least, and Fasta valiantly ignored them, kept her eyes on Henrik—until finally Johan and Konsta broke away from the rest, and stalked over toward them.

Fasta stifled a groan, but Henrik caught it anyway, and whirled around, eyes narrowing. His anger spooling up sudden and sharp in the air, strong enough that Fasta purposefully nudged her foot against his beneath the table.

"Heard you're at it again, Hallen?" Johan said coolly, folding his arms over his chest. "My pay wasn't enough for you? Had to go sneaking around in the storage room?"

Henrik's eyes briefly closed, and Fasta could feel him fighting down his temper, dragging in a deep breath. "Fuck off with this, Falk," he said, clipped. "It wasn't me."

But Johan loudly scoffed, and gave an exaggerated roll of his eyes. "Yeah, sure," he snapped. "It was a job only an earth-mage could have done. And we all know there's only one earth-mage here who's hurting for coin!"

His voice was loud enough to carry to the nearby tables, and the room was slowly but inevitably going silent. "And I heard," Johan continued, his dark eyes contemptuous, "that a certain close family member of yours has fallen out with his very generous sponsor, and had his patronage cut off. Thinking he's probably got some big bills due?"

Gods curse this interfering bastard—Fasta couldn't fathom how she'd ever found him attractive—and across from her Henrik's face flushed red, his eyes blazing. Looking like he might crush Johan into the floor at any moment, and Fasta's hand snaked across the table, and circled around his wrist.

"This is appalling behaviour from you, Johan," Fasta hissed toward him. "I thought you were better than this. Spreading malicious gossip about people you don't know, and making serious accusations without any proof whatsoever!"

"Oh, they'll be proven," Johan said grimly. "They essentially already are, since the directors have gone and put *him* on probation!"

Gods, how did he know that, and Fasta viciously glowered up at him, clenched her fingers tighter onto Henrik's straining wrist. "As a *precautionary measure*, based on external pressure only," she corrected him. "Until they find the actual culprit. And I will remind you, Johan, that Henrik had an airtight alibi, and he also allowed you to tear apart his entire room, and you found *nothing*!"

Johan opened his mouth to argue, but he was *not* going to keep maligning Henrik publicly like this, and Fasta pushed the bench back, and shoved up to her feet. "Also, if Henrik were in need of funds, for any reason," she said coldly, "I can assure you, I would *insist* that he take them from me!"

Johan's eyes narrowed, clearly reading the implications of that, and Fasta spun away, and stalked toward the door. And thankfully Henrik didn't hesitate, and only followed her silently out of the room.

"You don't need to keep jumping to my defense, Fass," Henrik said wearily, once they were outside, and again walking on the road toward Elgin's estate. "There's no point. They're gonna think whatever they want to think, no matter what you say."

Fasta frowned at him, kicked at a rock with her foot. "But they're supposed to be your *friends*, Harry," she countered. "At least, some of them. It's utterly *appalling* that they've all suddenly decided to treat you like a common criminal!"

But Henrik only shrugged, his eyes held straight ahead on the road. "It's not the same as it is with you," he replied. "I'm not one of *them*, and I never have been, and that means they'll turn their backs on me as soon as it's convenient for them. It's not like it's a surprise."

The way he said it, so cold and matter-of-fact, twisted in Fasta's gut. "But you've socialized with them for *years* now," she snapped back. "And you've probably slept with at least *half* of those girls."

It still hurt to think of that, that he'd always done that so easily, while Fasta had to go through all these plans and payments and rules—but Henrik shrugged again, his mouth tight. "Sure, they'll laugh with me, get drunk with me, get off with me," he said. "But they do all that shit with their servants, too."

Fasta couldn't help a wince, partly because yes, her own first kiss had been with one of her father's stable hands—and also because, maybe, Henrik was implying something about her. About... *them*.

"Look, you know I don't see you like that, Harry," Fasta said, searching his face. "Right?"

Henrik kept staring straight ahead, and he was quiet for long enough that Fasta's heartbeat began hammering, leaping into her throat—but then he nodded, bumped his elbow against hers. "Yeah," he replied. "I know."

He even twitched a smile toward her, but there was something almost sad in it. And Fasta should have pushed it further, but suddenly she couldn't bear to hear more of it. Couldn't bear to even think about people who took what they wanted from Henrik, made him into what they wanted, used him for their own ends...

Have it your way, you spoiled-rotten little brat. Again.

"So do you think this is slate beneath us right now?" she asked him, too loudly. "Or shale?"

Henrik's brief sideways glance was perhaps too knowing, but he gamely replied, and then shot back a question of his own. And soon they were caught in another one of their usual discussions, though it felt a little strained, and Fasta didn't miss Henrik's body slowly stiffening as Elgin's front gate finally came into view.

But when the gatekeeper waved them in, Henrik didn't protest, and followed Fasta up the cobbled drive. Straight toward where Elgin was already waiting for them, looking excessively handsome in his well-fitted riding clothes, with his dark hair slicked back from his face.

"My saviour has returned!" he said, with a grin and a wink at Fasta, and a mock little bow. "Thanks for coming back, you two. And I love the look, it's great."

He nodded meaningfully toward them, and Fasta blinked down at herself, and at Henrik. They were both wearing their long brown work tunics, which were functional as opposed to fashionable, with strategically placed pockets and straps for various tools. The one difference between them, however—Fasta felt her face heating—was that hers was accented, perhaps rather incongruously, by Henrik's new pendant, resting heavy and warm between her breasts.

Elgin clearly hadn't missed it, judging by the way his eyes lingered there, and it belatedly occurred to Fasta that maybe Henrik had given her the pendant for just this reason. And maybe she should have been offended or alarmed by that, but there was only warmth, bubbling in her chest, pooling in her groin. Because no matter what, it proved that he still wanted her. They could still make this work. Right?

"Um, thanks," Fasta told Elgin, with a distracted smile. "And were you able to contact the quarry? Will they be delivering the stone we need?"

"Yes indeed, it'll be here this afternoon," Elgin replied. "So where should we begin?"

Usually Fasta and Henrik would have agreed on that before they arrived, but they'd clearly both been avoiding the subject, and Fasta shot Henrik a swift, questioning look. This job would fall more on him than on her, with a lot of magical effort spent holding up buildings and hauling rock around, in which case, he was the one who needed to make the call.

"We need to start with the house," Henrik said firmly, fixing his eyes toward the northeast corner. "Specifically on that corner. It's not safe the way it is now, and puts your whole household at risk. You get any kind of earthquake or attack, or even a really heavy rainfall, and that whole side of the house could collapse, and kill everyone inside it."

Elgin's eyes had followed Henrik's, his brow furrowing. "Good to know," he said. "But that kind of work will take days, at minimum, right? Does it really need to be our first priority? Clearly it's been rained on for years, and we don't even get earthquakes around here, do we?"

They didn't, not that Fasta had ever been aware of, and beside her she could feel Henrik's mounting tension, his clear disbelief. "It's not *safe*," he repeated, in a low growl. "It needs to be dealt with."

"Yes, I heard," Elgin said, his voice light, though his eyes had gone just as flinty as Henrik's. "And I *am* dealing with it, that's why you're here. I'm saying, however, that in terms of priorities, there are a few other things I'd like to address first. That corner has been like that for a century, surely it can hold off for another week or two."

He wasn't entirely wrong, and Fasta shot Henrik a warning, quelling look. It wasn't their job to argue with clients, and at this point they could not afford to make enemies of Elgin, not with that infuriating probation preventing Henrik from taking on any other jobs beyond this one.

"We'll focus on whatever you need, Elgin, of course," Fasta cut in. "Is there somewhere else you'd like us to begin?"

The smile Elgin gave her was broad and grateful, and also a bit sheepish. "Well," he said, "I've actually got a little soiree coming up, with some family, and old friends. It'll be my first time hosting in the place, and I'd like it to be in good shape."

Fasta nodded, easily understanding this, because in Elgin's circles, hosting a party at one's new house was the expected thing to do, and postponing it for too long could be seen as stingy, or secretive. And the house would have to look good, and appear to be in good condition, if Elgin didn't want to become a subject of gossip or ridicule.

But Henrik beside her was sputtering, staring back and forth between them. "Wait, you don't honestly mean that?" he demanded. "You're putting off crucial structural repairs for cosmetic ones? So you can impress people at a *party*?"

Fasta bit back a groan, gave a warning squeeze to Henrik's arm, while trying to smile at Elgin. "Henrik's just concerned for your wellbeing," she said. "But of course you need to be ready for the party, so we'll get started right away. Where should we begin, the ballroom?"

"Please," Elgin replied, looking visibly relieved as he turned and strode off toward it. Leaving Fasta and Henrik to follow, which Fasta did, casting a pleading look toward Henrik over her shoulder.

He finally followed, not looking at either her or Elgin, and he didn't speak while Elgin escorted them around the ballroom, and pointed out the areas he'd like to focus on first. All of which were indeed cosmetic, but it was a large enough room that these alone would take days, possibly even weeks.

"I should probably mention, Fasta," Elgin began, as Henrik knelt and started sweeping out broken stone from behind the worst-looking wall. "Your father's coming to my party. And most of our old set from the Academy."

Fasta couldn't hide a faint flinch, but she managed a nod, and knelt down to help Henrik. "Sounds like a big crowd," she replied, as steadily as she could. "What's your guest list, a few hundred?"

She could feel Elgin watching her, shifting on his feet. "You should come, Fasta," he said. "People ask me about you all the time, you know."

Fasta's eyes darted up, narrowing on his face, and Elgin raised his hands, flashed her a rueful smile. "And no, I don't tell them anything," he added. "But it would be great to have you there. It would be a real coup, on my part."

Fasta frowned down at the wall, at where Henrik was pulling out larger chunks of stone, letting them drop to the floor with perhaps more force than necessary. "Well, thank you for the invite," she said, "but I'm really too busy with work right now."

"Yes, that's what they tell me you always say," Elgin replied. "But hey, if you're working for me, and I want you there, what's stopping you?"

Fasta reflexively glanced toward Henrik, who was glowering at the wall, yanking out another stone with a sharp jerk of his hand. "Look, Elgin," Fasta said, squaring her shoulders, "I'm just not interested anymore. I'm finished with it."

"With what?" Elgin asked, and when Fasta frowned up again he looked genuinely curious, his head tilted. "Your friends? Your *family*?"

Henrik's movements briefly hesitated at that, a rock hovering in mid-air, and Fasta took over his hold on the rock, set it down to the side. "No," she said tightly. "My father and I write every month, I visit him whenever I'm close enough to stop in, *and* he can come see me whenever he wishes. As can any of our old friends."

Elgin finally fell silent, maybe digesting what that meant. That Fasta's father did not visit, never had, and neither had any of her old friends. And Fasta didn't even hold it against them, because it was her own life choices that had created that gulf, that had taken her to places that they couldn't follow, couldn't comprehend.

"Well, if you change your mind," Elgin said, "let me know, will you? I'd honestly love to have you there."

Fasta gave him a polite but noncommittal smile, and finally Elgin wandered away, leaving her and Henrik alone in the cavernous room. And while Fasta kept working, pulling out rocks, Henrik had hesitated, and when she glanced up he was looking at her, his eyes unreadable.

"If you want to go, you should go," he said, quiet. "Don't let me stop you."

Fasta shrugged, and kept working. "It's not you stopping

me," she replied. "And also, I don't want to go. I don't enjoy attending parties with you either, do I?"

Henrik's mouth twitched into a half-smile, but his eyes were still carefully distant. "I thought that was because you didn't like watching my *transparent and frankly ludicrous attempts to entice unsuspecting women into my bed*."

It sounded vaguely familiar, and Fasta winced. "Did I say that?"

Henrik's smile on her went warm, maybe even affectionate. "A year or so ago, last time you came out with me. You were very, *very* drunk."

Oh. "Well," Fasta began, then hesitated, because it was telling that Henrik had remembered every word of that, wasn't it? "You've also said some very unfortunate things while drunk, Harry Hallen."

She attempted a glare toward him, but Henrik actually grinned back, broad and stunning. As if he remembered that, too, and wasn't particularly bothered by it. And blinking toward him, it occurred to Fasta that she hadn't seen him look this relaxed in days, or maybe weeks. And maybe it had something to do with how she'd refused Elgin, just now. How she'd told the truth, and made it clear that Henrik was more important. Proving this to him.

"Wanna have a few drinks tonight, then?" Henrik asked, as his big hand gripped on her knee. "Just me and you? Stop by a pub on the way home?"

Fasta's heartbeat skipped, and her face flushed sudden and hot. "Maybe," she replied, breathless. "As long as I don't have to watch you make any of those, uh, attempts. On other people, I mean."

Her face flushed even hotter, because maybe that was betraying herself too much, reminding them both that she still had a problem with that—but Henrik's eyes kept glimmering warm on hers, his hand gently squeezing at her knee.

"Nah," he said, lightly. "I already know who's gonna be in my bed tonight. Right, buttercup?"

Fasta's head ducked, but she couldn't help smiling back, the whole world suddenly warm and bright and alive. Because Henrik was gorgeous, and brilliant, and here, and yes, yes, she would still make him hers. She *would*.

"Yes, my lord," she whispered. "I can't wait."

20

The rest of the morning passed swift and easy, marked by a sudden, welcome return to Fasta and Henrik's usual way of working. Trading comments and praise back and forth, helping each other with the tricky bits, catching each other's eye with pleasing frequency. And it helped that the job itself wasn't as far beneath their skills as Fasta might have first thought, thanks to the excellent earth-mage artisans who'd built the house centuries before.

"What do you say to lunch?" Fasta asked Henrik around noon, as she stood and stretched her arms over her head. "Maybe off the grounds somewhere?"

Henrik stood up too, and he smiled back at her, his eyes warm, his hand briefly brushing against her waist. "Yeah, sure," he said. "I'd love to."

They ate out in a nearby field, sitting across from each other on giant rocks Henrik had dredged up. Talking animatedly together about the job, which had somehow seemed to revert back into a normal job again, despite a few pointed comments from Henrik about nobles and their fucked-up priorities.

The rest of the afternoon went quickly too, and by the end

of it they'd finished restoring one of the ballroom's walls in its entirety. It was the shortest wall, so this one room would still take at least another week. But it certainly looked much better, and to Elgin's credit, he freely acknowledged that when he came in again, late in the afternoon.

"Wow," he said, walking down the wall, trailing a hand against the stone. "I can't even tell where you changed it. Is this all new?"

He waved at a part of the wall that had previously been crumbling away, and Fasta nodded. "That, and all this here," she replied, nodding toward it. "We've already taken out the debris, so you'll have a few cartloads to get rid of."

Elgin still looked suitably impressed, and he slowly walked down the length of it, and back again. "It looks really, really great," he said. "No wonder I had to go to such lengths to get you here."

He shot Fasta a saucy smile, and though she smiled back, she could feel Henrik stiffening beside her. And they'd been doing so *well* until now, damn it, and Fasta quickly made the appropriate arrangements for the next morning, and ushered Henrik out.

"So the little fucker actually admits it," Henrik snapped, once they were walking out toward the gate. "How much time and money do you think he put into getting us there? Getting *you* there?"

Fasta sighed, and a daring, perhaps inappropriate part of her leaned over, and slid an arm around Henrik's waist. Where Elgin or any of his servants might still see them, and Henrik wasn't her boyfriend, but she shoved those thoughts back, and gave him her most beseeching look under her eyelashes. "*Harry*," she said, half-exasperated, half-amused. "Forget him. The job itself isn't terrible, right? Maybe we'll even have fun with it."

Henrik's glance down at her was unreadable, but he didn't resist, didn't tense against her touch. "I can't forget him, or have fun, I have to work for that wanker for *months*," he said, though his voice was more tired than angry. "It would really help if you told me you think he's a skinny spoiled little arsewipe, and you would never let him touch you again if he was the last person in the realm. And also, you think his artwork is shit."

That was new, and it hadn't occurred to Fasta that Elgin being an earth-mage, and an artist, would make him more threatening to Henrik, somehow. But it did make sense, in a way, and Fasta dragged Henrik bodily to a stop, put both hands to his muscled upper arms, gave him a little shake.

"Look, Elgin's a skinny spoiled arsewipe," she said firmly. "And I'd never let him touch me again if he was the last person in the realm. And also, his artwork is well done, but also pretentious and overbearing, and I would *never* want it in my house."

Left unsaid was the fact that Fasta's house was currently full of Henrik's work—had been half-built by Henrik, for gods' sakes—but the way Henrik was looking at her suggested he hadn't missed that, so Fasta kept going, digging herself deeper. "Meanwhile, your artwork is brilliant, your work in general is *spectacular*, so much that I've been attached to your hip for five entire years. *Also*, I want you so much I'm paying you to fuck me, and if you don't do it again tonight, I honestly think I will *die*, Harry."

Henrik's shoulders sagged, and he let out a choked chuckle, his eyes crinkling at the corners. "Oh, you'll get it, buttercup," he replied, husky. "The question is, how much else you're gonna have to do to earn it."

Fasta's face burned, even as she grinned back toward him, and clasped his hand in hers. And then they walked together like that, talking and laughing, while warmth bubbled higher and higher in Fasta's belly. They were doing this. She was proving this.

They stopped in one of Skent's dim, bustling pubs for their drinks and supper, and ate together at the bar. Where Henrik was friendly to the barmaids, and various women he seemed to know, but not nearly as flirtatious as Fasta had seen him previously. Even as he put back one drink, and then another, his eyes, his attention, stayed fully focused on her.

"I was thinking, Fass," he said, leaning close to speak over the noise of the pub, "we should put in a loft at the cottage. A place for both of us."

Now that was an idea, and Fasta considered it, even as her hand crept over to squeeze at his thigh in silent approval. "We'd have to raise the roof," she told him. "Change the bracing. Maybe a hammerbeam?"

"Yeah, that's what I was thinking too," Henrik replied, his eyes bright and eager. "Like this"—he demonstrated with his hands—"or this. Do you have some paper?"

Fasta did, of course, and she pulled it out of her trouser pocket, along with a pencil. And soon they were deep in discussion, debating this option versus that option, Fasta drawing while Henrik spoke, and his warm hand settled wide and possessive on her back.

A few drinks later, they'd finally agreed on a plan, and the pub's din had grown ever louder, clanging through Fasta's skull. So much that she couldn't quite hear what Henrik said when he leaned over to speak to the nearest barmaid, and then dropped a few coins into her hand.

"Hey," Fasta said, frowning at him, because she was sure they'd already paid for their drinks, and also, those coins had definitely amounted to more than that. "Why are you *paying* her?"

She was being jealous, her distant thoughts shouted, and suspicious, and Henrik wasn't her boyfriend—but he didn't seem to notice any of it. Instead, he only stood to his feet, one of his hands grabbing for Fasta's, the other for an empty wine bottle on the bar.

"C'mon," he said, and Fasta willingly let him pull her away. Not toward the door, but in the opposite direction, toward a set of back stairs. Up to a second floor, and down a dim hallway, and then into a small wood-panelled room, with a large, curtained bed in the middle of it.

The comprehension hit Fasta all at once, and she whirled around to glare at Henrik, who had already locked the door, and was now prowling around, inspecting the bedsheets and the hangings, and lighting the lamp on a small side table. "Wait," she said. "You *paid* for this room."

"I did," said Henrik, now putting his hands to the iron bed frame, clearly feeling for anything unsavoury hiding inside. "And it's clean, they usually do a decent job."

Usually. "You've done this *before*?" Fasta demanded, high-pitched. "Rented rooms in a pub to fuck random women in?"

Gods, she was supposed to be keeping her mouth shut about this, but Henrik's eyes looked smug, almost triumphant as he strode back toward her. "Yep," he said coolly. "And if you don't want me to start doing it again, you better start proving to me what a good little servant you are."

The dizzying hunger swarmed Fasta all over, and she betrayed a harsh shudder, a breathless gasp. "What do you— what do you want, then?" she breathed. "My lord?"

It had slipped out far too easily, but that was definitely a flare of approval in Henrik's eyes. "Want you naked, and your hair down," he murmured. "Obviously."

Obviously. Fasta shuddered again, but then she lurched into motion. Tugging out her braid, and then yanking at her tunic, hurling it off over her head. Feeling her new pendant shift and settle between her now-bared breasts, and she put a hand to the stone, shot Henrik a questioning look—but he shook his head, slow and certain.

"No, keep it," he said, husky. "New rule. You always keep that on, unless I tell you."

Another helpless gasp escaped Fasta's throat, but she rapidly nodded, and then kicked off her boots, and her trousers. Leaving her standing there in the middle of the room, breathing hard, dressed in only Henrik's pendant.

And for a long, hanging moment, Henrik just stood there, and looked at her. His eyes lingering on her face, the pendant, her breasts, her groin, and Fasta could almost feel the heat following his gaze. Pooling tighter, harder, and then wrenching even deeper when he stepped closer, and then walked in a slow, torturous circle around her.

"On the bed," he said from behind her, his voice low. "On your hands and knees. Knees wide."

Oh, gods. Fasta's legs buckled a little, but she went, fighting to keep her steps smooth, her head high. Feeling Henrik's eyes prickling on her skin as she climbed up onto the bed, and then knelt like he'd said, with her knees spread, her bare arse facing out toward him.

It was a deeply compromising position, and highly humiliating, and it was perhaps only the lingering alcohol that kept Fasta from shaking, or hiding, or backing down. Because there was still just silence from Henrik behind her, no words or movement, and she dragged in a trembly breath, let it out.

"Is this what you wanted?" she asked, into the silence. "My lord?"

There was a huff of breath behind her, and then the unmistakable sound of his footsteps, coming closer. "No," he said, rough, and the single word was almost shocking, sending a hard, forceful chill up Fasta's back. "When I tell you to do this, you show me everything. Every time."

Fasta's breath was already heaving, the heat in her face almost unbearable, but she repositioned herself, arched her back, spread her legs wider. Definitely showing him now, but— oh *fuck*—she felt a stinging little slap to her arse, sending another wrenching shudder up her back.

"Not good enough, buttercup," Henrik said, voice cool. "I want *everything* wide open to me. Ready to be fucked. You understand?"

He punctuated it with another slap, not hard, but enough to set Fasta's whole body trembling. While she tried, almost desperate now, to tilt herself out more toward him, to open wide to the cool air. To let Henrik see all of her, bared and ready for him, wet and inflamed and quivering.

"Better," Henrik breathed, and Fasta twitched at the sudden, jolting feeling of a single warm, thick finger, touching light against her. Tracing the exposed wet crease of her, from the bottom all the way up, lingering on the most secret shameful part of her, and then back down again, slow.

"Tell me," Henrik's voice said, "what you want right now."

What you want. That single finger was tracing upwards again, sliding slowly over her swollen trembling wetness, and Fasta gasped for breath, tried to think. He wanted her honesty, right? Her truth. She had to prove this...

"I want your mouth on me," her traitorous, appalling tongue said, making her entire body go rigid with it—but Henrik actually chuckled behind her, low and approving, as the pressure behind that slowly stroking finger gently deepened.

"Nice try, buttercup," he said, and there was another thrilling little slap to her arse, even as the finger kept stroking. "Maybe someday. If you're very good."

Fasta let out an unintentional moan, rubbed herself back against that tantalizing finger. "What's involved in being very good?" she breathed. "My lord?"

There was another slap, more pressure from that finger as it slid up again, lingered on that place where no other person had so much as ever touched. "You take my dick here," he murmured, "and I'll think about it."

Oh hell, because yes, Fasta had occasionally used her smaller implements for such things, had heard friends whisper and giggle about actually doing it with their partners in bed. But she had never once attempted it in person, like this, and Henrik couldn't want that, could he? *I will use you,* he'd told her, what felt like years ago. *I will fuck you every way I can, I will make you kneel and crawl and beg for me in the dirt, I will teach you some fucking lessons...*

"But," she gulped, as that tantalizing finger slid lower again, delved just the slightest bit against her slick wetness. "Your dick is *huge*, Harry."

"My lord," he corrected, with another light slap to her arse, but he huffed a low laugh, too. "And that's the whole point, buttercup."

Gods, that was hot, and impossible, and Fasta groaned aloud as that thick finger slipped further into her wet heat, and out again. "Do other women?" she gasped, even as she hated herself a little for asking. "Do that, I mean? With you?"

The finger went in again, deeper this time, and the accompanying slap was harder, louder, for the first time hinting at actual pain. "Yeah, sometimes," he replied. "A few."

And now Fasta was picturing that, gods curse him, and a sound almost like a growl escaped her mouth. Making Henrik laugh again, and now there was a second thick finger along with the first, delving slow and purposeful inside her.

"You don't like that, do you, Lady Valgeirr?" he asked, as the fingers slid in all the way, out again. "Me fucking other women. Or being *their* lord."

Fasta gasped again, pushing back a little, fighting to breathe against the full tight invasion of those fingers. "No," she managed. "I hate it."

It was humiliating, but it was truth, and those fingers pushed in deeper, harder. "Why?"

Why. It was so hard to think, but Fasta's mouth opened on its own, the words just spilling out. "Because I want you all to myself," she gasped. "I want you to be only *mine*. And even *thinking* of you doing this with anyone else makes me feel *sick* inside."

There was another low laugh from behind her, those

fingers twisting in deep. "Good," Henrik breathed. "So what are you gonna do to stop me?"

Oh gods, the spiking jealousy was choking her, and Fasta pushed back more, took those fingers harder, stretched and shameless and hungry, the slick sounds now audible in the air. "Whatever you want, my lord," she choked out. "Take me any and every way you want. Make me your favourite servant."

There was a soft groan behind her, oh, and with audible wetness those fingers finally slipped out. Seeking up higher, to that secret untouched pucker of skin, even as—Fasta's entire body flinched—something cold and hard pressed below, against where his fingers had been. And when she whirled around to look, it was the glass wine bottle Henrik had brought up from the bar. With its tapered long neck, widening steadily to a bulbous round base, bigger around than Henrik's entire hand. And she could even feel that he'd sealed off the head, turning it into another... *implement.*

Henrik's face was flushed, his hair tousled, but his eyes on hers were glittering, insolent. "What," he said. "Backing down already?"

He accompanied the words with another firm slap, and oh, the sight of that, of his big familiar hand actually *doing* that, made Fasta cry out, far too loud. "No," she gasped, "gods no, please don't stop."

Henrik's eyebrows rose, even as unmistakable satisfaction flashed across his eyes. "You sure?" he asked, and already there was the shocking feel of that glass bottle, slowly pushing, slowly breaching. Much larger and harder than his fingers had been, and Fasta gasped aloud, arched her back, let herself feel it, cold and demanding and glorious.

"I'm sure," she managed. "Please, Harry, fuck me with it."

Henrik's lashes fluttered, and his hand gave a telltale circling motion that meant, *turn around, away.* So Fasta did, blinking down at the bed, breathing hard, while the whole world condensed to the feel of that hard cold glass, pressing steady and slow inside. Already becoming thicker, wider, and she gritted her teeth, tried to breathe, to welcome it, through the pulsing flares of curling sweeping pleasure.

And then it stopped, just staying there, and Fasta hauled in thick gulping breaths, let her body adjust to it, stretching open around it. And it was almost working, almost, when there was the sudden, shocking feeling of those fingers again, brushing soft against that secret, appallingly exposed, stretched-out pucker of skin.

"Beg me," his voice murmured behind her. "If it's what you really want."

Oh fuck, and Fasta could hear the blood pounding, impossibly strong in her ears. Even as her body reflexively tightened, pushed away at the hard glass of the bottle, but Henrik's hand, or maybe his magic, held it there, solid and deep inside her.

"Beg me," he said, commanding now, even as he gave another slap to her arse. "Or are you lying to me?"

"No," Fasta gasped, immediate, breathless. "My lord. Please, touch inside me. Fuck me. Do whatever the hell you want with me."

She was rewarded with another husky laugh, a slap that was more of a grab, fingers lingering tight. "Good girl," he said, streaking more warmth up her back, and then—*oh*—there was his finger again. Still slick and slippery with her own wetness, and sliding up warm against that hard resisting knot of skin.

"You gotta relax," he said, and his voice was almost soft, gentle. "Let me in."

It felt almost impossible, what with the hard bottle still wedged so deep below, but Fasta took a deep, shaky breath. Let it out, all the way, while those fingers touched, stroked, caressed.

"Good girl," he breathed. "Again."

So she did it again, even as he eased away a little with the bottle, making it somewhat, partially, easier to breathe. And then there was pressure, more pressure, his voice murmuring praises again, and Fasta couldn't even hear it as that slick finger finally slid a little inside.

She cried out loud and long with it, because it was the strangest feeling, thrilling and wrong and deeply powerful. And impossibly, frantically full, stretched, with so much inside of her, how could her body possibly take this much, how could it feel so fucking *good*—

And already Henrik wanted her to take more, because the finger was slowly pushing deeper, even as the bottle did the same. And there were no thoughts anymore, no logic, no comprehension, just Henrik doing this to her, Henrik filling her impossibly full, impaling her, dominating her body, her mind.

"Tell me," he said from behind her, even as his finger slid out, and then back in a little, so foreign, so strange. "How it feels."

"Impossible," Fasta gasped, and that was truth, too. "So much. Oh gods, so much. So good."

Henrik gave another low chuckle, a twitch of his finger deep inside. "Beg me for more, then."

Beg him. And Fasta couldn't even comprehend what *more* might mean, but she instantly nodded, jerky and fervent. "Give me more, my lord," she breathed. "Give me as much as I can take. *Please.*"

There was another swat to her arse, and then—Fasta blinked—the pendant around her neck lifted off, away. Soaring through the air back toward Henrik—she could hear the chain clink as he caught it—and then his finger slipped out of her, leaving that part of her suddenly empty, hollow. Until—Fasta gasped, whipped her head around again—there was something blunt and cool pressing there instead. The pendant's smooth, teardrop-shaped stone, with the chain still attached, fucking *hell.*

"What?" Henrik said, his eyes challenging, as the stone pressed harder, as both of his hands gripped to her arse, pulled her a little wider apart. "There a problem, Lady Valgeirr?"

Fasta's entire body was shaking again, and maybe even more so when Henrik's eyes dropped, watching what he was doing. Using no hands on either the bottle or the stone, just his eyes, and the stone was pushing harder, twisting, looking for a way inside...

"Open up," Henrik ordered, his eyes back on hers, his hand giving a sharp slap to her arse. And fuck, but somehow Fasta actually did, and she could feel the stone finally pushing through, slipping all the way inside, leaving only the chain trailing out behind it.

And gods, this was fucked up, and *so* fucking hot, because Henrik's eyes were still looking, watching with greedy, glittering appreciation. And Fasta's shaking arms almost buckled at the feel of that rock slowly moving inside, going up further, dragging the chain deeper inside after it, of course Henrik could do that, but what in the ever loving *fuck*—

And then it stopped, finally, the chain vanished almost all the way up inside, and curse him, there had never been anything like this, Fasta's thoughts twisting and bending and shouting. And finally her arms stopped supporting her entirely, her breasts and face dropping hard against the bed, but her arse was still up behind her, her eyes craning to look back, catching on the sight of just the end of that chain, a single silver loop that Henrik was carefully slipping his finger into—

And then he pulled, slow and long and torturous, even as the bottle below—the bottle Fasta had almost forgotten about—pushed in deeper, harder, wider. Enough that she shouted, damn near screaming with it, oh gods oh *gods*—

"Such a spoiled-rotten little brat," Henrik's voice said, his face now a deep red, his glinting, fevered eyes flicking up brief to her face. "Fussing like this at your lord, while he's here fucking your tight little arse with actual *jewels*."

Fasta shouted again, her entire body wavering on the bed,

her fluttering eyes fixed to the sight of that chain, still hooked in his finger. And he just kept pulling, deliberate and agonizing, every loop of the sliding metal chain a perfect, shocking jolt to the senses. Until it finally stopped, finally meeting resistance, because Fasta could feel the stone there, lurking close inside, very nearly popping out again. Somehow firing the dizzying sensation even stronger, wringing another scream from her mouth—and Henrik's hand slapped again, hard, to her arse.

"Quiet, Lady Valgeirr," he said, his voice hoarse. "Else I'll need to come over there and shut you up with my dick."

Gods, *gods*, Fasta gasped, choked, swallowed, dragged in air. Couldn't think anymore, nothing left beyond this, Henrik was doing this to her, she was proving this, yes, yes, more, *please*—

"Then do it," she gasped back at him. "Please, my lord, come choke me with your dick."

There was a strange noise behind her, another slap to her arse—and then, oh hell, the sound of footsteps. Unsteady, but closer, here, and she felt strong hands guiding her up, tilting up her head. And there were fingers sliding into her mouth, pulling it open, and before Fasta could think or breathe or follow, her mouth was full of him, blunt hot hardness everywhere, in her eyes her nose her throat, shoving back rough and deep, so strong and so unexpected she gagged on it, her eyes watering, her breath thick and dragging.

But it was perfect, it was everything, exactly what she'd needed, his cock in her mouth, his strong hands in her hair, the bottle and the jewel both buried deep behind. Henrik using all of her at once, making her his, doing what he did with those other women, yes, yes—

"Look at me," he said, breathless, and Fasta fought to blink her watering eyes open, to find the blurry shape of him, even as that glorious cock pulled out, and slammed deep again. And kept doing it, even as her body kept being invaded behind her, just sheer sensation colours smells, the feel of him, the taste of him, so good so strong so deep and dizzy and overpowering, everything, hers...

The ecstasy flashed and burned, slamming into Fasta like a sledgehammer. Wrenching and wringing through her trembling invaded body, seizing against the bottle and the pendant, screaming through her choked occupied mouth. Stronger than anything she had ever, ever known, ever imagined, crushing her beneath its weight—

And crushing Henrik too, his body stiffening, his thrusts stopping, bright breathless relief—and then there was that taste of him, harsh and bitter, pulsing out into her mouth. While he shouted too, bending almost double over her, emptying himself into her, hers, hers, *hers*...

It felt like a chant, droning and distant, tilting Fasta's body strangely far away—but the choke in her throat dragged her back, for a jolting dangling instant. Because she had to breathe, had to swallow, couldn't move, it was only those hands in her hair holding her up now, rough and powerful and she needed to prove it, needed to show him, be a good servant a good friend a spoiled-rotten little brat...

Without warning the hands holding her up loosened, and Fasta's entire body sagged forward. Forgetting how to breathe, or move, or *be*, and her eyes had almost fluttered closed when her throat finally coughed on the thickness blocking it, closing it off.

She spat it out onto the floor, her head hanging over the side of the bed, and she couldn't even find the strength to wipe her mouth, to move back onto the bed. Just stayed there while the room spun, tilted sideways...

"Fasta," came a voice, distantly, urgently. "Fass. Talk to me."

Fasta couldn't find any words, or the will to move, and there were hands again, far gentler this time, moving her, pulling her back onto the bed. Turning her over, and then all the hard things were pulling out of her, disappearing, leaving her naked, alone, empty.

"Fasta!" said his voice, louder now, together with a gentle shake to her shoulders. "Look at me!"

That voice was everything, all-powerful, had to be obeyed, and Fasta's eyes blinked open. Finding brightness, first, and then Henrik's familiar face, his eyes wide and blown-out and looking more afraid than Fasta had ever seen him.

"Say something," he ordered, and Fasta pulled in breath. Couldn't quite open her mouth, though, or make it speak, and suddenly Henrik was gone, and now back again, stuttering images across her eyes.

"Here," he said, and that was the feel of his waterskin, nudging against her mouth. "Drink."

Drink. Fasta was suddenly parched, craving water, and she gulped the cool liquid back, until there was none left. Until there was only Henrik's face, Henrik's eyes, hovering over her. "Talk to me," he said, his voice hitching. "What hurts."

Nothing hurt, precisely, though a distant part of Fasta registered that she was exhausted, and tender, especially down below. And that the room had finally seemed to stop tilting, thankfully, and she swallowed hard, looked at those eyes. "I'm fine," she said, though her voice sounded thick, slurred. "I think."

Henrik's eyes closed, briefly, his shoulders shuddering, and then he abruptly stood, and turned, and walked away. Stopping halfway across the room, just standing there with his hands on his face, his shoulders rising, falling, rising again. Leaving Fasta feeling alone, suddenly, and bereft, and strangely, inexplicably afraid.

"Harry," she croaked, toward his back. "Wait. Did I fuck that up, I'm sorry, I—"

The words choked off, with only sobs lurking close behind them, and Henrik spun around again, his face drawn, white. And then he took two big lurching steps back toward her, until he was here again, leaning over her, looking at her with those strange, darkened eyes.

"Don't you dare apologize to me, love," he said, and his hands were suddenly on her face, their touch warm, careful, almost reverent. "You didn't fuck anything up. You were beautiful, you were perfect. I'm the one who fucked it up."

Fasta wasn't following, and his eyes briefly squeezed shut, his head jerking a hard shake. "Should've been more careful," he said, his voice thin. "Didn't realize I was losing you, at the end. You gotta *say*, love, remember?"

His voice was pleading, shimmering as intent as his eyes, and Fasta nodded, as fervently as she could. Of course she would, anything to make this work, and he nodded too, his hands still tight on her face, his eyes too bright, too close.

And suddenly she needed more of him, needed to touch him to hold him to know he was real, and her hands were clinging to him, tugging him down toward the bed. "Stay with me," she whispered, and it came out urgent, desperate. "Don't go. Please."

Why she thought he wanted to go, she wasn't certain—maybe that strange brightness in his eyes, the strained tautness all over his big body. But then he twitched a nod, and sank down to sit on the bed beside her. "I'm not going anywhere," he said, hoarse, but his mouth was grimacing, his breaths heaving too hard. "I'll be close by. Bring you anything you need."

His arm even settled heavy over her shoulders, his big hand rapidly rubbing at her bare upper arm. But Fasta wanted more, needed more, all of him, hers, and she clutched harder at him, yanked him closer. "But," she gulped, "I want you to hold me, Harry, sleep all night with me again, *please*."

Henrik's body stiffened against her, his gaze fixed on the opposite wall, even as his big hand kept rubbing her arm. "I'll stay close by," he said again. "Keep a close eye on you. But we're not gonna cuddle all night like that. Remember?"

Fasta's head shook back and forth, while Henrik's shoulders heaved, and his other hand rubbed over his eyes. "I'm sorry," he added, his voice thick. "I still just need—some space. Need to keep it separate. You're not my girlfriend, Fasta, you're not, you're *not*."

She wasn't, she wasn't. He wasn't. He wasn't hers, not even after all that, even after he'd hurled her full of such unthinkable pleasure, filled her with his own pendant, made her confess how jealous she was of his other partners, how she wanted him all to herself, not hers, not...

"You stay," he said, a little steadier, as he shifted himself sideways, and shoved up to his feet. "Get comfortable, and get some sleep. I'll stay up, keep an eye on you, and go get you more water. Is there anything else I can do? Anything else I can bring you?"

Fasta had to shake her head, because if she spoke she would start sobbing, and her hand gave a shaky wave that said, *Go, then, if you want. I don't care.*

Henrik hesitated, searching her face, and then he reached for a nearby blanket, and settled it gently around her shoulders. "Good girl," he said thickly. "I'll be back soon, yeah?"

Fasta still couldn't speak, just held herself still as he slowly eased backwards, and strode toward the door. Giving another long look over his shoulder before he stepped out, shutting the door quietly behind him, the lock clicking itself sharp into place.

And finally Fasta just let the sobs take over, consuming her, wrenching her apart from the inside out.

21

Morning found Fasta sore, and exhausted, and alone.

The room was bright—too bright—and she groaned, rubbed at her eyes. She'd slept deeply, not waking even once, and a careful exploration of her limbs suggested that they were all in working order, if rather tender all over.

The room was empty, with no sign of Henrik in it, no clothes or bedding to be seen, and Fasta's head was suddenly flooded with that, with the truth of that, with what it might mean. He hadn't stayed. He'd gone. Where? With who?

She pushed herself up in the bed, wincing again at the soreness, fighting off the visions of how she'd gotten that way. The image of Henrik standing there over her, his eyes on fire, his chest heaving. *Good girl. Beg me for more. Again.*

And then he'd refused to stay. Gone somewhere else, maybe with someone else. *You're not my girlfriend, Fasta, you're not, you're not.*

The wetness was already prickling again behind Fasta's eyes, and she shoved up to her shaky feet, grabbing at the little side table for balance. And there—her body stilled—was her pendant. And a note.

The note was written with her own paper and pencil—Henrik must have taken them from her pocket—and as usual his penmanship was scratchy, almost illegible. *I'm going off to the job*, it said. *Meet you there soon?*

Fasta stared at the note for too long, and then reached down, picked up the pendant. It looked deceptively innocent, benign, shiny and flawless, but she could feel Henrik on it, even stronger than before. Could smell the soap, because he must have cleaned it, and left it here.

A rebellious, whispering part of Fasta thought that maybe she should just leave it, or throw it in her pack, let him wonder what she'd done with it—but instead she lifted up the heavy length of it, settled it around her neck. Looked down at it, and then made herself find her clothes, which were draped neatly over the end of the bed.

Her waterskin was there too, heavy and full, along with a small basket of dried meat and fruit, and Fasta took a long, gulping drink, and ate a bit of fruit, too. Which helped a little, clearing at least a corner of the mess in her head, enough to remind her that she was supposed to be at work, and she was very, very late.

She washed quickly, dressed quickly, packed quickly, and a stilted question to the barmaid downstairs proved that Henrik had indeed paid for the room in full, and that he'd already left. And maybe this wasn't unexpected behaviour from him, either, judging by the barmaid's too-aware smile, tinged with pity and perhaps contempt.

A quiet walk in the morning sun should have improved Fasta's mood, but it didn't, especially since she felt more demoralized, more exhausted, with every step. Henrik hadn't stayed. He'd left without her. What would he say now, where did they go from here?

She walked through Elgin's grounds unimpeded, thankfully avoiding any interactions with either Elgin or his servants. But when she reached the ballroom door, she hesitated, her heart-beat hammering into her throat.

Because yes, there was Henrik. His back was toward her, his big hands were working on the wall, and every movement was familiar and suddenly breathtakingly, exquisitely painful.

Henrik's head whipped around, maybe feeling Fasta there, and now there was no choice but to keep walking. Trying to keep her steps as smooth as possible, to hide that still-radiating exhaustion, to hold her head high, keep her eyes dry.

"Hey, Fass," Henrik said, and though his mouth was smiling, his eyes were tired, wary, with dark circles under them. "How are you feeling? Did you sleep all right? And get my note?"

His eyes flicked downwards, briefly, toward the pendant, and Fasta made herself nod, and turned her gaze to the wall, where it was solid, familiar, safe. "Yes, thank you," she said toward it. "What are you working on?"

Henrik told her, his voice stilted, while Fasta only distantly listened, keeping her eyes on the wall. And then she nodded when he'd finished talking, and started doing the next thing that needed being done.

She could feel Henrik's eyes studying her, but he didn't speak again, and finally he resumed working, too. And this, Fasta could at least understand, at least she knew where she stood, stone and mortar and structural integrity. *You hold the wall while I sweep out behind it, I'll make a diagram of what I mean, yes, that's fine, thanks.*

Fasta was almost grateful when Elgin finally showed up, just before noon, and started waxing poetic again about how brilliant they were, and how fabulous the ballroom was going to look for his party. And then about the party in general, and the guest list, and his wizened old neighbour who'd only agreed to come if he could bring his gigantic dog.

It passed the time, at least, and though Henrik was almost entirely silent beside her, Fasta found that she didn't quite care.

Elgin was being kind, friendly, treating her like an actual person, rather than a pariah who he couldn't be in the same room with, even after he'd given her the most brutally thrilling fuck of her entire life.

"You know, Fasta," Elgin said finally, after she'd made a few halfhearted attempts at conversation, "you're looking a bit peaked. Why don't you two come join me for lunch? Cook's doing up baked quail, I know that was always your favourite."

He glanced at Henrik as he spoke, including him in the invitation, but Henrik's eyes were hard, forbidding. "I brought lunch," he said flatly, but he stopped there, didn't clarify whether he'd brought enough for Fasta. Which he usually did, and did this mean he didn't want to even *eat* with her anymore, either?

"And you, Fasta?" Elgin asked, quirking his mouth into a smile. "Are you this well prepared, too?"

Fasta wasn't, because she—maybe stupidly—always left their food to Henrik. It was one of those things they just did, without discussing it, but a sideways glance at him found his eyes still forbidding, cold. Not saying, *I brought your lunch*, or *stay*, or even *I like you, I'm sorry.*

Fasta swallowed, gave a jerky shrug. "Sure, why not," she said. "Thanks."

Elgin's eyes lit up, and he immediately started talking again, something about how his cook was one of the greatest accomplishments of his adult life, and Fasta only wanly smiled as she cleared up the last of what she'd been doing. And when she shot Henrik a swift, apologetic look, he wasn't looking back, was just gazing blankly at the wall.

That was clear enough, at least, and Fasta followed Elgin out of the ballroom, and down toward the large, well-appointed dining room. The long oak table was already set for one, but after a quick request from Elgin toward the kitchen, a pretty blonde maid appeared with another setting for Fasta.

"Come, have a seat," Elgin said to Fasta, after murmuring

his thanks toward the maid. "You really do look a bit off. Everything all right?"

Fasta shrugged, and sat down carefully in the oak chair, which was thankfully padded on the seat. And while it was admittedly lovely to sit, she still found herself eyeing the beautiful brocade tablecloth, the silverware, the crystal wine glasses. It had been so long since she'd eaten like this—months ago, during her last strained visit to her father's—and there was a brief, longing vision of Henrik, eating out on rocks in the sun.

"You're not sick, are you?" Elgin asked, looking genuinely concerned across the table. "If you want to take some time off, you honestly can. My party be damned."

His voice was convincing, even if his eyes weren't, and Fasta attempted another smile. "Thanks, but I'm fine," she replied. "And I know how you feel about that party. If I take off, you'll have every stonemason in the county here first thing tomorrow morning."

Elgin grinned, and took a sip of the wine the maid had just poured into his goblet. "I'm not sure I'd risk it," he said. "I think your partner might kill me if I tried that. We both know he's just looking for a reason at this point."

He said the words lightly, cheerfully, but Fasta still almost spat out her first sip of the excellent wine. "Henrik doesn't want to *kill* you."

Elgin laughed, his head tilting back, showing off the attractive line of his clean-shaven jaw. "Oh, yes, he does," he said. "I think he would take great pleasure in it. Strangle me with his bare hands, most likely. Maybe castrate me first."

Fasta had no idea what to say to that, and thankfully just then more maids came out, carrying plates of food. Which—Fasta's mouth watered at the sight—held not only roasted quail, but seasoned greens, and fresh berries, and dumplings. All very artfully arranged on the plate, and when Fasta glanced up, Elgin was smiling, making a *go-ahead* gesture toward it.

"Told you my cook was a revelation," he said. "It'll do you a world of good, Fasta."

It did smell—and look—delicious, and Fasta's first careful bite proved that it tasted delicious, too. Even so, it still felt strange to be sitting here, eating like a queen, while she knew Henrik was out there somewhere with his simple packed lunch, eating alone.

"So what's going on with you and the big guy, anyway?" Elgin asked, his voice conversational. "Is it just fucking? Or more than that?"

Fasta nearly choked on her greens, and with effort she swallowed, and glanced up at Elgin's eyes. Which weren't judgemental or critical, just curious, and Fasta pulled in air, let it out. How had Elgin *known*? And Henrik had wanted to keep it secret, right? Maybe especially now?

"Um," she said, stupidly, and took another breath. "Why do you ask?"

Elgin chuckled, and gave a vague wave of his fork. "Because it's obvious there's something going on," he replied. "You're constantly in each other's space, you defer to him like *he's* the one in charge, you wear matching outfits, you wear *that*"—he nodded toward the pendant—"and also, he wants to kill me."

Elgin flashed her a saucy smile, as if daring Fasta to challenge any of that—but when she didn't speak, he wryly shook his head, and stabbed a piece of quail with his fork. "I didn't know big guys were your thing," he said lightly, raising his eyebrows at her, and popping the quail into his mouth. "Or maybe back in the day I'd have eaten more."

Fasta tried to smile back, but abjectly failed, and instead took a long, fortifying drink of wine. "It's, um," she began, and then took another drink, tried again. "It's complicated."

Her thoughts were swarming with Henrik again, off eating alone somewhere, leaving her alone, slamming himself into her mouth, calling her a good girl—and across from her Elgin nodded, gave her an understanding smile. "Because he's a commoner, right?" he said, with a shrug. "I understand that. Have your fun, but keep it quiet. Only go public if it's actually got a future."

Fasta blinked at him, and carefully speared another bite of quail on her fork. "You don't think Henrik has a future?"

Elgin laughed—but then it faded, suddenly, and he cocked his head, studying her. "Oh," he said. "You're actually asking. I mean, sure the guy's got a future—he seems perfectly capable, right?—but not with *you*, Fasta. Not like that. Your father would lose his *mind*."

The words scraped, rankled, but Elgin kept studying her, his eyes too intent. "Your father would cut you *off*, Fasta," he added, with rising disbelief. "You would lose *everything*. You haven't actually *thought* about it, have you?"

Fasta jerked a shrug, her face heating, because maybe she *had* thought about it, oh gods. "I just think it's ridiculous," she said. "That social standing matters that much."

Elgin was still staring at her, and he set down his fork. "Well, it does. Not because it makes you too good for him, or whatever. But you just have completely different lives and experiences. You're looking at the world from an entirely opposite perspective."

Fasta shrugged again, frowned down at her half-empty plate. "You say that like it's a problem."

"It *is* a problem," Elgin replied, his voice flat. "Unless you really want to grovel and feel guilty for the rest of your life, about something you have no control over? Those people think we're oppressors, Fasta. They resent us. They want to bring us down to their level, and *punish* us."

Fasta couldn't deny it, because a few recent political uprisings would prove her wrong—and even worse, more vivid visions of Henrik were marching across her thoughts. *You spoiled-rotten little brat. I will make you kneel and crawl and beg for me in the dirt. I will teach you some fucking lessons, Lady Valgeirr.*

And maybe Elgin had caught that, because he leaned back

in his chair to look at her, wineglass in hand. "You would never be happy," he said firmly. "And you can't honestly think he would be happy, either. Especially once the money's cut off."

That rankled too, and Fasta frowned at him. "Henrik doesn't care about my money."

Elgin's eyebrows shot up, and he gave her a grim smile. "Sorry, Fasta, but I guarantee you he does," he said. "They all care about the money. Honestly, how much have you given him over the years? Directly or indirectly?"

Fasta couldn't help a wince down at her plate, and Elgin laughed, not unkindly. "Look, I've been there. I'm not judging you, I swear. But it's why we marry each other, and only fuck around with them. Right?"

It made sense, maybe, and it was what plenty of people in that circle did—including Fasta's father himself, whose marriage to her long-dead mother had been in name only. But it still felt wrong, and a glance up at Elgin showed him looking apologetic, maybe even sympathetic. "I understand, Fasta, I really do. But there's no reason to risk the rest of your life over it, is there? Especially when you can still get what you want without it."

Fasta frowned again, but Elgin shrugged, his gaze shifting past her to the wall behind her head. "Look, we're all adults, right?" he said. "I'm not the kind of guy who'd begrudge you some fun with a good-looking hulk on the side, or even some coin going into his pocket. As long as it's discreet, and goes both ways. And the kids are mine."

The room felt quiet, suddenly, too close and cramped, and Fasta stared at Elgin, caught in the implications of that. Wait. He was—offering? He *was* offering, right?

Elgin's eyes flicked back to hers, briefly, and there was a faint betraying flush on his cheeks. "Just throwing it out there," he said, a little too casually. "We always got along, understood each other, didn't we? And now that I've got this place, my family's after me to settle down, set up with a couple heirs. And

I want my kids to be smart, and well-bred, and hopefully decent earth-mages, too."

Fasta's mouth fell open, her thoughts swirling in a dozen directions at once. "Uh, you're aware that magic heritability isn't entirely predictable," she said, because maybe that was the only thing she could cling to, at the moment. "Right?"

"Of course I am," Elgin replied, with a shrug. "But I'd be a fool not to try to increase my chances, wouldn't I?"

Gods *damn* him, and suddenly Fasta snapped back into a too-vivid memory of sitting down at her desk, with tears in her eyes, and a quill in her hand. *Elgin cares about his own amusement more than he cares about me,* she'd written, and then she'd stared at it, made herself take in the truth of it. *Elgin will do whatever he pleases, even if it hurts me. Elgin lies to me. Elgin ignores me. Elgin has probably cheated on me.*

She'd never been quite sure of that last point, but looking at his handsome face across the table, she was calmly, distantly certain of it. "How many children are you expecting here?" she asked, for reasons she couldn't quite explain. "On what kind of timeline?"

Elgin shrugged again, pursed his lips. "Three?" he said. "Maybe more, depending on where the magic situation lands. And starting somewhat soon after the wedding, right?"

Fasta twitched, and kept staring at him. "And what about my work? My career?"

Elgin looked back, his head tilting sideways. "What about it?" he asked. "You wouldn't actually want to keep doing it full-time once you have children to look after, would you?"

Fasta had never honestly considered that question—children had always been some far-off vision, something to think about later, at an unspecified future date—but now, suddenly, the thought of abandoning her career, raising Elgin's three or more children, living forever trapped in Elgin's house, subject to Elgin's rules and preferences, was very much like Fasta's worst possible nightmare.

"Yes, I would want to keep working," she said, lifting her chin. "We would be able to afford as much help as we wanted, right? Especially once you gained my father's settlement, and access to my accounts. There would be no reason for me to stop."

The look on Elgin's face was one Fasta hadn't seen in years, but she still remembered it, all too clearly. "Look, Fasta, I understand that your work is fulfilling for you, and fun to play around with," he replied, his voice calm. "And I'd have no objection to you doing a bit of consulting, a few special projects here and there. But doing what you do now, getting up and putting on that outfit and trudging off every morning to dig in the dirt like a *commoner*? It's ridiculous."

Ridiculous. And this was as far as Fasta needed to go with this particular conversation, and she dropped her napkin on the table, pushed her chair back. "I'm flattered by the offer," she said crisply, "and I'm honoured that you still think so highly of me. But I wouldn't be happy with that life. I'm happy now."

Elgin stood up too, his jaw suddenly tight, his eyes cool. "Are you, though?" he shot back. "Honestly, Fasta? Because to me, you look pretty miserable right now. Like you're worn out and exhausted, and you've been bawling your eyes out all night long."

He waved sharply toward her face, and Fasta's cheeks heated as she shoved to her feet. "I appreciate your concern," she said, just as coolly. "But I should return to work. Thank you for lunch."

With that, she spun on her heel and walked out, without looking back. Just needing to get away from him, from the creeping prickling possibility of it, of *that*. Of leaving Henrik, walking away from her drawing, her desk, abandoning long days spent working together out in the sun, in exchange for a gods-damned *prison*.

Elgin didn't follow, thankfully, and when Fasta stalked back into the ballroom, Henrik was already there. Working with his back to her, mortaring the section they'd started on that morning, and the familiar sight of it seemed to settle something in Fasta's chest.

"Hey," she said to him once she'd approached. "Looks good, Harry."

Henrik didn't look at her, didn't take his eyes off the wall, and Fasta put a brief, unthinking hand to his arm—and then flinched as he jerked his arm away. Not hard, but enough to send her back a step, to dredge up the sudden swirling misery.

He still didn't speak, didn't stop his mortaring, and Fasta stared at him, tried to breathe over her loudly pounding heartbeat. "You're angry with me," she ventured, carefully, toward his back. "About lunch?"

Henrik's jaw spasmed in his cheek, his hand hurling mortar onto the wall with unnecessary force, and Fasta let out a slow breath. "Look, I didn't think to bring any lunch," she said. "And you didn't say anything about bringing mine, either, and why would you, since we weren't even home last night? And I hadn't eaten yet today, and was hungry. And I thought you *liked* it when I eat."

Henrik's shoulders hunched, the mortar slapping even harder against the wall. "Yeah, but I *always* bring your lunch," he countered, and Fasta could taste his anger now, simmering low in the air around him. "I have every day for *years*, you think staying the night at a pub is gonna change that somehow? Or maybe you just wanted it to, so you could go off with him instead?"

Fasta's eyes were prickling, blinking too hard, and suddenly she was just tired, so damned tired of everything. "Harry," she said, a little desperate. "I didn't mean anything by it. I thought—I thought maybe you didn't want to. You didn't want to be around me last night, did you?"

It came out bitter, maybe even accusing, and finally Henrik spun to face her, his eyes glinting. "Look, I *did* want to be around you last night," he countered. "But like I said, I just needed a bit of space."

Fasta gritted her teeth, blinked the wetness away. "But you also said," she began, "it could be us again. After."

Henrik shook his head, and ran an agitated, mortar-stained hand through his hair. "Not straight away after, for fuck's sakes," he replied, hoarse. "You think I can just flip that shit around in my head? I need time to separate it, to spread it out, so I don't break my damned *mind*. And I told you that from the start, and if you can't respect my one biggest rule in all of this"—his eyes glinted on hers—"then maybe we need to just call this whole deal off."

What? Fasta's panic kicked and surged, sudden and far too powerful, and her hand clutched tight to his arm. "No," her voice choked, on its own. "*No*, Harry!"

Henrik grimaced and rubbed his eyes, like she was just making it worse. Like maybe he *would* call it off for good, if Fasta kept pushing it. And suddenly she couldn't think, couldn't bear this right now, and she took a gulping breath, an unsteady step backwards.

"I think—I'm not feeling so well," she stammered. "I might—go back. See you later."

She didn't listen for his answer, couldn't stand to hear it, and instead just turned, and covered her eyes, and fled.

22

Fasta's goal upon reaching Coven Manor was just to rest. To sleep off the bitterness and exhaustion, and all the aches and memories Henrik had left behind.

But once she'd collapsed into bed, her traitorous body wouldn't even sleep. Just tasting Henrik on her sheets, feeling Henrik all over her room, even all over her skin.

Finally she gave it up and trudged down to her workroom, which, while still full of memories of Henrik, didn't reek of him quite so strongly. Enough, at least, that she could make an attempt at drawing, a stupid useless diagram of what she would do with Elgin's ballroom, if it were actually hers. Put in windows here, divide it here, turn it into a cozier space with a little seating area off to one side...

But it was ridiculous, because Fasta knew very well that Elgin, like her father, would have certain ideas of how things should be done, how his grand manor should look. And allowing one's daughter—or even one's wife—to wield that amount of control was simply not done. Right?

Fasta scribbled out the drawing, and rubbed painfully at her eyes. Elgin wasn't her father. He hadn't been trying to insult her. And here, alone, in the silence of her workroom, she could admit that he was, objectively, probably not the worst possible choice for a husband. Yes, he was selfish, arrogant, set in his ways, but he was also cheerful, charming, handsome, pleasant. And Fasta could believe, very easily, that he would give her space, would have fewer expectations around manners and customs than most men of their station. He understood earth-magic. He would let her still have Henrik.

And gods, *why* was she even thinking about this, and Fasta was almost grateful when she heard a sudden knock on the door. At least, until she glanced up, and found—Kjaran, looking both smug and cagey at once.

"What is it?" Fasta asked with a sigh, as she waved Kjaran inside. "Do you need something?"

Kjaran shot a furtive glance around the workroom—Fasta couldn't recall her ever being inside it before—and then down to the scribbled-out diagram on Fasta's desk. "I heard you had returned early," she said, "and wanted to ensure nothing was amiss with the job. Is the Earl of Valkin satisfied with your work to date?"

Of course, that was what Kjaran cared about, and Fasta gritted her teeth, and nodded. "Yes, he is excessively pleased, of course," she replied. "And the job is proceeding according to schedule. Henrik had to finish some mortaring before we could continue, so I returned here to sketch out our next steps."

Kjaran seemingly accepted this, and nodded as she came a step closer. "I also wished to mention," she said, pointedly now, "that it is being said, by several sources, that Mr. Hallen's younger brother has recently and mysteriously come into a large sum, which he has used to pay his overdue tuition at the Academy."

Gods *damn* it, how did everyone know *everything* around here, and Fasta bit back a groan, fought to keep her eyes steady. "It's not mysterious in the least," she said coldly, "because I gave it to him."

Kjaran blinked at her, twice. "That is an exceedingly generous gift."

Fasta didn't reply—it was up to her what to do with her own funds—but Kjaran didn't seem deterred. "Do you not think, however," she went on, "that given the current— *climate*—surrounding Mr. Hallen, such generous gifts may be quite unwise?"

The current climate. Fasta's patience was fraying very thin, and she raised her eyebrows, gripped her hands together. "What kind of climate is that?" she asked, clipped. "The kind where one of your most accomplished specialist employees is being victimized by false accusations, and the administration of this facility is doing *nothing* to find the true perpetrator? A course of action that I continue to find *deeply* offensive?"

Kjaran blanched, and took a tiny step backwards. "On the contrary," she said archly. "In consultation with my director colleagues, we have, in fact, decided to pursue several initiatives to help identify the perpetrator. Just yesterday, we brought a tracking specialist in to review both crime scenes, and we have made a comprehensive list of all the missing items, and their market values."

She said it triumphantly, like it was a grand concession for Fasta's sole benefit, rather than the bare minimum they should have done. "And?" Fasta shot back, too sharp. "What did the tracker find in the storage room?"

Kjaran hesitated, her mouth pursing. "Nothing out of the ordinary," she said finally. "Only signatures that would have been expected to be there. Staff and employees retrieving items, the servants cleaning."

"And can you tell me the stolen items?" Fasta asked. "Or can I review the list?"

She fully expected an instant refusal, but Kjaran kept glancing uncertainly down toward Fasta's drawing, and finally gave a helpless shrug. "If you must," she replied. "But you'll need to review it in my office, under my direct supervision."

It was something, at least, and Fasta immediately stood, trying not to wince at the still-lingering aches. "Fine," she snapped. "Let's go."

Thankfully, Kjaran again didn't argue, and Fasta followed her down the stairs toward her office. They passed a few people along the way—including Thora and Runar, the latter of whom took one sweeping look at Fasta, and gave a deeply disapproving frown—but Fasta ignored them, ignored everyone, until they were safely inside Kjaran's office.

"This is the list of stolen items," Kjaran said, and Fasta snatched the sheet from her hand, ran her eyes down the length of it. It was, to her rising dismay, an excessively long list, and most of the items, at first glance, were valuable, and definitely earth-mage-adjacent. Gold jewelry. Silver coins. Marble figurines. Gleaming looking-glasses. Artisanal ceramics.

But then, near the bottom, there was a set of game pieces made from whale teeth. Snapping Fasta's narrow eyes up toward Kjaran's watching face, as she jabbed her finger at the paper. "You do realize," she said, "that most earth-mages—including Henrik—aren't able to isolate or manipulate bones and teeth? And if it was truly Henrik, digging through that room feeling out valuables, he wouldn't have picked this up?"

Kjaran came around to look at the paper, her lip curling. "Surely anyone could have simply seen them sitting there, and realized their value."

"It says they were in a box," Fasta countered, frowning down at the list's careful script. "And also, it's highly doubtful that Henrik would even *fathom* that a game made of teeth would be worth that much money."

Unsurprisingly, Kjaran didn't look convinced, and Fasta sighed, handed back the paper. "Do you also have that list of everyone your tracker isolated as being in the storage room?"

Kjaran fussed again over that, mumbling about confidentiality and permissions, but Fasta stood her ground, and soon found herself in possession of another sheet of paper, with a list of names. Indeed mostly servants, and almost a dozen of her fellow mages. Including—she frowned—Merton, and Johan.

"You realize that there are any number of plausible suspects on this list?" Fasta demanded, jabbing her finger toward it. "And that Henrik is *not*, in fact, on the list?"

Kjaran began babbling again, this time something about motives and eyewitness accounts to the previous two incidents, and Fasta finally thrust the sheet back, and asked to be kept informed on any future developments before stalking out again. Feeling even more enraged than before, and after a minute spent glaring at the wall, she spun around and headed for the back hallway, toward that damned storage room.

The room's entrance was tucked away in a small nook around a corner, easily hidden if you weren't looking for it, and Fasta hesitated outside it, looking it over. The door was cladded in metal, in an attempt at security, and her touch against it revealed several locks, both inside and out. The largest lock was keyed, so servants could open it, and probably any competent earth-mage, too. But another lock—Fasta frowned, felt again—was made with some kind of string, clearly to prevent any earth-mages from entering. The string would need to be teased out from the other side, somehow, likely with a specific kind of tool, perhaps made to collapse and expand.

It meant that getting in there would have been tricky, even for Henrik, because—Fasta slid her hands across to the door's other side—there were also two sets of hinges, both on the inside, one set made of iron, and one wood. And while Henrik was deeply intuitive with wood, and could do things with it that most non-mage carpenters couldn't, wood still wasn't stone, and it was unlikely even Henrik could have removed those hinges from this side. Right?

Fasta glowered at the door, chewing her lip, hands on her hips—when behind her, there was a sound. And with it a distinctive taste in the air, one that set her heartbeat hammering, her stomach clenching in her gut. Henrik.

When she turned, he was standing there behind her, leaning against the wall, looking at her. Still wearing his work clothes, his arms crossed over his chest, his eyes unreadable. And Fasta couldn't bear to fight with him again, not now, so she lifted her chin, and waved irritably toward the storage room door.

"Come and feel this thing," she said. "Do you think you could open these latches?"

Henrik blinked, but then walked over, and spread both hands against the door. "The metal ones, sure," he replied. "But this string contraption—no, not unless I'd seen what they use to open it. Could probably make a copy, in that case."

That had been Fasta's thoughts too, and she gestured at the hinges on the other side. "And what about those wooden hinges?"

Henrik moved his hands accordingly, spread his fingers wider. "Could probably pry them off from the inside with something metal—a chisel, or even a sharp piece of steel. But getting them back on right afterwards would be a mess, though."

Fasta nodded, glared back at the door again. "Yes, that's what I thought," she said. "You would think Kjaran could have at least *asked* you."

Henrik shrugged, like he'd never expected any of this to be fair in the first place. And he was probably right, damn the entire *world*, and Fasta gave the door a too-hard kick that sent a flare of pain jolting up her leg.

"Look, Fass," Henrik said, quieter now. "You don't have to do this."

Fasta swallowed, and kept glaring at the door. "I don't?" she asked, as steady as she could. "So what, I should just sit back and wait until they pin these thefts on you for good? Have you forgotten, Harry, that you're only one step away from being *fired?*"

She could feel Henrik stiffening beside her, could taste his anger curdling in the air, so depressingly familiar from the past few days. And suddenly Fasta was just too tired, too worn out for all of this, and she turned back toward him, pulled herself to her full height.

"Go on, then," she said, voice flat. "Snap at me some more. Tell me I'm wrong, or lying to you again. Or whatever it is you think of me these days."

Henrik's eyes shifted, his throat bobbing, but he didn't deny it, and Fasta's eyes were prickling again, the hurt and the memories lurching up too present, too powerful. Him leaving last night, him slamming himself into her mouth, him with the pendant. *Such a spoiled-rotten little brat. You're not my girlfriend, Fasta. Beg me for more.*

He still wasn't speaking, wasn't even trying, and Fasta took one more gulping breath. "You know, I thought we were *friends,*" she said now, toward his chest. "You never used to raise your voice at me, or ignore me. You would never have abandoned me when I needed you."

The prickling behind her eyes was too close to burning, to spilling out, betraying her, and she looked away from him, blinked as hard as she could.

"So I think," she said, "I think maybe you were right. This was a bad idea. And we *should* just end it. For good."

23

Fasta didn't wait for Henrik to reply. Just turned, and started walking, not thinking, not breathing. And not stopping, not even when she could suddenly taste him behind her, too close.

"Fass," he said, but she didn't care, couldn't. Just kept going, until Henrik's hands caught around her waist. Pulling her bodily to a stop, turning her back to face him, because he could do that, because he was still Henrik, and Fasta only blinked at his chest, didn't even try to get away.

"Listen to me," he said, strangely breathless, and those strong hands maneuvered her over to the wall, to the hard bracing stone of it. Setting her gently against it, spreading his own hands to the stone on either side of her, trapping her there. "*Please.*"

As always, the stone helped, solid and steady and connected to the earth. Enough that Fasta could look up, find those painful grey eyes. "What," she said.

Henrik dragged in a breath, closing his eyes, maybe feeling the stone, too. And the taste of his anger and frustration slowly flattened, pooling into something else, something too close to misery.

"I'm sorry, Fass," he said, his eyes blinking open again, holding hers. "You're right. I should have done better last night. Shouldn't have snapped at you like that today. Shouldn't have said a damned word about lunch, about Bryant, about any of it. It was petty and jealous and not my place. I *know*."

Not his place. Fasta's stomach uncomfortably hitched, and Henrik drew in another sharp inhale, let it out. "And I know it's not an excuse," he said, "but this whole thing is really messing with my head. Like I keep telling you, I'm trying to keep it separate, keep it professional, but I *can't*. I'm *fucked* with it, Fass."

His voice caught, his eyes squeezing shut again, and before she could stop it, Fasta slipped her hand up against his chest, felt the rapid beat of his heart through his tunic. And she shouldn't ask, she'd agreed to keep it professional too, but...

"Why?" she whispered. "Is it affecting you so much?"

Henrik's eyes blinked open, stared at hers for an instant—and then he laughed, harsh and bitter, not a laugh at all.

"You have to ask?" he said, incredulous. "Because after all these years, I *finally* get to have you. I get to have you in every sick, twisted way I've ever wanted. And it's so much fucking better than I ever even *dreamed* it could be, and I can't stop thinking about it, about how perfect it is, about what I want to do with you next. All while the rest of you"—he jerked a wave at her body, her head—"is further away from me than ever, gets further from me every fucking *day*."

Fasta swallowed, and Henrik barked another bitter laugh, shook his head. "And maybe I even want it that way," he added, "I need it that way, 'cause otherwise—"

His voice choked off, and Fasta put her other hand to his chest, spread her fingers wider. Looked at him, waited, while he sighed, lowered his head, until his warm forehead rested up against hers. "Otherwise I'm never gonna get over you," he said, quiet. "*Never*."

It was like the world had gone still, breathless, with Henrik so close, all around her, touching her, letting her touch him.

Saying he did care, he did want her, he *did*—and Fasta dredged up her own courage, searched for truth. "What if," she whispered, even as one of her hands slid around his back, pulled him a little closer. "What if I don't want you to get over me."

Henrik gave another one of those bitter laughs, his head shaking against hers. "That's so fucking *easy* for you to say," he replied, his breath warm, close, on her face. "But what happens when you get on with the rest of your life, like you're supposed to. When you settle down with some rich arsehole, and forget all about me."

The visions of Elgin swirled in Fasta's head, and her hands gripped Henrik tighter, pulled him closer. "I could never forget about you, Harry," she breathed. "Even if I *did* marry some rich arsehole, I'd still want to work with you. And probably"—she pulled in more breath—"all the rest of it, too."

Henrik recoiled, suddenly, staggering back and away, and too late, Fasta heard what she'd just said. She'd let Elgin infect her head, damn the bastard, and she'd just told Henrik she wanted to keep him as a sidepiece, maybe a servant, a *pet*...

She was already shaking her head, clutching hard for Henrik's arm—and though he didn't push her away, he was staring at her with cold, glinting eyes, his chest heaving with his breath.

"And *that*," he said, voice flat, "is *exactly* why we need to keep it separate. Because in the end, Fasta, this is all going *nowhere*. Do you really think I'm gonna hang around and be the other guy in your fucked-up rich marriage? Hasn't it ever crossed your mind that maybe I want my own family? My own wife? A partner who's just *mine*?"

Fasta couldn't quite breathe, couldn't reply, because maybe she hadn't thought about that, had never even asked. And Henrik was shaking his head at her, his eyes still cold and angry, his hands in tight fists at his sides. "Look, we both know exactly where this ends," he snapped. "And you might as well admit it, that end is coming sooner rather than later—so I need to be in this for *me*. Doing what I can, getting whatever I can from you, without losing my fucking mind. And then I need to get the hell out, for good."

What? It was like he'd slapped Fasta across the face, and she wildly shook her head, fumbled to touch him, to drag him back toward the wall, toward safety. He couldn't honestly think that, this couldn't be how he felt, he was supposed to be *hers*—

"You can't mean that," she said, pleaded, to his glittering grey eyes. "You're just—using me? Getting what you want from me?"

Elgin's voice whirled up again, far too strong—*they all care about the money*—and Henrik sagged against her, his breath still heaving too fast. "I'm trying," he said, quiet. "Fuck, Fass, I'm trying."

Gods damn it, damn him, and something wrenched in Fasta's gut. Something hopeless, desperate, and she clung tighter to him, pulled him closer. Just needed to touch him, to show him, prove this couldn't be true, he had to want her, he *had* to care—

And he did, yes, yes, because he wasn't pushing her away. And instead, he even drew her sideways, around that corner toward the storage room. Where they were almost fully hidden from view, and he could lean in big and powerful, blocking Fasta close against the wall.

"You can't," Fasta said to him, for reasons she couldn't explain, even as her hands slid back against his broad chest, felt the strength of it under his tunic. "Think of this like that. Like we're just—*using* each other."

"Why the fuck not," Henrik replied, breathless, as his big body ground up against hers, his forearms to the wall on either side of her head. "It's what it fucking *is*."

But he didn't believe it, not really, and Fasta hooked her leg up around him, pulling him harder. "For you, maybe," she gasped, and in reply Henrik gave that bitter laugh, yanked up her other leg, too. So he was the only thing holding her up, pinning her between him and the wall, pressing that bulging hardness in his trousers right where she wanted it. And *gods*, he was strong, and were they really going to do this here, in a hallway, when anyone could just walk around the corner and see them—

"And for you," Henrik growled against her ear, followed by the sudden, intoxicating feel of his teeth, nipping gentle at her neck. "You *want* to be used. You want to be fucked, pounded, *owned*, until you can't take it anymore."

Fasta couldn't help a strangled gasp, and Henrik laughed again, the sound streaking straight to her groin. "Aw, yeah, you love it," he breathed, with another soft bite of his teeth. "You loved it last night, when I used every hole you have all at once. You loved having this"—she felt a tug of his magic on her pendant—"deep up inside you. Admit it."

Fasta gasped again, arching her neck, silently pleading for more—and he laughed again, bit at her ear, ground that hardness forceful against her. "You should've seen yourself," he breathed. "High and mighty and *perfect* Lady Valgeirr, in a cheap tavern, on her hands and knees with her arse up in the air, like a good little servant. With my chain hanging out of you, and a wine bottle halfway up inside you, and my dick buried deep in your mouth."

Oh *gods*, his voice, his smell, his strength, tangling with the memory of him the night before, so strong and so vividly real, more real than anything, anyone, had ever been. "I'm gonna be dreaming about that for weeks," Henrik whispered, as that hardness ground tighter, exactly where it needed to be. "Months. *Years*, probably."

Fuck. Fasta's trembling hands found his hard arse, dragging him even closer. "Me too," she gasped back, and she meant it. "Never felt *anything* like that before. Need you to do it again."

Henrik laughed again, not so bitter this time, but more husky, hungry. "What part?"

"All of it," Fasta whispered, and then groaned at another

nip of his teeth against her skin. "But maybe with your cock *there*, this time. Like you said."

Henrik didn't need her to explain what she meant, judging by the deep growl in her ear, the almost-painful press of his groin against hers. "Yeah?" he rasped. "You mean that?"

Fasta nodded, gasped again. "Never have before," she breathed. "With anybody. Want it to be you."

Henrik's breath against her ear caught, choked—and one of his hands clutched to her face, tilting it up. Which meant he was holding her up entirely with just one hand—but then it all vanished into nothing, because he leaned in, and kissed her.

It was hard, aggressive, demanding, and Fasta hurled herself back into it, sinking her hands into his hair, clutching her legs tighter around him. Gods, it was so good, the taste of him, the feel of him, the magic sparking under her skin. He was everything, glorious, *hers*—

But suddenly he pulled away, breathing hard, turning his head, averting his eyes. Saying, maybe, that he wasn't supposed to be doing that, but Fasta didn't care, pulled his face back in, kissed his cheek, his jaw, his neck, everywhere she could reach.

"Let me suck you," she whispered, between kisses. "I want you in my mouth. Want to taste you."

Henrik betrayed a helpless, breathless groan, his head tipping back—but it was a yes, it *was*. And when those strong hands set her down, Fasta instantly sank to her knees on the hard tiled floor. While Henrik fumbled with his trousers, shoving them downwards just enough to pull out that swollen ruddy cock.

Fuck, he was gorgeous, jutting out so thick and demanding toward her. And for a hanging, hovering breath, Fasta could only stare at it, drink up the sight of it, here before her eyes. Wanting her. *Hers*.

She shoved forward in a single frantic movement, and sucked him deep. Burying him all the way to the base, his blunt head spasming and prodding into her throat. And yes, this was right, this was perfect, almost overpowering, just on the edge of pain. Her lips stretched tight, her jaw still tender from the night before, her eyes watering as she blinked up at Henrik's flushed, watching face. *You always look at me*, he'd told her, *when my dick's in your mouth.*

"Good girl," he gasped, patting her cheek, and he gave an experimental little thrust, sinking a little deeper. "Dunno why you can remember all these rules just fine, and none of the other ones."

Fasta couldn't follow that right now, could only suck on him, hold his watching eyes. While he twitched a wry little smile back toward her, and slid a slow, deliberate hand into her hair. "New rule," he breathed, soft. "When I finish in your mouth, you swallow all of it. No spitting, no choking. You understand?"

Fasta moaned around him, and attempted a nod. Making him smile again, sly and wicked this time, and this was how it was supposed to be, Henrik smiling at her, pleased with her, hers...

"A good servant," he said now, almost conversational, as he slid his other hand into her hair, "would let her lord use her mouth, as hard as he wanted. And"—he slid himself out slow, and then back in—"she'd keep sucking as hard as she could, the entire time. No matter what it looked or sounded like."

Fasta blinked up at him, dragged for air, while his hands spread wider on her head, his thrusts still slow and steady into her throat. "Are you a good little servant, Lady Valgeirr?" he whispered. "You gonna do this with me? Be here with me the whole time?"

Fasta nodded again, almost desperate, but Henrik didn't smile this time, didn't change that slow, agonizing slide between her lips. "And if you're not," he continued, harder, "if you feel yourself starting to lose it, go somewhere else, and you can't tell me—you tap, however you can. Like this."

He demonstrated, three quick taps to her head, gentle but

distinctive. "Another new rule," he murmured. "One you're not gonna break on me, 'cause we need to keep you safe. You understand, buttercup?"

It sent something swerving in Fasta's chest, and she fervently nodded, holding his eyes. And he nodded too, quick and relieved, as he took another slow, agonizing slide out—and then he slammed back in, so hard that her head would have bounced off the wall behind her, if he hadn't been holding her still.

"Good girl," he breathed, his lashes fluttering, as his hands went wider, stronger, on her head, and he sank in again, again. "Just like that. *Fuck*."

Fasta kept holding his eyes, drinking up his pleasure, his praise, his thick hungry fullness everywhere, the impossible dragging craving. "Such a greedy, spoiled little cockslut," Henrik whispered, with another bracing, head-swirling slam inside. "Love having my fat commoner dick in your mouth, don't you. Love having your face fucked."

His eyes were imperious, commanding on hers, and Fasta rapidly nodded, silently pleading for more, more, *more*. And yes, he saw it, he knew, sinking harder, faster, rougher, until she could scarcely hold the suction, the saliva escaping her lips, dribbling down her chin...

"Suck harder," he breathed, with another jolting gouge inside, but despite Fasta's best efforts, her mouth wasn't cooperating, going wetter, sloppier around him. Making noises that would have been highly embarrassing, if she'd had the presence of mind to think about it, if there was anything else in the world than taking him, pleasing him, being a good servant for him—

But then, suddenly, he stilled, with his hands tight on her head, his cock plunged deep inside. And his eyes weren't looking at her anymore, they were looking sideways, around the corner, toward something—

The awareness rushed Fasta all at once, even as she heard

the unmistakable, too-loud sound of a giggle, too close. And when her frantic darting eyes looked, there were two of Coven Manor's maids, standing there in the corridor, with red faces. One of them doing the giggling, and the other staring at Fasta, and looking deeply and thoroughly shocked.

This was definitely where Henrik should have backed off, covered them up, made excuses and apologies—but he wasn't moving, and the maids weren't leaving, either. As if they *wanted* to see this, and Henrik seemed all too willing to oblige, just standing there rock-hard and unmoving, buried deep in Fasta's throat.

"Could you excuse us?" he said, his voice remarkably calm, in control, even as his thick wet cock slowly slid almost all the way out of Fasta's stretched-taut mouth, showing those watching eyes far, far too much. "We'll be done soon."

The first maid giggled again, and then had the audacity to curtsey back toward him before tugging the second maid back around the corner. While Henrik's cock slammed back in, hard, his hands giving Fasta's head a meaningful little shake, snapping her gaze back to his smug, glittering grey eyes.

"Forgetting the rules, buttercup," he murmured, and in reply Fasta immediately sucked as hard as she could, even as her still-shocked eyes blinked up at him, not quite believing that he'd just done that. That he'd let people see this—had let them see *much* more of it than he'd needed to—had wanted them to see Fasta's messy red face, with his cock filling up her mouth, *fuck*—

And he was enjoying her reaction to it, the bastard, his eyes glinting with triumph, as his hips kept slamming in, crushing his groin's coarse brown hair against her face. "Yeah, they saw you," he breathed, as he swelled even fuller in her mouth. "Rich perfect ice queen Fasta Valgeirr, on her knees in a back hallway, sucking my filthy commoner dick."

Fasta glared up at him, even as more furious heat burned through her entire body, and she sucked him harder, heard those humiliating sounds escaping from her swollen, stretched-out lips. While Henrik smiled sharply back toward her, and huffed a sound that might have been a laugh, or a groan.

"So offended," he breathed. "So prim and proper, even now. You should *see* yourself, see how your lord fucking *owns* you—"

His voice broke, and he swelled even fuller, gouging hard into Fasta's throat—and then he cried out, too loud, one of his hands gripping against the wall, hard enough that Fasta could feel it crack beneath his fingers. While his other hand held Fasta's head still, and that thick bitter fluid poured out of the blunt end of him, filling her mouth full of his pleasure, his approval, yes, *yes*.

Fasta groaned too, fighting with effort to gulp it all back without gagging, to swallow every last drop, just as he'd ordered. And she somehow managed it, except for a small trickle she couldn't quite catch, leaking out the corner of her mouth.

Henrik had begun softening between her lips, his grip loosening on her head. And with a low hiss, he drew himself out of her, and tucked himself away again. But his eyes were still glittering on hers, and his big hand slid to her hot cheek, gave it a firm little pat.

"Better, buttercup," he murmured, as his hand slid sideways, catching the streak of wetness on her chin—and then, oh hell, he slid it between Fasta's lips. Making his silent command very clear, and she eagerly obeyed, sucking off his finger until all the bitterness had faded.

"Good girl," he breathed, as he slid that finger out, and then reached down, guided Fasta's arm upward. "Good enough that maybe you'll get a reward, yeah?"

Fasta blinked as she stood, wavering on her feet, and Henrik's strong hands steadied her, set her back against the wall. And then he leaned in too, resting his forearm against the wall beside her head, while his other hand curved against her neck, and then stroked downwards. Caressing over her shoulder, down over her breast. *Touching* her.

Fasta trembled all over, because he hadn't once done this before—had he?—and oh, it felt good. His hand so warm and careful, almost reverent, as it kept stroking her, easing steadily downwards. Until it was nudging beneath the band of her trousers, slipping into her coarse hair, teasing her legs apart.

"Want you to come for me," he whispered, hot into her ear, as those thick, work-roughened fingers explored lower, delved into her swollen tender wetness. "Can you, like this?"

Fasta nodded, breathless, head arching back against the wall, and she gasped at the feel of two of those fingers, sinking in further. Making her clench tight around them, and she'd been craving this so much, was still craving this, needed more of him, needed everything, *hers*...

Those fingers slid until they were buried all the way up inside, his bulky knuckles pressing thick and hard below, and Fasta rocked herself against them, reckless and urgent. Not caring right now who saw, not even if more maids came around the corner, found her writhing against the wall, with Henrik's hand deep down her trousers.

"You like that?" Henrik whispered. "Like me playing inside you? Using what's *mine*?"

Fasta groaned and dragged for air, for truth. "Yes," she gasped, as he pushed harder, his big palm rubbing up hard, just where she wanted it. "*Gods*, yes. So good."

"You want more, then?" Henrik asked, circling his palm, radiating the jolting pleasure wider. And Fasta could only nod, quivering all over, and that was the unmistakable, thrilling feeling of his blunt third finger, pushing up with the others. Feeling big, painful, impossibly powerful, and she fought to relax, to open for it, to breathe...

Henrik kept pressing, seeking, gentle but inexorable, and his knee nudged up between hers, pushing her legs wider apart. Giving him better access, until the third finger finally slipped in, tight and wedged and close.

"Fuck," Fasta gasped, her eyes fluttering, while Henrik gave that low chuckle of his, making her body squeeze tight around those fingers. And in return, he huffed a low, approving laugh, his tongue brushing against his lips.

"Gonna leave you so stretched out, when I'm finally done with you," he murmured, his eyes glittering with the promise of it, the heady threat of it. "Gonna make you fit me, and *only* me, so no other dick will please you *again*."

Oh, gods, and Fasta groaned again, ground herself helplessly down against those hard invading fingers. "And I fucking mean it, Lady Valgeirr," he hissed. "I'm gonna leave you loose, gaping, wide open. Big enough to get my whole *hand* into."

Fucking hell, the absolute bastard, because Fasta betrayed an embarrassing little cry, her body driving down hard onto those fingers—and then, *yes*, she pitched over the edge. Into the unravelling screaming pleasure, pulsing out fierce and dizzying, swallowing everything in its furious flaring strength.

When it finished Fasta felt weak and trembly all over, Henrik's fingers far too uncomfortable—and he carefully pulled out, patted gently against her, and then drew up the waist of her trousers. "Better?" he asked, husky, and Fasta jerked a nod, had to close her eyes, search for her voice again.

"Thanks," she finally whispered, between breaths. "*Gods*, Harry."

Henrik chuckled, still warm enough that Fasta's eyes blinked open, found his again. And her hands had found him too, trailing up against the solid wonderful strength of him, and he wasn't moving away, wasn't stopping her. Even though his eyes had gone careful again, with that too-familiar distance in them.

"All good?" he asked, neutrally, clearly meaning that this was over now. That this was him needing to separate it, maybe—but he was still here. Still taking care of her, keeping his word to her. After he'd touched her like that, and given her all that pleasure, too.

It twisted something deep in Fasta's belly, something almost like hope. They could still do this. She could still control this. And she could keep her word to him in return, she could...

So she swallowed, and nodded, and shoved herself off the wall, standing on her shaky legs. "Yes, of course," she told him, taking a tentative step forward. "Though honestly, Harry, 'We'll be done soon'? Really?"

Henrik chuckled again, as his strong hand gently gripped under her elbow, guiding her up the corridor. "What, are you upset?"

Fasta took a moment to consider that, and then—to her own vague surprise—shook her head. No, she wasn't upset. And while being exposed sucking Henrik in the back hallway wasn't exactly ideal, it had still been so, so good. The way he'd looked, the things he'd said, his hand touching her, inside her...

"No, it's really fine," Fasta said, and she could almost taste Henrik's relief as he led her around the corner, up the stairs. "Although," she added, without thinking, "did you really need to show them that much of you?"

Henrik's sideways glance toward her was nonplussed, maybe surprised. "What, my dick?"

There were no other people around in the corridor, but Fasta's face still furiously heated, even as she attempted a noncommittal shrug. To which Henrik chuckled again, shaking his head, his hand tightening on her elbow.

"You get caught sucking me off in a back hallway, and you're complaining that I showed them my dick?" he said, his voice warm, almost affectionate. "Priorities, Fass."

Fasta's face flushed even hotter, and she lifted her chin, moved her gaze straight ahead, to where Henrik was all but propelling her up the stairs. "Um, where are we going?"

He laughed again, and nudged his elbow into her side. "You're going to bed."

Fasta blinked, frowned at him. "What? Why? It's not even suppertime yet."

"I know," Henrik replied, as they climbed the last set of stairs. "And don't argue with me, you're going. You're sore, and exhausted. And I've still got plenty of food left in my pack if you want some."

Right. Because Fasta had skipped out on their lunch, to eat with Elgin instead, and she winced. "Sorry."

Henrik shrugged, and pulled them to a stop outside his own bedroom door, releasing the latches with a wave of his hand. "Just gonna grab a few things," he said, "and I'll come stay with you again."

Right. Because of course they were still doing that, giving Henrik an alibi, protecting him from any further accusations. But Fasta still frowned at his back as she followed him inside, and she settled her hand against the closest boulder, breathed in its quiet solid steadiness.

"You're sure you still want to?" she asked, carefully, and Henrik glanced over his shoulder from where he was making a precarious pile of random-looking rocks, with a few books hovering on top. He always used shaved-thin rocks for bookmarks, and this was precisely why, clever earth-mage that he was.

"Sure," he replied. "Why wouldn't I?"

Fasta took a breath, dropped her gaze to the boulder under her fingers. "Because you didn't want to. Last night, in the pub."

Henrik exhaled, heavy, and then turned around to face her, balancing the entire teetering pile on only a few fingers of his hand. "Look, Fass," he said, and he sounded exasperated, maybe even curt. "Yeah, I should have stuck around this morning and waited for you. I *know* I should have. But"—the pile on his hand slightly twitched—"it wasn't like I was off downstairs getting drunk, either. I was with you all night, just sleeping on the floor. And after I left you that note this morning, I waited outside until I felt you get up, knew you were all right."

He had? Fasta blinked at where Henrik was rubbing both hands at his mouth, while his pile kept levitating in midair, swaying dangerously back and forth. "It's not that I didn't want to see you," he said, quieter. "Like I said, I just—needed some time to get my head back straight again. And also, I thought you'd know I was there. Can't you usually tell where I've been?"

His eyes darted sideways toward her—that wasn't something they'd really admitted, or discussed before, because maybe it was betraying too much intimacy between them—but he was right, that was true. Fasta should have been able to feel him there. Maybe she would have, if she'd properly tried.

"I usually can," she admitted, though she couldn't quite meet his eyes, and instead she reached up, pulled a few of the books off his swaying pile to safety. "I think I was just—too distracted. Again."

Henrik's sideways glance was understanding this time, and with an easy gesture of his hand, he added a few more books to Fasta's pile. "You don't mind me spreading out a bit, do you?" he asked. "In your room?"

Fasta didn't mind, even if it did look like a mess, once they'd gotten all of Henrik's possessions inside. She usually kept things very tidy, with clean uncluttered surfaces, but she had to admit it was strangely comforting to see all Henrik's rocks and books lying about, almost entirely covering her small desk, and half of her clear floor space.

"Into bed with you," Henrik said lightly, so Fasta quickly changed, and slipped her tired body into bed. While Henrik settled himself at her desk, facing sideways from her, and then began moving the rocks about, putting them into some semblance of organization. Doing it all in complete silence, without so much as a thunk or a rattle, perhaps out of consideration for Fasta—and something swooped in her stomach as she watched him pull over a book, flipping it open with one hand, while he kept silently moving rocks with the other.

"Do you realize, Harry," Fasta said, because she couldn't seem to stop herself, "that by tomorrow, everybody's going to know?"

Henrik glanced over, even as the rocks kept moving, arranging themselves into haphazard rows on the desk. "What, that you were on your knees in the back hallway, sucking me off?"

There was something almost amused in his voice, and Fasta's stomach swooped again. "You don't care, though?" she asked, and she propped up her head on her hand to better look at him. "I thought keeping this secret was one of your rules."

Henrik snapped one of the rocks into his hands, and then pressed his hands together against it, his knuckles white, his muscles straining under his tunic. Trying to change the rock's density, Fasta knew, because he'd been working to refine that lately, across a variety of practical applications. He was always refining so many things, always working so hard, and she swallowed as she watched, as the warmth of his magic flickered all through the room.

"Yeah, I can let that rule go," Henrik said, finally, once he'd released the rock, which began spinning in midair before his eyes. "Like I said, I need to get everything I can out of this. And everybody here knowing I had Lady Fasta Valgeirr on her knees for me, sucking my commoner dick"—he shrugged, gave Fasta a twisted little smile—"that's a major achievement for a guy like me, yeah?"

A sudden heat pooled in Fasta's groin, even as she frowned, and jerked up higher in the bed. "I wish you wouldn't talk about this like that," she said. "Like it's all just a—transaction. Just us *using* each other."

Henrik's shoulder shrugged, his eyes narrowing on the rock still spinning in front of him. "Well, sorry, but that's what it is," he replied, voice thin. "You're the one who just told me you're planning to marry some other rich guy, right? Try and keep me on the side?"

Fasta grimaced, dropped her gaze to the bed. "Look, I didn't mean it like that."

There was an instant's silence, in which she could feel the rock setting down, could feel Henrik turning in the chair to face her. "Then what did you mean?"

Fasta glanced up again at his flat eyes, and suddenly found that her brain was empty, useless. "I—I don't know," she said, as her cheeks prickled with sudden heat. "Honestly, I haven't really thought about it."

Henrik's mouth thinned, and another rock from behind him snapped into his hand, his fingers squeezing tight. "Yeah, I can believe that," he replied, clipped, "because it's already all laid out for you, isn't it? You fool around with this, with me, have a few thrills playing games in the dirt with a commoner— but once you get bored, or it stops being convenient for you, you'll jump right back in line, like a proper heiress should. You'll go back to your father, settle down with some rich arse-hole who's never worked a day in his life, and start having his kids."

Fasta's mouth felt oddly dry, her heartbeat kicking off-kilter in her chest, as Elgin's face, Elgin's words, again loomed behind her eyes. *It's why we marry each other, and only fuck around with them.*

Henrik had been watching her too closely, maybe waiting for her to refute that—but now he sighed, and snapped the rock sideways into his other hand. "And look, it's not like it's a surprise," he said. "I know my place in this, and I know I need to do a better job of remembering that. And I *will*. But"—he took a breath—"just to make it extra clear to you, I'm not staying around afterwards to be your sidepiece, or your secret boyfriend, or your pet. Once this is over, I'm done."

Fasta stilled in the bed, staring blankly at his face—he didn't really mean that? But his eyes were very steady, very certain, and the truth of it clutched almost painfully around her chest. He was supposed to be hers, she was supposed to be in control, making this work...

"What if," her thin voice said, too quickly. "What if—there is no one else. What if we just kept—doing what we're doing."

Even the thought of it was a strange, staggering relief, shimmering bright and hopeful—but Henrik's brows furrowed, his fingers gripping white on the rock. "What, you just keep me as your personal paid fucktoy, *forever*?" he snapped. "Fuck, no."

That was painful too, enough to make Fasta wince, and Henrik rubbed at his eyes. "Look, I don't mean this is bad right now," he said, his voice strained. "It's not. It's the opposite. But like I said, I want my own family someday. My own wife. And I know very well that's never gonna be you. *Never.* And if I have a wife, I'm sure as hell not gonna be able to keep working with you after all this, let alone go sneaking around with you behind her back. I wouldn't do that to somebody I loved."

Fasta didn't miss the criticism in that—the fact that she, perhaps, would do that—and she desperately fought for a reply. "But," she began, "back—back at the start of this, that first night—you said—maybe. We could try it. In ten years."

Henrik barked that too-familiar bitter laugh, shook his head. "You think I honestly believed you'd still be around in ten years? If you really had been, then yeah, I'd have thought about it."

Something clamped tight in Fasta's throat, and she squeezed her eyes shut. "So by doing this with you now," she said, high-pitched, "I've ruined it for the long term? For good?"

She was suddenly close to weeping, oh gods, but Henrik was silent, unmoving. "Look, Fass, I'm sorry, but it was never gonna happen," he said finally, quietly. "It never is. This is it, for us. I'm a poor lowborn commoner, you're heiress Lady Valgeirr. End of story."

Fasta couldn't look at him, couldn't trust herself to speak, and she heard him sigh again. "So your choice is," he added, harder, "we can either call it off now, like you said you wanted downstairs, or you can respect my rules, respect my position, until it's over. No getting mad at me for not giving you everything you want, and not being your boyfriend, since that sure as hell isn't what I am. We keep it separate, 'cause that's the only way I can do it without losing my head. So"—he pulled in another breath—"what do you want?"

Fasta still couldn't look up, could only blink at the bed, fight back that quivering lump in her throat. "I want *you*, Harry."

There was a too-still silence, broken only by the sound of that rock, snapping back into his other hand. "Right then," he said, gruff. "So let's enjoy it while it lasts."

It felt almost impossible to nod, but Fasta managed it, even might have managed a smile. "All right," she whispered. "I'll try."

24

The next morning, Fasta woke up resolved, refreshed, and grimly determined.

She still had Henrik, for now. She still had him in her room, in her bed. And even if she still couldn't bear to think about the rest of it—*I'm not sticking around to be your sidepiece, or your secret boyfriend, or your pet*—she could try to enjoy this, like he'd said. She could try to keep showing him. She could try to make him stay...

It helped that he was still here, that his rocks were all here, that she could reach and draw the nearest rock into her hand, curling her fingers tight around it. And that Henrik was lying there half-awake on the bare floor, watching her do it through heavy-lidded eyes, and now raising his own hand in silent invitation.

Fasta shot the rock toward him with as much speed as she could muster, and Henrik grinned at her as he easily caught it. And then he wound up his arm, hurled it back—but it was way too early, and Fasta was far too uncoordinated, and with a flail of her arm she shattered the rock into sand, making it rain down all over her bed.

"Too slow, buttercup," Henrik said cheerfully, as he reached out and sucked all the sand back up into his fingers, before it wedged itself into Fasta's bed. And then he tossed the remade rock back to her, lightly this time, so she could catch it without difficulty.

"Show-off," Fasta said, and Henrik grinned again, and snapped the rock back into his hand.

"You like it," he drawled. "Admit it."

Fasta wasn't admitting anything, but she couldn't seem to stop smiling at him as they went down to breakfast together, and ate companionably across the table from each other. The stories of their escapade in the back hallway had clearly already been making the rounds, judging by some of the looks they were getting—but if Henrik noticed, he certainly didn't seem to care.

And, Fasta realized, as Henrik nudged her plate closer toward her, shot her a meaningful look—she still didn't care, either. Quite the opposite, maybe, because there was something almost thrilling in everyone knowing it, looking at them, thinking they were actually together. A *couple*.

It made a brazen part of Fasta reach over, between Henrik's bites, to wipe some spilled sauce from his stubbled chin. An action that he didn't even blink at, and—Fasta's breath came out sharp—he then exacerbated by grasping her hand, bringing it up to his mouth, and sucking her finger clean, with far more lingering tongue than necessary.

Fasta could feel the watching eyes, the heat flooding to her cheeks, and Henrik finally released her finger with a distinct little *pop*. And with a look that said, *what are you going to do now?*—and that shocking, depraved part of Fasta actually brought the finger to her own mouth, and slowly sucked it clean again.

Henrik's eyes visibly darkened, and his grin was dangerous, approving. "Good girl," he murmured. "If you keep it up, maybe you can do that to my dick later."

Fasta nearly choked, and Henrik huffed a low, satisfied

laugh as he returned his attention to his breakfast. And once they'd finished, he gave the still-watching room even more of a show as they walked, settling his hand wide and possessive against the curve of her arse.

It was delightfully, thoroughly reassuring, and the walk back to Elgin's passed easily too, with the familiar discussion of all the usual things they talked about. Fasta's recent research, the book about rock transitions that Henrik was currently reading, ore and deposits and the job. Like nothing had changed between them whatsoever.

There was no sign of Elgin when they arrived, which suited Fasta just fine, and which made for an equally easy work morning—until Henrik went out to use the outhouse, and Elgin suddenly materialized from nowhere.

"You're back," he said lightly, leaning casually against the wall where Fasta was working. "Thought maybe I scared you off for good yesterday."

Fasta spared him a brief glance, but knelt and kept working. "No, but you were right, I was feeling ill yesterday," she replied. "My apologies for not informing you before I left."

But Elgin didn't immediately reply, and instead just kept standing there, his gaze prickling on her shoulders. "I realized, after," he finally said, "that I probably came on way too strong. Didn't I?"

Fasta angled another glance up, attempted another smile. "No, it was fine. I appreciated your honesty."

Elgin shook his head, and gave a dry little laugh. "I thought you might. And yet, you still spurned me with all the disdain of a goddess. As you probably should have, I'll admit."

His expression was serious now, his arms folding over his chest. "I came off like a bloody tyrant," he said, quiet. "And look, we both know I like having my way, but I also want you to know that more than anything, I'd want you to be happy. And if you wanted to keep working for a while, or put off having kids, I'd respect that. I promise."

Fasta swallowed, and then stood up, brushing off her hands. So she could look at Elgin's handsome face, his sober dark eyes, while her thoughts curdled with memories of kissing him, touching him, craving him so desperately. Needing him, but not being needed in return.

"Look, Elgin, I really am flattered," she told him. "And I have many good memories from our time together. But this"—she waved at him, the house, all of it—"isn't what I want anymore, in my life."

Elgin's throat bobbed, his mouth tightening. "But maybe you're forgetting, Fasta," he replied, "that this"—he mimicked her wave at him, the house—"doesn't have to be your life, if you don't want it to be. Sure, we'd own this property, whatever—but we'd also have enough money to make your life whatever you please. You want to travel, or study, or work, or just hunker down in a cottage in the woods? You can do all of that, and more."

Fasta blinked at the cottage mention—she hadn't mentioned that to him, had she?—and then shrugged, shook her head. "I'm sorry, Elgin," she said. "I'm just not interested anymore."

Elgin's head tilted, his eyes watchful on hers. "In me?" he asked. "Or in what I have to offer?"

Fasta hesitated, and her thoughts darted to Henrik, to their conversation the night before. "Both," she said, and she meant it. "I'm sorry."

Elgin's eyes remained carefully cool, even as his mouth twisted into a wry smile. "I suppose I should have expected that," he replied. "Ruined things between us worse than I thought back in school, did I?"

Fasta sighed, as more visions of Henrik swarmed behind her eyes. *I wouldn't do that to somebody I loved.* "Maybe," she told Elgin. "It wasn't a great way to treat someone you supposedly cared about."

Elgin grimaced, traced a circle on the floor with his

gleaming boot. "I was a selfish little shit, I'll admit," he said finally. "Any chance of proving to you that I've changed since then?"

Fasta grimaced too, and jerked a helpless shrug. "I don't know," she replied. "Probably not, Elgin. I'm sorry."

He was watching her again, his dark eyes strangely unblinking, and finally his mouth twitched into another smile. "Spurned again," he said lightly, with a grave shake of his head. "I'll have you know, Fasta, I was planning to give you the most spectacular engagement ring you've ever seen in your *life*."

"Were you really?" Fasta asked, feeling strangely, deeply relieved. "What was it?"

Elgin grinned at her, and it looked genuine this time, warming his dark eyes. "Black diamond," he said. "Came across it months ago in a pedlar wagon, of all places. Two carats, flawless."

Fasta gave a low whistle, because that was indeed an impressive stone, and exceedingly rare. "Was it already set?"

"Nope," Elgin replied, with another shake of his head. "I was planning to get it done to your specifics, with the jeweller and metal of your choice. I know how particular you are about such things."

Fasta's thoughts darted to Henrik again, to the heavy chain currently hanging around her neck, and how she'd told him she didn't care about expensive jewels. And she didn't—in truth, she'd choose Henrik's pendant over Elgin's black diamond any day—and suddenly there was a disconcerting new vision, blazing behind her eyes. Henrik making a ring, maybe one to match her pendant, with his magic shimmering all over it...

"Well, that's very thoughtful," she told Elgin, a beat too late. "And certainly an impressive effort, too. Custom jewelry is sure to warm all but the coldest earth-mage heart."

Elgin merrily laughed, tipping his head back. "Clearly I should have started with the ring, like most rational fellows would have. Maybe"—he arched a brow at her—"I'll keep it around, just in case?"

Fasta didn't have the heart to refuse him again, especially since they seemed to be back on good terms, and replied with a shrug and a noncommittal smile. Which Elgin seemed to understand perfectly anyway, judging by the rueful grin on his mouth.

"All right, I'll stop," he said, and his grin faded, his head tilting to the side. "And listen, Fasta, there's something else I wanted to mention to you. You didn't see anything suspicious around here yesterday, did you? Anyone out of the ordinary?"

Fasta blinked, but shook her head. "No, just the servants. Why?"

Elgin's mouth pursed, his eyes gone grim. "Well, I've been working on a commission," he said. "A carving out of pure amethyst. Small, but obviously pretty valuable."

Fasta nodded, trying not to imagine the kind of client—probably a man like her father—who would commission an entire sculpture out of pure amethyst. "Has something happened to it?"

"Yes, it's gone missing," Elgin replied flatly. "Yesterday. I was down there in the morning working on it, and when I went back in the evening, it was gone."

Gone. Fasta's heartbeat skipped, her thoughts suddenly darting to Johan, Kjaran, that damned storage room. And the fact that Henrik had been alone here yesterday afternoon, curse it, and he was already on probation, and what if—

Elgin's eyes on Fasta were careful, wary, almost like he'd followed that thought. "And look," he said, "I'm sorry to ask, but I've heard there's been some funny business at your work lately...?"

Fasta shook her head, so hard the room spun. "No," she snapped. "I mean, yes, there has been, but it has nothing to do with Henrik. Or me. I'm very, *very* certain of that."

Elgin's eyebrows rose, but he nodded. "All right," he replied.

"I'll take your word for it. But if you do see anything, hear anything, could you please let me know?"

Fasta nodded too, and let out a slow, heavy exhale. "Of course. Had the sculpture been fully carved? How big was it?"

"About this," Elgin said, making a pie-sized shape with his hands. "And yes, I was almost done, *and* it was a true-to-life human likeness, which makes it all the more infuriating."

"You still do those?" Fasta asked, her mouth twitching up. "I thought you always hated them."

"Yep, still do," Elgin said gloomily. "But the commission came in before I landed this place, and the price was right, so..." He shrugged, gave an exaggerated sigh. "Now I'll be paying for my hapless greed for *months*. More fool me."

Fasta's smile drew higher, at which inopportune time, Henrik strode back into the room. He'd been gone for an excessively long while, and he was clearly well aware of that, fixing Elgin with a look of purest dislike.

"Did you realize," he said, clipped, "that you have a sinkhole behind one of your barns? And that your barn was this close"—he made a pinching gesture with his fingers—"to falling in?"

"It was?" Elgin asked, looking briefly and truly alarmed. "With the *horses*?"

But Henrik scowled, shook his head. "No, the other one," he snapped. "With the chickens."

"Oh," Elgin said, with a shrug, his face clearing. "Well, then. Were you able to save the poor dears?"

Henrik rolled his eyes and stalked over to the wall, which Fasta had entirely stopped working on. "Yes," he replied, frowning at the stone. "You should really have the rest of the grounds surveyed, though."

"Well, isn't that something you can do?" Elgin asked, with a conspiratorial wink over Henrik's shoulder toward Fasta—and though Fasta's mouth slightly twitched, she absolutely did *not* need to get involved in this. And also, thanks to several unfortunate incidents they'd dealt with in the past, she knew Henrik was right, and sinkholes definitely weren't a laughing matter.

"Well, if you want the grounds surveyed, of course we'll survey them," Fasta told Elgin, putting a warning hand to Henrik's stiff shoulder. "Or would you prefer that we continue here?"

Elgin shot Fasta a longsuffering look behind Henrik's back, but sighed. "Fine, I'll go take a look around, if I must. You two stay here, that party's my top priority."

With another wink toward Fasta, Elgin spun and strolled off, leaving Henrik sputtering with rage. "That useless lying *snake*," he growled, once Elgin was well out of earshot. "How much you wanna bet he fucking *made* that sinkhole? It sure as hell wasn't there yesterday!"

Fasta didn't need to get into this, either, and she settled a hand to Henrik's back, and then slid it—perhaps presumptuously—around his waist. "Thank you for fixing it," she said, resting her head briefly on his shoulder. "I wish I'd been there to watch you do it."

Henrik shot her a narrow look, but didn't shift away from her touch. "So what did he want?"

Fasta's thoughts stilled, suddenly—telling Henrik what Elgin had truly wanted could very well end with bloodshed— and she shrugged against his shoulder. "He was telling me about this sculpture he's working on," she said. "Made of pure amethyst."

Henrik snorted, clearly finding that as ridiculous as she did, and turned around, frowned down at her. "That's all?"

Fasta shrugged again, dropped her eyes to Henrik's tunic. "He was also telling me about this stone he found. A two-carat black diamond."

She could almost feel Henrik's displeasure, seeping deep and powerful into her skin. "Thought you'd like that, did he?" he growled. "Well, let's show him what you *really* like."

Fasta blinked at him, and then at the sight of his hand reaching up, and snapping the stone off her pendant. Leaving the chain hanging empty around her neck, while the streaked grey stone flipped easily through Henrik's fingers, and then rose to hover in front of Fasta's eyes.

"New rule," he murmured. "Wherever this goes on you, it stays there. Until I say so."

Fasta nodded, but she wasn't at all following—at least, until Henrik plucked the stone from midair, and slid it down inside the front of her *trousers*.

"*Harry*," Fasta breathed, shivering at the touch of that cool silky hardness against her skin. "We're at *work*."

"So?" he asked, his voice and eyes challenging, as he slid the stone further, lower, oh *gods*. "Open up."

Fasta gasped, but her feet had already shifted apart, a little awkward, while Henrik's fingers nudged gently up against her slippery heat. Stroking soft at first, familiar, and then—Fasta's breath caught, her lashes fluttering—there was the hard stone, delving up between. Pushing further, further, until she could feel it settling there, cool, heavy, deep inside.

Henrik's fingers, Henrik's hand, slid back out, pulling up her trousers, straightening out her tunic. And then he patted lightly against her belly, while—Fasta gasped again—the stone *moved*. Moved *inside* her, first easing up and down, and then drawing outwards in a slow, torturous circle.

"It stays here," he whispered. "Until I say so."

Fasta jerked a shaky, helpless nod, earning another approving pat of Henrik's hand to her belly. "Good girl," he said, with a teasing, crooked smile. "Now you gonna get to work, or what?"

It was the strangest feeling, keeping that stone inside, while Fasta's body outwardly did all the mundane things she was supposed to be doing. Making sketches, holding up walls, mixing mortar, and then even following Henrik outdoors—walking a little more carefully than usual—for lunch.

"You good?" he asked, once they'd sat on their rocks, and he handed over the salted meat he'd brought her. "Doesn't hurt, does it?"

Fasta shook her head, took a careful bite. "No," she said. "Just feels very—*there*. And very distracting."

She could feel her cheeks flushing, and even more so when Henrik raised his eyebrow at her, and—she almost choked— the stone made another one of those thrilling little circles inside. "Now?" he asked, and Fasta tried and failed to glare at him, to which he only grinned back.

It wasn't until after they'd gone back to work that Fasta truly realized the extent of what this meant, because when Elgin sauntered in to check on their progress, Henrik was perfectly civil to him, even cooperative, explaining what still had to be done, and how much longer they expected this room to take. While Elgin's eyes darted, first, toward Fasta's stone-less pendant—and then, tellingly, down toward her belly.

Fasta's entire body flooded with heat, and she swiftly knelt and began mixing more mortar. But the damage had clearly been done, because Elgin was icily courteous to them both, and stalked off with his jaw set, his hands in fists at his sides.

"You bastard," Fasta breathed at Henrik, once Elgin had gone. "Did you know he would know?"

Henrik shrugged, but his eyes were satisfied, maybe even smug. "Not for sure," he said, as his hand spread against Fasta's belly again, making the stone slide up and down inside. "He hasn't done a single twitch of earth-magic in front of me, how am I supposed to know how good he is?"

Fasta attempted a glare toward him, but failed miserably, especially when his hand slid down a little further, and cupped warm and protective against the curve of her. "Right now, this is mine," he murmured, "to do whatever the hell I want with. And if he doesn't like it, too fucking bad for him."

Fasta could only nod, gulp for breath, and Henrik's

answering half-grin was teasing, triumphant. "Good girl," he said. "Now get to work."

Henrik liked watching her try to work like this, Fasta soon realized, liked watching her fight to ignore it, liked seeing her heated cheeks. Liked moving that stone, occasionally, just when she least expected it, making her gasp, making her look at him.

"Your control is shit today, Fass," he told her, late in the afternoon, when it took her three tries to place a simple stone. "Any particular reason?"

Fasta did glare at him, successfully this time, and he laughed out loud, put a wide, warm hand to her back. "Wanna head out for the day, then?" he murmured. "Put you outta your misery?"

Fasta fervently nodded, but the long walk back to Coven Manor didn't exactly help—only made things worse, in fact. So much so that by the time they'd eaten a hearty supper—with Henrik darting her amused glances the entire time—and finally, *finally* returned to Fasta's room, she was damn near frantic with the furious desperate craving.

"You bastard," she gasped at him, even as she clung to him, put her hands to his stubbled face, his back, his arms. "I am going to *murder* you."

"Nah, you're gonna obey me," Henrik said coolly, though his eyes looked just as hungry as she felt, his cock fully hard through his trousers. "Clothes off. On the bed. On your knees, arse up."

Oh *hell*, and it was only seconds before Fasta was doing it, legs apart, showing him everything, just the way he wanted it. Or, rather, mostly the way he wanted it, but she couldn't get the position quite right, not if she still wanted to keep that stone in place, damn him and his rules.

She could feel Henrik's eyes on her too-exposed body, could feel him coming closer—and then a gentle swat to her arse. "You can do better than this, buttercup," he drawled. "C'mon, you know the rule. Show me."

Fasta took a shuddery breath, tried again—but it wasn't happening, not with that stone there, and Henrik clearly knew that, judging by his breathless laugh behind her. "Fine, fine," he said, with a light little slap between her legs, making her jolt. "Give it here."

Oh thank *gods*, and Fasta groaned aloud as she pushed the stone back, felt its polished weight finally, slowly sliding out of her, lingering there—and then dropping, with a wet little thud, into Henrik's waiting hand below. And that was definitely a groan from behind her, and when she glanced back, Henrik was looking down at the stone in his hand, his chest heaving, his eyes darting up to meet hers.

"Good girl," he whispered, and then he moved, unsteady, to stand nearer her face. The front of his trousers bulging out beautifully toward her, enough to make Fasta's mouth water— and so damned distracting that she almost didn't notice him reaching down, attaching the stone back to its chain, still hanging around her neck.

"Got this all wet," he said, his fingers shaking just slightly as he raised the stone to show her, and his other hand stroked at her mouth, tugging her bottom lip downwards. "Suck it clean for me."

Gods damn him, but Fasta frantically nodded, and groaned aloud as he slowly slid the warm, slick stone all the way between her lips, leaving the chain hanging out. And the stone did taste of her, salty and a bit sour, and as Henrik watched, she sucked it in further, swirled it around with her tongue.

Henrik betrayed another strangled groan, his eyes wide and dark, and Fasta's hungry body took the liberty of sitting up a little, enough that she could reach with both hands and touch that bulge in his trousers, slide her fingers up tight around it. And he wasn't stopping her, just watching, so she untied his trousers with shaky fingers, pushed them down until his bare cock bobbed out, swollen and flushed and gorgeous.

She moaned around the stone at the sight of him, at the sight of her hands touching him. One hand sliding hard up the thick length of him, the other one curling close around those heavy hanging bollocks below. Like she was allowed to be there, allowed to do this, and a swift, furtive glance up at his eyes confirmed it, because he was still just watching her, his eyes half-lidded, heavy, hungry.

"Faster," he breathed, his hand sliding into her hair, and Fasta complied, drinking in the feel of it, the sight of her fingers curled around his thick shaft. Sliding forward and back, now, pointing him straight out toward her, milking him, bringing a little bead of wetness to his slit. And if only she could suck him, kiss it off, but her mouth was otherwise occupied at the moment, the chain still hanging from between her lips, jangling with the movement of her hands.

"Good girl," Henrik whispered. "Don't stop."

Fasta didn't, couldn't, and that silken length swelled even fuller beneath her hands, as Henrik's breath came scattered, ragged. His bollocks pulling up tight under her fingers, that slit leaking a little more, and Fasta needed to see this, so urgent she could barely breathe—

Henrik let out a low cry, even as his free hand came up, gripped around hers on the length of him, the other hand still holding tight on her hair. Pulling her closer, because, what the *hell*, he was gasping, aiming himself, straight toward her face. And now spraying himself out, spurts of his sticky white wetness clinging and catching all over Fasta's cheeks, her chin, her nose, her eyelashes. Even to the chain, still dangling out her mouth.

Henrik kept gasping, staring at her with hooded glittering eyes, while Fasta stared back, still too stunned to move, to think. Even when his fingers came up, smearing against the thick stickiness on her cheek, making even more of a mess.

"Fuck," he whispered. "Been wanting to see you like this for *years.*"

Fasta could only blink at him, her eyelashes already starting to stick together, and Henrik reached and pulled on the chain, tugging the stone out of her mouth. Replacing it now with his wet, sticky finger, sliding slick and bitter-tasting between her lips.

He didn't even have to tell her to suck it off, and he watched as she did it, still with that glinting, commanding look in his eyes. And then he wiped his finger in more of the mess, and again slid it between her lips. And then again, and again, as if he meant to feed her every last drop.

"Gods, you look good like this," he finally breathed. "Beautiful ice queen Fasta Valgeirr, on your knees, with a commoner's filthy fresh spunk sprayed all over your perfect face. You love lapping it up like this, don't you? Showing me just how greedy and spoiled-rotten you are?"

Gods curse him, because Fasta shuddered and groaned around his finger, and he laughed, low and approving. "Think you deserve a reward for this, buttercup," he murmured. "Touch yourself. Now."

Fasta couldn't help another groan, and her hand instantly darted downwards, grinding just where she wanted it. While Henrik's fingers kept doing this, kept wiping off her face, feeding himself to her slowly, intently, purposefully. And he was audacious, impossible, and she still couldn't believe that he'd done that, that he would dare to spray off on her face, or that it would feel so damned *incredible*—

She came with a shout, almost biting down around his finger, and Henrik laughed again, breathless and triumphant. While his other hand caught her chin, tilted it up, his eyes glittering on hers. As if drinking up the sight of her, the undeniable, visceral truth that she was his. And as if she was showing him, proving this to him, making him hers...

But then his eyes shifted, flattened, and Fasta fought back

her wince as he dropped his hands, and took a careful step backward. "You mind cleaning up the rest?" he asked, his voice light again, conversational. "Get dressed, too, will you?"

Right. Because they were keeping this separate. Because he wasn't her boyfriend. And Fasta made herself nod, though she couldn't quite meet his eyes, and the euphoria was plummeting again, twisting into something dark and cold, clenching deep and miserable in her stomach.

But cleaning up was an excuse to disappear into the water closet, at least, and if Henrik noticed how long Fasta spent in there, or that her eyes were red when she came out, he didn't comment. He was sitting at her desk, working with his rocks again, and he darted her a brief, searching glance before handing over his waterskin toward her.

"All good?" he asked, too casually, once Fasta had taken a long drink, and then curled up in bed, the blanket pulled halfway up over her face. But at least he was speaking to her, that was something, and Fasta choked back the words that so desperately wanted to come out.

Please, touch me, she wanted to say. *Please hold me. Please pretend it matters, that you care. Please promise you're not just checking off a list of ways you want to punish me, teach me a lesson, treat me like a spoiled-rotten brat.*

And Fasta wasn't supposed to lie, but maybe right now there was no other option. Just like there'd been no way to tell Henrik about Elgin's proposal, earlier today. Right?

So she took a breath, held his eyes. "Yes," she said, and it came out sounding almost like truth. "I'm fine."

25

That night, Fasta's dreams were dark, twisting, uncomfortable. Full of Henrik saying *no, I'm not your boyfriend, you spoiled-rotten little brat.* Henrik baring his teeth at Johan, Henrik shouting at Kjaran, Henrik burying Elgin under a crashing wall of stone. *My amethyst carving,* Elgin's echoing voice shouted, *you stole it, you fat jealous commoner...*

Fasta snapped awake into the early morning light, breathing hard, clutching her chest. Gods damn it, those thefts, looming like a cloud, a curse. Dumping all this extra pressure onto them, trapping them into this job at Elgin's, crushing them under accusations and assumptions and guilt.

Fasta's eyes flicked down to Henrik, lying sprawled and sleeping on her floor, his bulky arm thrown over his eyes. Truly, it was no wonder he'd been edgy lately, angry, frustrated with people like Johan, like Elgin, like... like *her.* All of them using him for their own ends, throwing around their wealth and power to make him perform. *I'm not your pet...*

Fasta swallowed, shook her head. She could still find a way to address this. She could focus on finding out who was trying to frame Henrik, and clear up this entire stupid mess for good. And maybe then…

She groped at the nightstand for some paper and pencil, and began making a comprehensive list of suspects. Johan remained at the top of the list, of course, and next was Konsta, and another one of Johan's friends, a fire-mage named Alik who was apparently friendly with Andreas' wealthy former patron. Merton would have also been near the top of the list, except for that pesky fact that he was also an earth-mage, and therefore wouldn't have been able to isolate those whale teeth, either.

"Who else have you crossed lately?" Fasta asked Henrik, once he'd yawned awake, and blinked up at her from the floor. "Or do you have any enemies I don't know about?"

Henrik shot her a disbelieving look, and scrubbed at his eyes with his palms. "That's not a *list*, is it?" he demanded, his voice thick with sleep. "Really, Fass? You're not even out of *bed* yet."

Fasta made a face at him, and in reply Henrik raised a hand, and snapped the pencil from her fingers into his own hand without even looking. "No work in bed, buttercup," he said. "New rule."

Fasta should have protested, told him he was supposed to be keeping it separate, or something—but she was too busy blushing to manage it, and Henrik lumbered to his feet, and rustled his big hand against her hair. "Actually," he added, "no work before breakfast. Aren't you supposed to be doing your deep thinking anyway? Settling down your brain, instead of riling it up?"

He meant her morning meditation, a practice that Fasta had entirely neglected these past few days, and she winced, earning a satisfied grunt from Henrik's throat. "Then that's what you do in the mornings from now on, buttercup," he said. "No exceptions, unless I say so."

Fasta's head ducked, her face flushing even hotter, and

Henrik gave another pleased-sounding grunt, and walked off to the water closet. Leaving her to sit there, blinking after him, but then she obediently crossed her legs, closed her eyes, and breathed. Tasting the rocks, the earth, the magic, Henrik, herself.

It did help, settling the dreams and the list and the accusations to a quieter part of her mind, to be evaluated and assessed later. But right now, Henrik was still here, and she could still try to enjoy this. She *would*.

It helped that Henrik grinned at her when he came out and found her meditating, and then kept his hand on her back as they went downstairs. And next they ate a hearty breakfast together, with Fasta once again cleaning her plate, thanks to a pointed glance from Henrik's glinting grey eyes. And then the walk to Elgin's passed easily too, with plenty of easy conversation between them—and even Elgin himself was all smiles when they arrived.

"There's only a few days left until my party, you two," he said cheerfully. "How's that ballroom shaping up? Are we still on schedule?"

They were, of course, and Fasta gave Elgin a quick overview of their current status, during which his eyes darted down to her pendant—thankfully still intact—and then back to her face. He looked almost amused, rather than affronted like the day before, and Fasta had an uneasy suspicion that she'd be seeing him again soon, no doubt the minute Henrik had gone off somewhere else.

"Can I come with you?" she asked Henrik, halfway through the morning, after he'd reluctantly muttered something about needing a leak. "To the outhouse?"

Henrik blinked at her, twice, and then barked out an uncertain, disbelieving laugh. "What, you want to watch?"

Fasta shrugged uncomfortably, and darted a furtive glance toward the door, where Elgin was liable to walk in as soon as

Henrik left—and the understanding instantly flicked across Henrik's eyes.

"Oh," he said, softer now. "Yeah. Sure. Thanks."

So Fasta accompanied him out toward Elgin's servant outhouse—which was perched rather precariously over a running stream, so it didn't stink, thank the gods. And while Fasta had fully intended to wait outside while Henrik did his business, he'd been eyeing her on the short walk there, his gaze growing saucier with every step. And once they reached the outhouse, he swung the door open, and ushered her inside.

"You wanted to come," he murmured at her, his hand lingering on her back as she stepped into the small wooden hut. "You get what you pay for, buttercup."

So Fasta watched, half-embarrassed, half-curious, while Henrik emptied himself into the latrine, his hands deft and familiar on his half-hard cock. And once he'd shaken himself off, put down the seat cover, and then sprawled down onto it, his cock was fully hard, and jutting straight out toward her.

"C'mon, buttercup," he said, raising his eyebrows, giving himself a slow stroke up with his hand. "You know you want to."

Fasta *did* want to, curse him, and she soon found herself in the humiliating, appalling position of kneeling in a filthy, rickety outhouse, with her head buried in Henrik's lap, his cock plunged deep down her throat. While his hands caressed her head, his low voice telling her what a good little rich girl she was, on her knees in a dirty outhouse, sucking off his filthy commoner dick.

It was impossibly arousing, impossibly thrilling, and when Henrik finally shot out down her throat, Fasta groaned aloud with it, fought to swallow all of it. Needed to prove herself to him, to please him—and when she finally lifted her head, her face entirely clean this time, he *did* look pleased, his eyes dazed and content.

"Such a good girl," he whispered, and he actually bent

down, and gave her a soft, lingering kiss on the mouth. Perhaps the warmest, loveliest kiss he'd ever given her, his tongue sliding languorous up against hers, maybe tasting himself all over it. "Keep it up," he said, once he'd pulled back, "and maybe I'll actually fuck you tonight."

It was a glorious, mouthwatering thought, and something he hadn't actually done—Fasta's thoughts flicked backwards— since that time in the forest, when Runar had berated him for being too rough afterwards. And for the first time, it occurred to her that maybe that had been intentional, on Henrik's part. That maybe he'd really meant it, when he'd said he couldn't stand to hurt her.

She became almost sure of it that night, when instead of actually putting his cock anywhere near her, Henrik demanded that she stretch herself out for her lord, give him a good show. And then—Fasta almost wished herself elsewhere—he pulled out nearly every one of her bedroom's hidden personal implements, and dropped them onto her bed. Bottles, polished stones, another slim feathered quill, even a long, thick piece of steel pipe.

"Found those, did you?" Fasta asked, with as much coolness as she could muster, as Henrik chuckled, and held up his hand—and into it snapped perhaps the most humiliating one of all. A thick, bulbous, round-headed steel hook, which had been mounted on the opposite wall at just the right height, ostensibly meant for holding up Fasta's coat.

"Found all of 'em, buttercup," he said, his voice warm. "Even this one, which I have to admit was a surprise, even for a confirmed greedy cockslut like you. Now which ones are you gonna use for me tonight?"

Fasta chose the least intimidating ones, obviously, and Henrik didn't protest, or push. Just watched, at first, and then joined in, moving them with and without touching them, until he and Fasta were both shaky and gasping, and he used his own hand to spray off, all over her breasts this time. And then he again stroked his hands into it afterwards, bringing them to Fasta's mouth. While she nodded and gasped and licked his slick fingers clean, drinking up the truth of him, still not quite believing this was real.

Afterwards he again gave her water, and stroked her hair, and helped her into her sleeping-shift. But then he kept his distance, sitting down at her desk to fiddle with his rocks, rather than holding Fasta, or praising her, or any of the other things she might have liked him to do. But she made herself shove down the longing, made herself think about something, anything else. Because she was still showing him, proving it. In control. Right?

But the unease kept gnawing, and once Fasta was settled in bed, she again yanked out the list of theft suspects she'd been working on that morning. Running her finger down the list, Johan, Konsta, Merton, maybe Henrik's previous bedpartners, maybe even Kjaran herself?

"I think we should meet with Kjaran again in the morning," she said, toward where Henrik was frowning at a hunk of sandstone. "See if she's actually done any more investigating into all this."

Henrik's stone abruptly flattened into a pile of sand, pooling off the side of Fasta's desk. "You go see her if you want," he replied, snapping the sand back onto the desk with a flick of his hand. "I'm not involving myself in any more of her shit. Also"—his head turned toward Fasta, his eyes narrowing—"is that your *list* again? Give it, Fass."

Fasta blinked, but obediently handed it over, to where Henrik balled it up, and shoved it into her desk drawer. "I told you, no work in bed," he said flatly. "Especially after I get you off like that. You're supposed to be lying there happy and blissed out, thinking about which one of *those*"—he jerked his head toward her pile of implements, still embarrassingly present on the floor beside her bed—"you're gonna use for me tomorrow."

Oh. The heat swarmed Fasta all at once, along with that tantalizing, wonderful promise of *tomorrow*—and suddenly it again seemed easy to clear her head of thefts and accusations and investigations. And instead to lie down, and close her eyes, and let sleep come.

The next morning Fasta did meet with Kjaran, but only after asking Thora to sit with Henrik in the dining hall while she was gone, again making sure that he was never left without an alibi. Thora tolerated the imposition with good grace— Fasta had never once seen her even slightly annoyed—while Henrik frowned toward Fasta, and picked at his half-full plate of food.

The meeting with Kjaran ended up being as useless as it was infuriating, as the extent of the directors' ongoing efforts was apparently filing a revised report with the Board. And when Fasta returned to the dining hall, she ignored Henrik's all-too-clear impatience, and instead turned her attention to Thora's face, her quiet blue eyes.

"Look, Thora," she said, "do you think your magic might be any help in sorting out these accusations against Henrik? Perhaps you could somehow project who the culprit might be?"

Henrik groaned aloud, but Fasta continued to ignore him, and waited as Thora glanced uneasily across the room, toward where Runar was casually chatting with none other than the pretty, vivacious Ilsa. "Um," she said. "Perhaps?"

"Good," Fasta said firmly, as she dropped herself next to Thora on the bench. "What do we do?"

It turned out that she only needed to sit there, fighting to ignore an increasingly aggravated-looking Henrik, while intently thinking about taking different courses of action. Accusing one suspect, tracking another, catching another. All while Thora's elegant hand remained firmly clamped to Fasta's arm, her eyes distant and glazed.

But once Fasta had gone through her list, and then some,

Thora pulled her hand away, and shook her head. "I'm sorry, Fasta," she said, with genuine regret in her eyes. "There's nothing conclusive that I can see right now, from any of that. I wish I could be more help, but—"

"But Thora has work to do," interrupted a voice behind them, and when Fasta glanced up it was Runar, frowning down at them with obvious disapproval, as he spread both of his hands rather possessively against Thora's slim shoulders. "And our work is a *much* more important use of her skills than whatever the hell this is. Don't you two have work to do too? Pleasing some rich noble to try to get *him* out of his... *difficulties*?"

He jerked his head toward Henrik, and then toward Johan and his buddies, who were eyeing them from across the room. In fact, there were multiple sets of eyes watching them, many with clear suspicion and perhaps even dislike, and Fasta hurriedly said farewell, and ushered a still-frowning Henrik out of the room.

Henrik's mood didn't improve throughout the morning, despite a variety of attempts at conversation on Fasta's part. An ill-advised mention of her ongoing investigation plans only seemed to make things worse, especially when she suggested— foolishly—that an interview with Johan might be worth pursuing next.

"You don't honestly *mean* that?" Henrik asked, glowering at her from behind a bucket of mortar, which was currently pouring itself behind their half-finished interior wall. "You want to go give that prick another chance to accuse me of petty theft, and try to get in your trousers? No, Fasta. Leave it *alone*."

The rational response would have been to argue, and tell Henrik that interviewing Johan—trying to either slip him up, or fish for more clues—was the next logical step, if they were really trying to sort this mess out. But instead, Fasta found herself considering Henrik, feeling that telltale taste in his magic, tilting toward misery, or maybe even shame—and then, with a slow, purposeful flick of her hand, she splashed some of the mortar out of the bucket, and onto his already-splattered tunic.

"Oh, *fine*, my lord," she said primly. "But I'll have you know, I am *not* happy about it."

She punctuated it by pouting, crossing her arms over her chest, and sticking her tongue out at him. All of which felt ridiculously juvenile, but she was rewarded first by the flash of astonishment through Henrik's magic, and then the twinge of amusement, and perhaps heat, that flicked across his grey eyes.

"Too bad, buttercup," he said, with more warmth than Fasta had yet heard from him today. "And if you're gonna keep talking back to me, I'm gonna have to deal with you later. Maybe even bend you over my knee, and teach you a lesson you won't soon forget."

Fasta betrayed a low, breathless groan, and Henrik's replying grin was dark, wicked, full of promise. Enough to ensure that Fasta's petty misbehaviour continued for the rest of the day, encompassing everything from sighs and eye-rolls, to outright disobedience of his perfectly reasonable work-related direction.

"You have been trying my patience all day, you spoiled-rotten *brat*," Henrik growled, once they were finally alone in Fasta's bedroom again, back at Coven Manor. "I think you're long overdue for a good hard spanking, don't you? Remind you who's boss around here?"

He'd latched the door behind them, his big body now prowling toward Fasta across the room, and she couldn't help a shaky gasp, despite her best attempts to roll her eyes at him. "A spanking from you won't affect me in the least, you great *beast*," she said. "I mean, you don't even have a *paddle*."

The amusement flared again across Henrik's eyes, and he deliberately raised his hand, and flew one of his larger stones across the room toward them. It was already thinning, length-ening, and by the time he'd snapped his fingers around the handle, it was indeed a large, flattened paddle, complete with a little hole in the end to hang it up with.

"Oh," Fasta said, eyeing it with genuine trepidation. "Oh, damn."

Henrik chuckled, low and triumphant, and firmly clapped the paddle against his other palm. "What was that again, buttercup?"

The heat flared behind Fasta's cheeks, and deep in her groin—and then it fired even hotter when Henrik strode to the bed and leisurely sat down on the edge of it, legs wide, eyes cool and insolent. "Now," he drawled, patting his knee, "come here."

Gods. Fasta stared at him, her body quivering all over, and Henrik raised his eyebrows, and smoothly flipped the paddle in his palm. "The longer you disobey me, Lady Valgeirr," he said, "the worse your punishment gets. Now come *here.*"

He accompanied the order with a magical tug on Fasta's pendant, and finally, somehow, she went. Lurching the rest of the way toward him, her body shaky and sparking, her eyes trapped on the sight of him, like this. Imperious, gorgeous, powerful, every single fantasy come to spectacular life, sitting here on her bed, with his legs spread, and a stone paddle in his big hand. Hers, yes, please, *hers...*

"Better," he purred, as his other hand reached over, and yanked out the drawstring of Fasta's trousers. Making them pool at her feet, leaving her whole lower half naked and exposed, and Henrik once again patted his knee, his eyes brazen, commanding. "Now come."

But Fasta couldn't seem to move, or breathe, and something flared, hard and hot, in Henrik's eyes. And suddenly the world was moving, she was moving, his strong capable hands yanking her body down and over his lap, oh gods.

It meant she was lying face-down on the bed over his muscled thighs, her bare arse up and exposed to the cool air, and Henrik's big warm hand was already there, palming against her arse-cheek, while the other hand gently shoved her still-clothed torso down toward the bed. "Arse up, legs spread, buttercup," he said. "You know the rule."

Oh, hell, and Fasta's face burned with shame as she obeyed. Shifting herself under his grip, spreading her knees wider on the bed, aiming her tailbone upwards, so every secret part of her was on display, opened wide for Henrik's watching eyes.

And yes, she could feel him watching, his gaze prickling against her exposed clenching wetness, and she jolted all over at the feel of his finger, trailing slow and torturous down her exposed crease, all the way, and then back up again.

"Are you ready for your spanking, Lady Valgeirr?" he murmured. "Are you ready for the punishment you deserve?"

Fasta gulped for air, her wet heat clenching against that still-trailing finger, and her desperate, craving body somehow bared itself even more, her legs spreading wider, her arse thrusting up against the warmth of that tantalizing finger.

"Yes, my lord," she whispered. "Please. I'm ready."

There was an instant's hanging, hungry silence—and then a shocking, wonderful jolt as the stone paddle slapped against her arse. Not painful, rather more careful and purposeful, but even so, Fasta cried out, her body scrabbling under Henrik's strong hand, still pressing her torso to the bed.

"How's that, Lady Valgeirr?" his husky voice said, and there was another purposeful slap of the paddle against her arse, sending streaks of pleasure down Fasta's legs, all up her spine, deep into her groin. "Is this gonna help you learn your lesson for me?"

Gods, this was good, unbelievably good, and Fasta gulped for more air, heard her mouth say words she hadn't at all intended. "No," she gasped, "I can barely *feel* it. Thought you were stronger than this."

There was a guttural-sounding groan above her, and then another strike of the paddle, harder this time. Still not bringing actual pain, but just more swirling pleasure, and Fasta's audacious arse gave a little wriggle, almost as if taunting him. "That's all?" she heard her appalling mouth say. "You can't do better than that, arsehole? I mean, *my lord*?"

The next strike was better, the pain soaring and firing, enough to bring another cry to Fasta's mouth, stealing her breath away. "How do you like *that*, then, you disobedient little brat?" came Henrik's ragged voice from above her. "Or do I have to give you more?"

"More," Fasta gasped, without thinking, and she felt a twitch of magic in the air—and then the sight, out the corner of her eye, of one of her most humiliating implements, rising up from where she'd stashed them under the bed. The thick, gleaming length of steel pipe.

"Will this help, Lady Valgeirr?" Henrik breathed, and Fasta jolted at the feel of the cold steel, already rubbing strong against her slick, spread-apart wetness. "Do you need to be fucked while I spank you?"

Fasta urgently nodded, her traitorous body already shoving back against that delving steel. Fighting to spread herself apart, to open enough to welcome it inside. And yes, yes, its smooth coldness kept sliding, pushing, harder and harder against her—then it was *there*, sinking inside her slow and sure, without even a touch of Henrik's hands.

The thrill the heat was everywhere, rising and rising, and the next strike of the paddle against Fasta's arse was stunningly intense, setting every nerve screaming, her body twitching and gripping around that invading steel pipe. Gaining even more strength from it, somehow, earth inside her and against her, both striking and giving, deep and powerful and whole.

"Better, Lady Valgeirr?" Henrik's gasping voice demanded above her, as that paddle struck again, and again. Leaving Fasta's arse decidedly tender now, hotter and hotter with each sting of stone, but it was still so good, impossibly good, better than anything ever, ever had been, chasing out every thought in her head but this—

And this, now, was the feel of Henrik's strong, capable hand, sliding around the length of pipe still jutting out of her, spreading her literally dripping wetness against his fingers. "Look at you, Lady Valgeirr," he murmured, every word a stroke of light, of heat, to Fasta's craving body. "Your disobedient arse bright red from my paddle, jammed full with a fucking *pipe*, and still dripping wet for more. Do you need to be spanked even harder, my high and mighty little cockslut? Do you need to feel the real strength of your lord?"

The words set Fasta's whole body convulsing, her head desperately nodding—and then she shouted, flailing, as that hard stone paddle slammed against her arse, again and again and again. Truly showing all of Henrik's strength, now, her entire body jerking with each strike, stretched and swollen and shrieking beneath him. Feeling both his hands on her now, one pressing her down, one fucking her with the steel, while the paddle kept striking on its own, sparking stars behind her eyes, every thought vanished, only earth and truth remaining, inside her against her all around, her body utterly prostrate for it, humbled and disciplined and laid bare, for him.

Her release came like a long-awaited avalanche, charging down a hillside, crashing against a cliff with furious force. Driving a frantic shout from her mouth, her body writhing and clenching over her lord's knee, her wetness dripping and spurting against his still-sliding fingers.

When it was done she was left trembling and wrung-out all over, her arse hot and smarting as her body collapsed down onto Henrik's lap. Feeling the distinct sensation of sticky wetness at his groin, too, and there was the heady, dizzying realization that he'd come from that too, without even once being touched.

"*Fuck*, Harry," Fasta breathed, and she wasn't supposed to be calling him that, but his hand between her legs was still warm, familiar, caressing, and she felt the steel pull out, and fall to the floor with a thunk. "*Gods*, that was good."

His laugh above her sounded choked, his slippery hand now sliding up to stroke gently against her stinging, smarting arse-cheeks. "You sure, Fass?" he said. "'Cause I sure as hell didn't go easy on you."

Fasta could only shudder in reply, the warmth radiating out from his still-stroking hand, and unfurling all over. "Gods, yes," she breathed. "You're *brilliant*, Harry."

Her throat choked off, betraying too much, and there was an instant's silence from Henrik, his chest rising and falling against her. "Well, *you're* a glutton for punishment," he said finally, his voice attempting to be casual, but still slightly wavering. "Still staggers me a bit. Prim and proper Lady Valgeirr, bent over a lowly commoner's knee with her arse up, begging for a paddling."

Fasta laughed, or perhaps groaned. "You're not a lowly commoner, Harry," she heard her shaky voice say. "You're— *you*."

Henrik's chest rose and fell again, his hand stiffening slightly against her skin, while something seemed to stiffen in his magic, too. "And you," he replied, his voice carefully neutral, "are exhausted. And you're gonna be sore, if you aren't already. You have some kinda salve we can put on this?"

Fasta's heart skipped as she nodded—what did he mean, *we*?—and then pointed a shaky finger toward one of the glass jars on her dressing table. And with an easy flick of his fingers, Henrik snapped the jar through the air, and into his hand.

"Let me know if this stings," he murmured, as he twisted the lid open, and the pungent smell of ointment filtered through the air. And then—Fasta closed her eyes, let out a shuddering exhale—his big hand gently settled against her arse, smearing the cool sticky salve against her hot smarting skin.

"Oh," Fasta gasped, with another helpless shudder, while Henrik briefly paused to scoop out more salve, and then kept stroking it against her. His touch gentle, almost reverent, in a bizarre, dizzying contrast to what he'd just done moments ago, and Fasta had to fight back the sudden urge to beg him to hold her, to kiss her, to do it all over again...

"Better?" he asked, far too soon, his voice again distant, professional. "Think you feel good enough to get dressed again?"

His hands were gently nudging at her now, wanting her to get up. Still wanting to keep it separate, even after something like that, and Fasta blinked back the rising wetness behind her eyes as she nodded. She'd agreed to this. That had been absolutely brilliant. It was *fine*.

"I think so," she croaked, as she staggered unsteadily to her feet. "Thanks."

Henrik was still sitting on the bed with the jar in his hand, and that telltale splotch on the front of his trousers. And his eyes on her were too aware, too regretful, and he took a heavy breath.

"My pleasure, Fass," he said, so quiet she barely heard it. "And you're brilliant too, you know."

It was enough to bring a genuine smile to Fasta's face as she went for the water closet, ignoring the still-smarting heat in her arse with every step. It was fine. Everything would be fine. She would show him. He would see.

26

Fasta awoke the next morning to a pleasantly sore arse, and to a sight she'd never properly seen before. Henrik, standing up with his back toward her, taking off his tunic.

Fasta blinked and shoved up in bed, greedily drinking up the view. Despite everything they'd done so far, Henrik's rules had still prevented her from seeing him undressed—and his shoulders were just as broad and powerful as she'd imagined, his arms and back corded with thick, rippling muscle. There was a smattering of freckles across the pale skin of his shoulders, and a trail of light brown hair at his lower back, leading downwards toward the hard curve of his arse, still hidden under his low-slung trousers.

The heat pooled to Fasta's groin, her breath heaving out—loud enough that Henrik's head jerked toward her, and he yanked on a new tunic with disappointing speed. Only then did he fully turn around, coming over to rustle a big hand in Fasta's hair.

"Sleep all right, buttercup?" he asked. "How's your arse?"

Fasta slightly winced as she shifted on it in bed, and Henrik clearly caught that, his brows furrowing. "Put some more salve on it, then," he said. "After your quiet time. Which I want you doing a bit longer this morning, yeah? Clear your head out."

Fasta ducked her head, and attempted to obey. But even though she focused on her meditation as intently as she could, afterwards the memories of the night before wouldn't seem to stop blazing behind her eyes. Henrik with that look on his face, that paddle in his hand. *Are you ready for the punishment you deserve?*

"What's with you today?" Henrik asked, halfway through the morning, and Fasta realized she'd once again stopped working, and instead was just staring at him again. At where his rolled-up sleeves bared his thick, powerful forearms, spattered all over with the white mortar he'd been slapping onto the stone. "We're not gonna finish this on time, if you keep disappearing on me like that."

He had a point, because Elgin's rapidly approaching party was now only a single day away. Servants had been milling in and out of the ballroom all morning, cleaning and setting up tables, while casting increasingly uneasy glances toward the still-unfinished wall, and the associated mess emanating out from it.

"Um," Fasta said, trying and failing to think up some excuse, and Henrik stepped closer, his eyes suddenly far too aware on hers.

"Truth, buttercup," he said, his sticky hand tipping up her chin. "You know the rule."

But that rule was still by far the hardest one to keep, and Fasta shot a furtive glance down toward Henrik's sweat-drenched tunic, clinging close to his broad chest. "J-just, uh, distracted," she stammered. "What with the view, and all."

Henrik's eyes flickered with amusement, his mouth twitching up. "Oh yeah?" he replied. "You been standing here just looking this whole time, winding yourself up, and making me do all the damn work?"

Fasta's heart skipped, even as her eyes darted down again,

lingering on Henrik's broad shoulders this time. While he chuckled, and gave a grave shake of his head. "Such a hopeless, spoiled little brat," he murmured. "This what you want, then?"

His other mortar-spattered hand dropped to his trousers, and then—Fasta gasped aloud—he pulled out his bare cock. It was already hard and flushed and swollen, and now streaked with white mortar, too.

"Um," Fasta said, helplessly, because yes, he was audacious, and gorgeous, and the *sight* of that, jutting out so incongruously between his mortar-spattered work clothes, was doing strange fluttery things to her head, her groin.

"Well?" Henrik said, his voice infuriatingly cool. "This what you need right now, Lady Valgeirr? Some filthy commoner dick?"

Fasta couldn't stop staring, could only spare a swift, surreptitious glance up toward his face. "Um, yes," she managed, finally. "But—the *servants*, Harry."

Henrik shot a disdainful glance around the room, which was admittedly empty at the moment. "What servants? I don't see any."

Fasta sputtered, her mouth opening and closing, because he knew perfectly well the servants had been in and out all morning. But he only stepped closer, nudging her back against the still-wet wall behind them.

"You know what, Lady Valgeirr," he said, taunting, as his sticky hand rose to the neck of Fasta's work tunic, tugging at the top button. "I think it's *you* who's distracting *me*."

Fasta gasped again, because the button had popped open, and Henrik pulled open the next button, and the next. Opening the tunic all the way to the waist, and though she had on a finer tunic beneath, it also had fine buttons, which Henrik pulled apart with a single jerk of his finger.

"Yeah," he said, husky, as he shoved both tunics aside, and used his sticky hands to pull both her breasts out into the room's open air. "Definitely you distracting me."

Fasta's breath heaved, making her mortar-streaked bare breasts swell and jiggle embarrassingly, but oh, Henrik liked that, he wanted that, his eyes lingering with open appreciation on the sight. And then, oh hell, his finger dipped into the mortar, and marked her pink nipple with sticky dripping white.

"The servants," Fasta gasped again, with a desperate glance toward the door, but Henrik gave a distracted wave of his still-dripping hand, and the door swung closed. Not quite all the way, not enough to alert the servants to any surreptitious goings-on, but enough that someone would have to walk in and around behind the door to see them.

"Now listen here, buttercup," Henrik murmured, his eyes flicking from Fasta's white-tipped breast to her face. "Not all of us are spoiled-rotten princesses who can stand around showing off all day. Some of us have a load of work to do before tomorrow, you understand?"

Fasta's breasts kept heaving, and Henrik flashed her a broad, dangerous smile. "So instead of distracting me," he continued, with a tweak at her white-streaked nipple, "you might as well make yourself useful. On your knees."

Fasta couldn't think, could only obey, sinking hard to her knees on the cold stone. Feeling Henrik's sticky hand brush brief and approving on her hair—and then it dropped to her mouth, pulling her bottom lip down. And then, in a single fluid movement, he slid that thick, mortar-streaked cock smooth and slick into her throat.

Fasta groaned around him, shocked and appallingly aroused, and her eyes snapped up to his face, following his rule. But he wasn't looking back, because—the heat fired hard, dazzling, between her legs—he was *working*. Picking up a rock, slamming it back into the wall, slapping mortar from the nearby bucket up onto it.

"What, princess?" he said, with a cool glance down toward her. "Told you, I have work to do."

Oh hell, he couldn't possibly be doing this, but he picked up another stone, thrust it into the wall. Thrusting his hips a little into Fasta's face, too, in a clear silent order, and she belatedly dragged in a breath, and started sucking.

Henrik's answering hiss was barely audible over the slam of another stone pounding into the wall, and then shaving off smooth. Shuddering a surge of magic into the air as he did it, and damn that felt good, and Fasta groaned again, gripped both hands to his still-clothed arse, pulled him deeper, sucked harder.

He didn't seem to notice this time, didn't spare her a single downward glance, and gods, it was breathtaking, he was breathtaking. All his strength and skill, the heft and pull of his magic, his focus—all of it on other things, more important things, because Fasta was just his servant, sucking him off, hungry and desperate, gouging his cock deep into her throat.

But even when she gagged on him, he just kept working, his eyes narrow and focused. His big hands slamming another rock into the wall, and then slapping more mortar against it, hard enough that Fasta felt it spatter against her cheek. And somehow it only spurred her on faster, sucking harder, keep serving her beautiful brilliant lord, making him *hers*—

"Don't swallow this time," came Henrik's low order, as another stone slammed into place—and then his huge hot cock juddered, pumping out, spraying into her mouth. Swarming her with thick sticky bitterness, but she couldn't swallow, she had to serve her lord, hold it there...

Henrik still wasn't looking at her, his eyes now flickering past the door, toward the hallway. And then, in a flurry of motion, he yanked himself out of her still-full mouth, tucked himself away, and spun Fasta bodily around, so she was facing the wall.

"Here," he said, shoving his bucket of mortar toward her. "Spit."

Fasta spat without thinking, lost in the sheer tilting relief at having obeyed him, pleased him, not wasting a drop. Until—her whole body froze—she heard the unmistakable sound of voices, coming toward the door.

She only barely managed to pull her tunic together in time, but Henrik was already working again, slamming another rock into place. While the servants spilled into the room—there had to be at least ten of them—all carrying armfuls of linens, and chattering together about the guest list.

Fasta's heart was furiously hammering, but Henrik looked entirely unaffected as he nudged the bucket of mortar toward her with a white-spattered boot. "Mix that up, will you?" he said, his voice perfectly calm and ordinary—while Fasta stared at him, and then down at the bucket. At what she'd just spat into it, pooling white and thick above the rest.

Henrik again didn't seem to notice, just slamming another rock into the wall, but then he paused long enough to raise an eyebrow at her. Saying, *are you really gonna defy me on this*, and of course Fasta wasn't, and with a wave of her shaky hand the mortar churned together, blending it all in.

"Thanks," Henrik said, with a saucy grin, and Fasta stared again as he raised a wet, viscous blob of mortar from the bucket, and slapped it to the wall. "Good work, buttercup. Bryant will appreciate this."

Gods, he was appalling, audacious, incorrigible. And if Fasta had been distracted that morning, she was almost useless throughout the afternoon, especially when Henrik began murmuring, at inopportune times, what a good girl she'd been, what she'd looked like sucking him, choking on him.

They worked late that night, and by the time they were back at Coven Manor Fasta was almost frantic, clinging to him, kicking off her clothes the instant her bedroom door had latched behind them. "Fuck me," she breathed, between kisses, into his willing mouth. "Please, Harry."

Henrik laughed, shoving her off onto the bed, though his hands kept touching her, gripping and stroking at her breasts, and then more gently over her still-sore arse-cheeks. "Not yet," he said, glancing purposely over his shoulder, toward that damned bulbous steel hook, mounted innocuously on Fasta's wall, still with her coat hanging on it. "You gotta show me all your secrets first. Remember?"

Fasta froze on the bed, and Henrik snapped the hook across the room into his fingers, sending the coat collapsing to the floor. "I've been very, *very* patient," he said, voice low, running his thumb over the hook's blunt steel end. "Wanna see what you look like, when you fuck this."

Even the thought of it was humiliating, and desperately thrilling, and Fasta's face burned as she watched Henrik float the hook back to the wall, clicking its fastening mechanism tightly into place. Leaving it just poised there, jutting out from the wall at precisely the right height, waiting.

Fasta couldn't breathe, couldn't look at Henrik, but she somehow walked her unsteady, tingling naked body over toward that wall. And then, gripping at the nearby dressing table for balance, she bent herself double, spread her legs, and impaled herself back, slow, onto that thick, jutting steel.

Henrik had come over to stand beside her, getting a better view, and gods knew what he saw as Fasta kept pushing back, further and further. Until that cold steel was all the way inside, her wet heated body pressed up firm and flush against the wall's cool plaster.

"Shame on you, Lady Valgeirr," Henrik murmured, as his warm hand stroked against her, sliding up and down the rest of her too-exposed crease. "Fucking yourself on a damned wall. Dangerous, is what it is, 'cause what if the wall fucks back?"

What? Fasta's eyes darted up, searching Henrik's face, but he held his gaze intent on the wall. And then—she gasped— the steel inside her began to shift, to change. Growing—wider. Not so much at the base, at the part of her against the wall— but *inside.*

"Oh," she gulped, helpless, breathless. "Harry."

Henrik instantly met her eyes, and the steel stilled inside her. "What?" he asked. "Does it hurt?"

Fasta shook her head, because no, it wasn't painful—just full, taut, and she cried out as she felt it shifting further, stretching wider. Forming itself into something that felt very like a round steel ball inside her, pushing her out on every side.

"Still good?" Henrik breathed. "You'll tell me if not, yeah? Or tap?"

Fasta urgently nodded, gasping for air. Feeling the hunger skitter and surge, needing her body suddenly to move, to thrust or rock or *something*—but then came the abrupt, shocking realization that she couldn't. The ball was far too big to pull out, and she was—*trapped*.

She let out a ragged moan—she was trapped to a wall with a steel ball, oh *hell*—and Henrik chuckled, his fingers still sliding soft, proprietary, against her. Even slipping down in between to feel it, where the still-slim part of the hard steel jutted inside.

"Such a spoiled, greedy little cockslut," Henrik's husky voice said, as those lingering fingers slid upwards again, until they nudged against that tight, stretched-out pucker of heat. "Stuck to a wall, and still not happy. You still need more, don't you?"

His fingers hesitated, because he was asking, making sure— and Fasta nodded again, and convulsed all over. The movement rocking her a little, giving her a vivid reminder of just how trapped she was, how big that steel ball was inside. And how it wasn't Henrik's finger nudging into her arse now, but instead— more cool hard steel. More of the hook, because he was changing the density, drawing out more from the wall just for this, oh fuck.

"There we go," he said, hoarse, as that steel settled closer, feeling like a slim, silken finger, easing its way inside. "That what you need, buttercup?"

Fasta nodded again, even as her fluttering eyes darted

toward the dressing table, and her tall jar of oil. And Henrik clearly followed that, reaching out a hand, snapping the jar into his fingers.

"Even better," he murmured, and she shivered at the feel of the cool oil drizzling onto her crease, slicking around the jutting steel. "Now you're gonna take even more for me, aren't you?"

Fasta moaned and nodded again, needing this, needing more. "Yes," she gasped. "So much more, Harry. My lord."

He softly laughed at that, as the cool steel kept sliding in further, harder, everywhere. "You are *shit* at that rule, buttercup," he whispered, but he almost sounded pleased. "Such a greedy, disobedient little brat."

His other hand lightly slapped at her still-tender arsecheek, and oh, that was good too, drawing another desperate moan from her mouth. While Henrik chuckled again, and gave her another little slap, harder this time.

"Look at you," he said, hoarse. "Prim and proper ice queen Lady Valgeirr, with her arse still bright red from a spanking, trapped on a wall, getting both holes used at once. Begging to have them stretched out even more."

Fasta's moan was more like a cry this time, her body spasming and convulsing, filled to the brink. With all that solid steel buried in both places at once, trapping her there, and then—she cried out again—they began *changing*. The ball deep inside her slimming, narrowing, while that slim tendril further up began... thickening. Widening. Stretching her, just like he'd said.

"Oh, fuck," she gasped, arching and gulping for breath, as the steel finger kept swelling, opening her around it, until the stretch felt almost unbearable, utterly overpowering—and then, oh, it softened again. Growing slimmer, easier, while the ball below swelled out again. Spreading and splitting her around it, until she was impossibly stuffed, shouting and incoherent, pleading for more.

Henrik was gasping too, now, his own cock visibly straining against his trousers. "Yeah, you love this, don't you?" he drawled, through dragging breaths, as he alternated the size again, and then again. "High and mighty Lady Valgeirr, getting fucked senseless by her bedroom wall. Even more shameful than being fucked by a filthy commoner, isn't it?"

Fasta gulped and heaved for air, and desperately blinked up toward his hooded, blown-out eyes. "W-would you?" she gasped. "P-please, Harry? I've shown you, I've been good, I—I need you. *Please.*"

Henrik's eyes squeezed shut, his body betraying a convulsive little quiver—but then he waved a hand toward the wall. And in a sudden movement, the steel broke fully free of the wall, releasing her—but it also meant it was still inside her, still filling her in both places, oh hell.

"We'll see how good you've been, Lady Valgeirr," Henrik rasped, as his firm hands gripped her hips, and turned her around away from him, resting both her arms against the dressing table. "How wide you've opened up for me."

Gods damn him, because it meant—he was looking. There. Seeing it, watching it, as both jutting steel lengths grew smaller and thinner again, and then began... sliding out. Moving with dizzying, agonizing slowness, bit by minuscule bit, and Fasta's jolting brain fought down the mortifying vision of what it must look like. Her body birthing both of them at once, feeding them out of her, until she could feel their weight tilting downwards—and with a slick, humiliating sound, they both wrenched free, and fell to the floor.

It left her empty, trembling, wide open and exposed, and this was even more humiliating, somehow. Especially since she could feel Henrik's eyes, looking, judging—and then came his slightly shaky fingers, trailing up her crease, slipping smoothly into both gaping holes with astonishing ease.

"Yeah, I suppose this is good enough," he breathed, as two fingers scissored in and out of her slack arse. "You ready to take a fat commoner dick up here, Lady Valgeirr? Ready to be defiled?"

Oh, hell, yes, and Fasta babbled and begged for it, glancing desperately over her shoulder to where Henrik had the oil in hand again, pouring it out onto his straining, weeping cock. And then he slicked himself all over, stroking up and down, before setting the oil aside, and easing himself forward. Toward her. Toward... *there.*

Fasta shouted at the touch of it, that thick blunt head settling hot against her gaping crease, and then—pushing. Slow, careful, gentle, but still so unthinkably huge, impossibly overwhelming. Opening her up even wider with every sliding press, stretching her as full as she could go, oh fuck—

"Good girl," Henrik gasped behind her, both hands gripped firm at her arse, holding her open and still for him. "Look at you, taking me so good like this. Opening your untouched, perfect little hole so wide for me. Making me your first."

Gods, yes, and Fasta writhed and arched for it, opening even wider, taking even more. "Yes," she croaked. "Yes, Harry, yours. My first. My everything. Mine. *Mine.*"

Henrik groaned too, making one last burning push—and then he was inside. Buried all the way, his hips jutted up hard against her, his invading pole swelling and spasming deep within, while she clutched back at it with all her strength. Fuck, it was good, it was perfect, she needed more—

He drew out just slightly, just enough to feel the drag and the loss—until he pushed back in again. Making both of them shout in unison, now, lost in the heat and craving and triumph. Whipping up wilder and hotter as he thrust in again, and again, and again, so good, so close, *hers*—

The release crashed through Fasta with stunning, staggering force, wrenching her tight around him, breaking her into light and ecstasy. And oh, hell, Henrik was breaking too, shouting as he bent double over her, his big arms cradling tight around her, his face buried in her neck. "Fuck," he moaned, as his body kicked and pulsed, ground as deep as he could go. "Oh, fuck, love, so good, so fucking *good*."

Fasta could only shudder and nod and arch closer, pressing up into his warmth, his pleasure, his praise, his safety. Into the way he was slightly shaking too, just as lost as she was, crushed beneath the pleasure and the relief.

She couldn't have said how long it was before he drew out, or where he'd found the rag he'd nudged up against her. Or even how they got to the bed afterwards, collapsing down together onto it—but it was so right, so good, so perfect. Henrik not pulling away this time, and instead lying here tangled up with her on the bed, still holding her with his safe strong arms.

"It was good, Harry?" Fasta's breathless voice asked, just needing to hear it again, to hear his praise, his voice. "You liked it?"

Henrik rumbled a low, shaky growl into her hair, and oh, that was a press of his warm lips against her sweaty forehead. "Fuck, yes, love," he replied, hoarse. "Loved being your first like that. You gorgeous, perfect girl."

He'd loved it. *You gorgeous, perfect girl.* Every word a bright, dizzying thrill, vibrating into Fasta's chest, shouting of relief and joy and triumph. She'd shown him, she'd proven it, she was his, he was hers. *Hers.*

And he was, he *was*. Because that was his warm callused hand, settling wide on her face, tilting it up—and then he kissed her. His lips so soft, so tender, treasuring her, adoring her. *Gorgeous*, he'd called her. *Perfect.*

Fasta shivered and moaned beneath the kiss, and then kissed him again, again, again. Drinking it up, drowning in it, lost in the certain undeniable truth of it.

She was smiling when he finally drew back again, and her own shaky hand found his face, kept it close. "Really?" she whispered, without even knowing it. "We're all settled, then? You're mine?"

But then—stillness. Blankness. Henrik's too-close eyes

blinking at her, once, twice—and in a sudden jerky movement, he shoved backwards. Yanking up his sagging trousers as he reeled to his feet, and staggered away from the bed.

Oh. Fasta's heart plummeted, her eyes suddenly prickling, and she shoved up too. Blinking toward where Henrik was turned away from her, breathing hard, dragging both hands down his face.

"What is it, Harry?" she asked, too thin. "What's wrong?"

But he didn't instantly reply, and maybe—maybe Fasta already knew. And the longer she stared at him, the deeper the certainty went, plunging into dread and misery and something almost like anger.

"I just need—" Henrik began, his voice muffled against his hands. "Just need—a minute. Straighten out—my head."

But Fasta's misery kept deepening, burning into the disappointment, the anger. "But you were—happy, just now," her voice said, almost plaintive. "You said—you wanted it. You wanted—*me.*"

A harsh sound scraped from Henrik's mouth, not quite a laugh. "Yeah," he said, still not looking at her. "And I've also told you, again and again, how I want to keep it separate. And I'm not your boyfriend. Remember?"

There was a brittle edge on his voice, echoed in his stiff back, his hunched shoulders. All of it rankling painfully through Fasta's gut, and she searched for an answer, for something to cling to. But her thoughts were juddering too hard, swaying too fast, and what was true, what could she say...

"But you're still—my best friend, Harry," she finally said. "And my partner. And I've been very generous to you, I've helped you so much, I've even been running this whole investigation to keep you from getting *fired*, and—"

But no, damn it, that was the wrong thing to say—and even as she belatedly clamped her mouth shut, Henrik jerked around to look at her, his eyes bright and incredulous.

"Really?" he said, too sharp. "I owe you for that now, too? I never asked you to do that, Fasta. *Never*."

Fasta's mouth opened and closed—no, but yes, he needed this job, he needed her... right? While Henrik shook his head, and barked a hard, grating laugh. "Look, if anything," he said, "I asked you *not* to do all that investigating, because I don't fucking care who did it. And you didn't listen to me, *again*."

Fasta stared at him, as her heartbeat skipped in her chest, and the room spun sideways. Wait. Henrik didn't—care? About—who was framing him? About his *job*?

"What do you mean, you don't—care?" she croaked, between heavy breaths. "Why? You don't want to keep your *job*?!"

Henrik grimaced, but the truth of it was too clear, glinting in his eyes. He didn't care. He didn't want to find out who'd framed him. He wanted to be *fired*?

"Look, maybe I *don't* care," he finally said, his voice thick. "Maybe I'm sick of being trapped here in this shitty little box, full of people who mock and disrespect me. And no, it doesn't matter which one of them is trying to get rid of me, because"—his shoulders heaved—"they all think the same fucking thing. Not one of them will be sad I'm gone. Except you."

The room was spinning faster, and Fasta rapidly shook her head. "But what about," she gasped, "your bills? Your family? How will you *live*? No other job will pay you nearly as well, you know it won't!"

Henrik grimaced again, and ran his hand through his hair. "Look, you paid me—a lot for this," he said, his voice stiff. "Two years of my usual salary. I used half of it for Andreas' tuition this year, and he only has one year left after this, so..."

His voice faded, his mouth twisting, and Fasta gaped at him, while shock roiled through her body. Henrik had asked for two years' tuition. For enough to cover all the rest of Andreas' schooling. As if... as if...

"You *planned* this?" she choked out. "You planned to get

everything you needed from me up front, so you could *leave* me?!"

Henrik's hand twitched out toward the bed, as though to touch her, but then it dropped again, closed into a fist. "I'm not *trying* to leave you, Fass," he said stiffly. "I'm being pushed out. And we both know they're gonna get their way sooner or later. That's just—how it is."

How it is. No, no, it wasn't, and Fasta whipped her head back and forth, fought down the lurking scream in her throat. "No," she choked. "They can't. And *you* can't. You're mine, Harry. *Mine.*"

The words echoed, dangled, and damn it, Fasta should not have said that again, should never have said it out loud. Should have known how Henrik would hear it, staring at her like that, his swallow audibly bobbing in his throat.

"No, Fasta," he said, his voice very steady. "We've talked about this, again and again. You *agreed* to this. I'm not your property, or your pet, or your boyfriend. And I'm sure as hell not gonna hang around here forever to be your cheap thrills on the side, while you live your real life with someone else!"

Fasta couldn't hide her flinch, and she tried to glare at him through the filmy wetness in her eyes. "You know that's not what I meant!" she countered, between gasping breaths. "I just thought maybe—we could keep doing this!"

But Henrik's eyes flashed, his jaw flexing in his cheek. "And I said, I don't *want* to keep doing this," he growled back. "And you didn't listen to me, again! Just like you can't even give me a few minutes when I need it! Can't you see"—he dragged in breath—"how you're acting just like every other rich entitled noble in this fucking place? Thinking you get to control my fate, my choices, my *life*? Just because you have more *coin*?!"

He almost spat the last word toward her, and his voice kept ringing, loud and furious through Fasta's ears. *Just like every other rich entitled noble. Thinking you get to control my fate...*

Henrik really... saw her like that. As an entitled spoiled

noble who only wanted to get her way. It hadn't always been a game, with all his comments calling her high-and-mighty Lady Valgeirr. A spoiled-rotten little brat.

That had been... *truth*.

And at the start of all this—how had Fasta forgotten?—Henrik had told her he didn't trust her. He'd made that very clear. And maybe... maybe that meant she shouldn't have trusted him, either.

And suddenly Fasta couldn't face this, couldn't bear it. Could only fix her eyes past him, hold her head high, try to keep the sobs pressed down tight into her throat.

"Then I beg your forgiveness for my selfish, spoiled weakness, Henrik," she said, as coolly as she could manage. "Take all the time you need to yourself. And"—she had to choke it out—"I wish you all the best in your future endeavours. Good night."

And with that, she grasped for her clothes, stalked for the water closet, and slammed the door shut behind her.

27

When Fasta came out of the water closet, Henrik was gone.

It was her fault, maybe, because she'd stayed in there for way too long, gulping back sobs, and hearing Henrik's words repeat over and over in her head. *I don't want to keep doing this. Just like every other rich entitled noble. Thinking you get to control my fate...*

Fasta should have gone out and tried to find him, especially since a single misstep was liable to get him fired. But then again, he *wanted* to be fired, he wanted to *leave* her—and finally Fasta ended up curled up and weeping in bed, trying and failing to sleep.

But maybe she'd gotten far too used to Henrik being there, because her sleep was fitful and broken, interrupted by tedious, circling dreams. And when morning finally came, Henrik still hadn't returned. She was still—alone.

She briefly considered staying in bed all day, blocking it all away—but Elgin's party was that evening, and the work on the ballroom still wasn't done. So she finally dragged herself out of bed and dressed, even as the misery kept shouting and rattling through her skull. Where had Henrik gone? Had he really left her, forever? He'd said he wanted to leave, right? He'd *planned* to leave her, all this time?

The sobs quivered again in Fasta's throat, and finally her shaky hands rose up, and carefully took off Henrik's pendant. Setting it there on the desk, amidst the rest of his rocks and stones. He didn't care. He thought she was a spoiled-rotten noble. He wanted to *leave*.

She kept her eyes intently averted from Henrik's latches as she left the room, and locked the door behind her. But when she passed by Henrik's own door in the corridor, she still couldn't help hesitating, giving a firm rap against it, while her heartbeat lurched into her throat.

But there was no answer, and she could feel that he wasn't there. Just like he wasn't downstairs, either, and she was unsurprised when she finally dragged herself into the dining hall, and confirmed it.

"Have you seen Henrik?" she asked a few people, servants and a group of air-mages eating, but they shook their heads, and one of the air-mages gave a grating laugh. "No, and good riddance," he replied. "Though I *would* like my shit back before he gets fired."

Fasta stared at him, and he at least looked away, the redness creeping up his neck—but he didn't speak again, and Fasta spun on her heel, and stalked away. To where she very nearly ran into Thora, who was carrying a half-full tray of food, and almost dropped it—but fortunately the tray was metal, and Fasta caught it, just in time.

"Thank you," Thora said, her too-perceptive eyes searching Fasta's face. "And hey, if you're looking for Henrik, Runar said he saw him go out last night."

Out. Maybe to the cottage then, or to an inn, or to one of those secret establishments he'd talked about, and Fasta couldn't think about that, not now. "Right," she dully replied. "Thanks."

Thora smiled again, but Fasta couldn't bear her sympathy,

either, and she staggered away, out toward the road to Elgin's. Walking faster than she meant, because maybe—maybe Henrik would be there. Maybe they could still talk, though what else was there to say? He wanted to leave. He didn't trust her. He thought she was a spoiled entitled noble. He always had.

But when Fasta arrived at Elgin's, she nearly sobbed again at the sight of the cavernous ballroom. The servants had clearly continued their preparations into the night, and it looked admittedly lovely, replete with tables and linens and banners and fresh-cut flowers—but there was nobody in it. No Henrik.

Maybe it meant they really were finished, then, and Fasta made herself go to the last little bit of wall they'd had left. It wasn't even that important, just tidying it all up once the mortar—*that* mortar—had dried. Making sure the repaired parts of the wall blended with the rest, that Elgin's partygoers wouldn't even notice a difference.

"You're here early," said a voice behind her, and Fasta wearily turned around, and found Elgin. He was dressed in what must have been his work clothes, with stone dust on his hands and in his mussed-up dark hair, and it distantly occurred to Fasta that he looked much better like this, rather than with the tailored outfits and shiny boots and perfectly slicked hair.

"Just wanting to finish in time for the party," Fasta replied, with a dismissive wave of her hand. But Elgin's eyes kept lingering on hers—which were no doubt red and swollen— and then dropped to where Henrik's pendant should have been. To where Henrik's pendant was now not.

Damn it, that had been a short-sighted decision on Fasta's part, because something shifted in Elgin's eyes, and he stepped closer. "Everything all right, Fasta?"

Fasta couldn't help a reflexive wince, but lifted her head. "Yes, fine."

Elgin didn't push it, thankfully, and leaned against the wall beside her, his dark eyes sober. "Come to my party tonight," he said, soft. "Take the rest of the day off, rest up, get ready. It'll make you feel better, I swear."

Fasta gulped down a breath, and shook her head. "I'd really rather not."

"Oh, come on," Elgin said lightly. "Relax and enjoy yourself for once. There'll be plenty of music and drinks and dancing, all your old friends, even your father. And the kitchen's putting on an amazing spread. It'll be fun."

Fasta didn't want to reply, or even think about it, and Elgin sighed, nudged her foot with his boot. "Look, you deserve it," he murmured. "You've worked wonders on this place these past few weeks. I'll even tell everybody what a spectacular job you did, and you'll be swimming in work for *months*."

The words pulled at something, something important, and Fasta narrowed her eyes, studying him. "Would you give Henrik credit, too?" she asked. "Give him a good reference, if people asked?"

Elgin pursed his lips, and shrugged. "Sure, why not. Any particular reason?"

Fasta's lip quivered, and she reached for the wall, spread her hand against the solid cool stone. "Because," she began, between shaky breaths, "he's planning to move on soon."

Elgin didn't look surprised, and if anything, there was more sympathy in his eyes than Fasta might have expected. "Sorry to hear that. I know you two had your"—he paused, waved vaguely, made a face—"thing."

Fasta's eyes wouldn't stop stinging, and she wiped at them, tried to smile. "Yes," she said. "We did."

Elgin twitched a crooked smile back, and his hand carefully reached out, clasped lightly against Fasta's arm. "Well, then you'll have to come tonight," he said firmly. "You'll have fun. I'll personally make sure of it. You'll see."

It was generous, and familiar, and kind, and Fasta so desperately wanted some kindness right now. And when Elgin held out his arms, and raised an eyebrow at her, Fasta sagged forward, her arms circling around his waist, while his tightened around her shoulders, and held her close against him.

He still smelled the same, scented with oil and perfumes, so unlike Henrik's delectable smell of earth and sweat and magic. But Elgin was here, and Henrik wasn't, and Fasta pathetically tried to squeeze what comfort she could from this, from the fact that *somebody* cared, even if she didn't quite care back.

But then she felt a strange little prickle, running up her spine. And when she twitched to look over Elgin's shoulder, she froze all over, because—damn it, of *course*—Henrik was there. Here. Standing in the doorway, staring at them, his hands in fists, his face shocked and pale.

Fasta's heartbeat stuttered, her breath choking in her throat, and she shoved Elgin away—but it was too late, because Henrik had already spun around, and stalked out. Leaving her, again, and Fasta blinked at Elgin, at the strange glint in his dark eyes. Why had she hugged him? Why had she let him hug her? She didn't even *like* Elgin, it was giving him entirely the wrong impression—

"Please—excuse me," she said to him, as smoothly as she could. "For a moment."

She didn't wait for his answer, just rushed off toward the door, toward where Henrik was already gone. But she could see him up ahead, striding swiftly down the drive, and she jogged after him, her breaths short and frantic.

"Harry!" she called. "Wait!"

But Henrik didn't wait, just kept walking, not looking back, not even acknowledging her. And after last night, after today, suddenly something crumpled in Fasta's thoughts, wrenching the misery into something not unlike rage.

"Stop ignoring me, Harry!" she shouted, even as she caught up to him, and grabbed his arm. Which he snatched away, but she grasped it again, and hurled herself in front of him. "I'm *trying* to talk to you!"

Henrik's eyes glittered, and his lip curled, his hands still in fists at his sides. "And I'm trying *not* to talk to you right now," he bit out. "I need to get away from you, and calm the fuck down, before I do something I'll regret."

But he couldn't leave again, he *couldn't*, and Fasta kept gripping his arm, too close in his space. "So that's it?" she demanded. "You just get to walk away from me, *again*, and I just have to stay behind and deal with it?"

"Yes, you do," Henrik shot back. "Because the *one time* I actually leave you—the *one fucking night*, after you all but *told* me to get the fuck out—the next morning here you are, without my pendant, and all over *him!*"

"I was *not* all over him!" Fasta countered, but Henrik was already walking away again, and she had to run to catch back up. "He saw I was upset, and he gave me a hug. That's *all!*"

They were already out of the gate, down onto the road, and Henrik shot her a look of purest contempt. "That was *not* fucking all," he growled. "I saw the whole thing, Fasta. He asked you to his shitty party, you essentially said yes, and then there you were, right where he fucking wanted you."

Gods *damn* it. Fasta flailed for breath, for focus, for words. "It was nothing," she insisted. "It was less than nothing, Harry."

"Bullshit," Henrik snarled, and he finally stopped walking, and rounded on her. "Stop *lying* to me, Fasta. That smug snake has been trying to slink into your bed since the first minute we *got* here, and you haven't done *squat* to get rid of him!"

That was so unbelievably unfair, and Fasta glared up at him, at his furious eyes. "I *have*," she shot back. "I told him flat out that I wasn't interested. *Twice.*"

"Oh yeah?" Henrik demanded. "'Cause I sure as hell haven't seen *anything* except you giving him all the deference and sucking up that he wants, 'Oh of course we'll fix that, of course we'll do that, that's our job, we're here to help', constant absolute *bullshit!*"

Fasta pulled herself up to her full height, and glowered down her nose at him. "Because I was trying to keep you *employed!*" she shouted. "Because I thought you actually *cared* about me!"

"Of *course* I care about you!" Henrik roared, and he looked ready to punch something, to explode something. "I care way too fucking much, I care enough that I will *murder* that bastard before I see him married to you!"

"Oh, you will not," Fasta snarled back, "because I already told you, just like I told him, I am *not* marrying him!"

Henrik's eyes shifted, changed, and his hand snapped up to grip Fasta's arm. "You told him you weren't marrying him," he repeated, hollow. "*When.*"

"When he asked me," Fasta replied coldly, raising her chin. "That day he invited me to lunch. And again the next morning."

Henrik stared at her, like she was something foreign, something he didn't understand—and then he pulled her sideways, off into the trees. And Fasta wasn't even fighting him, maybe because a twisted part of her knew this meant he really did care, he wasn't walking away—

"That bastard asked you to *marry* him," Henrik repeated, once they were well into the trees. "And you didn't *tell* me?!"

The fury flared harder in his face, in his eyes, but Fasta didn't care, wasn't afraid. "No, I didn't tell you," she snapped, "because I knew you'd fly into a jealous rage over it, just like you're doing now! I told him no, what the hell does it matter?"

"Because it fucking matters to *me!*" Henrik shot back. "Because you *promised* me you'd stop lying! You *promised* you'd stop protecting me! It was part of the fucking *deal*, Fasta!"

"Yes, well, you clearly don't care about the deal," Fasta snapped, "because you're *leaving* me!"

Henrik growled, the sound low and guttural in his throat, as his hand spasmed against her arm. "And you're not listening to me, *again!*" he hissed. "You don't always get to have your way, Fasta! You can't just get everything you want! At some point

you're gonna have to make some sacrifices, and face the consequences!"

The words struck at something, too deep and painful, but
Fasta shoved it away, gave a trilling little laugh, and shot him
her most disdainful look. "Oh, really?" she asked coldly. "Then
show me some consequences, Harry! If you really want to be in
control so much, then teach me. Punish me. I'm right here,
what the hell are you waiting for?"

There was an instant's hanging, twisting silence—and then
Henrik was half-shoving, half-dragging her to the nearest tree.
While a chunk of stone flew up through the air, clamping itself
hard against Fasta's wrists over her sleeves, then thrusting them
against the tree's rough trunk. Holding her there, trapping her
there with no escape, and yes, yes, that was exactly what she
wanted.

"Fine," Henrik's voice hissed behind her, even as his hand
swatted at her still-clothed, bent-over arse. "Now listen to me,
Fasta. You *told* me"—his hand swatted her again—"you wanted
this, over and over again. You *agreed* to my rules. You *promised*.
And this whole damned time, you've kept pushing me,
breaking my rules. You're still trying to control everything, and
get what you want from me!"

Fasta shook her head, and shoved back harder into those
tantalizing strikes of his hand. "And you haven't been breaking
the rules, either?!" she demanded, breathless, over her shoulder. "You *liked* me breaking your rules. You *liked* me calling you
Harry. You *are* jealous of Elgin, and don't try to deny it!"

Henrik's growl was even louder this time, and then she felt
him doing something behind her, maybe snapping something
off a tree. "I'm not trying to deny it," he hissed back. "I know
I've fucked it up, but I'm still trying to do my best for you, to
give you what you want from me—"

"Then do it, Harry!" Fasta demanded. "Be a better lord, and
teach me a damned lesson! Like I'm *paying* you to do!"

There was another instant's strange, hurtling silence,

followed by the sound of something hissing through air. And then, suddenly—pain. Not sharp, but still shocking, and when Fasta's head whipped around Henrik was holding a slim, supple switch in his hand. He was swatting her arse with a *switch*, oh *gods*, yes, please—

"Is this what you want, Fasta?" he demanded, as he snapped the switch again, as more flickering wonderful pain bloomed up in his wake. "This is better? Good enough for you?"

Fasta let out a helpless, hungry groan, even as her entire body shuddered, as her hands pulled at the too-strong stone. "Better," she gasped back, over her shoulder. "But still not good enough."

"Yeah, typical," Henrik snarled, and then snapped the switch again, as more flickering wonderful pain bloomed up in his wake. "Never satisfied, are you, Lady Valgeirr? Even now"— he paused, gasping, and the switch slapped again, harder this time—"when I'm giving you *exactly* what you want from me, again!"

Fasta was trembling all over now, and it wasn't at all from pain, but from the firing ravenous pleasure. And she just needed him to keep going, just needed him to take this where it led, please—

"And you know what else?" he asked, with another mouth-watering strike of the switch against her arse. "I could've been fucking around on you this whole time, but I *knew* you didn't like it, so I haven't so much as *looked* at anyone else since we started this! You, meanwhile"—the switch struck again, hungry stars spiralling everywhere—"get fucking *proposals*, let the *worst* arsehole of rich entitled arseholes hang all over you, let him make it all too clear that I'll never measure up. I'll *never* be good enough for you!"

I'll never be good enough for you. The world slowly stilled around Fasta, those words falling heavy into place, and behind her Henrik barked a sad, bitter laugh. "And he's *right*," he said, thin. "I'm not. Even if I hadn't fucked this up as much as I have.

You'll go to his party tonight, he'll ply you with drinks and music and everything you've ever said you liked, and you'll fall right into his arms, just like you're fucking supposed to. And I'll never see you *again*."

The hurt in his voice was real, palpable, echoed too strong in the swing of his hand, the sting of the wood striking Fasta's arse, again and again. All of it stuttering and surging together, driving through all her fraying control, and she bent forward more, exposed herself more, yanked desperately at those stone cuffs. Letting herself drop into the sensation, the pain, the freedom, the relief, the truth...

"*No*," she gasped at him. "I *won't*, Harry. I don't want Elgin. I told him. I don't want him, I don't want what he's offering. And he offered me wealth, and freedom, and continuing my work, and even a cottage in the woods, and I said *no!*"

She waited for another lash of the switch, but nothing came, and when she glanced over her shoulder Henrik was staring at her, his eyes unreadable, strange. "He offered you a cottage," he repeated, his voice blank. "In the woods."

Fasta gulped for air, and twitched a fervent nod. "Yes," she choked out. "And I said no. I want *our* cottage, Harry. I want what *you* can offer me. I want *you*."

There was more stillness behind her, and more truth kept bubbling up, breaking through all Fasta's defenses, all her control. "I want you, Harry," she repeated, and that was true, so true it hurt. "I still want you. I'd walk away from him a hundred times over, if I got to have you. I—I love you."

I love you.

There was a sudden, hurtling silence, stillness everywhere, and that truth kept echoing, sparking under Fasta's skin. "I love you, Harry," she said again, into the silence, her voice cracking. "I've loved you for years. Since the first day you walked onto my job site."

It kept ringing through the air like a song, like breaking dazzling light, and Fasta shivered all over, closed her eyes, sagged against the strength of the stone cuffs holding her up. She loved Henrik. She always had.

"Don't, Fasta," came Henrik's voice behind her, hushed. "You're lying again. You *have* to be lying."

She was lying—was she lying?—and Fasta took a breath, shook her head. "I'm not," she managed. "It's true, Harry. I love you. And I can't *stand* the thought of losing you."

A strangled sound choked through the air, and Fasta could feel Henrik backing away—and then suddenly the stone holding her wrists fell away too, crumbling toward the earth. And when Fasta staggered around to look, Henrik was staring at her with strange, unblinking eyes, his face haggard and pale, the switch falling from his slack hand toward the earth.

Fasta blinked back at him, rubbed at her wrist—and then gasped at the sudden, stinging pain. And a searching glance downwards found her sleeves bunched and torn ragged, her skin scratched and battered from where it had scraped against the tree's rough trunk.

She belatedly clutched at her sleeves, trying to pull them down so Henrik couldn't see—but his too-quick hand snatched around and grasped her forearm, holding it up to the light.

"Fuck," he whispered, and his face looked even more haggard than before, his eyes shadowy and appalled. "Fuck me," he said, and he backed away from her, stumbling over a root behind him. "Gods *curse* me, Fass. I'm sorry. I'm so, *so* sorry."

His eyes were still so dark and strange, pleading along with his voice, and Fasta took a breath, let it out. "I'm *fine*," she began, but Henrik cut her off with a strangled-sounding groan, a hard shake of his head.

"Don't," he said. "*Don't*. I won't believe you."

But he lurched forward again, his hands gentle on her face, though he wasn't meeting her eyes, was blinking at something beyond her. "You should have tapped," he said now, his voice just as strange as his eyes. "Or told me to stop. Why didn't you?"

Fasta put her hands to his, fought down her wince at the feel of the sleeve brushing at her sore skin. "I didn't want to," she said, and in reply Henrik made a harsh choking sound, deep in his throat. And too late Fasta realized that he was actually gulping back sobs, that water was brimming in his eyes, that she had never seen him look like this, so lost and empty and broken.

"Tell me you didn't mean it," he said, his too-bright eyes pleading on hers again, his hands spasming on her face. "Tell me you were lying."

But Fasta could only hold his eyes, and shake her head. She hadn't been lying. He'd broken through all her barriers, all her control, and found truth inside.

"I wasn't lying," she said, quiet but sure. "I love you, Harry."

Henrik flinched, his eyes briefly squeezing shut. "You can't," he said. "You *can't*, Fass."

She couldn't. And as Fasta stared at him, at the pain on his too-close face, it occurred to her that maybe—maybe he didn't feel the same way. Maybe he really didn't care.

And that had the awful ring of truth about it, didn't it? Because he was the one who'd wanted to leave. The one who'd left her last night. The one who'd told her he couldn't trust her. The one who'd just accused her of trying to control him, to get what she wanted from him...

Never satisfied, are you? Have it your way, you spoiled-rotten little brat. Again.

"I—I'm sorry," Fasta said, too quickly, almost tripping over the words. "If I'm controlling you again, trying to get what I want from you, like a rich noble, a spoiled brat. I don't mean to, I—"

She couldn't make sense of it, couldn't find a way through it, and Henrik flinched backwards, his hands abruptly dropping from her face. "No," he gulped. "Don't apologize, please. I just—"

He just what? But he didn't finish, rubbing a trembling

hand at his mouth. And his eyes kept blinking, his head shaking, and he'd backed away a little more. While Fasta's desperate confusion swung up higher, clenching tight and breathless around her chest.

"You what?" she asked, choked. "*Please*, Harry."

Henrik's throat bobbed, and he shook his head again. "I can't," he said, and his eyes were still so bright, so strange. "I can't, Fasta. This"—he waved at her, at them—"needs to end. For good."

What? Fasta's body recoiled, her breath rattling in her lungs. "It does?" she asked, and it came out high-pitched, plaintive. "You—you really still—want to leave? Now?"

Henrik squeezed his eyes shut, his shoulders heaving. "I—I need to, Fasta," he said, and his voice sounded flat, almost deadened. "I should never have touched you in anger like that. I just hurt you, *again*. And now you come out with—with saying you *love* me? I have ruined this beyond my worst *nightmares*, I've made you fucking *delusional*, and"—he drew in a ragged breath—"there's no *way* you mean any of it. No way we can get over this."

No, no, no, and Fasta just wanted to sob, to scream. "I *wanted* all this, Harry," she croaked. "And I *did* mean it. I'm not delusional. I love you. I did before all this, and I will after it's done. I *swear* to you, Harry."

But Henrik was still backing away, he was still leaving, oh gods, oh gods. "*No*," he said, strangled, pained. "No. This has to be over. Please, Fasta. Please don't fight me on this."

But Fasta wanted to fight him, needed to, and had already raised her chin, begun to protest—but suddenly he was here again, his hands clutching at her shoulders, and—Fasta blinked—his mouth was pressing against hers. Hard, desperate, despairing.

"No," he said again, once he'd pulled away, far too soon. "This is my last rule for you. You let this go. Let me go. It's done, Fass."

His voice cracked, but his eyes were determined, his mouth set. He really meant it, he did, and Fasta's face burned with misery, her eyes already streaking wetness down her cheeks, her head shaking so hard her braid swung out behind her.

"Please, Harry," she said. "Please, we can talk about this, we can work through this!"

But Henrik was backing away again, shaking his head. "You—go home, go see a healer, eat, get some rest," he croaked at her. "And I'll come get my stuff later. After we've both had some time. Yeah?"

There was no agreeing to this, none, but Henrik wasn't waiting for her to agree. Because he was already walking away, and when Fasta lurched to follow there was suddenly a single stone rising between them, hovering in front of her eyes.

"Stop," he said, cold now, over his shoulder. "That's an order, Fasta."

An order. Like she'd agreed to. Like she'd promised.

So this time, she obeyed. Standing there, unmoving, watching Henrik walk away from her. Losing him, letting him go, because he wasn't hers. He wasn't. He'd taught her that lesson now, she'd finally learned...

And once he'd vanished from view, she sank to the earth, buried her face in her hands, and sobbed.

28

The walk back to Coven Manor felt endless.

Maybe it was endless. Maybe Fasta was stuck, forever, in one laboured foot in front of the other. Trapped in trees, and more trees, and the occasional person, the occasional voice, that wasn't Henrik.

She had to look like a mess, she knew, and she vaguely considered stopping to clean up in Skent, maybe even visit that healer, like Henrik had told her. But that meant even more walking, and in the end she just kept going, though more than once she had to go off and hide in the trees. Cover her eyes, try to breathe, let the sobs wrench out of her throat until she could find enough strength to keep moving again.

"What the *hell*," Runar demanded, once Fasta had finally reached Coven Manor, and trudged up the endless stairs to his workroom. "Was this—was this *Hallen*?!"

Fasta opened her mouth to speak, but nothing came out, and Runar made a soothing, shushing noise that was entirely at odds with the look on his face. "You're all right now," he said, as his hand hovered over her head. "You're safe now."

But maybe whatever Runar was doing was already working,

because Fasta felt compelled to drag in a breath, try to clarify. "It's not," she began, "what it looks like."

Runar's eyes went even more forbidding, and he glanced purposely from Fasta's face, toward her wrists, and then down to her arse. "Oh, really?" he asked, his voice scathing. "Your stress hormones are *obscene* right now, your wrists are both sheared raw, and what did he hit you with, a tree branch?"

Fasta grimaced, tried to shove the too-strong memories back, away. "I wanted him to do it," she said. "I could have stopped it. In an instant."

Runar's hovering hands were moving downwards, following his eyes, and he gave a disbelieving shake of his head. "You think this is some kind of *game*, Fasta?" he demanded, as his hand circled gently against her forearm, raising it to show her scraped, reddened wrist. "Do you realize Hallen could be put into *chains* for doing this to you? And that some of these marks could have been *permanent*? I mean, not that you're pristine to begin with, not like Thora, but don't make it even *worse*, for fuck's sakes."

Fasta blinked, because what was that supposed to mean, Thora was pristine, and she wasn't?—but then she lifted her chin, even as she winced at the feel of Runar's fingers brushing light against her wrist. "It *is* a game, with Henrik," she insisted. "I like it. I *asked* for it. If you want the truth"—she grimaced, made herself say it—"I *paid* him to do this with me, so I could get what I wanted from him."

The truth of it twisted more stuttering misery into her gut, and she didn't miss the brief widening of Runar's eyes, the little curl of distaste on his lip. "Well, if that's really the case," he said flatly, "then why have you been bawling your eyes out for the last hour? Or more?"

His eyes narrowed on hers, as if daring her to argue, and Fasta distantly realized that he was doing his truth-seeing thing on her, too. Which meant she had to be honest, if she didn't want Runar dragging Henrik to the constables, but even the thought of it made her throat close off, the wetness welling up in her eyes.

"Harry's leaving," she managed, scrubbing at the tear that streaked down her cheek. "Here. And me. For good."

The comprehension flicked through Runar's eyes, and his hand moved to Fasta's other wrist. "Surely you can't be surprised," he said, though his voice was gentler than before. "If he was smart, he'd have taken off weeks ago. The rumours about him have been vicious."

Fasta took a gulping breath, scrubbed again at her wet cheek. "He didn't steal anything. He wouldn't."

Runar shrugged, his hand still lightly touching Fasta's wrist. "It doesn't matter," he said. "What matters is that it looks like he did. And no one's been able to prove otherwise."

"Yes, because there's been no actual investigation," Fasta countered. "They haven't even *tried*."

"Of course they haven't," Runar replied, without looking up from whatever he was doing. "You think they want to risk accusing Falk of lying? With his uncle being who he is?"

Despite everything, the injustice of that still rankled, and Fasta frowned as Runar sank to kneel beside her, his hand hovering over where the switch had struck her hip. "But Johan can't even be mistaken?" she asked. "Not even when it's obvious that Harry's being *framed*?"

Runar shrugged again, gave her a cool glance under dark eyelashes. "Maybe if you could prove who it was, and exactly how they did it, and how Falk was fooled," he said. "Can you?"

Fasta grimaced. "No," she said, with a sigh. "And I've tried, I've looked into it, as much as I can. It doesn't make *sense*. There's no *reason* for anyone here to try to get rid of Henrik."

Runar made a little spinning motion with his finger, and Fasta obeyed, turning so her back was toward him. "Sure there is," came his voice from behind her. "Hallen's not from the right kind of background, he was never professionally trained, he's taking up a valuable position here, and there have always been whispers that he's only got the job because of you. Also, he can be kind of an arsehole."

Fasta shot a frown down over her shoulder, toward where Runar's hand was, embarrassingly, hovering over her still-tender arse-cheek. "Henrik's not an arsehole," she snapped. "Everyone likes him. He's *much* more popular than I've ever been."

Runar snorted, and rolled his eyes. "Yes, because you don't have to care," he replied. "He does. It still doesn't mean he's ever belonged here. Or that any of these people really give a damn about keeping him here."

The words echoed too closely what Henrik had said, and Fasta's tired thoughts were floundering, losing her point. "But," she said, "the girls care, at least, they'd *have* to, he's been with so many of them!"

Runar huffed a too-loud sigh, like Fasta was being deliberately obtuse. "Yes, because he's decent-looking, and he has a big dick, and he's got the background he does, which means he's *safe*," he said flatly. "Again, it doesn't mean they care about him beyond getting what they can from him. Especially when he consistently treats them after like he does."

Fasta still wasn't following, and frowned again over her shoulder. "Like how?"

Runar huffed a disbelieving laugh, and finally stood up again, and went over to his washbasin in the corner. "You're really asking me this?" he asked, as he started scrubbing his hands with soap. "Hallen pays attention to a girl only long enough to get up her skirts. After that, she might as well not exist, because he's way too busy slinking around after *you*."

Oh. Fasta blinked at Runar's back, and then down at her wrists, which looked perfect, smooth, with no sign of injury whatsoever. "But Henrik doesn't really—*want* me," she said, quiet, and there was that wetness again, lurking behind her eyes. "He—he's been planning to *leave*, all this time."

Runar scoffed, barely audible over the splash of water on

his hands. "You can't honestly be this dense," he said, and then shot an assessing look over his shoulder, his eyes narrowing at where she was rubbing absently at her healed skin. "Actually, never mind. Clearly you can."

Maybe Fasta should have been insulted, but suddenly she was just too tired, and Runar wiped off his hands on a nearby rag, and turned to face her. "Hallen worships the ground you walk on," he said. "Or at least, he used to. Before he started beating you with *trees*."

Fasta started to protest, but Runar's eyes were forbidding again, and he waved her away. "Go away and get some sleep, for gods' sakes," he said. "And try considering the fact that Hallen leaving is a good thing. Probably the best possible outcome, under the circumstances."

The best possible outcome. The wetness in Fasta's eyes was already welling up again, and she turned toward the door—but then paused, her hand gripping too tight on the latch. "Thank you, Runar," she said, and she meant it. "You've been so kind. If there's ever any way I can repay you—"

Runar snorted behind her, and she could almost picture him rolling his eyes at her back. "If you really want to repay me," his voice said. "You can forget about Hallen, and move on with your life."

Forget about Hallen. Move on with your life. And it probably made sense, Fasta thought dully, as she shut the door behind her, and trudged up the stairs toward her bedroom. It would be the reasonable thing to do. The best thing. What Henrik had wanted her to do.

But her bedroom door had Henrik's latches. And she stared at them, blinking hard, before she undid them, and stepped inside. And found herself faced with a room full of Henrik's rocks, Henrik's books, Henrik's smell, Henrik's memories.

It was all just—there, like he'd come back at any moment. Like he'd pick up a rock, break it apart, put it together again.

Toss it to Fasta, maybe, or hold it out to her, say, *What do you think?*

The pendant was still there too, right where Fasta had left it, and she swallowed as she picked it up, traced her finger against the intricate chain, the smooth, perfect cut of the stone. *You could keep it,* he'd said that day, and Fasta could still remember how he'd looked as he'd said that. Like he hadn't been sure she would want to.

The water was welling up in her eyes again, and Fasta didn't wipe it away this time. Just let it fall, even as she lifted the pendant, dropped it again over her head, felt it settle heavy and familiar around her neck.

Henrik had made it for her. And her fingers closed around the smooth stone, stroking against it, as the tears dripped off her chin. He'd made it with his hands, his magic, his heart.

Of course I care, he'd said. *I care way too fucking much.*

The sobs lurched out of Fasta's throat, too strong, and she grasped for the nearest rock, held it as she wept. As she felt the traces of Henrik in it, on it, it had been his, touched by his hands, brought here, left here...

Her hands groped for the next rock, and the next one, not even looking through the water in her eyes. Just feeling her way, one by one, almost like she could still feel him, like he was still here. Rough, hard, strong on the outside, but inside something else, something solid and generous and kind.

I'm never gonna get over you, he'd told her. *I finally get to have you. And it's so much fucking better than I ever even dreamed it could be.*

There were more rocks, more stones, and Fasta needed to touch them all, every one. Needed to know he'd been here, needed to feel his strength, his truth, his care. And Fasta clung to the next stone, searched for the next—

But it was a box. A wooden box, carved by Henrik, and it had been buried under the haphazard pile of his clothes in the corner, and why had she never seen it before? And Fasta's hands slid over it, memorizing it, because it was just like Henrik's workmanship, simple, strong, clean, effective, and these were Henrik's latches, even more intricate than the ones he usually made.

But Fasta knew Henrik, *knew* his magic, and her fumbling hands unthinkingly opened the latches, one by one. Just needed to prove it, to feel it, to feel him...

The box's lid popped open on a little spring, held up with delicate steel arms, and Fasta fingered gently at them, smiled at them through the water in her eyes. And then she wiped at the water, because beyond the workmanship, there were—*things* in this box.

She should have closed it. Should have realized, then, that Henrik hadn't wanted her to know about this, and he would have had his reasons why. But these were Henrik's things, tasting so strong of him, like he'd touched them often, and Fasta's only thought was to touch them too, to feel, to *know*.

On top were several folded sheets of paper, and Fasta pulled one out, carefully opened it. And twitched another watery smile, because it was a pencil-drawn portrait, one she actually had seen, ages ago. Of a thinner, younger-looking Henrik, curls askew on his head, with his arm slung around the shoulder of a slim, grave-looking boy with dark hair, and a distinct resemblance around the mouth. It was his brother Andreas, and standing in front of them were Hilda and Elsie and Chloe, all short and adorable with their mussed-up blonde ringlets.

Henrik had hired an artist to do this, Fasta remembered, with the first full pay he'd earned from her, before he'd left home to travel and work with her. And she could still remember how he'd shown this to her, shy and a little proud, and how her stomach had flipped, almost like it was doing now.

Are you sure you're comfortable with leaving them? she'd

asked, and the look Henrik had given her had been serious, so intense she'd had to look away.

Yeah, I am, he'd said. *This is the opportunity of a lifetime, Lady Valgeirr, working with you.*

Fasta wiped again at her eyes, and pulled out the next paper, opened it. And this—she blinked—this was a clipping from one of the city papers. And it was a portrait of—them. Her and Henrik, together.

Earth-mage duo saves village from landslide, the headline shouted, but the rest of the article was missing, because Henrik had just kept the drawing. A drawing that showed Fasta standing there, straight and serious, her blonde braid trailing over her shoulder, while beside her Henrik was grinning, and pulling her toward him, his arm close and familiar around her waist.

Fasta couldn't remember ever seeing the drawing before— though she remembered the landslide, of course, a year or two before—but now she couldn't seem to stop staring at it, at Henrik. The relaxed set of his shoulders, the telltale grin, the crinkling at the corners of his eyes. And that familiar big hand, just visible on the other side of Fasta's waist, with its fingers spread wide, maybe even possessive.

It was almost painful to look at, and Fasta abruptly folded it away, pulled out the next. And this one was familiar, suddenly, even by the touch of its thick velvety paper, and the memory was here, sudden, too close.

Wait, you're burning that? Henrik had asked, years ago, frowning down at where Fasta had tossed a pile of papers onto the fire. They'd been travelling, and she had brought some old papers in her bag to use as kindling, and Henrik had plucked this portrait out of the flames, and stared at it. *It's you, Fass.*

Fasta had shrugged, not meeting his eyes, because it was a portrait her father had commissioned, on her nineteenth birthday. And at his insistence she'd suited up properly, with the dress, the diamond earrings, the intricately plaited hair, and the portrait proclaimed her every bit the titled heiress, down to the distant coolness in her eyes.

I only did it for my father, Fasta had told Henrik, bitterly. *And immediately afterwards, he told me that if I quit construction for good, he would double my dowry. As if he was doing me a favour.*

Henrik hadn't spoken, but he'd slid nearer to her on the log they'd been sitting on, and settled his heavy arm over her shoulder. Pulling her close, into the warm solid safety of him, and Fasta could still remember how grateful she'd been to him for that. For not defending her father, or asking about the amount of said dowry, like every other person of her acquaintance would have done.

Still seems a shame to burn it, though, he'd finally murmured, once the fire was crackling bright and merry in the dark. *Especially when the artist actually did a decent likeness of you.*

She could still remember how Henrik had looked when he'd said that, his eyes carefully on the fire, and she hadn't argued when he'd slid the portrait into his nearby pack. Clearly intending to keep it, and somehow he had, for all these years.

Fasta's eyes were watering again, her breath coming out hitched and shallow, and she made to put the portrait back in—but then she hesitated, blinking down at the remainder of the box's contents. It was all just—stones. Light, dark, rough, smooth stones, in a variety of colours and shapes.

And Fasta knew how Henrik felt about stones, but it was odd that he'd choose these ones to lock away, and none of the rest that were lying about her room, or his. Was there something special about these ones? Memories she wasn't aware of?

She trailed her fingers through them, frowning, because they didn't even really feel like Henrik. Not the way the rest of them did, the way they should—

But then her finger brushed up against something else, underneath. Something that felt markedly, fundamentally different from the rest. Not a stone at all, she realized, as her fingers closed around it, drew it out. Because it was—

It was a *ring.*

Fasta's breath caught, held, and she held the ring up to the light—and then went stock-still all over. Because it wasn't just any ring. It was a ring made of beaten, intricately twisted silver, and set with a distinctive grey-and-white streaked stone.

It was a ring made to match Fasta's pendant.

It had the exact same stone, polished silken and smooth. The same silver. Even the same kind of intricate twisting the pendant's silver had, but smaller, more delicate, even more beautiful.

How had Henrik done this? When had he done this? *Why?*

Fasta's heart was pounding, so loud it echoed through the room, and her shaky hand took the ring, turned it over—and then she slid it slowly, carefully, onto the ring finger of her left hand. Where it settled perfectly, fitting heavy and powerful against her skin.

It was hers.

29

Fasta didn't know how long she sat there, staring at that ring, listening to her heart try to pound out of her chest.

I want my own family someday, Henrik had said. *My own wife. A partner who's just mine.*

The words kept repeating, again and again, and Fasta couldn't stop staring, couldn't stop thinking. Because Henrik had kept saying that could never be her. And that he hadn't wanted to be her servant, her boyfriend, her pet...

But now here were all the other things he'd said, tumbling harsh and powerful through Fasta's head. *This is it, for us. I'm a poor lowborn commoner, you're heiress Lady Valgeirr. You'll fall right into his arms, just like you're fucking supposed to, and I'll never see you again...*

I'll never measure up. I'll never be good enough for you.

Gods *damn* it, and Fasta rubbed at her face, her eyes. Feeling the weight of that ring on her finger, and she closed her other hand around it, squeezed too tight. Could feel, could almost see, when he'd made it, quietly, carefully, here, glancing at her while she'd slept—

I'll never be good enough for you.

Fasta's breaths were coming shallow now, her heartbeat thumping faster, the grief deepening in her gut. Because that had been the real issue all along, hadn't it? The quiet, reeking truth, seething beneath all this mess, all this time. Fasta had paid Henrik to be intimate with her, because he hadn't wanted to risk it otherwise. *There's no future in it*, he'd told her, way back at the start of this. *It would only last until you got sick of me, and found some rich lord to marry.*

And Fasta had never... argued that. Had never fully... faced that. Right? Henrik had kept saying it, again and again, and in return, Fasta hadn't been willing to give him anything beyond just keeping on, just as they were. Trapping him where she'd wanted him.

But—why? Because it really was true, what she'd told Henrik back there, in the woods. Wasn't it? *I want our cottage. I want what you can offer me. I want you. I love you.*

But already the familiar panic was scraping up too, clawing at Fasta's throat, and swarming her with visions of—her father, *No, Fasta, you can't do that. No, you can't eat that. You can't wear that. You can't plant a garden. You can't change your bedroom like this. You can't build your own house. No, no, no...*

Fasta shook her head, hauling in deep dragging breaths, counting rapidly to ten. No. She'd rejected that life. She'd rejected her father, rejected Elgin, rejected polite society's standards and expectations for her. And instead, she'd clung to her earth-magic, to this prestigious position at Coven Manor, to Henrik. She'd carved out her own way. She'd taken charge of her own life. She'd found control. Control. *Control.*

It swayed and crumpled in her gut, spasmed in her chest. Because yes, being in control had helped her. It had saved her. It had given her everything she'd wanted...

Until it hadn't. Until Henrik, until those thefts. But Fasta had kept clinging to that control, craving it, even as she'd so desperately wanted to give it back. Even if there'd been no pleasure or relief in the world like Henrik taking charge of her, taking that control from her, making her kneel and beg and scream.

And Henrik—Henrik had seen that. He'd known. *You're still trying to control everything. You don't always get to have your way. You're gonna have to make some sacrifices, and face the consequences.*

Fasta swallowed, rubbed at her eyes, because until all this, she hadn't really needed to make any sacrifices, had she? As it stood, she would still be welcomed back to her old life, if she chose. She could still fit in again. She would still have her father, her wealth, her inheritance. Everything could still be fine.

But if she were to go ahead with this? With... *marrying* someone like Henrik? The backlash would be instant and permanent. There would be manipulations and entreaties and probably threats. It would mean saying goodbye to Fasta's old life, and her inheritance, and probably even her father, forever.

But... it wasn't like it was illegal, either. No, marrying a commoner wasn't *done*, but neither was working a day job, or throwing over all your old friends, or paying your colleague to be your lord. Right?

Fasta's heart was pounding still louder, thundering through her chest and her head, because suddenly she could see it, could almost taste the tilting, mouthwatering possibility of it. Waking up beside Henrik every morning. Working with Henrik every day. Living together with Henrik in a house they'd made...

Fasta's head snapped up, suddenly, her heartbeat racing, because—Henrik. The cottage. Henrik would have gone to the cottage. Right?

And suddenly she desperately needed to find him, to see him again. To face him, and be honest with him. To ask, and to listen to his answer. His truth.

She grabbed for her pack, hurling things into it, and though the familiar panic kept whispering—*your inheritance, your reputation, your father*—she didn't listen, didn't hesitate. Until, suddenly, there was the strongest thought of all, and it was Henrik himself, looking at her like everything hurt.

Please don't fight me on this, he'd said. *This is my last rule for you. You let this go. Let me go. That's an order.*

But then Fasta blinked down at that ring again, still there on her left hand. Still whispering of Henrik, and the sacrifice he'd maybe wanted her to make. And gods knew she'd broken so many of his rules already, hadn't she? And half the time he'd wanted her to? What did one more matter?

And with a choked little laugh, Fasta threw the pack on her back, and yanked open the door.

30

Fasta had never made the trip to the cottage in so little time.

It was like she was being driven, compelled, perhaps by that strange new weight on her finger, so close, so strong. She needed to see Henrik. Needed to talk to him. Needed to tell him the truth.

Because she hadn't told him the truth, all this time. She hadn't told him he mattered. She hadn't told him he was good enough. She'd been so afraid, so desperate to keep that control over him. To keep him where she'd wanted him. To make him *hers*, when it was still his own choice to make.

And though giving him that choice was still an alarming, unsettling prospect, swirling up that familiar scraping panic, it was still a relief, somehow, too. And Fasta let out a heavy breath as she jogged up the last hill, and the cottage's gabled roof came into view through the trees.

She ran down the hill toward it, her heartbeat thundering in her chest—and it wasn't until she reached the door that she hesitated, and the world spun to a stop. Because—she put her hand flat to the door's familiar wood exterior—Henrik wasn't—here?

The hopefulness plummeted in her gut, and she blinked at the closed door, spread her fingers wider against it. No, Henrik wasn't here. He hadn't been here. And what did that mean? Where had he gone?

She thrust her other hand to the door, pressing harder, like maybe that would make him appear—but no. Nothing. No Henrik. And the sobs were suddenly too close, lurking in her throat, because this was where he should go, where else would he go...

Back home, maybe. Or to Andreas. Or to an inn, any inn, anyplace. He could have gone straight to the bank, he could have taken that insurance she'd set aside, he could have done anything.

But—without his clothes? His things? He surely wouldn't go far without his things?

But no, no, because despite Henrik's attachments to his rocks, to this cottage, he had never actually needed much, had always been able to get by on almost nothing. Food, a waterskin, a bit of coin, the clothes on his back. And he'd probably even had his pack with him when they'd fought, Fasta couldn't even remember, *damn* it—

She sagged against the closed door, rubbing her face, trying to think. She could search. Could try to find him. But what if he didn't want to be found? There were so many places, maybe she would never find him, maybe it was just too late.

Maybe he had already made his choice, back there in the woods. Maybe it really was over, forever.

The sobs did escape then, desperate and wrenching, swallowing her in their strength. Henrik was gone. And how the hell was she supposed to do this, how was she supposed to survive it, when she was alone, and the one person she loved more than anyone else in the world was gone.

She spent too long standing there, sobbing, just leaning against that closed door. Feeling the traces of Henrik in it, in the smooth line of the boards, the clever intricate latches. So careful and perfect, because Henrik protected his house. Henrik was adamant, stubborn, ridiculously possessive about the things he did care about.

Of course I care about you. I care way too fucking much.

The memory made Fasta stand a little straighter, blinking back the wetness in her eyes, and she swallowed hard, pulled in a breath. Remembering, now, all the other times they'd argued, and how—she swallowed again—he'd always come back. Because he did still care. He did.

It didn't line up, it wasn't quite right, and—Fasta blinked again, turned around to face the door—the latches weren't quite right, either. Or were they? The top two were fine, and so was the next, but then, this one—

She held her hand to it, frowned at it. It was almost right, almost fully closed, almost the way Henrik had left it. But not quite.

Fasta's heart began pounding again, and she swiftly, shakily undid the latches, top to bottom. Leaving that one for last, feeling again as she opened it how it wasn't quite right, had never felt that way before. Felt... wrong.

She stepped inside the cottage carefully, her steps quiet on the stone floor, but her first glance around showed nothing amiss. The room looked just the way they'd left it last time, and though the familiar, beautiful sight of it should have soothed Fasta's racing thoughts, the feeling of wrongness felt even stronger, stranger.

Nothing was out of place in the main room that she could see, or the sitting area. Her own room hadn't changed either, and she couldn't help a longing look at her half-finished mosaic before shutting the door again behind her. And then she frowned across toward Henrik's door, on the opposite side.

She'd never gone into his room without him before—it was his space, and she tried to respect that—but she slowly went over, put a hand to the door. The door that should have been latched too, but—wasn't.

It opened smoothly, silently—more of Henrik's excellent workmanship—and Fasta stepped inside. And then she instantly froze, felt the hair on the back of her neck stand up, because it was wrong. All wrong.

The slitted windows were still there, the brass bed solid and huge off to the side, the rocks scattered all over every surface, just like his room back at Coven Manor. But Fasta's eyes were lingering on the massive desk, which should have had those haphazard but somehow organized rows of rocks on it—but instead, the rocks were shoved over to the side, all jumbled together. And there, beside them, were—things.

Things that didn't belong.

Fasta's whole body flinched, and she stepped closer, stared. There was gold and silver jewelry. Cut stones, glittering in the light. A gaming board. A pouch, which—Fasta picked it up, shook it—had coin inside, and scented faintly of Johan's magic.

It was everything that had gone missing. All of it, down to Johan's pay, sitting right here in Henrik's bedroom.

And then—Fasta's legs staggered—there was a beautiful little sculpture, carved out of pure amethyst. Not quite complete, but the figure of a gowned lady rising out of it was so distinctive, so strangely familiar, that there was no question.

It was Elgin's missing sculpture.

31

Fasta sank down to Henrik's bed, rubbing her shaky hands against her thighs. What the hell. What the *fuck.*

It was wrong, like so much of this was wrong. It all said, it shouted, that Henrik had done it. Henrik had needed money, whether to pay for Andreas or to escape Fasta, escape his life—so he'd stolen all these things, hidden them here, until he could take them far away and sell them.

He'd had the incentive. He'd had the opportunity. He'd been alone, away from Fasta, at both Coven Manor, and at Elgin's property. He'd had enough time to get out here, more than once, and then come back to her, and pretend like nothing was wrong.

And maybe Fasta would have believed it, maybe. But she *knew* Henrik's magic, just as well as she knew her own—and even the barest brush of her hand over the stolen items was proof enough. Henrik had never touched them. He had never even gone *near* them.

And even if that hadn't been enough, there was still Elgin's amethyst sculpture. An item which—Fasta reached a trembly hand, trailed her finger against its smooth carved surface—betrayed the entire premise, and smashed it to bits.

Because Fasta knew—she was absolutely, positively certain—that Henrik would *never* have brought something of Elgin's into his room like this. He might have crushed it, turned it into something else, sold the stone. But to leave it like this—speaking so deeply of Elgin's wealth, Elgin's privilege, Elgin's skill—and let it defile this place that was so much his own? No. Never.

Fasta's fingers on the sculpture twitched again, and her head snapped around, because on her hand there'd been the slightest, faintest hint of cool air. A draft, and she and Henrik never tolerated drafts, so what the hell—

It was the window. One of their perfectly built, perfectly sealed windows, tall and slim, not unlike the shape of a human. And—Fasta's hand shot out, spread against it—it had been changed. Removed, maybe. Replaced.

It would have taken more than one excellent earth-mage, with a fair amount of construction skill, because the window was load-bearing, with a stone header at its peak. Someone would have had to hold up the wall, hold up the entire cottage, while someone else extracted the window, slipped inside...

The fury had been bubbling low in Fasta's stomach, but now it surged up into her hands, her thoughts. Someone was framing Henrik. Someone had broken into their cottage. Someone had trespassed on their property, and put their entire beautiful perfect *home* at risk, someone who maybe had no idea what the hell they were doing. What if they had damaged it? What if she'd come back to a *ruin*?

And also... where the hell was Henrik? He needed to know about this, he would be viciously enraged by this, he would jump into action and handle all of it for her, and...

Fasta grimaced and leapt to her feet, and then made a swift circle of the room, hands in fists at her sides. No. No. Henrik was gone. He'd made his choice. And when he came back—*if* he came back—she wanted him to know he could trust her. That she didn't see him as her servant, or her responsibility, or her pet. That she wasn't a fearful, spoiled-rotten brat, attempting to control him, expecting him to obey. She would respect him, and stand up for him.

And in doing so, maybe... she would respect *herself*. Stand up for herself, and for what she truly wanted. For what she'd been too afraid to face, all this time.

She spun on her heel and strode for her room, and grabbed for her pack. And then she stalked back to Henrik's room, and carefully filled the pack with all of the things that had been stolen from Coven Manor. The jewelry, the gaming board, the stones, Johan's pay. And on top, wrapped in cloth, Elgin's amethyst sculpture.

Fasta left the cottage the way it should have been left— Henrik's door carefully locked, all the latches properly shut— and then made the long, tedious trek back to Coven Manor. The pack on her back felt heavier and heavier with every breath, and she had to use more and more magic to hold it up, to keep taking one step after another.

You can't carry a pack of rocks for a half-day's walk? Henrik would have said, with that teasing grin of his. *Don't you remember when you made me carry that floor?*

It brought a rueful half-smile to Fasta's face, and she soldiered on, slower and sweatier with every staggering step. She was doing this. Not only for him, but for herself.

By the time she reached Coven Manor, it was early evening, and the corridors were bustling with people heading down to supper. And though Fasta could ignore their sidelong glances, she soon couldn't ignore their whispers, rising and scraping all around her. Whispers of *Hallen. Stealing. Fired...*

Fired.

That was new, but Fasta wasn't even surprised. And when she finally stalked into Kjaran's office, she was equally unsurprised by the row of smug, staring faces, waiting for her inside.

The three directors Kjaran, Argusson, Luda, and—Fasta's lip curled—Johan, and that scum *Merton*.

"What's this about?" she asked coolly, flicking her eyes between them. "Something to do with Henrik, I presume?"

Kjaran's lips curved unpleasantly, and her gaze slid sideways, toward where Merton was glowering at Fasta, arms crossed. "Your loudmouth commoner boytoy broke into *my* room this time," he said, his voice scathing. "Last night. Took every last copper and piece of metal he could *find*, and left my room a total *wreck*. As *revenge*, I can guarantee you."

The anger surged in Fasta's chest, and flared even higher at the sight of Kjaran's dismissive shrug. "There was no other choice," she added archly. "We have unanimously made the decision to fire Mr. Hallen from the Coven, and this facility, effective immediately. He is no longer permitted to step foot on the premises, and if he attempts to do so, we will immediately summon the proper authorities, and lay full charges. He will be fortunate to escape imprisonment, if not worse."

Fired. Imprisonment. Fasta stared at Kjaran's grim face, and then at Argusson and Luda and Johan, all regarding her with hard, unfriendly eyes. While Merton just looked downright vindictive, his beady gaze flicking up and down Fasta's slightly trembling frame with something not unlike glee.

And *this* was what Coven Manor supported. *This* was what earned protection and respect in this godawful hellhole, over Henrik's *years* of skill and dedication and accomplishments. This was what Fasta's fear had chosen, all this time.

Suddenly the decision was easy, obvious, as if it had been settled long ago. And in a swift, decisive movement, she yanked the pack off her back, and hurled it onto Kjaran's desk with a deafening, room-shaking *thud*.

"Bullshit," she growled. "Here's your proof. And also, I *quit*."

32

She quit.

Fasta flinched at the sound of those words coming out of her mouth, but she didn't take them back. She would stop lying, with both her words and her actions. She would speak truth.

"I quit," she said again, hearing the truth on her tongue, seeing its effect on the assembled faces. Surprise, from Argusson and Luda and Johan. A glittering-eyed anger, from Merton. And from Kjaran, a blanching, slack-faced dismay, her fingers gripping hard against her desk.

"You *quit*," Kjaran repeated, rising unsteadily to her feet. "*Voluntarily?*"

People didn't quit the Coven for Magical Advancement, Fasta well knew—except for one certain famous air-mage, several months before. And that had been a fiasco, prime gossip that had been rehashed endlessly in all the city papers, and as Fasta gazed with rising contempt at Kjaran's pale face, it occurred to her that perhaps this would be just as discussed. *The Earl of Dalreagh's daughter, sole heir to his immense fortune, has voluntarily taken leave of the prestigious Coven for Magical Advancement, citing...*

"Yes, I quit," Fasta said firmly. "Voluntarily. And if you refuse to cooperate with me yet *again*, I will publicly share the reasons why. Incompetent management, greatly reduced standards, and unfounded, *unconscionable* accusations against longstanding and exemplary colleagues!"

As she spoke, she'd reached down, and yanked her heavy pack open. And setting aside Elgin's wrapped sculpture, she dumped out the contents onto Kjaran's desk. The stones, the jewelry, the gaming board, the clinking pouch, all of it.

"I found this in the woods, a short walk from here," she said coldly. "As you may have done yourself, had you even *pretended* to pursue a legitimate investigation. And you will note, as I have, that there is *no* trace of Henrik's magic on any of these items. He's never so much as *touched* them."

The room's assembled eyes stared at the pile, and no one spoke. At least, until Johan stepped forward and plucked up the bag of coins, yanking its drawstring open and peering inside. "Yeah," he said, his voice stilted. "This is mine. And"—he brought it to his mouth, inhaled, and then grimaced—"yeah. There's no trace of Hallen on it."

Merton was frowning at the pile too, and after a minute's stillness he yanked up another pouch, and stuffed it in his pocket. Not speaking, not even acknowledging that Fasta had returned it, and she shoved down the almost overwhelming urge to hurl a rock at him, and forced her eyes back to Kjaran's pale face.

"You *will* compensate me for your utter *failure* to address this matter," Fasta said, her voice as imperious as she could make it. "And as compensation, here is what I want. You will give both Henrik and me *glowing* references. You will make it clear that we have both left voluntarily, on our own accord. And for the next year, you will forward me any and all requests you receive for my services, and Henrik's services. You will not attempt to fill those requests here, as you have ignored your

Earth department for years, and therefore have *no one* on staff with the requisite skills and experience."

Merton began sputtering again, but he was utterly outranked and outclassed, and Fasta shut him up with a disdainful wave of her hand. "If you fail to do this," she added, and she swept her eyes across Argusson and Luda, encompassing them as well, "I *will* ensure the truth about your blatant mismanagement is communicated to the public. Not only through my father's circles, but also through the city papers, which I am sure would be *very* interested in an exclusive interview with the Earl of Dalreagh's daughter."

The threat, while entirely empty on Fasta's part, had precisely the desired effect. Luda flinched, Argusson scowled, and Kjaran sagged back into her chair, her hands still gripping the desk. "We *did* look into it," she said, plaintive. "We were following the directives of the *Board*, and—"

Fasta's hand snapped up, in a silent order to stop, and Kjaran complied. "I want two weeks to sort out my affairs," Fasta said flatly. "After which I will keep you apprised of my whereabouts, so we're able to stay in contact."

With that, she grasped her now-empty pack, along with Elgin's sculpture, and spun on her heel, and strode out. No one attempted to stop her, but once she was out in the corridor, she heard the sound of footsteps, jogging up behind her. "Fasta," came a voice. "Wait."

Fasta hesitated, but warily turned, and found Johan. Gripping his pouch in one hand, and running his other hand through his dark hair. "Listen, Fasta," he said. "I'm sorry. About all this."

He waved at his pouch, at Kjaran's office down the corridor, and Fasta looked at his handsome face, and sighed. He'd been utterly infuriating, he'd helped to get Henrik *fired*, and what the hell else was there to say to that?

"Look, for what it's worth," Johan continued, "I know I had selfish reasons to want to suspect Hallen, but"—he winced, ran his hand through his hair again—"I wasn't making it up, all right? His signature *was* in my room, both times, when it's *never* been there before. No lie."

Fasta had a few ideas about that, and she twitched a tired nod, and turned to go—but Johan swiftly moved to block her path, and thrust the pouch in his hand out toward her. "Take this, will you?" he said, and his dark eyes were earnest, maybe even regretful. "Give it to Hallen. With my apologies."

Fasta blinked down at it, but then shook her head, and used a flare of magic to nudge the pouch back toward him. "Thank you," she replied, with a strange quaver on her voice, "but Henrik wouldn't accept it. He *hates* taking other people's money."

Johan looked suitably pained, and he nodded, stuffing the bag back in his pocket. "Fair enough," he said. "Will you at least pass on my regrets, then? I shouldn't have been so quick to jump to conclusions. I just"—he sighed, rubbed at his eyes—"I hated that Ilsa kept going off with him, you know? I know it's petty and jealous and so fucking stupid, but Ilsa and I grew up together, and we used to be—"

He didn't finish, but Fasta could follow all too easily, and suddenly that first night—that night when Henrik had kept flirting with Ilsa, and Johan had then asked Fasta to come upstairs with him—made so much more sense. Gods, maybe it even explained why it had felt so wrong with Johan, because maybe he hadn't even wanted it, either.

"I understand," Fasta said, with a reluctant but genuine smile toward him. "I wish you all luck, Johan."

Johan nodded, and that might have been a twitch of a smile on his mouth, too. "Same to you," he replied. "What are you planning to do next?"

It was a good question, a crucial question—but somehow, along the way, Fasta had already found the answer.

"I'm going to keep working," she said. "But this time, I'm doing it for *myself*."

33

Fasta walked up to her room with her thoughts still swimming, but her head was held high, her mouth set. She was doing this. She was being honest with herself.

And leaving Coven Manor needed to be part of her way forward. For too long, this place, this job, had been an excuse, a defense against the seemingly indefensible. A way to say, *I've traded my wealth for prestige. For a reputation. For the pinnacle of professional success.*

People like Fasta's father might not like that, but they understood it. Coven Manor was known the continent over, and placements were truly impossible to gain. It was a plausible reason for sacrificing one's privileged life of wealth and undeserved idleness.

But it wasn't what Fasta had truly wanted, was it? No. It had been another way to cling to her past, and her control. A reason to not take risks or make sacrifices. Even if Coven Manor had treated Henrik horribly. Even if he'd wanted to leave, maybe for longer than he'd ever let on.

Fasta shut her bedroom door with a sigh, and reflexively stroked at that ring, still so heavy and powerful on her finger. But maybe—maybe it was still a sign of her clinging to control, too. Making a choice for Henrik that he hadn't freely made himself.

But the thought of taking the ring off, risking it being lost or stolen—especially since the cottage—scraped painfully up Fasta's spine. And after a moment's consideration, she pulled the ring off her left hand, and slid it carefully onto the right. Where it only spoke of friendship, perhaps. Of... hope, for when Henrik came back. If he came back.

Next she went for her wardrobe, yanking it open, glowering at its contents. Most of her clothes these days were utilitarian, and very far from stylish, but she pulled out a silk blouse, and her dressiest pair of black trousers. She just needed to get into Elgin's party, and then...

She was frowning at her reflection in the looking-glass, trying to drag her fingers through the mess of her hair, when there was a quiet knock on the door. And once she went to open it, there was Thora, giving her a slow, genuine smile.

"I heard you quit," she said. "I'm so *happy* for you, Fasta."

She drew Fasta forward into a tight hug, and after an instant's hesitation, Fasta hugged her back. Feeling herself relax into Thora's arms, breathing in the light, delicate taste of her lovely, airy magic.

"Do you happen to know anything about hair, Thora?" Fasta finally asked, through her thick-feeling throat. "Because I'm terrible at it, and I'm"—she pulled back, tried in vain for a smile—"I'm going to a party."

Thora didn't even blink, but only gave a knowing smile back, and picked up Fasta's hairbrush from the dressing table. "Of course you are," she said lightly. "And of course I know hair, I have two younger sisters, don't I? Now sit."

Fasta gratefully sat, and watched in the looking-glass as Thora carefully teased out the plentiful knots in her hair, and brushed it until it was smooth and gleaming. And then she began twisting it up, too, into a fair approximation of the knots Fasta's servants had often done, and Fasta's eyes fluttered closed, her breath exhaling with genuine relief. Thora had never been one to pry, or ask questions about one's personal matters, and suddenly Fasta was deeply grateful to her for that, and for being one of her few real friends in this entire cursed place.

"I'm going to miss you, Thora," she said, earning a brief glance from Thora in the looking-glass. "Perhaps you and Runar could come visit, at some point? Wherever I end up?"

A distinct dismay flickered through Thora's eyes, her mouth twitching downwards. "That would be nice," she said noncommittally, and Fasta frowned at her in the looking-glass. Maybe she should leave it, but she was finished with lying, pretending, talking around things, instead of speaking truth.

"Why not?" she asked. "Is it because of your work? Or because of Runar? Whatever it is that's going on between you two?"

Because somehow, along the way with all this, it had become quite clear that there was *something*, and Thora gave Fasta a wan smile in the looking-glass. "A few reasons," she replied. "Let's just say"—her gaze dropped back to where she was sliding another pin into Fasta's hair—"you're lucky, Fasta. Both because you're getting to leave here for good, and because you have someone who cares so much about *you*."

She must have been referring to Henrik—and perhaps, also, to Runar?—and Fasta frowned back at Thora in the glass. "I'm sure Runar cares about you, Thora," she said. "He seems to think very highly of you, doesn't he?"

Thora laughed, low and bitter. "Runar thinks highly of my usefulness," she said, toward Fasta's hair. "And my suitability as an unsullied test subject who doesn't offend his delicate sensibilities. Though of course, despite that, he would still rather go off with girls like Ilsa, and—"

She broke off abruptly, blinking at Fasta in the glass—and then hurriedly returned her attention to Fasta's hair, sticking in one last pin before giving it a decisive pat. "There," she said firmly. "You're all set."

It was a highly impressive updo, but Fasta was still frowning at Thora, who was now looking back in the glass, her eyes almost pleading. Saying, perhaps, *please leave it*, and when Fasta nodded, Thora's slim shoulders rose and fell, and her mouth rose into a sincere, if wavering, smile.

"I'll try to visit," she said. "And I hope you have a wonderful time at the party."

Fasta barked a grim laugh, because this party was likely to be an utter disaster—but the knowing look in Thora's watching eyes suggested she already knew that, of course. And in a jerky movement, Fasta rose to her feet, and pulled Thora into another quick, fervent hug.

"Please do visit," she said. "And tell me if there's ever anything I can do to help. I mean that."

Thora nodded into Fasta's shoulder, betraying an almost inaudible sniff. But when she stepped back she was smiling again, and even gave Fasta a knowing little wink as she handed over Fasta's bag, with Elgin's sculpture safely inside.

"Thank you," she said. "Now go knock them out, Lady Valgeirr."

Fasta nodded, and almost managed a genuine smile. "Oh, I plan to," she said grimly. "With pleasure."

34

F asta strode up Elgin's drive with her bag in her hand, her head held high, and her determination deepening with every step.

She was addressing this. She was facing it with honesty, with truth. Even if that meant walking straight into Elgin Bryant's damned ridiculous party.

It was certainly an impressive affair, by the looks of it. The drive was lined with carriages and waiting grooms, smoking and chatting with each other, and at the end of the lane, Elgin's beautiful house was a beacon in the dark. With a wide-open front door, warm light spilling from the windows, and faint strains of music filtering across the grounds.

No one seemed to notice Fasta as she approached, and she hesitated a few paces from the front door, frowning. Perhaps it was just her usual aversion to these events, or Henrik's gnawing ongoing absence, or the goal she'd come here to accomplish—but something still felt... wrong, somehow. That same kind of wrongness she'd felt at the cottage, strong enough to flare gooseflesh up the back of her neck.

But she had a job to do, and she forced herself to step forward again, toward the door. Elgin's usual butler was

waiting, holding the door open, and Fasta could see him strug-
gling to place her, what with the markedly different ensemble,
the elegant pinned-up hair.

"Lady Fasta Valgeirr," she supplied crisply, putting him out
of his misery, which he returned with a relieved smile, a wave
of his hand inside.

"Of course," he said. "Won't you come in? May I take your
bag?"

"No, thank you," Fasta replied. "Is my father here? The Earl
of Dalreagh?"

This, of course, was another reason Fasta had come, and
the butler nodded, looking pleased. "Yes, he is already in atten-
dance. I'm sure he will be most delighted to see you."

That was a highly dubious claim, but Fasta nodded and
strode off toward the ballroom, and the sound of lush, lilting
music. The hallway was filled with people, all talking and
milling about, and though Fasta tried to keep her head down,
she could already feel their curious looks, likely in part due to
her not-quite-appropriate ensemble.

"Well, if it isn't Fasta Valgeirr!" came a voice, and when
Fasta's head snapped toward it, she found a familiar face from
the Academy. And though she vaguely smiled and kept
moving, she soon found herself hemmed in on all sides,
surrounded by familiar faces and tedious questions. How had
she been, where had she been hiding, they had heard about
that deadly situation at Coven Manor last year, and was it true
Fasta had known some of the people involved?

It all felt acutely uncomfortable, like an interrogation Fasta
hadn't in the least prepared for, but she fought to be polite, and
to dredge up all the various names. Most of her old crowd had
done quite well for themselves, judging by the clothes and the
multiple children wandering about, and they all seemed to
have settled down with each other, all perfect well-off happy
little families.

But Fasta had lived that life, she knew that life. And she

knew that at least some of the marriages would be in name only, the children raised on the other side of the estate, brought in only for supper and to show off to friends. She knew, too, that everything from their clothing to their latest vacations would be weaponized, ranked against the others, in a constant, silent competition that had no real winner.

"Have you kept up with your magic, Anka?" Fasta asked one of them, a rosy-cheeked woman who'd been an excellent earth-mage at the Academy—but Anka sighed, and shook her dark head.

"Not much, unfortunately," she replied, with a twinge of regret in her eyes. "Who has time, between managing the estate and the staff and the children?"

She snapped a finger toward the wandering children below, and two small girls immediately stepped forward, and gave matching curtsies toward Fasta. Both girls were fashionably dressed in frothy, frilly gowns, which were so long that the smaller one accidentally trod on her dress when coming out of the curtsey, and nearly pitched forward into Fasta's legs.

"Jane!" Anka snapped, and dragged the girl upward by the arm. "Apologize!"

The girl mumbled a very proper, well-spoken apology, her eyes darting between Fasta and her mother. While something gripped deep in Fasta's chest as she watched, because her own childhood had been so, so much of this—never performing properly, never measuring up. And along with all the rest of it, maybe this was part of why Fasta had never truly considered settling down and marrying, or having her own children, because this was precisely how it would be, wouldn't it?

"Oh, I'm quite all right," Fasta said brightly, as she knelt down before the red-faced girl. "And look what I found in the wall. It's"—she reached out, snapped over a random loose stone from the hallway's masonry, let the girl watch as she passed her hand over it—"a hedgehog!"

The girl gave a shout of delight that was probably far out of line with the rather warped-looking hedgehog, but she'd already clutched it to her chest, smiling shyly toward Fasta's face. "You're an earth-mage!" she said. "My mama used to be an earth-mage."

She said it quietly, like it was a closely guarded secret, and Fasta smiled back. "Yes, and a very good one," she said, with a warm glance up toward Anka, but Anka wasn't smiling back. In fact, she was looking rather appalled, and she clasped both her daughters' shoulders again, and steered them away.

Fasta sighed and stood again, turning back toward the ballroom—when suddenly, striding through the crowd up ahead, there was Elgin. Beaming straight toward her, and looking devastatingly handsome in his perfectly tailored suit.

"Fasta!" he exclaimed, holding out both hands to grasp hers. "You came! I am truly shocked. And *most* honoured."

As he spoke, he angled a brief, almost imperceptible glance down at the bag Fasta was still carrying, but then he stepped forward, and lightly brushed his lips to her cheek. "I'm so glad you're here," he said, into her ear. "Come, let me show you the fruits of your labours."

He stepped back, flashing her a saucy grin, and kept hold of her hand as he guided her down the corridor, toward the ever-increasing noise of music and chattering voices. "I've had so many compliments," he said, over the din. "You're truly a miracle worker. See?"

With a flourish, he waved her through the ballroom's entrance, and for an instant, Fasta stilled in place, blinking at the sight. The room was utterly transformed, lit up by hundreds of candles, and the open space was jammed with people dancing, talking, eating, drinking, laughing. It truly did look lovely, and like a wonderful success, and Fasta ought to have felt pleased and proud and gratified.

But instead, her determination only deepened, coiling with something much like anger, and the unease she'd felt since she arrived here seemed to worsen, too. Perhaps due to that very slight tilt in the floor, made a shade more prominent due to the crush of people weighing down the room.

"I couldn't have asked for a better showcase of the house," Elgin's voice said, tickling low and warm against her ear. "I owe you, Fasta."

His hand settled against her back, in something approaching an embrace, and Fasta swiftly stepped forward, into the room. "Is my father here?" she asked curtly, to which Elgin flashed her another warm smile, and once again put his hand to her back. Guiding her, ostensibly, toward her father, and Fasta let out a huff of irritation that Elgin either didn't hear, or chose to ignore.

"Here we are," Elgin said cheerfully, and yes, here was Fasta's father in the crowd, turning around to face them. He looked as regal as ever, his suit impeccably fitted, his dark hair becomingly streaked with grey. And while his eyes warmed as they met Fasta's, they also flicked purposely downwards, in a not-so-subtle critique of her not-so-suitable clothes, and her not-so-slender body beneath them.

"Father," Fasta said, with the little curtsey she knew he expected. "I hope you're well?"

He nodded, and gave a small smile back. "My prodigal daughter," he replied. "I am surprised to find you here, Fasta."

Fasta's frustration was already jolting higher, but she forced a tight smile, too. "I've been working with Elgin on the house for the past few weeks."

Her father nodded—so this clearly wasn't a surprise after all—and his gaze slid past her toward Elgin, who was still standing far too close by Fasta's side. "You clearly know my daughter's interests, Norberg," he said, with approval in his voice. "A rambling little spot like this would certainly keep her occupied."

Only someone of Lord Dalreagh's wealth would call Elgin's estate a *little spot*, but Elgin seemed unperturbed, his hand once again resting against the small of Fasta's back. "That's what I'm hoping, sir," he replied, with a wink toward Fasta. And wait, what was he implying, the *hell*—

"Elgin and I are working together in a purely professional capacity, Father," Fasta cut in, with a pointed look toward Elgin. "And Elgin, I regret to inform you that I'll be stepping back from the job. I've given my resignation to Coven Manor, effective immediately."

If Fasta's father had been any other parent, he might have protested, or demanded why his daughter would so casually throw away such a prestigious, impossible-to-obtain position. But he only blandly nodded, his eyes sliding back toward Elgin. "Well, surely you and Norberg can develop an alternate arrangement?"

An alternate arrangement. And beside Fasta, Elgin gave a sheepish grin, raising his eyebrows at her, like a hopeless lovelorn *innocent.* Like an arsehole who'd already talked to her father about this, and who'd clearly received his wholehearted endorsement.

"I'm afraid no alternate arrangement will be possible," Fasta said coldly. "I will be far too busy building my own business with Henrik."

That was a highly presumptuous thing to assume, Fasta knew—Henrik might not come back at all, and even if he was willing to hear her offer, he might choose not to accept. And she would respect his decision, she *would*—but right now, Henrik's name still felt like safety, somehow, like an irrefutable rejection of Elgin's offer. A rejection that Elgin clearly didn't miss, judging by his narrowing eyes, but Fasta's father just looked confused. "With *who*?"

Fasta sighed, rolled her eyes. "My *partner*, Father," she replied. "For the past five years. Henrik Hallen. You have met him, on multiple occasions."

The comprehension passed over her father's face, followed swiftly by disapproval. "Your *labourer*?" he asked, incredulous, and next to Fasta, Elgin actually snickered out loud. While the fury surged up hard in Fasta's stomach, and she wrenched purposefully away from Elgin, away from that still-too-present hand on her back.

"I realize that Henrik's background precludes you from judging him fairly, Father," she snapped. "But he is a highly accomplished earth-mage, and a very good friend."

Her father looked unimpressed, and his eyes slid back toward Elgin again. "Well, Norberg here is a highly accomplished earth-mage as well, is he not? As well as a longstanding friend of yours?"

Damn him, he was making his point very clear, offering Elgin his full support. Suggesting that this could—this *should*—be Fasta's future. And churning together with her anger was the unease again, that feeling of wrongness, of something almost like fear.

"Of course Elgin is accomplished, and a friend," Fasta gritted out. "But his values and his goals are very different than mine. I feel very strongly that it's best we remain friends."

Her voice came out clear, decisive, and in reply, Elgin and Fasta's father exchanged a swift, telling glance. One that said, on her father's part, *This again*, and on Elgin's side, *I know, I'm trying*.

Fasta's disbelieving eyes darted back and forth between them, while that feeling of being trapped, being wrong, kept wringing tighter. Tangling with a deep, hurtling loneliness, because she didn't belong here, she'd never belonged here, with these people who barely saw her, barely heard her, barely cared.

She had to fight down the urge to turn around and rush away, back out into the cool open darkness—but she made herself take a breath, gripping both hands at her bag. "Farewell, Father," she told him, as steadily as she could. "I'm sure our paths will cross again, and I will write you to confirm my future plans. And Elgin"—she met his eyes—"could we speak for a moment, please? Somewhere quiet?"

Elgin's narrow eyes flicked down to her bag, and then back to her face—but he nodded, and waved her out the door, and down the main corridor. Into a small sitting room that Fasta had briefly seen on their first day here, and it was warm and well-appointed, with a crackling fire in the fireplace.

"I presume this isn't the kind of invitation I was hoping for, then?" Elgin asked, as he shut the door behind them, muffling the lingering sounds of music and voices. "You have something for me, perhaps?"

Fasta couldn't read the tone in his voice, but his eyes were on her bag again, and she nodded, reached inside. "Yes," she said, as she unwrapped his amethyst sculpture, and held it out toward him. "I found it in the forest."

Elgin's eyebrows rose, but he took the sculpture from her hand, and set it carefully on a small side table. "Where in the forest?" he said. "If I may ask?"

That unease curdled again, even sharper than before, and the room suddenly felt too small, too warm—but Fasta took a breath, drew herself tall. She was being honest, and standing up for herself. She was.

"*Do* you need to ask?" she replied, as steadily as she could. "I expected you would know exactly where, Elgin."

The words rang through the small room, too loud and clear, and Fasta didn't miss Elgin's faint flinch, the slight widening of his eyes. Because yes, she was accusing him—and yes, he was guilty. Guilty of the thefts, the break-in, Henrik's firing. All of it.

"I've come to give you a chance to apologize, Elgin," Fasta said, holding his eyes. "A chance to make amends. To me, and to Henrik, and to everyone else you involved in this ridiculous scheme."

Elgin's expression didn't change, and for a moment there was silence, broken only by the crackling fire. But Fasta waited, holding her head high, while Elgin's throat swallowed, and he...

He *laughed.* Cold, bright, amused, as if Fasta had just made a hilarious, outrageous jest. "Really, Fasta?" he asked. "You dare to walk in here and blame me for this? *Me*?"

Fasta's eyes narrowed, her mouth opening—but Elgin shook his head, and came a swift, purposeful step closer. "Look, Fasta," he said, and his voice was different now, flatter. "You must see how this looks, can't you? My sculpture disappears from my house, while you and Hallen are working here, and then *you* happen to find it? Just lying about in the forest? Just like that?"

He laughed again, but his eyes were hard, his mouth thin. "Your labourer *stole* from me, and you're protecting him," he snapped. "And while I understand your sentiments, I am *not* willing to condone them any further. I'm reporting this to the proper authorities, Fasta. All of it. Hallen's not going to escape the consequences this time. And if you're not careful"—his mouth pulled into a cold, humourless smile—"you won't escape them, either."

The consequences. Fasta might well have laughed, if she'd hadn't been swarmed in jolting, dizzying rage. "Oh, bullshit, Elgin," she snarled. "You're the one at fault here, and you won't get away with this. You have no proof against Henrik. *None*."

"Oh, I have proof, Fasta," Elgin said, his eyes glinting with triumph. "Because earlier today, after you left, he came back here, alone. And he *threatened* me, within full hearing of half of my household staff!"

What? Fasta's thoughts scattered, flaring in all directions at once, because Henrik had—come back here? Where had he gone afterwards? And what he threatened Elgin with? What had he known? *How*?

"More bullshit, Elgin," Fasta made herself say, through clenched teeth. "There's no reason Henrik would have come back here, or bothered threatening you. He was planning to *leave*."

Elgin's eyebrows snapped up, and he gave another cold, scraping laugh. "Clearly he forgot that part," he said. "Because he spent a good quarter-hour raging at me about you. Some incoherent guff about a cottage, and how it was apparently a total outrage for me to *dare* to offer you a better *life*."

His voice sounded bitter, perhaps even angry, and Elgin never got angry—at least, not that Fasta could remember. But now he stepped toward her again, his eyes flinty and narrow. "I have no idea why you keep defending him," he said, his voice lower, harder. "You think I haven't noticed how he treats you? He orders you around, acts like he fucking *owns* you, makes you kneel and bleed and *beg* for him. And now he's a petty lying *thief*, too? You really think the authorities will overlook all that?"

Wait. No. Fasta's heart was hammering, her voice caught in her throat, and Elgin took another step closer. "I think they'll be *very* interested in his behaviour toward you, Fasta," he drawled. "Meanwhile, I'm here being *nice* to you, offering you wealth and opportunities and a life most people would *kill* for, and that's still not good enough for you?"

Damn it, damn it, Fasta just needed a minute to think, but her thoughts were still shouting and careening, pounding with the anger, the confusion, the rapidly rising fear. How had Elgin known all this, how much had he seen, where the hell was Henrik...

Her hand groped for the wooden door behind her, while Elgin came even closer, almost near enough to touch. "And you know, it's starting to seem to me," he said, even lower, "that there's only one possible explanation. You *like* how that stupid peasant treats you. You *like* being pushed around, being called a slut, being fucked within a breath of your life. Is that right?"

The pounding echoed in Fasta's head, louder and louder, and Elgin smiled as he leaned in, his hand spreading against the door beside her. "So maybe we need to try this again," he continued, his breath so close that Fasta could taste the wine on it. "Here's the deal, Fasta. You agree to give Hallen up, and accept what I'm offering you. And"—his hand rose to Fasta's chin, gripped it, hard—"if you're a good girl, I'll drop my charges against him."

Something dangerously dipped in Fasta's belly, and she couldn't move, couldn't breathe. "And I'll treat you just how you want to be treated," Elgin murmured. "You'll be my whore. I'll hold you down, wallop you with a stick, fuck you until you bleed. And you'll fucking love every second of it."

And then—Elgin's mouth. His mouth, pressing hot and hungry against Fasta's, teeth and lips and wine, magic that was cold and thin and *wrong*. And suddenly the world spun into focus again, sharp and brilliant and stunning, and that amethyst sculpture flew across the room, snapping into Fasta's hand—and she drove it up, hard, straight between Elgin's legs.

Elgin yelped with pain, his eyes rolling back, and Fasta hurled herself forward with all her strength, driving her shoulder into his chest, shoving him backwards. "What the *hell*, Elgin," she gasped at him. "How fucking *dare* you?!"

Elgin was still bent double, breathing heavy, but his eyes darted up to hers, and now it was Fasta stepping closer, looming up over him, brandishing the sculpture in her hand. "You've been following us," she hissed. "You've been spying on us. You arranged to steal all those items, and planted them in our cottage. You falsely accused Henrik of the thefts. And now you're trying to *blackmail* me into *marrying* you?!"

Elgin assumed an expression that tried to be shocked, but utterly failed, and Fasta glowered at him, gripped the offending sculpture in her hand. "It might have even worked," she gritted out, "if not for *this*. Because there's no way Henrik would have taken this, not in a million years. And the only connection to this was *you!*"

She knew that rising look in Elgin's eyes, that sulky petulant *how-dare-you* look, and with effort he stood up again, breathing hard. "You're swallowing Hallen's *lies*, Fasta," he spat. "The only connection was *him*. The arsehole who fucking *beats* you, who you keep defending for *ridiculous* reasons!"

But Fasta shook her head, gripped the sculpture tighter. "Henrik and I had an *agreement*," she said. "A *game*, that we both freely consented to. *You*, on the other hand, know far too much, and you've pushed me far too hard with this! If you really just wanted some earth-mage children, there are plenty of other willing women available who would give you much less trouble. Why keep trying with me? When we already tried and failed at this *years* ago, back when you *lied* to me, and *cheated* on me, and made it excessively clear that I didn't actually *matter* to you?!"

Elgin was still breathing hard, but he didn't reply, and Fasta felt her lip curling, her strength rising from the stone floor beneath her feet. "It's the money," she said, quieter. "Isn't it? You want my dowry, my inheritance. You probably even need it."

Elgin's eyes betrayed a telltale little flicker, and Fasta huffed a hoarse, flat little laugh. "You're still taking commissions," she said, waving the sculpture at him. "Of course you need the money. This place, your staff, your clothes, your standards of living—they're far beyond what you can actually afford. Right?"

It was such a common theme among their set—keeping up appearances to the detriment of everything else—and the truth of it was there, written all over Elgin's face. And how had Fasta not seen it before, how had she not guessed? Especially with him inheriting this new estate, and all the new expenses that would come along with it?

Elgin's shoulders rose and fell, and his jaw tightened, his hands clenching. "So what," he said. "Of course I wasn't going to bring up the money discussion with you until we were settled. It doesn't change a damn thing, Fasta. Especially the fact that your so-called *partner* is a common petty *thief* who treats you like shit. You'd be way better off with me."

Fasta laughed again, louder this time, the sound ringing through the small room. "I would be *miserable* with you," she corrected him. "I am finished with lying, with pretending, with putting on appearances, all of which"—she waved at Elgin, the house, the party—"is clearly your entire *life*! Meanwhile, Henrik has *always* been honest with me, has *always* respected my goals and my priorities, has *always* supported me!"

Elgin's mouth curled up unpleasantly, his eyes glittering and cold. "Sure he has," he said flatly. "So tell me, where is he now?"

Fasta took a step closer, and she briefly touched that warm, heavy ring on her finger, bright and solid and powerful.

"That's the question, arsehole," she said quietly. "You tell me. *Where is he?*"

35

The look on Elgin's face was exactly what Fasta expected. All innocent, confused, make-believe handsome *bullshit*.

"I have no idea what you're talking about, Fasta," he said. "Why the hell would I know where your labourer is?"

But Fasta stepped closer, the sculpture still clutched tight in her fingers. "Because," she snarled, "you've gone to a hell of a lot of trouble to set this up. Between hiring me, and spying on me, and arranging all those thefts, and planting the stolen goods in my cottage, and blaming Henrik. And then Henrik comes back here this morning, and probably accuses you of all of it—and you're just going to let him walk away, and wait for him to tell me what you've been up to? No *way*, arsehole. You're in this *way* too deep, and you're damned lucky Henrik didn't *murder* you!"

As she'd spoken, Elgin had kept that too-innocent look on his face—until the very last, when he betrayed a cold, mocking smirk. And Fasta had wasted two entire *years* of her youth dealing with his bullshit, and it was more than enough to whip up the soaring jolting gods-damned *rage*.

"Where is Henrik," she demanded again, harder this time. "*Tell me.*"

But she was getting the better of him, and Elgin had always, always hated that. And that smirk curled higher on his mouth, into an expression Fasta remembered all too well. The one that said he was about to do everything in his power to thwart her.

"I have no idea what you're talking about," he said coolly. "You're delusional, buttercup."

Delusional. Buttercup. They were Henrik's words, even spoken in an awful caricature of Henrik's accent, and Fasta's entire body froze, the rage blooming sharp and white behind her eyes.

"You little piece of *shit*," she growled. "Where is he? What the *hell* did you do to him?"

Elgin just laughed, tilting his handsome head back, while Fasta's rage jolted higher, harder. Together with a sudden screeching terror, because Elgin wouldn't actually *hurt* Henrik, or would he—

"*Tell me,*" she demanded, but Elgin only gave her that familiar old saucy smile, and shrugged his shoulders. And how the hell had she ever kissed this arsehole, loved this arsehole, given him *way* too much power over her...

"You really are losing it, *buttercup*," he drawled, and he made to step past her, toward the door. "Sorry to say, because I really thought we could be something. But it looks like you're way too busy rolling around in the *gutter*—"

The words broke off with a high-pitched shout, because the sculpture in Fasta's hand had broken apart into two jagged pieces. One of them jamming hard against the pale skin of Elgin's neck, and the other one hovering menacingly in front of his groin.

"What the fuck, bitch," Elgin hissed, as his hand grasped for the amethyst at his neck, fought in vain to pull it away. "That sculpture was a fucking *masterpiece*, how *dare* you—"

But Fasta's hand snapped out, and a hefty stone wrenched

from the nearest wall, flying into her fingers. "Then don't leave your masterpieces," she shot back, "lying around where they don't belong!"

And with a firm, furious flick of her hand, her stone transformed into a long, sinuous chain. A chain that easily shot through the small space between them, wrapping itself tight around Elgin's chest and upper arms, and trapping his arms down by his sides.

"You fucking *dare*—" he began, but there was already another stone in Fasta's hand, thinning and lengthening. And with another whip of her hand, it curled itself around his waist this time, pinning his forearms tight against him.

"Yes, I do dare," she snarled, as a third stone snapped from her hand, this time soaring down to circle around Elgin's ankles. Yanking itself slim and tight, while he flailed and staggered, fighting in vain to kick his feet free.

"Tell me," Fasta demanded, and with a purposeful wave of her hand, all three restraints pulled a twitch tighter. "Or this keeps getting more and more unpleasant."

Elgin was still hopping uselessly, writhing and squirming around in his fancy clothes, and Fasta crossed her arms, and waited. Glowering at him with rising, disbelieving contempt, because he was supposed to be an earth-mage, wasn't he?

"Pathetic," she said, and the next stone floated slowly, leisurely, from the wall into her outstretched hand. "I thought you kept up with your earth-magic. You can't even handle three measly rocks?"

Elgin's eyes glittered on the stone in her hand, and his throat convulsed, his lip curling. "I have better things to do," he said, hoarse, "than perform shitty common *labour* with shitty *building materials*."

The look in his eyes was triumphant, like this was the ultimate insult, even as Fasta had his gods-damned entire *life* in her hands. And suddenly she just felt drained, and sick, because she had loved Elgin once, and now here he was, mocking the entirety of her life choices, while she was threatening him, maybe even wanting to kill him...

She dropped the stone from her hand to the floor with a thunk, and Elgin's eyes followed it, and then darted back up to hers. "What are you waiting for?" he spat. "Too much of a pushover to finish the job?"

But Fasta was done, just done, with him, with this. And with another flick of her hand, the amethyst sculpture was back in one piece again, the broken edges blending seamlessly together, as though it had never been broken.

"Please, Elgin," Fasta said, with a heavy sigh. "For the sake of our friendship, for the good times we had. *Please* tell me where Henrik is."

But Elgin's head was already shaking, his eyes strangely, feverishly bright. "No," he said. "I won't. You're supposed to be *mine.*"

Mine. The word dragged up Fasta's spine, bitter and far too familiar, and blinking back toward him, she could suddenly feel the presumption in that claim, the pettiness, the selfish, spoiled-rotten *greed.* The way Elgin felt entitled to push past all Fasta's boundaries, and control her fate, her choices, her *life.*

Just like... just like she'd done with Henrik.

"No," she said, as she stretched out the stone in her hand, and slid it toward Elgin's feet. "I'm not yours, Elgin. And clearly"—she even managed a cold smile—"you need to be taught a lesson."

With that, her stone slithered up and around Elgin's ankle, joining onto the cuff she'd already made. And then its other end melded itself into the tile on the floor, and trapped him tightly in place.

"Enjoy your party, Elgin," she said, as she slung her bag over her shoulder, and spun toward the door. "And may we never meet again."

36

Fasta shut the door quietly behind her, and then sealed it into the stone on the inside. Confining Elgin firmly within, and muting his already-muffled shouts to a low drone, which Fasta entirely ignored.

Henrik was here. Somewhere. And Fasta didn't look back as she jogged down the corridor, her bag slapping against her shoulder, her fingers trailing against the stone wall. Henrik was here. He had to be here.

She ran up the back staircase, avoiding the party and the guests, and then sprinted around one floor, and then the next. Trailing her hand against the wall the entire time, because if Henrik had suffered here, if he was trapped and miserable here, it would be here in his magic, it had to be—

There was nothing on those floors, in that wing, so Fasta sprinted north, to where the next wing connected. Still touching the wall, searching for any trace of Henrik's magic, but right now it was only distant, faded, from long ago. Maybe from when they'd first toured the place, it felt like *years* ago—

But this had already taken too much time, and Fasta's fear pounded higher as she ran. At some point, someone would wonder where Elgin had gone, or maybe he would muster up enough earth-magic to break himself free. She had to keep running, had to find him—

"Where is Henrik Hallen?" she demanded, skidding to a stop beside the first servant she saw, a lovely blonde who blinked back at her through wide, fearful eyes. "Have you seen him?"

The servant stammered her refusal, even as something like awareness flickered through her eyes—so Fasta snapped another stone out of the wall, hovered it menacingly in front of her face. "Tell me," she demanded. "Is Henrik in the house?"

The servant rapidly shook her head, her eyes sparking with too-clear terror, and Fasta made the stone spin, fast and close. "Then where is he?" she hissed. "Outside?"

The servant nodded—yes, *yes*—and Fasta spun and sprinted toward the stairs, dropping the stone at the servant's feet. "Sorry," she called behind her, and she meant it. "Thank you."

If the servant responded, Fasta didn't hear it, because she was already racing down the stairs, her hands in fists. Outside, outside, Henrik was outside, where, why...

She burst down the main staircase, out past the blinking butler, out the front door. There was no time, Elgin would be following soon, where the *hell* was Henrik...

The panic shouted louder, her heartbeat clanging through her ears, and she forced herself to stop, in the middle of the moonlit lawn. Ignoring the strange glances from the random latecomers coming up the drive, and she squeezed her eyes shut, hauled in a long, dragging breath. Henrik was out here. *Where?*

Her magic was unfurling, somehow, seeking into the empty space around her, rippling out and across the dark lawn. Feeling for Henrik, feeling how he'd been here weeks ago, days ago, yesterday, today...

Until—there. *There.*

Fasta whirled around, and ran. Away from the house, away from that barn, veering off due north, and then east, because Henrik had been here, today. Here, and *here*, and Fasta could hear voices from behind her now, from the house. Coming closer.

"Harry!" she yelled, as she sprinted further, felt him fade, and then rounded back again. "Harry! Where *are* you?!"

There was no response, except for those voices from the house following her, and she circled back, toward where it felt strongest—and then stopped. Because all that was here was the outhouse, that one she'd sucked him off in that day, and *wait*, was that a *noise*—

In a breath Fasta was there, yanking at the closed outhouse door—and when it didn't open she crushed the latch, and finally ripped the door off by the hinges, and hurled it behind her. And inside, in the darkness—there was someone. *Henrik.*

He was curled up on the floor, wrapped with what looked like furlongs of woven rope, and his face in the dappled moonlight was half-covered in dried blood, his right eye swollen almost shut. His hands were bound behind his back, his feet lashed together, and Fasta fought down the furious, raging urge to go back in time, back to Elgin, and keep squeezing those stones until his breath stopped.

"Harry," Fasta choked, falling to her knees beside him, yanking at the ropes. "Harry. Oh gods, oh gods. Please tell me you're alive. *Please.*"

A strange noise scraped from Henrik's throat, and damn it, there was something in his mouth—an old, filthy rag—and she yanked it out, hurled it over her shoulder. "Gods *fuck* that arsehole," she gasped, and she cupped her hands on Henrik's face, desperately searched his eyes in the dappled moonlight from the open door. "Can you hear me, Harry? Can you *breathe*?"

Henrik's head twitched, and Fasta felt his chest move, rising purposefully against her. And Fasta half-laughed, half-sobbed, her hands running over his bloody face, his chest. Feeling for the ropes, trying to pull out the knots with her too-shaky fingers, and then snapping up the nearest sharp stone, dashing it to a point, and then using that instead.

"Harry," she said, putting her hands back to his face, as the stone kept working behind her. "What the hell. What *happened*?"

The ropes had been loosening as she spoke, and Henrik shoved to sit up, his hands and feet scrabbling against the filthy outhouse floor. "Bryant," he croaked, but his voice was all wrong, and Fasta groped in her bag for her waterskin, and held it to his lips. Watching, her heartbeat lurching, as Henrik poured water into his mouth, rinsed it out, spat on the filthy floor—and then just drank, and drank, and drank.

Finally he shoved the water-skin away, wiping at his face with the back of his hand, but maybe it had helped, because his eyes on her had gone focused, grim. "Bryant," he said, in a voice that sounded a little more like his. "And his servants."

That made more sense, somewhat, because there was no way Elgin could have done this to Henrik on his own—but at the same time, Fasta would have bet on Henrik against a dozen of Elgin's servants. "How?" she demanded, even as her hands kept stroking his stubbly face, his neck, drinking in the feel of him, *here*. "What about your magic?"

Henrik croaked a sound, something like a laugh. "One of them clocked me from behind," he rasped. "With a wooden club. Four other ones held me down, while Bryant shoved a cloth over my face. Must've had some kinda drug. Woke up in here a while ago."

What?! Fasta had already opened her mouth to demand why Henrik hadn't immediately used his magic, maybe caused a damned earthquake under the lawn—but then she felt the earth beneath her feet, and understood. The outhouse was perched over that deep-below stream, on several insubstantial wooden beams, and any kind of not-perfect magic on the earth beneath could have sent the entire structure falling.

"Was working on it," Henrik's hoarse voice said, clearly following Fasta's thoughts. "Head's still not quite right, from whatever they used. Didn't wanna drown myself, on top of everything else."

Fasta fervently nodded, and choked a half-laugh, half-sob. "Thank the gods," she breathed, feeling the wetness build behind her eyes now, despite the smile on her mouth. "Damn you, Harry, I've been losing it, looking all over, couldn't imagine where the hell you'd gone—"

Her voice broke off, the wetness streaking out of her eyes, and she couldn't quite look at him anymore. Because he *had* wanted to leave, after all, and maybe he still did. And she'd sworn to respect that, respect his choice, no matter what.

She yanked at the ropes again, pulling them down and off his feet, her hands trembling again. But Henrik was free, that was all that mattered, all she could stand to think about right now, and—

And then Henrik's fingers grasped her hand.

Fasta froze, because—her heart picked up, hammered double-time—that was the hand wearing the ring. Wearing Henrik's ring, that she'd found snooping through his private possessions, and then taken and worn, without even asking. And what was he thinking, why was he staring, what was that look on his face...

Fasta snatched her hand away, far too late, and gods it was stupid, because Henrik would still be able to feel it, even if he couldn't see it. And her face was burning, her entire body twitching, she should apologize, she should explain, offer to give it back, offer to help him leave...

Henrik's eyes were looking at her, so intent that it felt like a touch, and now his hand reached for hers again, and gently drew it back toward him. Toward where he could see it, see his ring on her hand, and something lurched in Fasta's throat, waiting...

"There they are!" shouted a familiar, gut-twisting voice. "My attackers! Get them!"

It was quite possibly the voice Fasta both least and most wanted to hear in this moment, and with a low growl she leapt out the outhouse door, dragging up every single loose rock she could feel in the earth around them. Hurling them up into something of a makeshift wall, hovering between her and Henrik and—Fasta growled again—*Elgin*. Still wearing his fancy clothes, but now flanked by a good half-dozen of his servants, all men, all carrying crackling torches that were far too bright in the dark.

"Oh, come *on*, Elgin," Fasta snapped, and she couldn't tell if she was more disgusted or enraged. "*You* assaulted Henrik, *you* trapped him in here, and then you tried to assault *me*! And you have the audacity to accuse *us* of attacking *you*?"

Elgin's smile back was cold, smug, superior. "I have witnesses," he said, encompassing his servants with a flourish of his hand. "That commoner oaf came onto my property this morning without permission, and threatened me. And a few hours later *you* come and do the same, and leave me tied up in my guest sitting room!"

The distinct sound of a snicker rose behind Fasta, and when she glanced over her shoulder, Henrik was sitting up in the outhouse door frame, his elbows resting almost casually on his knees. His face still looked awful, but he must have wiped away some of the blood, and even now, Fasta's belly still dipped at the sight of him, all coiled and broad-shouldered and beautiful.

"Did you really, Fass?" he asked her, almost conversational, despite the hoarseness in his voice. "What'd you tie him with, stone?"

Fasta blinked, but nodded, holding the hovering rocks steady. "Yes, from the wall," she snapped, frowning back toward

Elgin. "And it was surprisingly easy. For someone who supposedly calls himself an earth-mage."

Henrik chuckled again, the familiar sound making Fasta's belly dip again. "Yeah, I think by now we all know better," he said. "I'm willing to bet this piece of shit hasn't touched a rock in *years*."

Elgin clearly didn't like that, his eyes narrowing in the flickering firelight. "Says the scum who's too weak and pathetic to crawl his way out of an outhouse," he snapped, with a smug smile. "And whose mouth is full of shit. *Literally*."

The rage surged bright and painful through Fasta's thoughts, and her wall of rocks juddered menacingly toward him. "How *dare* you," she shot back. "After everything Henrik has done for you on this house. You're just jealous that he's better than you, in *every single way!*"

Elgin's eyebrows shot up, and he barked a loud, carrying laugh. "Him?" he demanded. "Better than me? The impoverished fat meathead who has to work like a *dog* to make a living? The guy who's only *ever* been with you for the money?"

Fasta's body stiffened, and she shook her head, and lifted her chin. "That's enough, Elgin," she hissed. "You have no idea what you're talking about."

But Elgin only laughed again, shaking his head. "You were always such a gullible innocent, Fasta," he drawled. "Believe me, we've all heard about his poor little brother, who's too good to suck some dick for his supper. And whose big brother, luckily"—he gave Henrik a sharp-toothed smile—"has absolutely no qualms about what he does for his coin."

Fasta's mouth fell open, because how the hell had Elgin known about that, too? And a searching glance over her shoulder showed Henrik looking grim, forbidding, but not moving, not saying a word.

"So here's the reality, *buttercup*," Elgin said, coming a step closer, with his servants close behind. "He's in it for the money. He doesn't give a damn about you. And"—his eyes sobered, held on Fasta's—"if you still want to make things right with me, it's not too late. You're better than this."

Better than this. The words were swarming, surging up against the disbelief and the rage, and Fasta pulled her body tall, and snapped the rocks still hovering between them into a perfect, precise grid.

"Fuck you, Elgin," she hissed. "You want to know who's only after me for the money, and who doesn't give a damn about me? *You!* Henrik is my best friend, and a brilliant partner, and one of the most powerful and accomplished earth-mages in the entire *country*. And he's loyal, he's honest, he's generous and gorgeous and an absolutely *mind-blowing* fuck. The complete and total opposite of *you!*"

Elgin kept smiling, and gave a slow, elaborate shake of his head. "Doesn't matter, sweetheart," he said. "You're still being hoodwinked, because *he's* still in it for the money! And you even told me yourself, he wants to leave you!"

Damn Elgin, because it was the one thing Fasta couldn't argue against, couldn't dismiss. And another glance over her shoulder toward Henrik showed him now rising unsteadily to his feet, leaning against the door frame, and staring at Elgin with something not unlike hatred.

But he still wasn't speaking, and that meant Fasta was on her own, staring down Elgin and his watching servants, staring down the truth. And—she took a breath, let it out—she was telling the truth. She was.

"I can't control Henrik's motives, or his decisions," she said. "He's not my property, or my servant, or my pet. But I still choose to trust him, and respect him. I still"—she swallowed, raised her chin—"I still love him."

The last came out quiet, too quiet, but behind her she could almost feel Henrik's surprise, the sudden taut tension in his magic around her. Feeling so suddenly close, now, and had it always been like that, but Fasta didn't dare turn around to see...

"So one last chance, Elgin," she said now, quieter. "Let's

agree to leave this, and part ways, and forget any of it ever happened. All right?"

It was maybe too big a concession, letting him get away with what he'd done to Henrik, but at this point Fasta would take it, if it meant they could just walk away. If they could just escape this cursed place forever, get Henrik somewhere safe, where he could rest.

"You think I'm just going to let you walk away?" Elgin demanded, into the silence. "When *he* threatened me, and *you* attacked me and confined me in my own house, at my own damned party? No way in hell. You're both getting what you deserve for this. Now, capture them!"

He raised an imperious hand toward the assembled servants beside him, waving them forward. And though Fasta braced herself for an attack, the servants—didn't move. Instead, they shifted on their feet, and glanced at each other with uneasy eyes.

"Uh, sir," said the tallest one, who Fasta vaguely recalled being named Denn. "She's the daughter of the Earl of Dalreagh. And he's *here*."

He nodded back toward the house, while Elgin rolled his eyes, and irritably waved him forward. "The Earl is a reasonable man," he said coldly. "He already knows something is deeply wrong with his daughter. This won't come as a surprise."

This Denn still looked unconvinced, but he stepped forward anyway, his eyes wary, his hands lifted. The others beside him did the same, while Fasta lurched a reflexive step backwards. Never in her life had she been in a fight like this, especially against multiple people at once, what the *hell* was she supposed to do—

But then—Henrik. Henrik's magic, in her breath, and Henrik's warm hand, spreading against her back. Henrik was here, standing behind her, touching her, and she let out a long, shuddery breath. Henrik was here.

"Just start walking, buttercup," he murmured, his breath warm against the back of her neck. "Toward the road. And spin the rocks around us, will you? Keep them close?"

It was a plan, it was something to cling to, and Fasta nodded, and obeyed. Staggering due east, toward the road, moving her makeshift wall into something resembling a tight, spinning shield, feeling the solid steady weight of Henrik's hand on her back.

"Get them!" came Elgin's voice from behind, making Fasta flinch, her rocks stuttering in midair—but Henrik was still here, his hand almost pushing now, guiding, leading.

"Keep going," he said, quiet. "Don't even look at them."

Fasta didn't, but Elgin had yelled something else, and now here was Denn again, dashing out in front of her. Trying to trap her here, block off any escape—but the whizzing rocks from her shield kept him from coming too close, and suddenly a half-dozen of those rocks left the shield and snapped sideways, circling sharp and menacing around Denn's head.

It was Henrik, of course, his hand still so warm and reassuring on Fasta's back, the taste of his magic jolting through the air. And yes, yes, if she and Henrik could keep doing this, keep walking, maybe they really could just leave—

But then Denn raised his hand. And as Fasta stared, Henrik's rocks circling his head fell to the ground, and smashed into sand at his feet.

"Wait," Fasta demanded, without thinking. "You're an earth-mage?! Since when? *How*? Where did you train?"

Denn blinked, while Henrik's hand tightened on Fasta's back. Still guiding her, so she kept walking, even as her eyes stayed on Denn, as the confusion jammed up her thoughts. Not only was Denn an earth-mage, but he was good enough to break stones without touching them? And to overpower Henrik's admittedly weakened magic? Why the *hell* was he working as Elgin's servant?

"Pretty sure they're all earth-mages, love," came Henrik's

voice, more strained than before, even as she felt a surge of his magic rising, soaring out behind them. "Who do you think Bryant gets to do his commissions? And all his spying and stealing, too?"

Fasta's head twisted around to stare at Henrik, digesting all that—but he wasn't looking at her. Because he was frowning toward the rest of the servants, who kept coming in closer, and as Fasta watched, one of them churned a hefty rock up from within the manicured lawn, and shot it toward them.

"They're throwing *rocks*?" Fasta demanded, her voice shrill, even as Henrik waved a hand, and the rock exploded into sand in midair, raining down over their heads. "At *us*? At *you*?"

Henrik huffed a shaky chuckle, even as another servant dragged up another huge rock, leaving a gaping, crumbling hole in Elgin's previously perfect lawn. "I'm weak and pathetic," Henrik murmured, and with a wave of his hand, a sharp surge of magic, the servant's rock plummeted to the earth. "Remember?"

Fasta couldn't help a choked laugh, but there was no time to talk, because the servants kept advancing, dragging up more rocks from the ground below. And though Fasta's makeshift shield was still spinning, still keeping them at a distance, she could feel unfamiliar magic now pulling at the shield's rocks, trying to break them apart.

It wasn't happening—Fasta wasn't the most in-demand builder in the country for nothing—but this wasn't something she could keep up indefinitely, either. And there were six servants, against only two of them, and Fasta swiftly calculated the distance to the road, wincing at the feel of even more rocks rumbling up under the servants' hands.

"Change of plans," Henrik's voice said, urgent in her ear. "To the house. Round the back."

It didn't make sense, because that was in the opposite direction of the road, but again, Fasta obeyed. Grasping Henrik's hand in hers as she headed due north, feeling how unsteady he still was, how running was entirely out of the question...

Another rock flew through the air, this time well over their heads, and Fasta belatedly realized that had been Henrik too, knocking it off course. And then another one, and again more magic pulling at her shield, trying to break it apart.

"You focus on the shield," Henrik ordered, even as Fasta felt more pull on it, obviously from the two servants lurking back, standing side by side. While Denn in front of her dragged up another rock from the earth, and hurled it straight at her face.

"Harry!" she gasped, because she couldn't break the rock and keep up the shield at the same time—but he was already here, his hand punching out over her shoulder, smashing the rock into smithereens just before it touched Fasta's shield.

"Wait," she breathed, because Henrik could've easily spun that rock around, shot it back at Denn's face. "You're not fighting back?"

It wasn't that Henrik wasn't strong enough—she could feel the magic in his touch now, could taste it, low and simmering and powerful. And despite his unsteadiness he was keeping up, they were almost to the house, another rock breaking apart before Fasta's eyes—

"Surround them!" came Elgin's voice from behind them. "Trap them against the house!"

Fasta and Henrik were indeed near the house now, backed up beside the old stone of the bulging northeast corner, the one Henrik had wanted to fix. And Henrik's hand was still in Fasta's, gripping hard, his face pale and shiny with sweat, his magic jolting through her fingers with every breath.

"No fighting back," he said, finally, in answer to her question. "Too risky. Exactly what he wants."

That was probably true, but all six servants were striding menacingly toward them, dragging up more rocks from under the earth. While Elgin watched from behind, a torch blazing in his hand, and Fasta's only defense was that still-spinning shield, the grip of Henrik's fingers on hers.

"Now!" Denn yelled, and the servants let their rocks fly, all at once—but a wave of Henrik's hand smashed them all into powder, dust in Fasta's eyes, her mouth.

"C'mon, fellas," Henrik said, and his voice was almost his own, his eyebrows lifted. "You can do better than that, can't you?"

The servants exchanged glances, and at a signal from Denn, they advanced closer, dragging up more rocks from under the earth. "Surrender," Denn ordered. "And nobody will get hurt."

Henrik smiled, and Fasta felt his magic touch her shield, expanding it out a little further, spinning it a little faster. "Nobody's getting hurt," he said, his hand squeezing tighter on Fasta's. "And if you fools back off now, we'll let this go. Last chance."

His eyes flicked back to Elgin, but Elgin just sputtered and shook his head in the torch's flickering light. "Stop talking and just fucking *take* them!" he shouted at Denn. "You can't deal with a few spinning rocks?"

Denn's eyes briefly closed, in something almost like exasperation, but when they opened again they were narrow, determined. "On three," he ordered, to the servants flanking him. "Pull up everything you can. One, two, three!"

The earth shook with the movement, with six earth-mages dragging up boulders from deep below. And Fasta's spinning shield faltered, Henrik's magic surging out and down and under—

The rocks flew toward them as one, fast and huge and deadly—but this time, Henrik's whole body leaned into them, against them. And instead of smashing into powder, the rocks shot toward the house, pounding into that weak, sagging corner.

Fasta could feel the house tremble, deep and wrenching in her bones—but no one else seemed to notice. Especially not

Elgin, who was shouting another order at the servants, and who in return—Fasta let out a gasp—dragged up more huge boulders from the earth below, quaking the ground beneath them.

"*Harry*," she breathed, her eyes panicky on his, because they couldn't let them hurt the *house*—but Henrik's face was grim, determined, focused. He was... *concentrating*, his magic reaching out deep below. Pushing, pulling, breaking.

The understanding shot through Fasta like a punch to the gut, and she gasped as the servants raised their boulders, let them fly. "Wait!" she shouted, but it was too late, because the boulders were in the air, and Henrik's whole body and Henrik's whole focus were with them, part of them, hurling them toward that same weakened corner.

The house's entire foundation lurched this time, slipping downwards. Only a little, probably not even a handsbreadth, but any more would be catastrophic, how did none of them *see*—

But they didn't even hesitate, just dragging up more rocks from the earth, and damn it, that was part of it, too. Weakening the ground below, weakening that corner from all sides, Henrik's magic pulling and pulling under there, until—

The foundation slipped again, and now Fasta could see the house's corner crumbling a little, as a few of the stones fell away. And gods, there were hundreds of people in that house, what the hell was Henrik *thinking*—

The next set of rocks hurled toward them, and again Henrik heaved them off course, straight toward the corner, smashing so forcefully into it that the earth below them rolled and heaved. Making Fasta's shield wobble, and several of the servants staggered sideways, while the house's corner slipped further, bulging out wide and dangerous.

"The house!" one of the servants finally yelled, snapping Elgin's eyes toward it—and then his face froze, shocked and pale in the torch's flickering light.

"You cheating *fucker*," he growled at Henrik, but Henrik didn't reply, and Fasta could feel that pull of his magic again, deep below. Splintering off even more of the house's foundation toward the earth, and even Elgin had to feel it this time, rumbling and shuddering beneath their feet.

"Fix this!" Elgin yelled at the servants. "Fix the house. Now!"

The servants were already scrambling, sprinting off toward the house, climbing over the crumbly, slippery earth. "Hold it up!" Fasta heard Denn's voice say, as the servants' hands shoved against the sagging corner—but it only slipped further, sending rocks raining from above this time, barely missing the servants' heads.

"It's not working!" one of them shouted, as he pulled a hand off, barely blocked another falling stone. "It's going to collapse!"

Denn shot a desperate look over his shoulder toward Elgin, and then braced himself on the earth, and pushed hard against the house. And he was clearly an excellent earth-mage, because Fasta could feel the house briefly stabilizing—that was, until another tug from Henrik's magic deep below set it staggering again.

"*Harry*," Fasta breathed, and she belatedly realized she was still spinning her shield, and let it drop. "Any more, it's going to go."

Henrik's eyes glancing toward her were focused, glittering, and Fasta realized, suddenly, that he was viciously, dangerously furious. That maybe he truly *would* smash Elgin's house, that Elgin had hurt them and insulted them in too many ways, that this was Elgin's battle to lose.

"Fix it!" Elgin hollered again, coming closer, his voice and eyes verging on frantic. "Obey me!"

But Denn at the wall shook his head, his feet sliding haphazard behind him. "We can't," he gasped. "It's too far gone. It's going to fall."

Elgin's eyes darted side to side, up and down, wide and white-rimmed in the light from his torch—and then he seemed to notice Fasta and Henrik there, still hand in hand, Fasta with her other hand gripped tight to Henrik's arm.

"You," Elgin said, advancing toward them. "*You* fix it. Now!"

Fasta could feel Henrik's surprise, the barely suppressed fury leaking into his magic. "What the fuck?" he said, and he actually laughed, hard and bitter. "We're not your servants, arsehole."

The panicked rage shot across Elgin's eyes, and he stepped closer. "Fix it," he growled. "Or else."

"Or else what?" Henrik shot back. "You're gonna report us to the authorities, and try to ruin our lives? Weren't you already doing that anyway?"

One of Elgin's servants yelled, barely jumping back in time to avoid a shower of rock from above, and Elgin betrayed a sound somewhere between a growl and a scream. "You're just going to let my house collapse with two hundred people inside?!" he shouted. "Do you want a fucking *massacre*? Her *father's* in there, for fuck's sakes!"

Henrik's eyes flicked toward Fasta, but she wasn't moving, because the house wasn't going, not quite yet. And she trusted Henrik, she was respecting Henrik's choices and his autonomy, and he deserved this, was entitled to this—and he somehow seemed to follow that, his chest rising and falling, his hand pulling Fasta closer, fingers spreading wide against her back.

"What's it worth to you, then?" he said to Elgin, his voice cool. "What are you gonna offer me to fix it?"

Elgin spluttered, his eyes darting between Henrik, his servants, and the still-crumbling corner, now exposing half of the thankfully empty room inside. "I won't bring charges against you," he said. "And I'll pay you double for the original job."

Henrik's hand in Fasta's spasmed, and he laughed again, brittle and cold. "Very funny," he replied, and he turned to go, tugging Fasta along with him. While the servants shouted again from behind, the earth rumbling below, and that wasn't any of Henrik's magic this time, all earth and physics and gravity.

Elgin yelled out another amount behind them, nearly double the first one, and Henrik hesitated, and glanced over his shoulder. "If you double that again," he said coldly, "I'll think about it. If you put it in writing. *And* make the transfer first thing in the morning."

Elgin flinched, his hands in fists at his sides, but the servants were yelling again, and the corner was almost entirely gone now, stone splintering and falling in a steady stream to the earth.

"Fine!" Elgin shouted, though the fury was clear in his voice, his eyes. "Do it!"

"In writing," Henrik said, and with another exasperated groan Elgin began searching his pockets, giving desperate looks toward the house. And Fasta finally took pity on him, and reached into the front pocket of Henrik's work tunic, and tossed over the paper and pencil she knew would be there.

"Fass, you witness it," Henrik said, as Elgin started scribbling. "Sign it."

Fasta went over to Elgin, a little warily, but he thrust the paper toward her without complaint. A brief read over it proved its legitimacy, and Fasta put her own signature to the bottom, and folded the paper into her pocket.

Henrik's glance toward her was brief, but grateful, and now he stepped closer too, crossing his arms over his burly chest. "You're also gonna clear me of any theft accusations," he said, "and give me a good reference. And, we're gonna need all these servants of yours, for the rest of the night."

Elgin spat out a curse, but Henrik only raised his eyebrows, and glanced purposely toward the house's still-collapsing corner. Making Elgin's eyes follow, and Fasta could see the fight finally leaving him, his slim shoulders sagging, his eyelids sliding shut.

"Fine," he muttered. "Fat piece of shit commoner *arsehole*."

Thank the gods, Henrik ignored it, and this time his eyes on the house were thoughtful, assessing. "You with me, Fass?" he asked, reaching out his hand, and she quivered beneath the surge of warmth, soaring up her spine.

"Of course," she said. "Always."

37

I f Fasta had ever doubted that Henrik was the greatest earth-mage she'd ever met, this decided it once and for all.

"Back off, all of you," Henrik said to the servants, as he strolled over to the precariously sagging corner, and pushed up his sleeves. "Take a breather, you're gonna need it."

And with that, he braced himself, and thrust both hands against what was left of the splintering wall. And in that moment, hanging and breathless, everything stilled, and stopped. The earth, the house, the crumbling, everything.

Everyone stared, a few of the servants' mouths dropping open, and Fasta gave a wry shake of her head, and stepped up beside Henrik. "Show-off," she murmured, as she reached and fished more paper out of his pocket, and smoothed it out against the now-solid stone. "What do you want me to calculate first? How much new stone we'll need?"

Henrik's grin was warm and beloved and familiar, and he glanced over his shoulder, toward where the quarry had delivered the stone they'd been using for the indoor walls. "Think we can get by with that?"

Fasta was already calculating it, breaking out the volume of what they needed against what remained, between the quarry and the usable remnants of the current wall, all scattered as rubble below them. "No, more," she said. "Unless you want to have to do this again in two years."

Henrik replied with a good-natured groan, a jerk of his head toward the still-staring servants behind them. "You, Denn," he said. "Take your strongest guy, and go digging for stones to match her specs. Take them from another building if you have to. And you two"—he nodded at two more of them—"bring over everything that's left from the quarry. Everyone else, start digging, we need this entire foundation uncovered."

Several of the servants glanced warily toward Elgin, but he waved them on, his eyes clouded and flat, and they scuttled away, following Henrik's instructions. While Henrik himself hadn't yet broken a sweat, now looking up at the decimated stone above, and down at the mess below.

"This wall was a bit off to start with, yeah?" he asked Fasta. "And that's why it originally gave out? Along with the shitty mortar maintenance?"

Fasta had still been making calculations, and she nodded, frowning down at her paper. "This part needs to move here," she said, as she pulled up a makeshift wall of earth to demonstrate. "Like this."

"Shoddy," Henrik said, gravely shaking his head, even as he flashed her a grateful grin. "Draw it up and show me?"

But he didn't even have to ask, because again, Fasta was already doing it, using one hand to calculate it out on the paper, while her other hand rested on Henrik's, her magic sinking down and into his. Brushing against where he was currently holding the wall, nudging it where it needed to go, and Henrik immediately complied, sliding several precarious tons of stone without even taking a breath.

"Better?" he asked cheerfully, and Fasta rolled her eyes at him, even as her hand slid up against his back. Just needing to touch him, feel his brilliant warm body under her fingers, his breath rising and falling, here, alive.

"Yes," she said, her eyes meeting his, and she could see his smile slowly fading, his eyes sobering—and then the wall slipped, just slightly, and he choked a breathless laugh as he turned back toward it, magic pulsing out deep. "Think I might've taken this a bit too far," he murmured at her. "As I seem to do."

Fasta chuckled and shook her head, and spread her own hands to the wall beside his, easing her magic in with his, too. Keeping the wall taut and straight, taking some of the pressure from him, while he turned his attention to the now-returning servants, lugging stone behind them.

"Bring that over," he said to Denn, who was singlehandedly dragging what looked like the bulk of it. "And you two, start taking out all this sand and rubble. You, go make some mortar. Fass, you go supervise, keep them in line? And I'll return the favour later?"

His voice had softened at the end, and he gave her a quick wink, a teasing twitch of a smile. And it was all Fasta could to keep from gasping, while the heat flashed through her thoughts, her belly, her skin.

"You will?" she murmured back, because she needed to hear it, suddenly so desperate she could barely breathe—and Henrik nodded, his eyes serious again, his throat convulsing.

"Yeah," he said, quiet. "If you don't hate me."

Fasta didn't hate him, could never, and somehow her arms hurled themselves around his waist, her face buried into his sweaty neck. While one of Henrik's hands snapped down too, pulling her tight and almost painful against his side, until the house under his other hand gave another little twitch, almost as if threatening to escape.

"Fucking thing," Henrik said gruffly, and when Fasta glanced up again his eyes were bright, blinking in the dim light. "When we're done, yeah?"

It was a promise, a real one, and Fasta nodded, and turned away. Feeling his eyes on her back as she went over to the servants and the quarry rock, and quickly evaluated the volume, the size, the type of stone.

"These need to be shaved square," she said, picking up a stone, and demonstrating. "Like this. Use this one as a guide."

They obeyed, just as the other servants were obeying Henrik, and together they slowly, surely, shaped the stones, placed them, poured mortar behind, sealed the front. Filled in the earth, packed it down, kept going, and going.

Henrik held the house up the entire time, giving orders and slamming rocks into place, helping the servants when they faltered. He was a good teacher, patient and authoritative, giving praise when it was due, and by the time the foundation was properly set, the servants were looking at him with respect, and maybe even admiration.

"Good work, fellas," Henrik said, hours later, once the surrounding earth was finally packed back in, the house's walls straight and sturdy again, the morning light just peeking over the eastern horizon. "And Fass, of course. Nicely done."

He grinned at her, his eyes tired but satisfied, and Fasta smiled back. While Henrik's gaze flicked to Elgin, who, to his credit, had entirely abandoned his party to stay out here and supervise. And who, to Fasta's mind, was damned lucky this had all happened out back, on the opposite end of the manor from his party, and that none of his guests had seemed to notice what had occurred.

"And my coin?" Henrik asked Elgin. "You'll have it in the morning at the bank in Skent, right? Unless you want all this work to undo itself?"

Elgin's hands twitched against his expensive suit, which was now spattered with earth and mud, but he jerked a stiff nod. "Yes," he said. "You'll get it. And then never show your face here again."

Henrik shrugged, and his gaze flicked to the servants, who

were standing off to the side, away from Elgin. "Fine by me," he said. "Though if any of your guys wanted to get in touch, do some real work, they'd be more than welcome."

The servants glanced at each other, a few of them shifting on their feet, and Henrik nodded, first at them, and then at Elgin. "Good luck, then," he said. "And next time your house is fucking broken, arsehole, *fix* it."

Elgin didn't deign to reply, but it didn't matter, nothing mattered, except Henrik stepping toward Fasta, and slinging his heavy arm over her shoulder. Drawing her close, his mouth pressing warm against her hair, before he pulled her away, toward the road, without another look back.

"Where do you wanna go?" he murmured, quiet, as they walked, and Fasta slid her arm around his waist. "Back to Coven Manor?"

Fasta shook her head against his shoulder, glanced up at his still-battered, tired-looking face in the faint morning light. "No," she replied, with a sigh. "We can't. I found out last night that they've *fired* you, Harry."

Henrik grimaced, but he didn't look surprised, not even a little. "'Course they have," he said, with a sigh. "So Bryant's plan worked after all. Get me well and permanently out of the picture, so he could get himself into it."

Fasta flinched, and frowned up toward him. "His plan *didn't* work," she countered firmly. "Because I quit, too."

Henrik's steps beside her faltered, his arm clenching tight around her shoulder. "Wait, *you* quit?" he demanded. "*Why*?!"

Fasta hesitated too, pulling back to meet his disbelieving eyes. "Well, I've been giving it a lot of thought," she said slowly. "And there's no reason for me to keep working at a place that doesn't respect me, and doesn't respect you. They threw you out on what essentially amounted to *hearsay*, Harry."

Henrik kept staring at her, perhaps hearing the anger in her voice, and Fasta took a long breath, let it out. "I only stayed there because it was—easy. Safe. A way to defend against my father, and society's expectations. A way to stay... in control."

Henrik's eyes flickered, and his chest rose and fell against her. "So what are you gonna do now, then?" he said, his voice careful. "Without the Coven?"

Fasta pulled in her courage, pulled in more breath. "I was hoping," she said, "to go into business for myself. And there's no obligation whatsoever, but I wanted to ask you"—she squared her shoulders—"if you might like to join me. As real partners, this time."

Henrik blinked, once, but he didn't speak, and Fasta fought down the whispers of suddenly bubbling panic. "I just thought—it could be good, right?" she said, high-pitched. "We could choose our own jobs, make our own rules, set our own schedule. And yes, it will be slow going at first, and a significant reduction in pay, while we rebuild our client base—but I made Kjaran promise to pass on any requests for our services, and that should help considerably, don't you think?"

Henrik just kept staring at her, as if he wasn't following, or maybe wasn't agreeing. While Fasta's panic pounded faster, a frantic drumbeat of uncertainty in her head, strong enough that she couldn't bear to look at him—so she gulped down a shaky breath, dropped her eyes to the road, made herself start walking again.

"But again, you don't—have to," she said, through her quivering throat. "I'll respect your decision, no matter what."

There was an instant's silence, but Henrik was still here, walking beside her, keeping pace. "Look, Fass," he said, his voice low. "You can't—you can't actually *want* to do all that."

"Why can't I?" Fasta shot back, the unsteadiness too close under her voice. "I told you, I already quit. I'm doing it for myself, whether you're involved or not. I even told my father."

"You told your *father*?" Henrik echoed, his voice rising, and Fasta nodded, frowned at the earth.

"I even told him I was doing it with you," she said thinly,

"not that I knew you would agree. But I just—I'm tired of lying, Harry. Tired of pretending to be in control. Pretending like everything is fine, when it isn't."

There was more silence, the only sounds their matching footsteps, and the morning chirps of birds in the nearby trees. "You were right, you know," Fasta continued, quieter, toward the road. "That you couldn't trust me. Because—I do lie a lot, and pretend. I avoid the truth, and act like everything is fine, even when it isn't. I think I justified it by feeling like I was protecting people with it, doing what was best for them. But I was really just protecting—myself."

She could feel Henrik's eyes on her, could almost taste the closeness of his magic. "Protecting yourself from what?" he asked, just as quiet, and Fasta snapped up a nearby rock into her fingers, squeezed it tight.

"From making the sacrifices," she said finally. "From facing the—consequences. Losing my family, my wealth, my security. Being cast out. Being... alone. But"—she took another breath, squeezed the rock into dust—"I already lost my family, years ago, and maybe I never even really had them to begin with. I'm already alone. I just"—she swallowed, fought to make her voice steady—"need to accept it, and move on."

She could hear Henrik's breath, suddenly, too loud beside her, and now here was the heat and weight of his arm, settling again over her shoulder. "I'm so proud of you, Fass," he said, his voice unsteady too. "I know how hard it must have been for you to face all that. And for what it's worth"—he took a breath—"you're not alone. You've never been alone."

Fasta gulped back a breath too, shook her head. "I appreciate that, Harry," she managed. "But you also—wanted to leave. You said we could never get over it. You ordered me not to follow you. And you had every right, and I want to respect your decision, and—"

But Henrik cut her off with a hard laugh, not quite a laugh at all. "Yeah, and it was a fucking stupid decision," he said, with a sigh. "Fuck, I'm sorry, Fasta. For all of it. For losing my temper. For hurting you. For everything I said. And especially for taking off on you like that."

Fasta blinked, swallowed, and Henrik drew her closer, gently squeezed his hand at her shoulder. "I should've known I just needed to cool off. By the time I got to the road, I was already cursing myself, and fully planning to crawl back and beg you to forgive me."

Wait, really? Fasta shot a surprised glance up at his face, at his grim, rueful eyes. "But what you said, about the cottage," he continued. "About Bryant offering you one. It started to make sense, that it could've been him and his servants behind all this, all this time. Working together with the servants at the manor to get rid of me, so he could get at you."

The possibility of Coven Manor's servants being involved had already occurred to Fasta too, and she nodded, took a deep breath. "It was the only explanation that made sense," she said. "The servants could have easily accessed all the rooms items were stolen from, and also could have taken something of yours to drag around Johan's room. Maybe even your laundry."

Henrik made a face, but nodded, too. "And they could've seen enough to know that you'd gone off with Johan that night, and that I'd be raging, which gave me a motive," he added. "And even those two maids who caught us in the back hallway had to be in on it, right? Pretty damn convenient for them to show up right then, unless they'd been following us, or trying to plant something, right?"

Right. It did make sense, and Fasta was still kicking herself for not seeing it earlier, too. "I didn't know for certain until I saw the cottage," she said. "And it had to be earth-mages who broke into it, so—"

"Wait," Henrik snapped, his whole body gone taut, his hand gripping Fasta's arm. "They broke into our *cottage*?!"

Fasta blinked, because right, how would he have known

about that? So she told him, as briefly as she could, about the latch, the stolen items, the draft through his bedroom window.

"That piece of shit *scumbag*," Henrik growled, once she was done. "I knew the arsehole *knew* about the cottage, but to actually fucking break *into* it? What if he'd fucked it up somehow? What if we'd come back to a total fucking *ruin*?!"

His sentiments echoed Fasta's so thoroughly that she gave a choked laugh, leaning closer up against him. "Probably a good thing I didn't tell you earlier, then," she said lightly. "You would have let his house collapse after all, wouldn't you?"

Henrik still looked enraged, but his arm tightened around her shoulder again, pulling her closer as they walked. "Probably would've murdered the bastard," he muttered. "I was already damned close, when I figured it out. I should have left it alone, and come after you instead, but I was so fucking furious, I thought I'd go deal with him first."

Fasta winced, because that had clearly been a patently ill-considered idea, and Henrik choked out another laugh. "Yeah, it was stupid," he said. "And I *knew* that, and by the time I got there I was half-thinking of backing off still—maybe just say I was picking up something I'd left there—but when I walked into the ballroom, there was Bryant. Pinning one of his servants up against the wall, and pumping away under her skirts."

Fasta winced again, but nodded, because it wasn't even a surprise, was it? Gods, Elgin had told her she could continue bedding Henrik if they married, and of course he would have done the same with whoever he pleased.

"I fucking lost it," Henrik said now, quieter, "because it was one of the blonde ones, and she had her hair in a braid just like yours, and I *saw* the look on her face. And he was doing it right out in the open, didn't even jump when he heard me walk in. Which means they all know. And he doesn't give a shit."

Fasta's stomach churned, but she nodded again, leaned closer into the warm safety of Henrik's shoulder. "So that's why he attacked you, and knocked you out," she said, and it wasn't a question. "He thought you'd tell me."

Henrik gave another tired laugh, his hand squeezing tight on her shoulder. "Right in one," he replied. "'Course, it didn't help that I was about to murder him anyway. And *then*, he had the gall to say it was just the same with me and you. That I was your servant, and *you* were the one taking advantage."

Fasta's fury toward Elgin was rising all over again, and it was echoed in Henrik's voice, hard and fierce. "I told him you would *never* take advantage," he said. "You never, ever did. You *paid* me, for fuck's sakes, as a *favour*, when I *needed* it. And you made damn *sure* I wanted it. The difference between him and you is night and day."

Fasta couldn't help a furtive, searching glance up, to where Henrik's eyes on her were just as fierce. "You were so fucking good to me, Fass," he said. "You always have been, in every single way. I don't even come *close* to deserving it."

They'd somehow reached the town gate of Skent, which was still closed, and Fasta was spared from replying while Henrik talked to the gatekeeper, and handed over a few coins. And then he led her through the town's quiet streets, toward that same inn they'd stayed in the week before.

"One room," Henrik said at the bar, handing over more coins, and Fasta didn't miss the same barkeeper's raised eyebrows between them, lingering on Henrik's still-bruised face. But Henrik didn't seem to notice, just guided Fasta up the stairs, down the hall, his fingers firm and familiar on her back.

He slammed the door shut behind them, latching it with a wave of his arm, and suddenly he was here, so close, his big hands cradling both sides of Fasta's face, making her look at him.

"I'm sorry, love," he said, and the truth of it was in his eyes, in the tightness on his mouth. "I'm so sorry. I've been way too rough with you, too hard on you. I should never have lost my temper on you like I did out there. Should never have walked away like that, and left you there alone. Should've held you, and kissed you, and told you that you're incredible, and gorgeous, and *perfect*, in every single way."

Fasta blinked at him, as he pulled in another breath, his throat bobbing. "And I should've done that so many times, throughout all this," he whispered. "Can't tell you how much I wanted to, all this time. How much I wanted to hold you, and treasure you, and *worship* you."

Oh. Fasta's heart skipped, and Henrik's hands stroked her face, his eyes blinking hard. "And how much I wanted," he croaked, "to beg you to take the money back. How much I hated even *thinking* about that coin you'd put in my account. How much I thought about going back on the deal, throwing over my sweet little brother, so maybe I wouldn't end up hurting you, and driving you away from me."

Fasta couldn't move, could only keep blinking at his too-bright eyes, feeling his callused hands tenderly stroking her face. "And this whole time," he rasped, "I've been lying, too. I've been protecting myself, at your expense. I've been telling you, and myself, that I would still walk away from you. That I *could*."

The words came out choked, almost desperate, and they took away Fasta's breath, her thoughts whirling and splintering apart. *I've been lying, too. Telling myself that I would still walk away from you.*

And it meant—it meant that Henrik couldn't walk away from her. Or wouldn't. And Fasta's hands found him too, frantic and craving and furious, pulling him close, dragging his mouth to hers.

And he was there, hot, fiery, demanding. Lips and teeth and tongue, pressure and heat and billowing hungry magic. Blasting straight through the tension and the tiredness, his hands wide and possessive on her arse, while hers were pushing him back, and back, until he was up against the bed, still ravaging her mouth, even as he dropped down flat onto his back, and yanked her up on top of him.

"You can't walk away," Fasta gasped, into his mouth, between kisses. "Never. New rule."

He groaned back against her, that stunning bulging hardness in his trousers already grinding up between her legs. "Why not," he breathed, making Fasta briefly snap back to look at him—but he wasn't protesting, he was asking, and there was a difference, there was.

"Because," she said, breathing hard, holding his eyes. "I'm sorry too, Harry. I was hiding the truth from you, all this time. Even though I promised you I'd tell it. And the truth is—"

Her throat had seemed to close off, her eyes caught on the look in his, and she made herself drag in air, put her hands to his chest, feel his own shuddering breath. She could do this. She could be honest. She would.

"The truth is," she said, "I love you, Harry Hallen. I always have. And these past five years—especially these past few weeks—have been the best of my entire life. And if you still want me"—she drew in more air, more courage—"I'll sacrifice whatever it takes to be yours. Forever."

38

Fasta's truth was met with silence, stillness, breath. With Henrik Hallen looking at her like that, like she was something exquisite, precious, unreal.

"You don't mean that," he said, his voice so soft, so choked. "You're lying, Fass. You *have* to be."

But Fasta gave a hard, deliberate shake of her head, holding the truth in her eyes, making him see it—and then she leaned down, kissed his mouth again, gentle this time, lips brushing lips. And next she kissed down his cheek to his stubbly jaw, his neck, his ear, feeling his arms circle around her, his body arching, his breaths coming ragged and shallow. Like he was agreeing, almost, actually believing her, and when Fasta's hands slid up under his tunic, he didn't even protest, didn't resist.

Oh *gods*, because it meant that Fasta was actually touching Henrik Hallen's bare belly, his bare chest, for the very first time. Feeling the softness over hardness, the tickling hair all over him, the silken warmth of his skin—and in a burst of daring she clutched for his tunic's hem, and tugged it upwards.

"Please," she breathed, because she'd still never seen this, had never set eyes on Henrik Hallen without his clothes on.

And suddenly the craving was shrill, demanding, all-consuming, her hands sliding hungry and everywhere at once.

"Please, Harry," she said again, pleaded. "Need to see you."

His face had flushed, his eyes oddly wary, but finally he twitched a nod. And then he reached and pulled the tunic up, and up, and off over his head.

Fasta gasped at the sight, her tongue brushing her lips, because good *gods*, Henrik was gorgeous. His bare chest broad and hairy and full, his shoulders bulky and powerful, his arms wrapped in thick ridged muscle. His belly below was soft and rounded, dusted with that same golden hair, and—Fasta couldn't help another groan—peeking out against it, jutting up out of his trousers, was the swollen, reddened head of that hard, thick, glorious cock.

"May I?" Fasta asked, breathless, pulling at the trousers, and though something strange again passed over Henrik's eyes, he nodded. And then she yanked the trousers down, and all the way off, revealing powerful thighs and more golden hair and the impossible, thrilling sight of that swollen ruddy cock, propped up against his slightly rounded belly, as if displayed on a stunning, obscenely arousing platter, just for her.

"Fuck," Fasta breathed, as her hands slid against that belly, around that perfect cock. "You're *gorgeous*, Harry."

He only kept staring at her, watching as she dipped downwards, and sucked the head of that cock deep into her mouth. Revelling in the taste of him, and in the strangled-sounding gasp from his throat, the seemingly reflexive, too-powerful grasp of his hands in her hair. Guiding her up and down, harder and faster, while she kept her eyes on his face, obeying his rules, even now.

But then his hands gripped tighter, pulling her up, and the head of his cock bobbed out of her mouth, slapping back against his belly. "What?" Fasta breathed, between gasps, because she was already close, just from this—but he shook his head, pulled her up further, looked at her with those strange, glittery eyes.

"You're lying again," he said, in a choked whisper, almost as if it hurt him to speak. "I'm not gorgeous, I'm pale and hairy and fat. And you're not gonna give me what I want, you never will, because you *can't*."

Fasta blinked at him, fought to reorient herself, to think over the pounding gasping hunger. "You *are* gorgeous," she managed, as her hands again stroked at his belly, his chest, the coiled strength of his shoulders. "Exactly what I like best. Big, bulky, powerful. What kind of earth-mage has no meat on his bones?"

Henrik's body stilled under hers, looking like he didn't quite follow, and a daring, rebellious part of Fasta urged her downwards, dropping her first-ever kiss to his pebbly pink nipple. And then to his other one, sucking a little this time, making that barrel chest heave up against her, his hand tightening again in her hair.

"No," he gasped, and his face looked pained now too, like Fasta was truly hurting him, somehow. "No. You *can't*, Fass."

She couldn't. The hurt plummeted in her gut, and Fasta blinked at him, at his miserable grey eyes. "Why," she said, through her too-thick throat. "I *adore* you, Harry."

His eyes closed at that, like she was still hurting him, and he gave a sharp, uneven shake of his head. "No," he said again, sounding almost desperate this time. "You can't give me what I want."

Fasta blinked at him for another long, dangling moment, and she groped through her memories, dragged up what he'd told her about this. "But you told me," she gasped, between breaths, "you want—a wife of your own. A family. Right?"

Yes, that was it, and Henrik twitched a small, almost imperceptible nod toward her. The pain still flaring through his eyes, because—because—

And I know very well that's never gonna be you. I'll never be good enough for you.

Right. And this was where Fasta needed more truth, needed to face her fear, to put the last of it out and bare between them. So she lifted her chin, drew in breath, dragged up her courage...

"So?" she asked. "You can't do that with me?"

Henrik's entire body under her flinched, his eyes snapped wide, genuinely shocked. "No," he said. "Of course not."

He said it like it was a foregone conclusion, like something long ago decided, and Fasta frowned down at him, her hands spreading against his bare chest. "Why not?"

Henrik blinked, and shook his head. "Because," he said, sounding almost confused, now. "Your title. Your inheritance. Your father. Your standing, your reputation. It would be a mess, a scandal, all over the papers. Your family would never talk to you *again*."

It was all true, of course, but Fasta had already considered it, decided it, what felt like ages ago. "I know," she said, and with a strange, irritated brazenness, she leaned over, pressed another slow, lingering kiss to that tantalizing nipple. "And I already told you, I've accepted all that. I don't care about any of that."

"But," Henrik countered, as his hand found her face, tilted her head up again. "You—you've always cared so much about that, Fasta. About the safety, and the coin. And you—you deserve it, yeah? It's the one damned thing you get from your fucked-up childhood, and you shouldn't have to give it up for me, you *shouldn't*."

Fasta's irritation curdled up higher, and she felt her frown deepening. "But I want to," she said, perhaps sharper than she meant. "And it's still my choice to make, Harry, not yours. Was Elgin right when he said you don't want me without the inheritance?"

Henrik's lip curled, in immediate and obvious revulsion,

and he gave another sharp shake of his head. "Of course not," he replied. "You know I don't want even another *copper* of your money, for as long as I live. But"—he took a breath—"it's still your right, Fasta. Your *life*. You can't just—*abandon* that."

"Why can't I?" Fasta shot back. "Who says? You? The Coven? The government? Do you really think an official would refuse to marry us? And even if they *did* refuse, if my father prevented it somehow, who's going to stop us from speaking our own vows, and setting up our lives on our own terms? Yes, my father will stomp and rage about it, and call me a horrible disappointment, but how is that any different than what he already does? And since when have I cared what he thinks anyway?"

Henrik was staring at her again, and his chest and belly under her were heaving, making her rise and fall along with it. "You," he began, and he squeezed his eyes shut, opened them. "You can't actually mean this, Fasta. You're—tired, or over-whelmed, or something. Sure, you like working with me, and fucking me, and playing those power-trip games with me. It's not the same as"—he pulled in another breath—"as *committing* to me, like that. *Forever*."

His eyes were serious, intent, maybe even pleading, and Fasta's heart was beating faster, her hand brushing reflexively against that ring of Henrik's on her finger. "I know," she said again, watching as his eyes darted downwards, lingering now on his ring, too. "I'm well aware of the difference, Harry."

His chest heaved harder, and Fasta twisted that ring on her finger, let him feel her doing it. "I love you, Harry," she whispered. "I want to commit to you. In whatever way makes this relationship work for you. And if that means getting married, then I want to get married."

It was there, it was said, and Henrik's mouth fell open, his eyes darting from hers, down to that ring, and back again. So Fasta held his eyes, and took her time sliding the ring off her right hand, letting it hover in the air between them—and then she slid it onto her left hand instead.

"*Fasta*," Henrik gasped, sounding almost strangled, even as his glittering eyes held to that ring on her finger. "You don't understand. I would want it to be—*normal.* Quiet, and simple, with none of the coin and servants and houses you're used to. I'm not gonna give you that kind of life, and even if I could, I wouldn't want to. You'd have to give up *everything.*"

Gods, Henrik was stubborn sometimes, and in a flash of irritation, or maybe insight, Fasta reached down, and pulled off her own tunic. Showing him everything beneath, hard nipples and jiggling breasts, with his pendant nestled close and familiar between them.

"I *know*, Harry," she snapped. "And in case you haven't noticed, this *is* my life. With you. Working with you and living with you and eating with you and talking to you and fucking you. Building an entire *house* with you, for fuck's sakes."

Henrik's eyes looked almost frantic, darting between her eyes, her breasts, her ring, and Fasta cupped his face in her hands, made him look at her. "You know me better than anyone else *alive*, Harry," she said. "Do you really think I'd be happy hanging off my father's purse-strings for the rest of my life, waiting for a payout? You think I want to live the way he thinks some proper lady should, hosting society parties and wearing impractical clothes and sitting all day in a house I can't *touch*?"

A flicker of comprehension passed across Henrik's face, thank the gods—so next Fasta shoved at the waist of her trousers, kicked them down and off her ankles. "And do you honestly think," she continued, harder now, "I'd be happy living with an arsehole like Elgin? Being lied to day in and day out, bearing him children he doesn't actually give a damn about, while he sneaks around my house—and my children's *nursery*—with the nannies and chambermaids?"

That flicker of understanding again shifted through

Henrik's eyes, and Fasta spread her now-naked body over his, and reached down between her legs, took his still-hard cock in hand, stroked its warm, silken skin.

"And do you really think," she added, breathless, "I'd be happy fucking some weak, pampered, flimsy little rich boy, who's not actually an earth-mage but pretends he is, and has no idea whatsoever how to please me? When I know how good it is with *you*?"

As she spoke, she guided him up, nudging that thick hardness against her waiting wet heat. And oh *hell*, he was still huge, the head of him not even breaching her, even as she lowered her weight onto it, slow.

"It's so *good* with you, Harry," she whispered, closing her eyes, willing herself to relax. "*So* good. I'll never, *ever* be able to get over it."

It was an echo of his own words from that day in the hallway, and she felt that jutting hardness vibrate against her, sinking a breath deeper—and she took another breath, spread her legs wider. "I love how big you are," she breathed. "How solid and sturdy and strong you are. You have the most incredible cock I've ever *seen*, let alone taken inside me."

That was definitely a gasp, another telltale quiver of that hardness against her, and Fasta bit her lip, let out a little cry. "And I love how you take charge of me," she choked out. "I love how you can take control, take all the pressure and fear away, and just let me be—*me*. No matter how wrong or shameful it is. And how you still want me like that, still want to take me, fill me, *own* me—"

Henrik's hands had settled against her hips now, guiding her downwards, gently deepening the pressure—and then it snapped, broke, as he sank deep inside. Impaling Fasta on the length of him, hot and powerful and *alive*, and she arched backwards, crying out, hands scrabbling at his chest. Fuck, *fuck*—

"Good girl," Henrik whispered, and Fasta's entire body

shuddered, spasming tight around him. Making him flare up again inside, and Fasta's wildly trembling body skittered down to collapse against his, her hands clinging to his shoulders, her face buried deep into his neck.

But damn, it was good, so good, especially with that wonderful, utterly new sensation of bare skin to bare skin, all down the length of her. The swell of his belly fitting up into the curve of hers, her breasts spilling out over his broad chest, her legs tucked close by his sides. And when his chest rose and fell, she went with it, that huge thrilling cock pinning her firmly in place.

"Fuck," she gasped against him, and in reply his hips canted upwards, his strong hands guiding hers down to meet them. And oh, oh gods, this was the best thing Fasta had ever felt in her entire *life*, and one of her hands again cupped his stubbly jaw, the other sliding deep into his hair.

"Fuck," she said again, shoving up to better see his face, his eyes. "Fuck, Harry, you're *everything*, and"—she cried out again, as his hips slammed up—"I need you, I need this. You have to want me. You *have* to believe me."

His hips thrust up again, his perfect cock grinding deeper, skin sliding slick and smooth and hot. "'Course I want you," came Henrik's voice, rough, his eyes almost painfully intent on hers. "How could I not. Gorgeous generous genius *perfect* girl."

Fasta gulped back something like a sob, and her eyes blinked hard, even as her mouth cried out its pleasure. "Then you won't leave," she gasped. "You'll stay. Right?"

Henrik's eyes were speaking again, saying something Fasta couldn't read, while his cock ground deeper, harder, distracting, *beautiful*. "You have to," she choked. "We'll keep working together, we'll put the loft in the cottage, you'll fuck me with anything and everything you can possibly *think* of."

Henrik betrayed a low, ragged groan, and his cock plunged in again, making her jolt all over. "You'd still want that?" he said, quiet enough that Fasta almost didn't hear it. "After what I did to you?"

After what I did. It took Fasta an instant to realize he meant in the forest, with the switch, and she clenched all over at even the thought of it, her eyes rolling back a little in her head. "*Hell,* yes," she gasped. "And maybe next time you could use a stone paddle again, so you could fuck my mouth at the same time."

There was a low rumble from Henrik's throat, somewhere between a growl and a laugh, but he wasn't arguing it anymore, he wasn't—and Fasta quaked beneath the hungry shouting hopefulness, the reeling slamming euphoria.

"And if I break the rules badly enough," she whispered, her breath hitching with every thrust, "you could use two paddles. Fuck me with the handle of one, spank me with the other, while your dick pounds my throat until I *choke.*"

Henrik's groan was low, guttural, powerful, his hips driving up again, again, again—and then he shouted, his body curling up hard, his cock spurting out deep inside. While Fasta's own body flashed and stretched and suddenly furiously broke, blazing out around him, hard enough to make her scream.

When it finished, Fasta felt shaky and tingly all over, her bare body splayed sticky and sweaty against Henrik's skin. But his arms were warm and heavy around her slippery back, keeping her there, and she sagged down deeper onto him, revelling in the feel of his softening cock inside her, his breath rising and falling through his heaving chest.

"*Gods,* Harry," Fasta breathed, raising her head enough to flash him a brief, genuine smile. "Remind me why we haven't done it like this before?"

There was an instant's quiet, a clench of Henrik's fingers against her back. "'Cause you paid me to be rough, and in charge," he murmured. "And I was already getting way too attached."

Oh. Fasta raised her head again, studied his hazy, shifting eyes. "So you do still like it when it's not rough, then?" she asked, and the surprise in her voice betrayed that she hadn't been quite sure. "You don't find it too boring?"

Henrik huffed a hoarse, incredulous laugh, his belly shuddering against Fasta's. "'Course it's not boring, love," he replied. "Gods damn it, do you really think I can only get off on being a demanding arsehole?"

Fasta's face heated, but she raised her eyebrows at him, because yes, that was almost all they'd ever done—but his face was flushed too, and he shrugged his shoulder against her. "Told you, before we started this, I only ever did that once in a while, in secret," he said. "You were never supposed to find out how much I liked that shit. Would've been thrilled to have you like this, for as long as you'd have put up with it."

Really? Fasta tilted her head, frowning down at him. "What do you mean?" she asked. "You were—*planning* to have me like this?"

Henrik's mouth betrayed an unmistakable grimace, his chest heaving out a slow breath. "Yeah, I was," he said, with a sigh. "After I walked in on you and Runar. Gods, I was so fucking jealous I couldn't even *think*."

Fasta kept blinking down at him, and he twitched a sad little half-smile toward her. "You were right, again," he continued, "that I did think of you as mine that whole time, yeah? You're just"—he exhaled again, stroked his hands almost reverently up and down her back—"you're everything I've ever wanted in a woman, wrapped up in a perfect, gorgeous package. Smart, generous, loyal, cool under pressure, brave as hell—and a brilliant earth-mage, too. I've just wanted you so damn much, all this time, and no way was I gonna sit back and let some other guy steal you away from me."

The heat streaked to Fasta's groin, burned in her cheeks— he really thought all that?—but she shoved her way through it, fought to find the point again. "So you mean," she began, "you'd already *decided* to do this with me—*before* I ever offered to pay you? You'd have done it for *free*?"

The look Henrik gave her was stubborn, but with a flicker of amusement, too. "I *did* do it for free," he countered. "That first time, in your workroom. And then again at the cottage. And if you hadn't have come up with the payment thing, you *know* we'd have kept doing it. Especially once I realized how perfect you are in bed, too. How"—his voice lowered—"you're such a shameless, mouthy, needy little brat for me. Just how I've always liked most, yeah?"

How he'd always liked most. It quivered more heat all through Fasta's body, while Henrik's hands kept stroking her, curving down to cup against her bare arse. "Not to mention those damned dildos of yours," he added, with a choked little laugh. "I think those *broke* me, Fass. Unlocked something I'm never gonna be able to put away *again*."

Fasta's breath shuddered out, her body quivering beneath his touch, clutching against his softened cock inside her. "But," she said, as she fought to keep digesting all this, reorienting it in her head. "But you still kept saying you wanted to leave. That you had to keep it separate. So you could go off and have your own wife someday."

Henrik let out a breath, his chest sinking under Fasta's. "Yeah, I did want my own wife, and a family," he replied, quiet. "Still do. But I told you, I was lying, too, 'cause I don't think I ever could've actually left you, for good. And the reason I really needed to keep it separate was so I wouldn't lose my shit and go on a murderous rampage when you dumped me over for some guy like Bryant. 'Cause we both knew that was gonna happen eventually, right?"

They were back to this again, and Fasta shook her head, held his grey eyes. "It was never going to happen, Harry," she said. "And it won't. I promise."

But those eyes shifted again, flickering in the rising sunlight through the window, and his hand rose to her face, his thumb stroking slow and gentle down her cheekbone. "Look, maybe you mean that now," he whispered. "But what happens in five years? Or ten? Or twenty? When you finally realize how much you've given up?"

Fasta's head tilted into his touch, even as her eyes frowned at him, her mouth gone tight. "Nothing happens," she snapped. "Because it's not going to happen. I want *you*, Harry. I want the life we have together, the life I've already lived for five whole *years*. I love *you*."

Henrik blinked, and again, his eyes bright, almost pained, on hers. "You can't mean that," he said, his voice so faint. "You *can't*."

Fasta sat up further, enough to glower down at him properly, and didn't miss his telltale glance up and down, lingering on her still-hard nipples. "Then tell me how I can convince you," she demanded. "Do I need to get on my knees with a ring? Tie myself up and beg you to spank me? Get rid of my birth control spell?"

Henrik's eyes fluttered, and he hissed a low, rumbling groan. "You can't actually want to have my kids," he breathed, though his eyes flicked to her breasts again, and then further down to her belly. "No fucking *way*, Fass."

Fasta kept glaring at him, and then leaned back down over him, this time settling both hands to the bed on either side of his head, giving him a damned good view. "Why the hell not," she said. "You essentially told me, back when we started this, that making me pregnant was your ultimate fantasy, didn't you? Also, our children would be *brilliant*, Harry."

Henrik groaned again, but there was a hard, betraying twitch of that cock, still inside her. "More like total *terrors*, Fass."

Fasta couldn't help a laugh, and she leaned down further, brushed her lips to his warm, willing mouth. "Probably," she murmured. "Knowing you."

But Henrik wasn't laughing, and his eyes were serious again, his hands gripping against her hips. "Fasta, your father would *murder* you," he said. "His only daughter, getting knocked up by a poor working *commoner*?"

Fasta lifted her chin, gave him her most imperious look. "You mean," she said primly, "having legitimate children with my legitimate, brilliant, gorgeous *husband*?"

Henrik gave another helpless, breathless groan—and in a sudden, swift movement, he flipped Fasta over onto her back. So easy, like she weighed nothing, and now he was on top, his body big and powerful and heavy over hers, his eyes hooded and hungry and demanding.

"Say that again," he breathed, so close. "Please, love."

Oh, *gods*, because his mouth had lowered to her neck, kissing and nipping, while his tousled hair brushed against her face, his powerful shoulders shifting over his huge muscled arms. And Fasta's whole body was arching against him, clinging to him, shuddering with need and relief.

"You'll be—my husband," she gasped, as he moved down to her collarbone, to the curve of her breast. "My own bossy, powerful, gorgeous husband. And you'll be—*fuck!*"

Henrik's mouth had closed over her hard nipple, drawing it deep inside, flicking it with his tongue, and the sight of this, the look in his half-lidded eyes as they met hers, fucking *hell*—

"You," she began, her breasts heaving against him, and her fluttering hands found his shoulders, all rippling breathtaking muscle. "You'll be a *brilliant* husband to me, Harry. You'll take care of me, and challenge me, punish me, reward me—"

His mouth groaned around her nipple, the vibrations soaring the pleasure higher, and Fasta gasped as he moved to the other one, took it deep. "You'll own me," she breathed. "For good. And you can do whatever you want with me. Give me new rules. Make me your dirtiest servant. Pump me full of your seed, and grow your children inside me."

Henrik's groan sounded guttural this time, and he raised his head, held Fasta's eyes as he moved his bulky body downward, settling between her legs. "Keep talking," he said, grasping her thighs, guiding them wide apart. "And I'll keep going."

Oh gods oh gods, Fasta couldn't even think, because there was only the image of this, the vision of this. Henrik Hallen's tongue licking his parted lips, his blond head hovering between her legs, down where he'd already filled her up once. Where she could still *feel* it, leaking out onto the bed, and he wouldn't *dare* go there now with his mouth—would he?

But his eyes were brazen, challenging, and—Fasta yelped—the first touch of his tongue between her legs was glorious, exhilarating, impossible. Making her entire body clench and heave, her fingers curling tight into his tousled hair, while his hooded eyes held on hers, waited.

"Oh," Fasta gasped. "Oh *gods*, Harry. I—I'll be such a good wife for you. You'll see."

He groaned again, but approval flickered across his eyes, even as his head lowered again, his tongue hot jolting ecstasy against Fasta's too-sensitive skin. While her traitorous legs spread wider, giving him better access, spilling out more of his thick seeping wetness onto the bed.

"I'll wear your ring and pendant always," she gasped, earning another rewarding, thrilling lick of that tongue. "I'll give you all my loyalty, my devotion. I'll worship you and *adore* you."

Henrik's tongue kept licking, his mouth gently suckling, just where Fasta craved it, and she couldn't help another cry, a hard spasm of her fingers in his hair. "I'll give you my body," she whispered, "and you can do whatever you want with it. You can open me up wide, stretch me out for you, watch me take the biggest bedposts you can possibly *make*."

Henrik's tongue was slipping inside her now, deep into his own mess, and Fasta's legs shook, her eyes rolling back, her hands tingling in his hair. "You'll be my only one, Harry," she breathed, or maybe sobbed, while the rising pleasure finally shattered, rocking through her in waves, again and again and again. "Forever. And everybody will know. *Everybody.*"

Henrik's tongue against her stuttered, jolting even more pleasure through Fasta's entire body, and his head lifted, his eyes dark, dazed, almost disbelieving. "You can't," he said, his chest rising and falling, but Fasta was so done with his protests, and she yanked on his hair, dragging him upwards again.

"I can," she breathed, as she wrapped her legs and arms around him, held him tight. "I will. I promise."

There was an instant's hanging stillness, his eyes blinking above her—and then his mouth, warm and soft and almost reverent against hers. Tasting of both of them, and kissing her with astonishing, breathtaking sweetness.

He was hard again, that cock silently demanding against her, and Fasta spread her legs wider, felt its thick length sinking inside. Just where it should be, just where she needed it to be, and the feel of it, his warm body inside her, above her, all around her, protecting her, was the most overwhelming, most spectacular thing Fasta had ever felt in her life.

He kept kissing her, his body now moving slow and powerful above her, inside her. Making her his own, in a way he never had before, and it was all she could do to hold on, to kiss him back, to keep the sobs from stealing their way out of her throat.

He came with a strangled shout, briefly breaking the kiss as he arched up over her, his cock pulsing out deep inside. Filling her, claiming her, owning her, while Fasta clung to him, drank him, adored him.

The feel of his full weight sagging back against hers was another kind of pleasure, all warm heavy contentment, and she reached for his face, pulled him back for another kiss. Slow and quiet this time, tasting oddly of salt, and when Fasta drew back, it was to the realization that his face was wet too, his eyes unmistakably red.

"You're gonna regret this," he said, his voice hoarse. "You will, love."

But Fasta shook her head, put both hands to his stubbly face. "We've already had this conversation," she whispered back. "I didn't regret it then, I won't regret it now. And if you truly do care about me, Harry, you'll respect my decision on this. Just like I promise to respect yours."

His eyes closed, briefly, something Fasta couldn't quite read passing over his face, and she could hear him swallow, could feel the slow, shaky exhale of his breath.

"Yeah," he said finally, slowly, the single word flaring an exquisite jolt of heat through her skin—and then again as he abruptly leaned backward, onto his knees, pulling her up with him. So he could look straight into her eyes, his expression sober and serious and watchful.

"Yeah," he said again, like he was bracing himself, his bare shoulders rising and falling. "Fass, my brilliant beautiful buttercup, my love"—he swallowed again, and his oddly shaking fingers brushed against her hand, settling against that ring—"will you marry me?"

The whole world slammed to a stop, caught on the truth of Henrik Hallen slowly sliding that ring off Fasta's finger, and hovering it in midair above his outstretched hand. Waiting, offering, not breathing.

"I'll take good care of you," he said, his voice low and fervent. "I'll be faithful to you. I'll do whatever I can to make you happy. I"—he took another breath, let it out—"I love you, Fass. Always have, and won't stop."

The wetness was streaking down Fasta's cheeks again, but everything was good and bright and right in the world. Henrik Hallen loved her, Henrik Hallen was asking her to marry him, Henrik Hallen was here, looking at her, waiting.

"Oh, Harry," she whispered, and with a twitch of his magic, or maybe hers, or both, the ring slid back onto her finger, where it belonged—and she flung her arms around his shoulders. "Yes. I will."

EPILOGUE

It was their first time ever having company, and the cottage was immaculate.

"Do you think we have enough food?" Fasta asked, biting her lip, frowning down at their fully laden dining table. "Or should I get more?"

Henrik glanced up from where he'd been giving the stone floor a final polish, sliding multiple pads of packed sand against it. "Gods, no, Fass," he said, and came over to look over her shoulder, while the pads kept circling on the floor behind him. "There's only two of them, not ten."

Fasta let out a little huff, because having company—having Henrik's brother, no less—felt like some kind of warped test of her down-home wifely abilities. Not that Henrik had ever suggested anything of the sort, but Fasta wanted to prove this, to them, and maybe herself.

"It's gonna be *fine*, Fass," Henrik said, as his warm mouth pressed softly to the back of her neck. "Andreas doesn't give a shit what the place looks like, or what we feed him. We're just showing off, at this point."

There was an undeniable trace of pride in his voice, and Fasta turned around to look at him, at his raised eyebrows and tousled golden hair and broad shoulders. Looking even broader in his rather fitted blue tunic, which had been one of Fasta's recent indulgences with their newly-earned money, and she settled her arms over those shoulders, let him pull her close.

"But he's your brother," she countered. "And he's going to go tell your mother. And *she'll* give a shit, I guarantee you."

That was perhaps a bit unfair, because Henrik's mother had been nothing but kind to Fasta, if rather shocked when they'd first told her the news of their engagement. But Fasta knew she'd had misgivings, that she still thought Henrik would be better off with some sweet country wench who would ply him with apple pies and cream.

"Well, *I* don't give a shit," Henrik said, his voice gone sharper, more authoritative. "So leave it, buttercup."

He softened the words with a light pat to her arse, and Fasta nodded, felt herself relaxing against him. It was one of their newer rules, Henrik having full veto power over her more obsessive and controlling tendencies, and it was surprisingly liberating, one of the many wonderful discoveries six months' worth of marriage had brought.

Henrik's head turned abruptly toward the door, just before Fasta heard the sound of their brass knocker, banging twice. Meaning that Andreas was here, and Henrik gave one more tap to Fasta's arse before striding over, undoing all the latches with a wave of his hand, and swinging the door open.

"Brother!" Henrik said, the delight clear in his voice, and Fasta only caught a glimpse of Andreas' slim, dark-haired form before Henrik bodily grasped him into a crushing bear hug. While behind them stood another slim young man, carrying a satchel, and blinking in at the cottage and Fasta with rather perplexed blue eyes.

"Welcome to our home," Fasta said, stepping forward, holding out a hand toward him. "I'm Fasta Hallen, Andreas' sister-in-law. Won't you come in?"

The relief was clear in the new arrival's eyes, and he gave Fasta a slow, appealing smile as he shook her hand. "Thank you," he said, his voice lilting with a slight eastern accent. "I'm Viktor. It's very kind of you to have us."

Behind him, Andreas had extracted himself from Henrik, and brushed off his rather rumpled travelling suit. "Fasta," he said, and his grey eyes behind his spectacles were warm as he leaned in for a hug from her, too. "It's so good to see you."

He smelled like earth, similar to Henrik but not quite, and as he stepped back again Fasta was relieved to notice that he'd filled out slightly since she'd last seen him, his cheekbones not as prominent in his pale face. "And you, Andreas," Fasta said, and she meant it. "How were your travels?"

Andreas angled a sideways glance at Viktor, and if Fasta wasn't mistaken, a slight flush was creeping up his cheeks. "Fair, thank you," he murmured, and then he stopped up short, blinking at something beyond Fasta's head. Making Fasta turn around to look too, but it was only the cottage's great room, with the loft's curved balcony above.

"*Gods*," Andreas said, and he elbowed Viktor's side, and shoved up his spectacles on his nose. "*This* is your place, Henrik? You said it was a cottage!"

Henrik and Fasta exchanged looks, and Henrik gave a wry smile. "Well, to Fasta's mind, it's a cottage," he said lightly, but she knew there was no malice in it, just teasing. "What do you think?"

Andreas was spinning slowly in place, his mouth hanging open, and Fasta followed his gaze, trying to imagine seeing it for the first time. It was bright, and welcoming, and they'd finally finished the great room, setting it with a mechanical brass chandelier and a huge stone fireplace. They'd also finally chosen furniture and furs and textiles, some of it wedding gifts, and under Henrik's strict, thrilling supervision, Fasta had made an admittedly suggestive abstract mosaic, which took up the whole of the opposite wall, and still made her feel warm every time she looked at it.

"It's absolutely delightful," Andreas said, with feeling. "It's perfectly balanced, beautifully laid out. Is this floor *one piece*, Henrik?"

Henrik's grin toward Fasta was rueful, and more than a little pleased. "Yes," he said. "Don't even ask."

"Hey, it was *your* idea," Fasta protested. "I only pointed it out!"

"Oh, but I *knew* you wanted it," Henrik said back, his eyebrows rising, his hand stroking against the small of her back. "I spoil you rotten, buttercup. Well"—he leaned in, his voice lowering—"when you're a good girl, at least."

Fasta felt her cheeks flushing, too obvious to the two pairs of watching eyes, and she cleared her throat, made herself step away from the warmth of that hand. "Um," she said, "maybe Harry can start supper, while I take you out to the guest house, get you settled?"

"There's a guest house, too?" Andreas echoed, and Fasta didn't miss his furtive glance toward Viktor. "For both of us?"

"Yes, of course," Fasta said, intentionally avoiding Henrik's eyes as she waved them out after her. They followed meekly through the trees, until Fasta stopped at the door of the snug new guest house they'd built, made of thousands of small stones mounted on a wood frame.

It wasn't quite finished, either, but after Fasta had opened Henrik's latches, she was rewarded with yet another gasp from Andreas. The house was small, but very comfortably appointed, with two canopied beds, a sitting area, a small side kitchen, and another hefty fireplace, with a fire merrily crackling in it.

"Please, make yourselves at home," Fasta said, gesturing between them and the beds. "Perhaps we can meet back at the cottage in a while for supper, once you're properly settled?"

Andreas nodded, again giving Viktor another telling,

lingering glance. "Thank you, Fasta," he said. "This is truly lovely."

Fasta waved it away, and made to leave—but Andreas stepped abruptly toward her, holding out a hand. "And wait," he said. "Fasta. I've—been wanting to thank you."

Fasta blinked, but waited, and Andreas cleared his throat, pushed up his spectacles. "Look, Henrik's never really said," he began, "how he got the payment for my tuition this year. But I know it was you."

Fasta wasn't quite sure how to reply, and Andreas took a breath, twisting his hands together in front of him. "You got me out of something I hated," he said, "and into what has unquestionably been the best year of my life. I know your own situation hasn't been ideal recently"—he swallowed, cleared his throat again—"but if I can ever repay you, I will happily, eagerly, do so."

He was referring to Fasta's father, of course, and to his inevitable reaction to Fasta's marriage. It had been thoroughly unpleasant, complete with lawyers and threats and *what-was-wrong-with-Norberg* rubbish, but in the end most of it had been kept out of the papers, and one of Fasta's regular letters to her father had even received an answer, a month or so before.

"Please, Andreas, don't concern yourself," Fasta said, and she meant it. "I am very well provided for, and our work these past few months has proven even more lucrative than we anticipated. And, to be honest"—Andreas was an adult, he deserved truth—"your situation was part of what brought Henrik and me together. So I'm very grateful to you for that."

Andreas' eyes perhaps saw more in that than Fasta would have liked, and he gave her a small smile. "Well, for what it's worth," he said, "I'm glad. Henrik's been hankering after you for years now. It's good to finally see him happy."

The heat pooled in Fasta's cheeks again, and she couldn't help fingering at her solid, familiar pendant—she still always wore it, along with her ring, and now matching bracelets for each wrist, too. "Thank you," she said. "He takes very good care of me."

Andreas nodded, again with that understanding in his eyes, and Fasta turned and left them, walking quickly back to the cottage. To where Henrik wasn't preparing supper at all, but was instead sprawled back on a chair, legs spread, spinning a ceramic plate before his eyes. And as Fasta watched, it snapped into a thousand tiny shards, whirling into a chaotic mess—and then fitting perfectly back together again, without even a single movement of his hand.

"Show-off," Fasta said, grinning at him, as he dropped the plate back to the table. "What are you thinking about?"

Henrik's shoulders slightly relaxed, and he patted his knee in silent invitation. Not even arguing with her assumption, because this was the kind of thing he always did when he was thinking, and Fasta went over and straddled his knees, settled herself down onto his warm, solid thighs.

"You didn't know about that, did you?" she asked now, tilting her head toward the guest house. "Andreas and Viktor? Like that?"

She leaned in, touched a brief kiss to Henrik's lips, felt his hands circle warm around her back. "No," he said, with a sigh. "Maybe I should've guessed, though. Between the way he talked about this Viktor in his letters, and that whole mess with that arsehole noble last year."

Fasta pulled back a little, searched his eyes. "Are you upset?"

Henrik considered that, and then sighed, shrugged his shoulder. "Nah," he said. "I can't be, can I? Far be it from me to judge somebody for what they get off on. Speaking of which"—he raised his eyebrows at Fasta, gave a teasing grin—"you should see what I made upstairs for you."

Fasta couldn't help a hard shiver, because the things Henrik had made for her upstairs were universally thrilling, and beautifully built, besides. "What is it?" she asked. "Something I'll like?"

Henrik's grin widened, going sharper, a little hungry. "Maybe," he murmured back. "Definitely something *I'll* like, buttercup."

The heat was already pooling in Fasta's groin, and she couldn't help a grinding circle up against him. Discovering, in the process, that the bulging hardness was already there in his trousers, too, jutting up strong and breathtaking, just where she wanted it.

"Tell me," she breathed, with another hard little circle against him. "Please, my lord."

The word had the same effect it always did, bringing that darkening edge to Henrik's eyes, and he slowly slid his hands up Fasta's spread thighs, under the edge of her skirt. She'd started wearing more skirts at home lately, at his request, and it was for just this reason, for giving him access whenever the hell he wanted.

"Not gonna tell you, buttercup," he murmured, as those fingers brushed up against the bare, spread-apart wetness between her legs. "It's a thing for showing."

Showing. Fasta's body clenched helplessly against those fingers, betraying her, and Henrik's smile turned cool, smug. "Look at you, already dripping wet for it," he murmured. "Such a greedy, spoiled-rotten wife. When I already gave you such a good plowing this morning."

It had been a good plowing, oh gods, with Fasta on her back on this very table, with her legs hiked up on Henrik's broad shoulders. And her whole body shuddered at even the memory, her eyes glancing back toward the table, her body grinding down hard against those still-exploring fingers.

"Please, my lord," she whispered. "Show me. I've been a very good girl today."

Henrik couldn't deny that, because his list of rules had become rather extensive, and Fasta could be very good at following them, when she wanted to be. Calling him only *Harry*, or *husband*, or *my lord*. Not getting herself off, or using any of their many implements, without his express permission. Always wearing his jewelry. Being unflinchingly honest with him. Obeying his heated commands without hesitation.

And still the most distracting—and perhaps currently the most arousing—was this one, the one that had Henrik's hand sliding further back, high up between Fasta's parted thighs. Feeling for the rounded, slightly protruding end of the smooth stone plug that he'd wedged deep into her tight, resisting body just that morning.

"Have you touched it?" he murmured, giving a careful circle of it inside, and the hunger pooled harder between Fasta's legs, betraying her against those still-delving fingers. "Once or twice," she admitted, against the smarting heat in her face. "Not breaking the rules, by taking it out, or getting off. Just—feeling it. And"—she took a breath, brought out truth—"maybe worrying a bit."

There were more teeth to Henrik's smile now, while that plug swelled even wider inside. "Worrying about what?" he asked, voice cool. "The fact that two earth-mages are visiting us, and are probably gonna be able to tell that you have my stone shoved up your tight little arse?"

Fasta gave a shuddering, trembly breath, and dropped her eyes, her head nodding. But now here was Henrik's hand on her chin, lifting her head again, making her look at him.

"Stop worrying," he said, his voice low, authoritative, firing another thrill of heat straight to Fasta's groin. "Your arse is mine, to do whatever the hell I want with. And if they're looking, they'll know it's my work, my magic, and therefore my problem to deal with. Not yours."

Fasta's body relaxed again, the breath heavily exhaling, and Henrik's eyes on her were warm, approving, maybe even hungrier than before. "Good girl," he murmured. "Maybe I *will* show you what I made you, then. Thing is, though, if I do, you'll have to use it."

More heat surged to Fasta's face and groin, and she shot a swift look over her shoulder toward the food-laden table, and then in the direction of the guest house. "*Now*?" she asked, breathless. "What about supper? And *them*?"

A single glance of Henrik's eyes toward the door sent all its latches clicking into place at once. "They can wait," he said, with a shrug. "Chances are, they're out there doing the exact same thing."

He probably wasn't wrong, and he raised his eyebrows at Fasta, waiting for her protest—but after another shaky breath, she nodded. Earning another approving look from his eyes, which were now—Fasta followed his gaze—flicking up to the loft, where something was rising over the railing, and slowly hovering downward.

It was—a chair. A normal-looking, sturdy-looking chair, with thick, wide-set stone legs and arms, and an upholstered seat and back. Looking like nothing out of the ordinary, and Fasta shot Henrik a nonplussed, uncertain look, which he returned with another one of those too-sharp grins.

"Get up," he said. "Go stand behind it."

Fasta did, walking a little awkwardly now, what with the increased width of that invading stone inside her. And then she glanced again at Henrik, raising her eyebrows in a silent question, because it was still just a chair, still just sitting there.

"Put your feet close on either side," Henrik said, gesturing toward its back legs. "And rest your arms down onto its arms."

Fasta blinked but obeyed, placing her feet up against the chair's back legs, and bending down to rest her forearms against its cool stone arms. Noticing, instantly, that this chair perfectly matched her body, that the padded back of it was the perfect height to cradle her hips, and—she gasped aloud—that it had metal straps, somehow, hidden inside. And they snapped out of the chair's arms and legs with a simultaneous clink, cuffing her wrists and ankles tightly against it.

"Fuck," Fasta breathed, because the result was that she was bent double over the chair's back, her legs spread, her entire body trapped in place. And—she gasped again—she could feel another ring of steel, curling out of the chair's seat, and circling up gentle and loose around her neck, bending her torso further down over it.

It meant that Fasta's feet were still flat on the floor, but only just, and she could feel Henrik sauntering over behind her, his hand sliding over her jutting-up arse, still thankfully covered by her skirt. "Tell me, buttercup," he murmured, husky, "what do you think?"

Fasta's face was pressed down against the chair's soft uphol-stered seat, and she could hear her heart thundering, the blood rushing to her head. "I think it's brilliant," she breathed. "I think you're brilliant. And I'm hoping this means you'll fuck me."

It was the right answer, judging by Henrik's low chuckle behind her, and his warm hands slid up Fasta's bare thighs, pushing up her skirt with them. "Right now?" he asked coolly, as his hands—and the skirt—curved up over her bare arse. "What if someone were to walk in?"

He settled the skirt up over Fasta's waist, leaving her whole lower body bare to the air, her legs spread wide. Meaning that everything between her legs was open, quivering, obscenely exposed to anyone behind her, and suddenly there was the distant, deeply alarming click of one of Henrik's latches, unlocking on the door.

"What if someone were to see you like this?" Henrik murmured, as his fingers brushed light against Fasta's spread-apart, dripping-wet heat. "Prim and proper Lady Valgeirr, bent over a chair with her arse up and legs spread, just begging to be fucked?"

Oh, gods damn him, and Fasta's body was already straining

against the cuffs, testing their strength. But there was no getting out without magic—Henrik's workmanship was top-notch, as usual—and if Fasta wanted to keep the game going, she didn't dare use magic, that was one of the rules.

"What if someone were to see," Henrik continued, his hand now rising to brush against that hard stone, still wedged inside, "what you have up inside you right now? What if someone were to come over"—there was another alarming click of a latch opening, behind her—"and watch what this looks like, coming out of you?"

The embedded stone plug was already moving, pulling against Fasta's clenching tightness, and she could feel her body resisting, trying to keep it there. Because it being there kept that part of her safe, protected, concealed—but then she flinched all over at the feel of something flat and hard and delightfully painful, striking against her too-exposed arse-cheek.

It was their favourite paddle, the one Henrik had made out of highly valuable pure white marble, calling it an appropriately posh tool to use on a high-and-mighty, spoiled-rotten princess like her. And it hurt like hell, and it was *glorious*, and Fasta's entire body shook, her mouth letting out a strangled little cry.

"Give this to me, buttercup," Henrik said, his hand still on the stone inside her, as the paddle slapped again, harder this time. "Now."

The warning was clear in his voice, and Fasta nodded desperately against the chair's seat, and tried to make herself relax. Tried to push the plug out, even, for Henrik's benefit, and he gave a low murmur of approval, his hand rubbing circles against her smarting arse, as the plug drew out of her with discomforting, humiliating slowness.

"Look at you," Henrik's voice murmured, as the plug finally pulled out all the way, and fell to the floor with an audible thunk. "Such a cockslut wife, exposing yourself like this.

Showing off both your tight little holes at once, all stretched out for your lord, ready for a good hard fucking."

His fingers had still been rubbing in Fasta's wetness, getting slick and slippery, and now they slid up to where the plug had been. Touching slowly, almost reverently, against the still-tender skin, and then slipping gently, easily inside.

"Look at you," he said again, though his voice was unsteadier than before. "Taking two fingers now, on the first try. Think you can handle three?"

Three. Fasta writhed against the chair, desperately now, and in reply there was another hard slap of that marble paddle against her arse. "Wrong answer," Henrik whispered, as those fingers kept working, invading deeper, spreading her wider, oh *fuck*. "You're my wife, you talk to me when I ask you a question. So tell me. Do you want three fingers? Or maybe"—his voice went deeper, hoarser, as his other hand palmed lower, against her trembling wetness—"you want my whole *fist* up there, like I did down here last week, until you were screaming my name?"

Gods *curse* Henrik, because even the memory of that was setting Fasta's entire body aflame. He'd worked at it all evening, whispering orders and praises, alternating fingers and stone and his glorious mouth. Until Fasta's entire body had been arched and spasming, her brain empty of all coherent thought, but for the sheer, pummelling, world-wrenching sensation of Henrik Hallen's hand, all the way inside her, breaking her apart.

"Well?" he murmured, with another stinging slap of that paddle. "Tell me what you want. Truth, buttercup."

His third finger was already poised there, waiting warm and powerful, and Fasta's breath heaved against the chair. "Oh gods," she gasped, her body clenching, twitching, dripping. "Oh, fuck. Your fingers. Three of them. Please, my lord."

She was rewarded with a low chuckle, with a gentle little circle of those two fingers inside. Stretching her out more, preparing her, before the third one slowly slipped inside—and Fasta let herself sink into the feel of it, the breath by breath experience of it. Her incredible husband gently filling her, stretching her, pushing her limits, giving her exactly what she needed, what she craved most.

"Good girl," he murmured now, burying those fingers deeper, all the way to the knuckle, as her body stretched wider, tighter, on the edge of pain. "Such a good wife. Gods, you should see yourself."

There was another click of a door latch behind them, hurling a sharp shuddering jolt up Fasta's spine, and bringing another chuckle to Henrik's mouth. "Scared someone will see you?" he breathed, as the fingers of his other hand slid below, brushing against her willing wetness, delving their way inside there too, oh gods, oh fuck. "Bent over a chair with your skirt up, your arse out, and your husband using both your holes at once?"

Fasta's mouth was whimpering now, her entire world caught on the sensation of this, on those powerful, purposeful hands, owning her, consuming her, driving the pleasure and the pain higher and higher. "Talk to me," Henrik said now, his breath sounding short, ragged. "Tell me how it feels."

Fasta gulped in one breath, another, tried to make her brain move, find words. "Feels—impossible," she gasped. "So much. So good."

Henrik groaned, and those fingers went harder, deeper. "What else?"

What else, oh gods, Fasta couldn't think. "You," she managed, helpless. "Need you. You're—everything. Husband. Lord. Genius. Best friend. *Hands.* Fuck. Just—*need.*"

It was babbling, verging on incoherent, but she could feel Henrik's approval, the warmth spinning out slow in the magic. "Need what, buttercup," he whispered, and there was a light, tantalizing slap of that paddle to her arse, even more sparks of swirling, sweeping sensation. "Tell me."

Damn him, his hands, and Fasta whimpered again, her whole body exposed, stretched, impaled, invaded. "Need more," she gasped. "Your mouth. Your *cock*."

Henrik gave another strangled-sounding groan behind her, and with a sucking, obscene-sounding noise, both hands pulled out at once. Leaving her suddenly cold, empty, gaping wide open, quivering all over, her mouth betraying a too-loud cry of protest, or maybe pleasure.

"Say that again," Henrik said behind her, and though he was trying to sound cool, she could feel the tension, could taste the hammering hunger in his magic. "You need what, buttercup?"

Fuck him, fuck her obnoxious gorgeous arsehole of a husband, and Fasta strained against the chair, tried to drive her trapped, still-empty body backwards, toward him. "Your mouth," she gasped. "Your cock. Anything. Please, Harry, my lord. Fill me. Please."

His breath was audible now, behind her, and without warning she felt him falter, sinking to his knees behind her. And now that breath was there, hot and close, kissing up the back of her bare thigh, firing flashes of pleasure all through Fasta's skin.

"Oh gods," she gasped, her legs trembling, and here were his hands, strong, steady, holding her still. "Oh gods, Harry, oh fuck, *please*—"

There was another shaky chuckle, more shivering heat of his breath—and then his tongue was *there*, oh fuck, oh hell. Licking flat and hard against her too-sensitive, swollen wetness, lapping it up, and Fasta jolted all over, and nearly screamed.

He chuckled again, did it again, deep, without hesitation. And fuck, he was good at this, had repeatedly proven that beyond all doubt, and the pleasure was already spooling up, close and hard—until like always Henrik eased off, because he could somehow taste it in her magic. And when Fasta's mouth whined her protest, he just laughed again, rising unsteady to his feet behind her.

"All good, buttercup?" he breathed, low. "Maybe I'll leave you here for a bit, go out and get them—"

The noise out of Fasta's mouth was something between a shout and a sob, while the world sparked, swam, spun. "You can't leave now, you can't, you *can't*," she pleaded, babbling again, but she didn't care. "Need you, need you, you *said*—"

"I didn't say shit," came his voice, but it was low, hungry. "You're the one supposed to be talking, wife. Convincing me."

Fuck, *fuck*, and Fasta dragged in air, grasped for coherent thoughts. "Need you," she managed, and as if to demonstrate, her exposed, quivering body pushed back harder, higher, like the wanton servant she was. "Need you inside me, filling me. Using me. *Please.*"

There was a wild, strangled instant of silence, but for their breaths, and the obscene, humiliating sound of Fasta's swollen wetness, opening and closing at nothing. Waiting, while Henrik watched, oh gods, until finally—finally—there was the feel of his warm hands on her arse, pulling her apart even wider, exposing everything.

"I'm only using you if I can fuck both of these," he whispered, but she could hear him opening his trousers. "And if you beg me to do it."

Oh, hell, but Fasta was too far gone to think, to care. "Please, my lord," she gasped. "Please, take me. Take me wherever you want. However you want."

But there was still no glorious hot invasion, only the sudden, shocking impact of that marble paddle, slapping up firm against her, as another latch across the room clicked open. "Not good enough," came his voice, breathless. "Say it. Beg me. *Truth*, Fass."

Truth. They'd worked on this, and it was still surprisingly difficult sometimes, even like this, with that paddle striking her again, stars and colour and surging soaring pleasure. "Oh," she choked out. "Oh gods. Please, Harry, husband, my lord"—she gulped back air, felt the stillness of his magic behind her— "please, fuck me. I'm all stretched out for you, ready for you, waiting for you."

There was no paddle this time, but nothing else, either. Just more hanging, twisting silence, their heavy breaths the only sound in the room, and Fasta braced herself, tried again. "*Please*, Harry," she begged, or perhaps sobbed. "Please. There's nothing I need more in the world than your cock"—she gulped back more air—"in both my holes, filling me up with your spunk. I need to feel you slamming into me, spilling out of me, owning me. *Please*."

And that was it, finally, thank the gods, because behind her Henrik let out a low, guttural groan. And there was an instant's shocking, jolting pleasure, as that swollen thick hardness finally nudged into her soaking-wet, quivering heat—and then slammed home with so much force that Fasta screamed.

"Fuck," Henrik gasped, grinding hard deep inside, and then drawing out, slamming back in. "Good girl. *My* girl. All mine, always."

It was enough to finally light the spark, set the flame—and the world exploded, pleasure exploded, light and black and colour behind Fasta's eyes. Making her entire body convulse against him, again and again and again, while her mouth babbled and begged, oh husband oh gods oh *please*.

Henrik's body shuddered behind her, his belly heaving, and that meant he was close too, Fasta could almost *taste* it. "Fuck," he whispered again, and he dragged all the way out, slow. "You look so good, buttercup. Feel so good. Better than anything else *alive*."

The pleasure was still sparking, tingling all through Fasta's skin, and the praise only made it stronger, brighter. "Please," she gasped, because that cock wasn't touching her again—until it was, now up higher, where it was harder, tighter, tenderer.

"All good?" he whispered, and Fasta nodded frantically,

heard him gasp as her body clenched along with it. And now here he was, hard hot beautiful, invading her, taking her, pressing slow and inexorable and thrilling inside.

The plug all day had definitely helped, as had his fingers, and it felt impossibly good, impossibly full. Like Henrik Hallen was penetrating her very soul, locking her against him, all primal heat and size and earth and power.

He was barely thrusting, his breath coming harsh and ragged behind her, and now it was Fasta pushing back on him, needing him, trying to drive him deeper. "*Please*, Harry," she gasped. "I need this. Need you. *Love* you."

It was enough to make him give a rumbling, growling groan, the sound shuddering through Fasta's bones—and then with a shout it was done, he was done. His whole body arching as he drove in deep, as deep as he could possibly go, spraying out inside her like he owned her, he craved her, he loved her.

"Fuck," he whispered again, once he'd finished, and Fasta could feel how hard he was breathing, how he was shaking, too. "*Gods*, love. One of these days you're gonna make me *explode* with how much I want you."

Fasta couldn't help a strangled laugh beneath him, and felt him carefully pull out, leaving her tender and dripping with his wetness. A sight that she could feel him drinking up for a minute, greedy bastard that he was, until he finally released the cuffs around her wrists and ankles with a loud *clank*, and carefully, gently wiped her up with one of the rags he always kept in his pocket, for just this purpose.

"Thanks," she breathed, once he'd finished and disposed of the rag, and she finally pushed her stiff, rubbery-feeling body up to standing again, met his eyes. Which were watching her, warily now, because he was still sometimes a little worried and regretful, after—but Fasta felt incredible, absolutely *wonderful*, and without hesitation she circled her arms around his waist, drawing him close.

"So good, Harry," she whispered, into his warm, broad

chest. "Gods, that was so good. *You* were so good. I loved it. Love *you*."

She could feel the tension in him easing away, and she stroked at his broad back, the hard curve of his arse. "The chair is absolutely brilliant," she said now, and in a flash of awareness she pulled out her wrist, smiled down at it. "And padded, too. So thoughtful of you."

She shot the smile up at him, her most winning and genuine one, and she could feel him relaxing more, his hands circling around her waist, his mouth kissing at her hair. "Not the prettiest, though, is it?" he asked, and with a nod of his head toward it, the shackles packed themselves back away, leaving only an innocuous-looking chair behind. "Wanted it to fit you properly, and not be unsafe, when you're strapped in. So the proportions are a bit off, for a chair."

But Fasta wasn't hearing it, and she extracted herself from Henrik's arms long enough to stride over and lower herself gingerly into the chair, taking care with her still tender-feeling arse. "It's lovely," she said, "and perfectly comfortable, too. Where would you like to put it?"

She stood up again, striding back over to fold herself back against Henrik's broad chest, and felt the surge of magic as he lifted the chair up, and then dropped it again, into what was definitely the most preferable spot, on the opposite side of the fireplace.

"That work?" he asked, and Fasta smiled at him again, let her hand wander back down to his arse.

"Perfect," she murmured. "Just like you."

He smiled too, relaxing a little more, and Fasta sank deeper into his chest, breathing in the succulent, earthy scent of him. Revelling in the feel of those strong arms stroking her, pulling her closer, warm, safe, loved.

"You're delusional, buttercup," he murmured, but his voice was soft, affectionate. "I just shackled you to a piece of furniture, and threatened to expose you to *Andreas*. For fuck's sakes."

He still sounded a little disgusted with himself, and this was something Fasta was still figuring out. Realizing how Henrik hated himself, sometimes, for wanting this as much as he did, and how that old rule of his about keeping things separate hadn't just been hard on her, but on both of them.

"Yes, and it was absolutely brilliant," Fasta murmured back. "Very resourceful of you. Such a clever husband. And"—she leaned back, and tilted her head toward where she could feel, of course, that there was no one outside the door—"I knew you'd never have actually done it. And if you'd even come *close*, I'd have been tapping so hard, you'd have had *bruises* afterwards."

She could taste Henrik's relief in his magic, in the air, as he smiled down at her again, his big arms tightening closer against her. "Good," he said, quiet. "Thanks, love."

He meant not just for remembering the tapping—which they still both had to use, sometimes—but also for reassuring him, reminding him that it still was a game, a choice, on both their parts. That they both held equal power in this quirky relationship of theirs. Henrik was the lord, but Fasta's submission was a choice, a gift, a truth all its own.

"And I'm still your best servant, too, right?" she asked him, just as quiet. "Better than any of those women at your establishments? Or at Coven Manor?"

Because sometimes—even after all this—sometimes Fasta still needed reassurance, too. Reminders that of all the women Henrik had taken—and especially the ones he'd taken like this—she was still the only one that mattered, the one he craved. The one he loved.

"*Gods*, yes, love," he breathed, his arms tightening even closer around her. "You're every one of my most fucked-up fantasies come to life, you know that? A smart, gorgeous, unbelievably accomplished earth-mage, giving up her pampered life of luxury, so she could *marry* me, and come here and submit herself to all my wildest shit, full-time, every day? Even to my ridiculous *furniture*? That's a *million* times better than random fucks with strangers, Fass."

Fasta couldn't help a relieved chuckle against him, especially when one of those hands gently wandered downwards, coming to spread wide against her belly. Which was still flat, for now, but maybe not for long, seeing how she'd finally gone to a healer—to a snarky-as-ever Runar, in fact—and had her birth control spell removed, just the week before.

"And look, this is some *permanent* kinky shit, Fass," Henrik murmured. "You're still sure, right? You promise me?"

The world was bright, and beautiful, because Fasta was safe in Henrik Hallen's arms, in the house and the life they'd made, and her smile up at him was wide, and true, and full of hope.

"Yes, Harry," she said. "I promise."

~

THE END

~

THANKS FOR READING!

Thank you so much for joining me for Fasta and Henrik's story! It was so satisfying to bring these two stubborn, kinky earth-mages together for their happily ever after.

If you'd like to spend more time in my Mages world, the first book in this series is *The Mage's Match*. The realm's most famous celebrity has lost his magic, and no one can bring it back... except for a poor, unfashionable commoner.

I also have a free Mages story for members of my mailing list! In *The Mage's Groom*, a haughty mage has been misbehaving, and now she's about to get the correction she deserves. Find it at finleyfenn.com.

Finally, if you enjoyed this book, I hope you'll share your thoughts! I'm always so, so grateful when readers leave reviews on my books, but I'd also be happy to hear your feedback on my Facebook group, Discord server, or Patreon. You can find them all linked on my website at finleyfenn.com.

Thank you again for joining me on this adventure! Hugs!

ACKNOWLEDGMENTS

As always, I'm so thankful for all the readers and friends who have shared their enthusiasm and appreciation for this series. Thank you so much!

I also want to thank the generous beta readers who took the time to give me their extremely helpful insights on this book: Anne-Marie, Ari, Jo Henny Wolf, Lauren Mauchley, and Mary Lynne Nielsen. I'm also deeply grateful to my proofreader Emmy at Bra Bedre Belt, and to my incredible author friends Lillian Lark and Lizzy Bequin.

I'm also forever thankful to my amazing Patreon supporters, my advance reviewers, my Skai Librarian Amy, and my brilliant Right Hand Marykate.

And finally, I need to thank my own stubborn magical husband, who has always been such a rock of love and support to me. Thank you, love.

ALSO BY FINLEY FENN

THE MAGE'S GROOM
The Mages: Bonus Story
with Email Signup

When a brilliant mage gives up and goes home, she finds her master waiting...

Greta Hendersson was supposed to do great things in life. Build a career, rack up accolades, make a perfect marriage.

But when her two-year relationship with the world's most famous air-mage blows up in her face, everything else falls apart, too. And all that's left is to go home...

To where her head groom has been patiently waiting. With a collar and whip in his hand...

FREE download!
www.finleyfenn.com

ALSO BY FINLEY FENN

THE LADY AND THE ORC

He's the most feared monster in the realm. And she's what he needs to win his war...

In a world of warring orcs and men, Lady Norr is condemned to a childless marriage, a cruel lord husband, and a life of genteel poverty—until the day her home is ransacked by a horde. And leading the charge is their hulking, deadly orc captain: the infamous Grimarr.

And Grimarr has a wicked plan for Lady Norr, and for ending this war once and for all. She's going to become his captive—and the perfect snare for Lord Norr.

There's no possible escape, and soon Lady Norr is dragged off toward Orc Mountain in the powerful arms of her greatest enemy. A ruthless, commanding warlord, with a velvet voice and mouthwatering scent, who awakens every forbidden hunger she never knew she had...

But Grimarr refuses to accept half measures—in war, or in pleasure. And before he'll conquer Lady Norr's deepest, darkest desires, she needs to surrender *everything*.

Her allegiance.

Her wedding ring.

Her future...

And with her husband's forces giving chase, Lady Norr can't afford to play such a dangerous game—or can she? **Even if this deadly orc's plans might be the only way to save them all?**

ABOUT THE AUTHOR

Finley Fenn is "the queen of dark orc romance" (Virgo Reader), and her ongoing Orc Sworn series has been praised as "sexy, romantic, angsty, and captivating ... utter brilliance" (Romantically Inclined Reviews).

When she's not obsessing over her stories, Finley loves reading, drooling over delicious orc artwork, and spending time with her incredible readers on Patreon, Discord, and Facebook. She lives in Canada with her beloved family, including her very own grumpy, gorgeous husband.

For free bonus stories and epilogues, special offers, and exclusive Orc Sworn artwork, sign up at www.finleyfenn.com.